"Was it real, wh

A long sigh shuddered through him before he spoke. "Real enough that we went through a lot of pain for each other. Real enough that sitting here together isn't some easygoing reunion."

Hearing that heavy sigh of his, she realized he'd suffered, too, more than she'd ever known. Somehow, that made her feel less alone. Yes, they'd hurt each other, but maybe they could help each other, too. Maybe the time had come for a coda of sorts, to bring their song to an end.

"Malcolm, what's Europe going to be like if just sitting here together is this difficult?"

"So you've decided to come with me? No more maybes."

She shoved to her feet and walked to him at the piano. "I think I have to."

"Because of the stalker?"

She cupped his handsome, beard-stubbled face in her hands. "Because it's time we put this to rest."

Before she could talk herself out of something she wanted—needed—more than air, Celia pressed her lips to his.

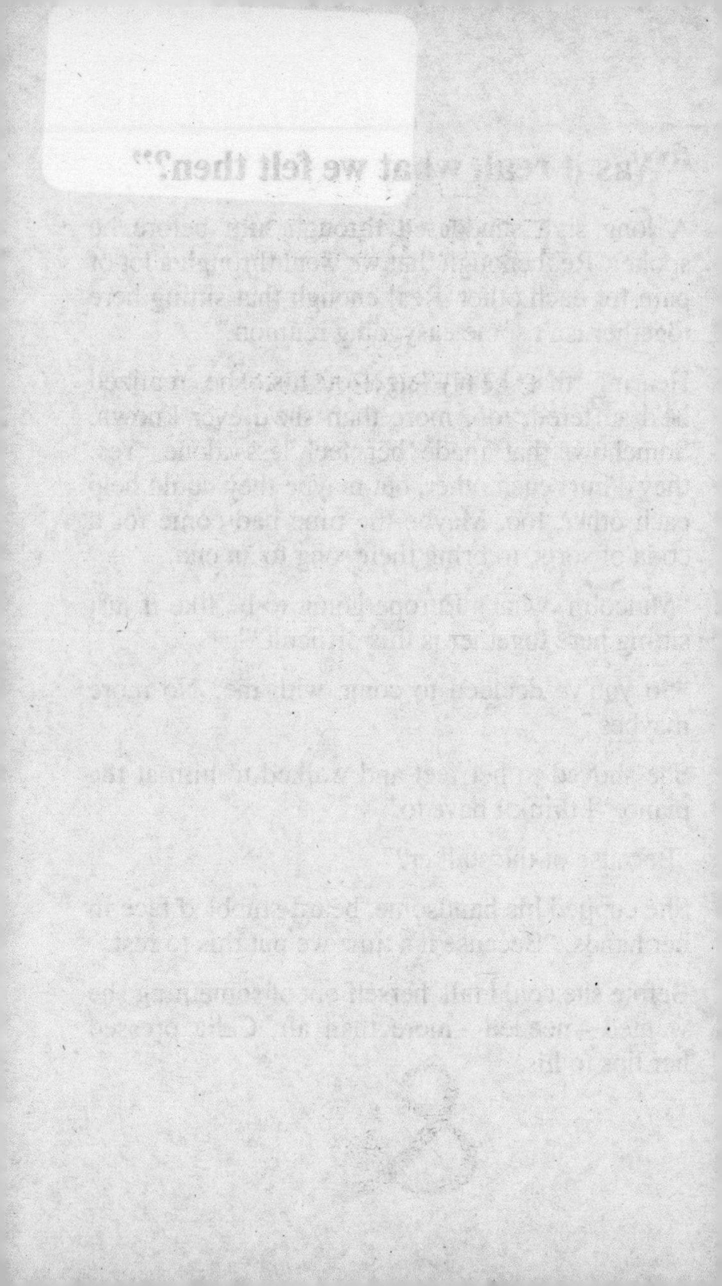

PLAYING FOR KEEPS

BY
CATHERINE MANN

Published in Great Britain 2013
by Mills & Boon, an imprint of Harlequin (UK) Limited,
Eton House, 18-24 Paradise Road, Richmond, Surrey TW9 1SR

ISBN: 978 0 263 90475 8
ebook ISBN: 978 1 472 00608 0

51-0613

Harlequin (UK) policy is to use papers that are natural, renewable and recyclable products and made from wood grown in sustainable forests. The logging and manufacturing processes conform to the legal environmental regulations of the country of origin.

Printed and bound in Spain
by Blackprint CPI, Barcelona

USA TODAY bestselling author **Catherine Mann** lives on a sunny Florida beach with her flyboy husband and their four children. With more than forty books in print in over twenty countries, she has also celebrated wins for both a RITA® Award and a Booksellers' Best Award. Catherine enjoys chatting with readers online—thanks to the wonders of the internet, which allows her to network with her laptop by the water! Contact Catherine through her website, www.catherinemann.com, find her on Facebook and Twitter (@CatherineMann1) or reach her by snail mail at PO Box 6065, Navarre, FL 32566, USA.

To the charter members of "The Tree House Club,"
karaoke singers extraordinaire:
Johnny, Tom, Elena, Lori, Mike, Vicky, George, Jerry,
Linda, Shawn, Chris, and Daphne.

One

Midway through the junior-high choir's rehearsal of "It's a Small World," Celia Patel found out just how small the world could shrink.

She dodged left and right as half the singers—the female half—sprinted down the stands, squealing in fangirl glee. Their footsteps rattled metal risers and squeaked on the gymnasium floor, the stampeding herd moving as one. All their energy focused on racing to the back of the gymnasium where *he* stood.

Malcolm Douglas.

Seven-time Grammy award winner.

Platinum-selling soft-rock star.

And the man who'd broken Celia's heart when they were both sixteen years old.

Celia hefted aside her music stand before the last of the middle-school girls rushed by, oblivious to her attempts to stop them. Identical twins Valentina and Valeria nearly plowed her down in their dash to the back. Already, a couple dozen students circled him. Two bodyguards shuffled their feet uncertainly while more squeals and giggles ricocheted into the rafters.

Malcolm raised a stalling hand to the ominous bodyguards while keeping his eyes locked on Celia, smiling that million-watt grin that had graced CD covers and promo shots. Tall and honed, he still had a hometown-boy-handsome appeal that hadn't dimmed. He'd merely matured—now polished with confidence and about twenty more pounds of whipcord muscle.

Success and chart-topping wealth probably didn't hurt.

She wanted him gone. For her sanity's sake, she *needed* him gone. But now that he was here, she couldn't look away.

He wore his khakis and designer loafers—sockless—with the easy confidence of a man comfortable in his skin. Sleeves rolled up on his chambray shirt exposed strong, tanned forearms and musician's hands.

Best not to think about his talented, nimble hands.

His sandy-brown hair was as thick as she remembered. It was still a little long, skimming over his forehead in a way that once called to her fingers to stroke it back. And those blue eyes—heaven help her—she recalled well how indigo-dark they went just before he kissed her with the enthusiasm and ardor of a hormone-pumped teenager.

There was no denying he was all man now.

What in the hell was he doing here? Malcolm hadn't set foot in Azalea, Mississippi, since a judge crony of her father's had offered Malcolm the choice of juvie or military reform school nearly eighteen years ago. Since he'd left her behind—scared, *pregnant* and determined to salvage her life.

Even though he showed up regularly in the tabloids,

seeing him in person after all these years was different. Not that she'd gone searching for photos of him. But given his popularity, she couldn't help but be periodically blindsided by glimpses of him. Worst of all, though, was hearing the sound of his voice crooning over the radio as she changed the station.

Now, across the room, he pressed a paper against his knee to sign an autograph for Valentina—or Valeria. No one could tell them apart, not even their mother sometimes. Totally beside the point, because watching Malcolm with the young girl twisted Celia's heart with what could have been if somehow, against the odds and all better judgment, they'd been able to keep and raise their baby.

But they weren't sixteen anymore, and she'd put aside reckless dreams the day she'd handed her newborn daughter over to a couple who could give the precious child everything Celia and Malcolm couldn't.

She threw back her shoulders and started toward the cluster across the gym, determined to get through this surprise visit with her pride in place. At least the nine boys in the choir were sitting on the risers, making the most of the chance to play with video games banned during class. She let that slide for now and zeroed in on the mini-mob collected by a rolling cart full of basketballs just under a red exit sign.

"Class, we need to give Mr. Douglas some breathing room." She closed in on the circle of girls, resisting the urge to smooth her hands down her sunshine-yellow sundress. She gently tapped Sarah Lynn Thompson's wrist. "And no pulling hair to sell online, girls."

Sarah Lynn dropped her hand to her side, a guilty flush spreading up her face.

Malcolm passed back the last of the autographs and

tucked the pen in his shirt pocket. "I'm fine, Celia, but thanks for making sure I don't go prematurely bald."

"Celia? *Celia?*" asked Valeria. Or was it Valentina? "Miss Patel, you know him? Oh, my God! How? Why didn't you tell us?"

She didn't intend to delve too deeply into those murky waters. "We went to high school together." His name was etched on the sign that proclaimed "Welcome to Azalea, Home of Malcolm Douglas" as if the town hadn't once tried to send him to jail because of her. "Now, let's get back to the risers, and I'm sure Mr. Douglas will answer your questions in an orderly fashion since he disrupted our rehearsal."

She shot him a censorious look that merely prompted an unrepentant grin in return.

Sarah Lynn stayed glued to Celia's side. "Did you two date?"

The bell rang—thank God—signaling the end of class and no time for questions after all. "Students, line up for your last class."

And wouldn't you know, both the principal and the secretary stood in the doorway as starstruck as their students in spite of the fact that both ladies were happily married and grandmothers. How had he gotten into the gym/auditorium without causing a riot?

Celia led the students to the double door, her sandals slapping the wood floor. Step by step, she realized the pair of guards inside were only a part of Malcolm's security detail. Four more muscle-bound men stood outside in the hallway while a large limo lurked beyond the glassed front entrance. Additional cars with majorly tinted windows were parked in front of and behind the stretch limo.

Malcolm shook hands with the principal and secretary, making small talk as he introduced himself, ironic as all get-out since at least half of the free world knew his face. "I'll leave autographed photos for your students."

Sarah Lynn called over her shoulder, dragging her feet on the way down the hall, "For all of us?"

"Miss Patel will let me know how many."

The last of the students stepped into the corridor, the door swooshing closed after the administrators left. How had their departure managed to suck all the air out of the massive gym along with them? She stood an arm's reach away from Malcolm, his two bodyguards looming just behind him.

So much for privacy.

"I assume you're here to see me?" Although she couldn't for the life of her fathom why.

"Yes, I am, darlin'," he drawled, his smooth baritone voice stroking over her senses like fine wine. "Is there somewhere we can talk without being interrupted?"

"Your security detail makes that rather moot, don't you think?" She smiled at the bulky duo, who stared back at her with such expressionless faces they could have been auditioning for positions as guards at Buckingham Palace.

Malcolm nodded to the stony-faced pair and without a word they both silently stepped out into the hall. "They'll stay outside the door, but they're here for your protection as much as mine."

"*My* protection?" She inched a step away to put a little distance between herself and the tempting scent of his aftershave. "I seriously doubt your fans will start worshipping me just because I knew you aeons ago."

"That's not what I meant." He scratched the back of his neck as if choosing his words carefully. "I hear via the grapevine there have been some threats made against you. A little extra security's a good thing, right?"

Perhaps some security from the temptation of having him around disrupting her well-ordered life, not to mention her hormones. "Thanks, but I'm good. It's just some crank calls and some strange notes. That kind of thing happens all too often when my dad has a high-profile case."

Although how in the world had Malcolm heard about it? Something uneasy shifted inside her, a stirring of panic she quickly squashed down. She refused to let Malcolm's appearance here yank the rug out from under her blessedly routine existence. She refused to give him the power to send her pulse racing.

Damn it all, she was a confident adult and this was her turf. Still, her nerves were as tight as piano strings. Fighting back the urge to snap at him for turning her world upside down, she folded her arms and waited. She wasn't an indulged, impulsive only child any longer. She wasn't a terrified, pregnant teen.

She wasn't a catatonic, broken young woman caught in the grips of a postpartum depression so deep her life had been at risk.

Her road back to peace had been hard-won with the help of the best shrinks money could buy. She refused to let anything or anyone—especially not Malcolm Douglas—threaten the future she'd built for herself.

Loving Celia Patel had changed his life forever. The jury was still out as to whether that had been a good or bad thing.

Regardless, their lives were linked. For nearly eighteen years, Malcolm had been able to keep his distance from her. But he'd never mastered the art of looking away, even when they were a couple of continents apart. Which was what had brought him here now, knowing too much about her life, too much about a threat to her safety that sent old protective urges into high gear. He just had to figure out how to persuade her to let him back into her life so he could help her. And by helping her, he could atone for how he'd wrecked their lives. Maybe then he could finally let go of a glorified puppy love that after so many years he doubted was real.

Although given his physical reaction to her at the moment, the memories of their attraction were 100 percent real. Once again, desire for Celia Patel threatened to knock him flat on his ass.

Hell, no, he hadn't been able to forget her even while across the world singing to sold-out stadiums. He certainly couldn't tear his eyes off her now when she walked only a step ahead. Her wavy dark hair hung loose halfway down her back, swaying with each step. The bright yellow sundress hugged her curves the way his hands once had.

He followed her across the gymnasium floor, the same building where they'd gone to school together. He'd performed on that stage in the junior-high choir to be with her. Taunts hadn't bothered him—until one stupid little idiot had said something off-color about Celia. Malcolm had decked him and gotten suspended for three days. Small price to pay. There was nothing he wouldn't do then for Celia.

Apparently that hadn't changed. One of his contacts had gotten wind of a case on her judge father's docket, a high-profile drug case with a kingpin who'd drawn a target on Celia's back. Malcolm had notified local authorities, but they hadn't bothered looking into the evidence he'd gifted them with. Evidence that detailed a money trail connecting a hit man to the suspected drug dealer.

Local authorities didn't like outsiders and were stubborn about their ability to handle matters on their own. Someone had to do something, and apparently that someone was Malcolm. Nothing, absolutely nothing, could derail him from his plan to protect Celia. He had to do this in order to make up for all the ways he'd let her down eighteen years ago.

She opened the door by the stage steps, her spine stiff and straight as she entered her small office lined with shelves surrounding a tiny desk. Musical scores and boxes of instruments packed the room—everything from triangles to xylophones to bongo drums. The smell of paper, ink and leather mixed with the familiar praline scent of Celia.

She spun to face him, her hair fanning gently, a strand caressing over his wrist. "It's more of a closet really, where I store my cart, instruments and paperwork. I travel from classroom to classroom, or we meet in the gym."

He adjusted the fit of his watch to cover rubbing away the sensation of her hair skimming his skin. "Just like the old days. Not much has changed here."

The police department was every bit as slack as before, swayed by the person with the most influence.

"Some things are different, Malcolm. *I* am different," she said in a cool tone he didn't recognize at all.

And he was a man who specialized in the timbre of the voice.

"Aren't you going to chew me out for disrupting your class?"

"That would be rude of me." Her fingers toyed restlessly with the ukulele on her desk, notes lightly filling the air. "Meeting you was obviously the highlight of their young lives."

"But obviously not the highlight of yours." Leaning back, he tucked his hands in his pockets to keep from stroking the strings along with her. Memories taunted him of how they'd played the guitar and piano together, their shared love of music leading to a shared love of each other's bodies. Had his mind exaggerated those memories into something more than they really were? So much time had passed since he'd seen her that he couldn't be sure.

"Why are you here?" The sight of her slim fingers moving along the strings damn near mesmerized him. "You don't have a performance scheduled in the area."

"You follow my tour schedule?" His eyes snapped up to her face.

She snorted on a laugh. "The whole freakin' town follows your every breath. What you eat for breakfast. Who you dated. I would have to be blind and deaf not to hear what the town has to say about their wonder boy. But personally? I'm no longer a charter member of the Malcolm Douglas fan club."

"Now, there's the Celia I remember." He grinned.

She didn't. "You still haven't answered my question. Why are you here?"

"I'm here for you." His libido shouted a resounding echo. Damn it all, why did she have to be even more lushly sensual now than she had been before?

"For me? I think not," she said coolly, her fingers still lightly stroking the ukulele with instinctive sensuality, as if she savored the feel of every note as much as the sound. "I have plans for tonight. You should have called ahead."

"You're much more level now than you were before."

Her expression flickered with something he couldn't quite grasp before she continued, "I was a teenager then. I'm an adult now, with adult responsibilities. So if we could speed this up, please?"

"You may not have kept track of my schedule, but I kept up with yours." He knew every detail of the threatening phone calls, the flat tire and the other threats increasing in frequency by the day. He also knew she'd only told her father half of what happened. The thought of each threat chilled Malcolm's ardor and ramped up his protectiveness. "I know you finished your music degree with honors from the University of Southern Mississippi. You've been teaching here since graduation."

"I'm proud of my life, thank you very much, far more than can be summed up in a couple of sentences. Did you come to give me a belated graduation gift? Because if not, you can go finish signing autographs."

"Let's cut to the chase, then." He shoved away from the door and stood toe-to-toe with her, just to prove to himself he could be near her and not haul her against him. "I came here to protect you."

Her fingers popped a string on the ukulele, and even though she didn't back away, her gaze skittered to the side. "Um, would you care to clarify?"

"You know full well what I'm talking about. Those crank calls you mentioned earlier." Why was she hiding the incidents from her old man? Anger nipped at his gut—at her for being reckless and at himself for having taken that tempting step closer. As if the room wasn't small enough already. "Your father's current case. Drug lord, kingpin. Ring a bell?"

"My father's a judge. He prosecutes bad guys and often they get angry, make empty threats." Her eyes met his again, any signs of unease gone, replaced with a poised distance so alien to the wild child she'd once been. "I'm not sure why this is your concern."

And there she'd hit on the truth. She wasn't his to watch over, but that didn't stop the urge to protect her any more than her dress could stop him from remembering what she looked like with only her long hair draped over her bare shoulders. His frustration snapped as surely as that nylon string. "Damn it, Celia, you're smarter than this."

Her plump lips pressed into a tight line. "Time for you to leave."

He gritted back his temper, recognizing it for what it was—frustrated desire. His attraction to her was even more powerful than he'd expected. "I apologize for being less than diplomatic. I heard about the threats on your life, and call me a nostalgic idiot, but I'm worried about you."

"How did you get the details?" Her face creased with confusion—and suspicion. "My father and I have made sure to keep everything out of the press."

"Dear old Dad may be a powerful judge, but his power doesn't reach everywhere."

"That doesn't explain how you found out."

He couldn't explain the "how" of that. There were things about him she didn't know. He kept much better secrets than her father. "But I'm right."

"One of the cases my father's prosecuting has gotten… messy. The police are investigating."

"You're really going to put your faith in the three-man shop they call a police department?" He couldn't keep the cynicism from his voice. "Security around you is awe-inspiring. I should get my men to make notes."

"No need to be sarcastic. I'm taking precautions. This isn't the first time someone has threatened our family because of my father's job."

"But this is the most serious threat." If he told her about the paper trail, he would have to explain how he got it. But that was a last resort. If he couldn't convince her to accept his help any other way, he would tell her what he could about the work he did outside the music industry.

"You seem to know a lot about what's going on in my life."

She studied him with deep brown eyes that still had the power to draw him in and lure him past reason.

"I told you, Celia. I care enough to keep tabs. I care enough to want to make sure you're okay."

"Thank you. That's…nice." Her braced shoulders eased, some of her defensiveness draining away, as well. "I appreciate your concern, even if it's a little confusing. I will be careful. Now that you've fulfilled your sense of…obligation or whatever, I truly do need to pack up and go home."

"I'll walk you to your car." He raised a hand and plastered on his best smile. "Don't bother saying no. I can carry your books, like old times."

"Except for your whole secret-service-style protective detail."

"You'll be safe with me." More than she could know.

"That's what we thought eighteen years ago." She stopped and pressed a hand to her forehead. "I'm sorry. That wasn't fair of me."

His mind exploded with images of their teenage passion, out-of-control hormones that had led them to reckless sex. A lot of sex. He cleared his throat. Too bad his brain still hitched on the past.

"Apology not needed but accepted." He knew he'd let her down then, and damned if he would repeat the mistake. "Let me take you out to dinner, and we can talk over an idea I have for making sure you're safe until the trial's over."

"Thank you, but no." She closed the laptop on her desk and tucked it in a case. "I have end-of-the-year grades to finish."

"You have to eat."

"And I will. I have half of a leftover panino waiting in my refrigerator at home."

She might be a more poised woman now, but there was no missing the old Celia stubbornness. She'd dug in her heels, and it would take serious maneuvering to budge her.

"Fine, then you leave me no choice. I'll talk now. This threat against your life is real. Very real. In my line of work—" his real line of work, which only a handful of people knew about "—I have access to security sources you can't imagine. You need protection beyond anything the local police department can provide and more than your father can buy."

"You're being overly dramatic."

"Drug lords, Celia, have unlimited funds and no scruples." He'd taken the fall for those types as a teenager to keep his mother safe. And it was his own fault for putting himself in their path by working in that club as a last-ditch effort to make enough money to support Celia and their baby on the way. "They will hurt you, badly, even kill you, in hopes of swaying your father."

"Do you think I don't already know this?" Her jaw flexed as she clenched her teeth, the only slip in her carefully controlled composure. "I've done everything I can."

He saw his opening and took it. "Not everything."

"Fine, Mr. Know-It-All," she said with a sigh, sweeping back her silky hair from her face. "What else can I do?"

Clasping her arms, he stepped closer, willing himself not to cave to the temptation to gather her soft body close against him and kiss her until she was too dizzy to disagree. Although if he had to use passion to persuade her, then so be it. Because one way or another, he would convince her. "Let my bodyguards protect you. Come with me on my European tour."

Two

Go on a European tour? With Malcolm?

Celia grabbed the edge of her desk for balance and choked back her shock at his outlandish offer. He couldn't possibly be serious. Not after eighteen years apart, with only a few short letters and a couple of phone calls exchanged in the beginning. They'd broken up, drifted away from each other, eventually cut off contact completely after the baby's adoption was complete.

Back at the start of Malcolm's music career, she'd been in her early twenties, under the care of a good therapist and going to college. She'd dreamed of what it would be like if Malcolm showed up on her doorstep. What if he swept her off her feet and they picked up where they'd left off?

But those fantasies never came to fruition. They only held her back, and she'd learned to make her own realities—concrete and reasonable plans for the future.

Even if he *had* shown up before, she wasn't sure then or now if she would have gone with him. Her mental health had been a hard-won battle. It could have been risky, in her fragile state, to trade stability for the upheaval of a life on the road with a high-profile music star.

But it sure would have been nice to have the choice, for him to have cared enough to come back and offer. His ridiculous request now was too little, too late.

Celia hitched her floral computer bag over her shoulder and eyed her office door a few short steps away. "Joke's over, Malcolm. Of course I'm not going to Europe with you. Thanks for the laugh, though. I'm heading home now rather than stick around through my planning period since, for the first day in forever, I'm not slated for bus duty. You may have time to waste playing games, but I have grades to tabulate."

His hand fell to rest on her bare arm, stopping her. "I'm completely serious."

Hair prickled. Goose bumps rose. And damn it, desire stirred in her belly.

After all this time, her body still reacted to his touch, and she resented the hell out of that fact. "You're never serious. Just ask the tabloid reporters. They fill articles with tales of your charm on and off camera."

He angled closer, his grip firm, stoking long-buried embers. "When it comes to you, I've always been one hundred percent serious."

And wasn't that an about-face for them? She used to be the wild, adventurous one while Malcolm worked hard to secure his future. Or at least, she'd thought he'd been serious about the future—until he'd ended up in handcuffs, arrested.

Her breath hitched in her throat for three heavy heartbeats before she regained her equilibrium. "Then I'll be the rational one here. There's truly no way I'm leaving for Europe with you. Thank you again for the offer to protect me, but you're off the hook."

He tipped his head to the side, his face so close a puff of her breath would rustle the stubborn lock of hair that fell over his forehead. "You used to fantasize about making love in Paris in the shadow of the Eiffel Tower." His voice went husky and seductive, those million-dollar vocal cords stroking her as effectively as any glide of his fingers.

She moved his hand slowly—and deliberately—off her arm. "Now I'm *really* not going anywhere with you."

"Fine. I'll cancel my concert tour and become your shadow until we're sure you're safe." He grinned unrepentantly, stuffing his hands in his pockets. "But my fans will be so pissed. They can get rabid sometimes, dangerous even, and above all, my goal is to keep you safe."

Was he for real?

"This is too bizarre." She clenched her fists to resist the urge to pull her hair—or his. "How did you say you found out about the Martin case?"

He hesitated for the barest instant before answering, "I have contacts."

"Money can buy anything." She couldn't help but think of how he'd once disdained her father's portfolio and now he could buy her dad out more than twice over.

"Extra cash would have bought us both some help eighteen years ago."

And just that fast, their final fight came rolling back over her, how he'd insisted on playing the gig at that seedy music joint because it paid well. He'd been determined for them to get married and be a family. She'd been equally as certain they were both too young to make that happen.

He'd gotten arrested in a drug raid on the bar, and she'd been sent to a Swiss "boarding school" to have her baby.

Even now, she saw the regret in his eyes, mixed with censure. She couldn't go down this path with him, not again. Tears of rage and pain and loss welled inside her, and while she understood how unhealthy it was to bottle her emotions, she refused to crumble in front of him.

She needed to get out of there before she lost it altogether and succumbed to the temptation to throw herself into the comfort of his arms, to bury her face in his shirt.

To inhale the scent of him until it filled her senses.

"Things would have turned out better for you with more financial options," Celia said, reminded of how he'd lost out on the promise of a scholarship to Juilliard. "But no amount of money would have changed the choices I made. What we shared is in the past." Securing her computer tote bag on her shoulder, she pushed past him. "Thank you for worrying about me, but we're done here. Goodbye, Malcolm."

She rushed by, her foot knocking and jangling a box of tambourines on her way out into the gymnasium. Malcolm could stay or go, but he wasn't her concern anymore. The custodian would lock her office after he swept up. She had to get away from Malcolm before she made a fool of herself over him.

Again.

Her sandals slapped an even but fast pace through the exit and directly into the teachers' parking lot. Thank heavens she didn't have to march through the halls with the whole school watching and whispering. Tears burning her eyes, she registered the sound of his footsteps behind her, but she kept moving out into the muggy afternoon.

The parking lot was all but empty, another hour still left in the school day. In the distance, the playground hummed with the cheers of happy children. What a double-edged sword it was working here, a job she loved but with constant reminders of what she'd given up.

Her head fell back, and she blinked hard. The sunshine blinded her, making her eyes water all the more. Damn Malcolm Douglas for coming into her life again and damn her own foolish attraction to him that hadn't dimmed one bit. She swiped away the tears and charged ahead to her little green sedan. Heat steamed up from the asphalt. Magnolia-scented wind rustled the trees and rolled across the parking lot. A flyer flapped under the windshield wiper.

She stopped in her tracks, her hand flying to her throat. Was that *another* veiled warning from her father's latest enemy?

Every day for a week, she'd found a flyer under her wiper, all relating to death. A funeral parlor. Cemetery plots. Life insurance. The police had called it a coincidence.

She pinched the paper out from under the blade, shuffling her computer bag higher up onto her shoulder. The flyer advertised…

A coupon for flowers? A sigh of relief shuddered through her.

An absolutely benign piece of paper. She laughed, crumpling the ad in her hand. She was actually getting paranoid, which meant whoever was trying to scare her had won. She fished out her keys and thumbed the unlock button on the key fob. Then she reached to slide her computer bag onto the passenger seat…

And stopped short.

A black rose rested precisely in the cup holder. There was no mistaking the ominous message. Somehow that macabre rosebud had gotten into her car. Some*one* had been in her locked vehicle.

Bile rose in her throat. Her mind raced back to the florist ad under her windshield wiper. She pulled the paper out of her computer bag and flattened the coupon on the seat.

Panic snapped through her veins, her emotions already on edge from the unexpected encounter with Malcolm. She bolted out of her sedan, stumbling as she backed away. Her body slammed into someone. A hard male chest. She stifled a scream and spun fast to find Malcolm standing behind her.

He cupped the back of her head. “What’s wrong?”

With his fingers in her hair and her nerves in shambles, she couldn’t even pretend to be composed. “There’s a black rose in my car—completely creepy. I don’t know how it got there since I locked up this morning. I know I did, because I had to use my key fob to get in.”

“We call the cops, now.”

She shook her head, nudging his hand aside. “The police chief will write it up and say I’m paranoid about some disgruntled students.”

The old chief would make veiled references to mental instability in her past, something her father had tried to keep under wraps. Few knew. Still, for them, a stigma lingered. Unfair—not to mention dangerous since she wasn’t being taken seriously.

From the thunderclouds gathering in Malcolm’s eyes, he was definitely taking her seriously. He clasped her shoulders in broad, warm hands, gently urging her to the side and into the long shadows of his bodyguards. Malcolm strode past her to the sedan, looking first at the rose, then kneeling to peer under the car.

For a bomb or something?

She swallowed hard, stepping back. “Malcolm, let’s just call the police after all. Please, get away from my car.”

Standing, he faced her again, casting a tall and broad-shouldered shadow over her in a phantom caress. “We’re in agreement on that.” He charged forward and clasped her arm, the calluses on his fingers rasping against her skin. “Let’s go.”

“Did you see something under there?”

“No, but I haven’t looked under the hood. I’m getting you out of here while my men make sure it’s safe before the rest of the school comes pouring out.”

The rest of the school? The sound of the children playing ball in the distance struck fear in her gut. The faces of her teacher friends and students scrolled through her head. To put an entire school in harm’s way? She couldn’t fathom whoever was threatening her would risk drawing this much attention—would risk this many lives. But there was definitely something more sinister about this latest threat, and that rattled her.

Malcolm tugged her farther from the vehicle.

“Where are we going?” She looked back over her shoulder at the redbrick building with the flags flapping in the wind. “I need to warn everyone.”

“My bodyguards are already taking care of that,” he reassured her. “We’re going to my limo. It has reinforced windows and an armor-plated body. We can talk there and figure out your next move.”

Reinforced windows? Armor plating? Security in front and behind? He truly did have all the money he’d once dreamed of, access to resources beyond her own local law enforcement. Enough resources to protect her from all threats, real or imagined.

She shivered in apprehension and didn’t bother denying herself the comforting protection of Malcolm's presence all the way to his stretch Cadillac.

Malcolm stopped seeing red once he had Celia tucked into the safety of his armored limousine and the chauffer was headed for her home.

Two of his bodyguards had stayed with her vehicle to wait for the police—and report the details back to him without the filter of local authorities. He didn't think there was anything else wrong with her vehicle, but better to be certain and put all of his financial resources to work. He'd done all he could for now to make sure Celia and the school weren't in danger.

He scrolled through messages on his cell phone for updates from his security detail, all too aware of the warm presence of Celia in the seat beside him. Once he had her safely settled, he would work with his contacts to find substantial proof to nail that drug-dealing bastard Martin for these threats. Malcolm had taken the fall for a drug-dealing scumbag in return for them leaving his mother alone. He hadn't known who to turn to then.

He wasn't a flat-broke teenager anymore. He had the resources and power to be there for Celia now in a way he hadn't before. Maybe then he could finally forgive himself for letting her down.

As they drove down the azalea-lined Main Street, he felt the weight of her glare.

Malcolm tucked away his phone and gave her his undivided attention. "What's wrong?"

"Something that just occurred to me. Did you put that flower in my car to scare me so I would come with you?" She stared at him suspiciously.

"You can't possibly believe that."

"I don't know what I believe right now. I haven't seen

you in nearly two decades. And the day you show up, offering to protect me, *this* happens. The thought that they were here, at the school, near my students…" Gasping for air, she grabbed her knees and leaned forward. "I think I'm going to be sick."

He palmed between her shoulder blades, holding himself back from the urge to gather her close, just to touch her again. "You know me. You know how much I wanted to take care of you before. You of all people know how much it frustrated me that my dad wasn't there to take care of my mom. Now, ask me again if I put the rose in your car?"

Sweeping her hair aside with her hands, she eyed him, her breath still shallow. "Okay, I believe you, and I'm sorry. Although a part of me wishes you had done it because then I wouldn't have to be this worried."

"It's going to be all right. Anyone coming after you will have to get through me," he said, tamping down the frustration of his teenage years when there hadn't been a damn thing he could do for Celia or his mom. Times were different now. His bank balance was definitely different. "The police are going to look over your car and secure the parking lot if there's a problem."

"Ten minutes ago you said the police can't protect me."

Dark brown locks slithered over his arm, every bit as soft as he remembered. He eased his hand away while he still could. He might not believe in the power of love anymore, but he sure as hell respected the power of lust. His body still reacted to her, but this wasn't just any woman who'd caught his eye. This was Celia. The power of the attraction—as strong as ever—had caught him unawares. But he'd come here to make up for the past. What they'd shared was over. "We still need to let the police know. Where is your father? At the courthouse?"

"At his annual doctor's checkup. His heart has been giving him trouble. He's been talking about retiring after the Martin case." She sagged back into the leather seat. "I can't believe this is happening."

He opened the mini-fridge and pulled out a bottled water. "No one will get to you now." He passed her the cooled Evian. "This vehicle is steel-reinforced, with bulletproof glass."

"Paparazzi can be persistent." She took the bottle from him, taking special care to avoid brushing his fingers. "Is it worth it living in a bubble?"

"I'm doing exactly what I want with my life." He had a freedom now that went far beyond the musician lifestyle, a side to his world with power that only a handful of people knew about.

"Then I'm happy for you." She sipped the water, all signs of her fear walled away.

But he knew what he'd seen, even if she was far better at hiding her emotions now than she'd been as a teenager. "Your school year finishes tomorrow. You'll be free for the summer. Come with me to Europe. Do it for your dad or your students, but don't let pride keep you from accepting my proposal."

She rolled the bottle between her hands, watching him from under the dark sweep of her eyelashes. "Wouldn't it be selfish of me to take you up on this offer? What if I put you in danger?"

Ah. He resisted the urge to smile. She hadn't said no. Something was shifting in her; he could sense it. She was actually considering his offer.

"The Celia I knew before wouldn't have worried about that. You would have just blasted ahead while we tackled the problem together."

A bump in the road jostled her against him. His arm

clamped around her instinctively, and just as fast his senses went on overload. The praline scent of her. The feel of her soft breasts pressed against his side, her palm flattened on his chest. And God, what he wouldn't give for a taste of her as she stared up at him. Her wide brown eyes filled with the same electric awareness that snapped through his veins.

Biting her lip, she eased away, sliding to the far side of the seat. Away from him.

"We're all grown up, and a more measured approach is called for," she said primly, setting the water bottle into a holder. "I can't simply go to Europe with you. That's just…unthinkable. As for my students, you already noted the school year's over, and if the threat truly is stemming from my father's case, it should be resolved by the time summer's over. See? All logical. Thank you for the offer, though."

"Stop thanking me," he snapped, knowing too well the ways he'd come up short in taking care of her and their child. This was his chance to make up for that, damn it, and he couldn't let it pass him by.

The limo cruised down the familiar roads of Azalea with blessedly smaller potholes. Not much had changed; only a few of the mom-and-pop diners had folded into chain restaurants near a small mall.

Otherwise, this could have been a date of theirs years ago, driving around town in search of a spot to park and make out. They'd both lost their virginity in the back of the BMW she'd gotten for her sixteenth birthday. The memories… Damn… Too much to think about now while trying to keep his head clear.

When he'd come up with the plan to help her, he hadn't expected to still want her, to be so pulled in by her. He'd dated over the years and could have any woman he wanted. And still, here he was, aching to take *this* woman. Had he gotten himself in too deep with his offer of protection? The prospect of touring Europe together, staying alone in hotels, suddenly didn't sound like such a smart idea.

"Malcolm?" Her voice drew him back to the present. "Why did you look me up now? I truly don't believe you've watched my every move for nearly eighteen years."

Fair enough. He had kept track of her over the years. But this time of year, thoughts of their shared past weighed heavier on his conscience. "You've been on my mind this week. It's the time of year."

Celia's eyes shut briefly before she acknowledged, "Her birthday."

His throat closed, so he simply nodded.

Her face flooded with pain, the first deep and true emotion she'd shown since he arrived. "I am sorry."

"I signed the papers, too." He'd given up all custodial rights to his child. He'd known he had no choice, nothing to offer and no hope of offering her anything in the foreseeable future. He'd been lucky not to be in jail, but the military reform school in North Carolina had been a lockdown existence.

"But you didn't want to sign the papers." She touched his arm lightly, the careful poise in her eyes falling away to reveal a deep vulnerability. "I understand that."

His willpower stretched to the limit as he fought back the urge to kiss away the pain in her eyes.

"It would have been selfish of me to hold out when I had no future and no way to provide for either of you." He shifted in his seat and let the question roll out that had plagued him all these years. "Do you think about her?"

"Every day."

"And the two of us?" he pushed, studying her hand

still resting on his wrist. Her touch seared his skin with memories and, yes, a still-present desire to see if the flame between them burned as hot. “Do you think back and regret?”

“I regret that you were hurt.”

He covered her hand with his and held tight. “Come with me to Europe. To stay safe. To ease stress for your old man. To put the past to rest. It’s time. Let me help you the way I couldn’t back then.”

She nibbled her bottom lip and he sensed that victory was so damn close….

The limo eased to a stop in front of her home. She blinked fast and pulled her hand away. She gathered her computer bag from the floor. “I need to go home, to think. This is all too much, too fast.”

She hadn’t said an outright no, and that would have to do for now. He would win in the end. He always did these days. His fame and position had benefits.

He ducked out of the car and around to her side to walk her to her door. He didn’t expect to come inside and stay the night, but he needed to be sure she was safe. His hand went to the small of her back by instinct as he guided her toward the little carriage house behind a columned mansion.

She glanced over her shoulder. “You already know where I live?”

“It’s not a secret.” In fact her life was too accessible. He’d seen too much corruption in the world. This kind of openness made him itchy.

Although he had to confess to being surprised at her choice for a home. The larger, brick mansion wasn’t her father’s house, as he’d half expected when he’d first learned of where she lived. She’d carved out her own space even if she’d stayed in her hometown.

Even so, the little white carriage house was a security nightmare. Dimly lit stairs on the outside led to the main entrance over her garage. He followed her up the steps, unable to keep his eyes off the gentle sway of her hips or the way the sunlight glinted on her silky dark hair.

She stopped at the small balcony outside her door, turning to face him. "Thank you for seeing me home and calling the cops. I truly do appreciate your help."

How many times had he kissed her good-night on her doorstep until her father started flicking the porch light off and on? More than he could count. A possessive urge to gather her close and test the old attraction seared his veins, but he was a more patient man these days. He had his eye on the larger goal.

Getting her to leave the country with him.

He held out his hand for her keys. "Once I've checked over your place, I'll be on my way for the night."

Just not far away.

Malcolm wasn't the same idealistic teen he'd once been. He'd spent every day at that military reform school plotting how he would show up at Celia's father's house. How he would prove he hadn't done a damn thing wrong. He was an honorable man who'd had his family stolen from him. He'd held on to that goal all through college, as well, playing music gigs at night to earn enough money to cover what scholarships didn't.

But he never could have foreseen the path to honor that would play out for him. He'd sure as hell never planned on being a music star with his face plastered on posters. He'd stuck with it for the money. Then surprisingly, his old headmaster had shown up in his dressing room after a concert with a crazy offer.

Malcolm's globe-trotting lifestyle offered him the perfect cover to work as a freelance agent for Interpol.

In that moment, Malcolm gained a strong compass for his life and he'd never veered from the plan. Until today.

Even after eighteen years, he couldn't look away from Celia. "The keys, please?"

Hesitating for an instant, she dropped the keys into his hand. He turned the lock—a lock he could have picked thanks to some skills he'd acquired along the way—and pushed open the door to an airy and light space with sheer frills, an antique upright piano and a lemony, clean scent.

He stepped inside to make sure there weren't any more roses—or worse—waiting for her. She disarmed the alarm, then walked beside him down the narrow hall leading toward the living area, clicking her fingernails along a panpipe hung on the wall. His sixth sense hummed on high alert. Something wasn't right, but his instincts were dulled around Celia, and damn it, that wasn't acceptable. He knew better. He'd been trained for better.

Drawing in his focus, he realized… Holy hell…

He angled back to Celia. "Did you leave the living room light on?"

Flinching, she gasped. "No. I never do…"

He tucked her behind him only to realize…a man sat on the sofa.

Her father.

Malcolm resisted the urge to step back in surprise. Judge Patel had gotten old. Intellectually, Malcolm understood the years had to have left a mark, but seeing that in person was…unsettling. He'd resented this man, even hated him at some points, but bottom line, he understood they both had a common goal: keeping Celia safe.

Malcolm was just better suited for the job, and this time, he refused to let Judge George Patel stop him.

Three

Celia could swear she heard Fate chiming with laughter.

She looked from her father to Malcolm, waiting for the explosion. They'd never gotten along. Malcolm encouraged her to think for herself. Her parents had pampered her while also being overprotective. They'd seen her relationship with Malcolm as dangerous. They'd been right, in a way. She had been out of control when it came to him.

However, their refusal to let her see him had only made her try all the harder to be with him. Malcolm had chafed at their disapproval, determined to prove himself. The whole thing had been an emotional train wreck in the works.

Could they all be more mature now? God, she hoped so. The thought of an ugly confrontation made her ill, especially at the tail end of a day that had already knocked her off balance in more ways than one.

Malcolm nodded to her father. "Good evening, sir."

"Douglas." Her father stood, extending his hand. "Welcome back."

They shook hands, something she wouldn't have believed possible eighteen years ago. Even if they were eyeing each other warily, they were keeping things civil. The last time they'd all been together, her father had punched Malcolm in the jaw over the pregnancy news, while her mother had sobbed on the couch. Malcolm hadn't fought back, even though he was at least six inches taller than her father.

Nervous about pushing their luck, she turned to Malcolm and rested her fingers lightly on his arm. "I'm fine now. You can go, but thanks again, truly."

She shuddered to think what it would have been like to find that macabre rose on her own and have her concerns discounted by the police again. This was not the work of some student pissed off over a failing grade. Malcolm seemed to grasp that right away. She hadn't considered until just this moment how much his unconditional belief meant to her.

He dipped his head and said softly, "We'll talk tomorrow. But don't say no just because I'm the one offering." Grasping the doorknob, he nodded to her father again. "Good night, sir."

And that was it? He actually left? No confrontation? Celia stood there stunned at how easily he'd departed. She wanted a proper goodbye, and it scared her how much that mattered. Although his final words swirled in her mind. Was she being contrary—like the old Celia—turning down a wise opportunity because Malcolm had made the offer?

She shook off the thoughts. Likely Malcolm just realized she was safely home, his duty done. After resetting the alarm, she turned back to face her dad. The familiarity of her place wrapped around her, soothing her at the end of a tumultuous day.

This little carriage house wasn't as grand as the historic mansion where she'd grown up or the posh resorts Malcolm frequented—according to the tabloids. But she was proud of it. She took pride in how she'd decorated on her own budget. She'd scoured estate sales and flea markets until she pieced together a home that reflected her love of antiques and music.

Her home had become a symbol of the way she'd pieced herself back together, reshaping herself by blending the best of her past and her future. Shedding the dregs, taking responsibility for her own messes, which also gave her the freedom to celebrate her own successes.

And in finding that freedom, being around her father had actually become easier. She wasn't as defensive, and right now, she was only worried—about him.

"What are you doing here, Dad? I thought you were at your doctor's appointment."

"News travels fast." He nudged aside throw pillows and sank back on the couch, looking weary with bags under his eyes and furrows in his brow. "When I heard about Malcolm Douglas's impromptu visit to the school, I told the doc to speed things along."

His shock of gray hair still caught her by surprise sometimes. Much like when she'd been stunned to realize her indomitable father was actually only five-six. He'd always had a larger-than-life presence. Yet the day her mother had died, her father had grown frail in an instant, looking more and more like Grandpa Patel—without the Indian accent.

Intellectually, she'd always understood that her mom and dad were older than her friends' parents. She'd been a late-in-life baby, born after her sister died. How strange to have a sibling she'd never met.

And yes, more than once, Celia had wondered if she would have been conceived had her sister lived.

She'd never doubted her parents' love or felt she was a replacement for the child they'd lost to cancer. But that loss had made them overprotective, and they'd spoiled her shamelessly. So much so that Celia winced now to think of what a brat she'd been, how many people she'd hurt.

Including Malcolm.

She glanced at her slim silver watch. "He showed up at school less than an hour ago. You must have rushed right over."

"As I said, small town."

There weren't many secrets around Azalea, Mississippi, which made it all the more miraculous that she'd managed to have a baby and give her up for adoption without the entire town knowing all the details. Malcolm had been sent off to a military reform school in North Carolina, and she'd been sent to Switzerland on an "exchange" program, actually a chalet where she'd been homeschooled until she delivered.

She swallowed the lump in her throat and sat on the arm of the sofa. "What did the doctor say about your shortness of breath lately?"

"I'm here, aren't I? Doc Graham wouldn't have let me leave unless she thought I was okay, so all's fine." He nudged his round steel glasses in place, ink stains on his fingers from making notes. Her dad didn't trust computers and backed everything up the old-fashioned way—on paper. "I'm more worried about you and your concerns that someone might be targeting you."

Her concerns? Did he doubt her, too? "How bad is the Martin case?"

"You know I can't talk about that."

"But it's an important one."

"Every judge dreams of leaving the bench with a landmark case, especially just before he retires." He patted the top of her hand. "Now, quit trying to distract me. Why did Malcolm Douglas show up here?"

"He heard about the current case on your docket, and somehow word got out about my reporting the threats to the police, which I find strange since no one here takes them seriously." Would they finally listen to her after today's incident?

"And Malcolm Douglas—international music star—came running after not seeing you for eighteen years?" Concern moved through his chocolate-brown eyes.

"Seems crazy, I know." She toed a footstool made of an old leather drum. "Honestly, though, I think it had more to do with the timing."

"Timing of what?"

That he even had to ask hurt her heart. "Dad, it's her seventeenth birthday."

"You still think about her?"

"Of course I do."

"But you don't talk about her."

She'd done nothing *but* talk about her baby in therapy—cry and talk more, until finally she'd reached a point where she could move forward with her life. "What's the point? Listen, Dad, I'm fine. Really. I have end-of-the-year grades to tabulate and submit."

Her dad thumped his knees. "You should move home."

"This is my home now," she reminded him gently. "I consented to letting you pay for a better security system. It's the same one at your house, as you clearly know since you chose the pass code. Now, please, go home and rest."

She worried about him, about the pale tinge to his

dusky complexion, the tired stoop to his shoulders. His job would be easier if she wasn't around since he wouldn't have to stress about her. Not taking Malcolm up on his offer suddenly felt very selfish. "Dad, I'm thinking about taking a vacation, just getting away once school ends."

"If you come to the house, you'll be waited on hand and foot." He continued to offer, and she continued to say no, a pact she'd made with herself the day she'd graduated from college at twenty-four. It had taken her an extra two years, but she'd gotten there, by God.

"I have something to tell you, and I don't want you to misunderstand or be upset."

"Well, you'd better spit it out, because just saying that jacked my blood pressure a few points."

She drew in a deep breath of fortifying air before saying quickly, "Malcolm thinks I should go on tour with him."

His gray eyebrows shot upward, and he pulled off his glasses and cleaned them with a handkerchief. "Did he offer because of the reports made to the police?"

She weighed whether or not to tell him about the incident with the rose, but then given how fast he'd heard about Malcolm's arrival, he would hear about the little "gift" in her car soon enough. "There was another threat today."

He stopped cleaning his glasses abruptly, then slid them slowly on again. "What happened?"

"A cheesy black rose left in my car." As well as the florist coupon in some kind of mocking salute. She tried to downplay the whole thing for her father, but her voice shook and she probably wasn't fooling him in the least. Still, she plowed ahead, trying her best to put his mind at ease. "Next thing you know, they'll be leaving a dead horse somewhere like a parody of *The Godfather*."

"This isn't funny. You *have* to move back home."

Seeing the vein at his temple throb made her realize all the more how her being around right now made things more difficult for him. "Malcolm offered the protection of his own security people. I guess crazed stalker fans rank up there with hired hit men."

"That's not funny, either."

"I know." And it wasn't. "I'm concerned he has a point. I make you vulnerable, and I placed my students at risk by waiting this long. If I go on his European tour, it will solve a lot of problems."

She didn't want her father to worry, but she had to admit there was something more to this decision than just her father. Malcolm had presented more than an offer of protection. He'd presented the chance to put their past to rest. Because he was right. The fact that she'd turned him down so promptly hinted at unresolved issues.

But could they really spend the whole tour together? A tour that lasted four weeks? She knew because, damn it, she periodically did internet searches on his life, wondering if maybe he would play at a local arena. He never did.

"That's the only reason you've made this decision?"

She hadn't decided yet. Or had she? "Are you asking me if I still have feelings for him?"

"Do you?" he asked and strangely didn't sound upset.

God, as if she wasn't already confused enough.

"I haven't spoken to him in years." Malcolm hadn't spoken to her, either, not since after the baby was born, and yes, that stung. "Aren't you going to push me again to come to your house?"

"Actually, no. Go to Europe." He studied her with those wise judge eyes. "Close that chapter on your life so you can quit living in limbo. I would like to see you settled before I die."

"I am settled," she said and then as an afterthought rushed to add, "and happy."

Sighing, her father stood, kissed her on top of the head. "You'll make the right decision."

"Dad—"

"Good night, Celia." He patted her arm as he walked past, snagging his suit jacket from the iron coatrack. "Set the alarm after I leave."

She followed him, stunned, certain she couldn't have heard what she thought she'd heard. Had her father really encouraged her to just pick up and travel around Europe with the former love of her life? A man reputed to have broken hearts around the globe?

Except, strangely, going to Europe with Malcolm was beginning to make sense. Going with him would solve her problems here, keeping her life ordered and safe. It was also her last chance to be with Malcolm, and the wild child she'd once been shouted for her go for it.

The newer, more logical side of her even answered that leaving with him would be the lesser of two evils.

Celia locked the door behind her father and keyed in the security code.

A noise from the hall made her jolt.

Her stomach gripped tight with fear and she spun around fast, grabbing a guitar propped against a chair and lifting it like a baseball bat. She reached for the alarm just as a large shape stepped out of her bedroom.

A man.

Malcolm.

He grinned. "Your security system sucks."

Malcolm watched the anger flush Celia's cheeks as her hand fell away from the alarm's keypad.

She placed the guitar on an armchair. "You scared the hell out of me."

"Sorry about that." He stepped deeper into her living room, a space decorated with antique musical instruments his fingers itched to try out. Later. First, he had business with Celia. "I thought I made it clear I'm worried about you being here alone."

"So you broke into my home?"

"Just to prove how crummy your security system is." He'd bypassed the alarm, climbed the nearby oak and made it inside her window in less than ten minutes. "Think about it. If someone like me—a plain ol' musician—could break into your place, then what about someone motivated to find you?"

"Your point has been made." She pointed to the door. "Now leave, please."

"But then you're still here, alone in the crappily secured apartment. My code of honor has trouble with that." He wandered lazily through her living room, inspecting the canvas over the fireplace, a sketch of band instruments and, below it on the mantel, an antique piccolo on a stand. "Gauging by your conversation with your dear old dad, you don't want to go to his place."

"You eavesdropped on my discussion with my father?"

"I did." He lifted the piccolo and blew into it, testing out a quick scale—not a bad sound for an instrument that appeared to be close to two hundred years old.

"You're shameless." She snatched the instrument from him and placed it back on the wall.

"I'm unrepentant, yes, and also concerned." He moved aside a brass music stand full of hand-scored songs—apparently for students, given her notes at the top—and sat on the piano bench in front of the old upright. "Since we're being honest, I heard it all, and even your father gave his consent for you to come with me."

"I don't need my dad's permission."

"Damn straight."

Watching him warily, she sat in a rocker by the piano. "You're trying to manipulate me."

"I'm trying to make sure you're safe—and yes…" He took her hand lightly in his. A benign enough touch. Right?

Wrong. The silkiness of her skin reminded him of times when he'd explored every inch of her. "Maybe we'll settle some old baggage along the way."

"This is too much."

He agreed. "Then don't decide tonight."

Her thick dark hair trailed over one shoulder. "We'll talk in the morning?"

"Over breakfast." He squeezed her hand once before letting go and standing. "Where are the sheets for the sofa?"

She gaped at him, smoothing her hands over wrinkles in her skirt. "You're inviting yourself to spend the night?"

He hadn't planned on it, but somehow the words had come out of him anyway, likely fueled by that reckless second when he'd touched her.

"Do you expect me to sleep on your porch?" He'd actually intended to sleep in the limo.

This was the man he was, the man he'd always been. He remembered what it was like for his mom living on her own. Call him old-fashioned, but he believed women should be protected. No way in hell could he just walk away. Especially not with images of the skirt of her dress hugging her soft legs.

"I would offer to get us a couple of rooms at a hotel or B and B, but we would have to drive for hours. People might see us. My manager likes it when I show up in the press. Me, though? I'm not as into the attention."

"Being seen at a hotel with you would be complicated." Her fingers twisted in the fabric she'd just smoothed seconds earlier.

"Very." He knelt in front of her, careful not to touch her just yet, not when every instinct inside him shouted to kiss her, to sweep her up into his arms and carry her to the bedroom. To make love to her until they both were too sated to argue or think about the past. He wasn't sure yet where he planned to go with those impulses. "So let me stay for dinner, and I'll bunk on your sofa. We won't talk about Europe tonight unless you bring it up."

"What does your girlfriend think of your being here?"

Girlfriend? Right now he couldn't even envision anyone except Celia. "Those damn tabloids again. I don't have a 'girlfriend.' My manager planted that story to make it look like I'm settling down."

Relationships were too messy, and more of that protective honor kept him from indulging in the groupies that flocked backstage. He "dated" women whose publicists lined up promo gigs with his publicist. As for sex, there had been women who kept things uncomplicated, women who needed anonymity and no strings as much as he did. Women as jaded about the notion of love.

"Is that why you're really here?" Her fingers kept toying nervously with the hem of her dress, inching it higher, revealing a tantalizing extra inch of leg. "You're between women and the timing fits?"

Something in her voice triggered warning bells in his mind. "Why is it so difficult to think I'm worried about you?"

"I just like my space. I enjoy the peace of being alone."

"So there's no guy in your life?" Damn it, where had that question come from?

A jealous corner of his brain.

She hesitated a second too long.

"Who?" And why the hell wasn't the man here watching out for her?

"I've just gone out with the high-school principal a couple of times."

The reports he'd gathered on her hadn't included that. His people had let him down.

"Is it serious?" he asked, her answer too damn important.

"No."

"Is it going to be?" He held up a hand. "I'm asking as an old friend." *Liar.* His eyes went back to her legs and the curve of her knees.

"Then you can ask without that jealous tone in your voice."

She always had been able to read him.

"Of course…" He winked. "And?"

She shrugged, absently smoothing the dress back in place again. "I don't know."

Exhaling hard, he rocked back on his heels. "I worked my ass off for that answer and that's all I get?"

"Pretty much." Hands on the arms of her chair, she pushed to her feet. "Okay. You win."

Standing, he asked, "Win what?"

"You can stay tonight—on the sofa."

He resisted the urge to pump his fist in victory. "I'm glad we're in agreement."

"You won't be so glad when you hear what's on the menu. I only have half a panino, barely enough for me. I was planning to shop once school finished."

"Dinner's on its way." He'd remembered about that

panino and had given his chauffeur instructions before he'd climbed the tree. He found the notion of an intimate dinner with Celia—discovering all the new secrets about her—stirring. "My very discreet driver will be delivering it."

"You already assumed I would agree? You're more arrogant than I recall."

"Thank you."

"That wasn't a compliment."

"That's all right." He soaked in the sight of her brown eyes flickering with awareness, her chest lifting faster with each breath. His hands ached to touch her, to relearn the curves, to find out if she still had the same sensitive areas and discover if she had new ones, as well. "It's for the best we don't exchange too many pleasantries."

She chewed the rest of the gloss off her bottom lip. "And why ever not?"

"Because honest to God," he growled softly, his body firing with a need that hadn't diminished one bit in nearly eighteen years apart, "I want to kiss you so damn badly it's already all I can do to keep my hands off you."

Four

Each seductive word out of Malcolm's mouth sent a thrill rippling through Celia. And not just his voice, but the strong lines of his handsome face, the breadth and power of his mature body—all *man*.

Teenage lust had ripened into a deeper, headier awareness. She still found him infinitely attractive, and the fact that she'd already been with him *many* times in the past only made that need edgier.

Dangerous.

Especially when they were only steps away from her bedroom.

She tipped her chin and steeled her will against temptation. "You used that line on me eighteen years ago. I would think your game would have improved since then. Or does being some kind of music legend make you lazy in the romance department?"

His head fell back, laughter rolling and rolling until he

scrubbed his hand over his face, grinning. "As I recall, my 'game' was just fine with you back then."

"Suffice it to say," she retorted, meeting his gaze with level strength, "my standards and expectations have changed."

"You want me to work harder." His eyes narrowed with the challenge.

"That's not what I meant." Her heart stuttered over a couple of beats before she found her balance and bravado again.

"What did you mean, then?" His hand grazed the keys of the upright piano, touching without stirring a note.

She shivered as she remembered the way he'd played so carefully over her skin long ago. "I was sixteen." She tapped out a quick tune on the other end of the keyboard, her nerves all too ready for an outlet. "Tough sell? I think not."

"My poor ego." He skimmed a scale.

"Sorry to have wounded you." She mirrored his notes. How many times had they done this?

"No, I mean it. You're good," he said without a trace of sarcasm. "It's nice to have someone who's real around me, someone I can trust."

"Am I supposed to cry for the poor little rich rock star?"

"Not at all." He slid onto the piano bench, his scale taking shape into a tune, the music relaxing and drawing her in at the same time.

Unable to resist, she sat down next to him and continued to twine her notes with his as easily as taking in air. "You know, one of the things that attracted me to you before was how you never seemed impressed by my father's wealth or influence."

"I respect your father—even if he did get me sent away

from you. Hell, if I had a daughter and—" His melody tangled. "Ah, crap. Okay, let me roll back that statement and reframe it."

"I know what you meant." Her hands fell to her lap, the piano going silent. "No parent would be happy about their sixteen-year-old having sex, much less reckless sex."

His face went dark with guilt, his hand gravitating to her face until he cupped her cheek. "I should have protected you better."

"We *both* should have been more responsible." She put her hand over his without thinking, her body going on autopilot around him as it always had, whether with touches or with music.

In less than a day, they'd fallen right back into the synchronicity they'd shared before, and God, that scared her spitless. She'd dated other men—slept with other men—but being with them never had this sense of ease. Already, she felt herself swaying toward him as his body leaned into hers.

Magnetic.

His hand still held her face, the calluses on his fingers familiar, a reminder of the countless hours he devoted to playing the guitar. Music hummed through her now, the sound of the two of them occupying the same space.

Her lips parted in anticipation—

The doorbell rang.

She jolted back as it rang again. How had she missed someone coming up outside?

Malcolm stood, his hand sliding away, then coming back to stroke her jaw once again. "That's dinner." He frowned. "And my phone."

He pulled his cell from his pocket.

"Supper?" she parroted, surprised she could even speak at all. She vaguely recalled him mentioning sending his driver/bodyguard for food. He had a whole staff at his disposal day and night, another reminder of how different their worlds were these days.

On his way to check the door, Malcolm said over his shoulder, "My chauffeur will set everything up while I take this call. All I need is a blanket and pillow for the sofa."

Before she could answer, he'd opened the door, waving his driver inside and stepping outside with his phone. Clearly, he didn't want her to hear his conversation. Which made her wonder a little about what he had to say.

And wonder a lot about *who* he said it to.

How the hell had he almost kissed her?

Malcolm gripped the wooden rails of Celia's small balcony landing just outside her front door. With ragged breaths, he drew in muggy night air as he listened to his driver setting up dinner inside. Bodyguards were stationed in the yard below and outside the brick-wall fence.

Malcolm's cell phone continued to buzz, and he knew he had to answer. And he would return the call—as soon as his heart rate settled back to normal.

He'd come here to make amends with Celia. To put his feelings of guilt to rest by helping her now like he couldn't before.

Where did sex factor into that?

It didn't. It hadn't. Until he'd seen her again.

These days he had control over his libido, enjoying healthy, safe relationships. He'd sure as hell never forgotten to put on a condom ever again. But he knew protecting Celia was about more than safe sex. That wouldn't keep either of them safe from the heartache of resurrecting something that was long done.

Plucking his phone from his pocket, he thumbed Redial and waited for Colonel John Salvatore to answer. His old headmaster from boarding school.

Now his Interpol handler. The man had traded in a uniform for a closet full of gray suits worn with a red tie.

"Salvatore here," his longtime mentor answered in clipped tones, gravelly from years of barking military orders.

"Calling you back, sir. Any word on Celia Patel's vehicle?"

"I checked the local department's report and they lifted prints, but with so many students in the school, there are dozens of different impressions."

His frustration ratcheted up. "And the security cameras?"

"Nothing concrete, but we did pinpoint the time the flyer was placed on the vehicle. We just couldn't see who did it. Kids were on lunch break, and a large group passed in front of the camera. Once they cleared, the flyer was under the wiper."

Malcolm scanned the street beyond the brick security wall, monitoring the lazy traffic for warning signs. "So whoever placed it there appears to be cognizant of the school's surveillance system."

"Apparently. One of my people is in between assignments and agreed to look into it."

"Thank you, sir."

Salvatore oversaw a group of freelance agents and field operatives, mostly comprised of former students. People who knew how to push the boundaries. Individuals with high-profile day jobs that allowed them to move in influential circles for gathering intelligence.

Except, today Malcolm needed Salvatore's help, and as much as he hated to ask anyone for anything, when it came to Celia…well, apparently he still had a weak spot. "I have a favor to ask."

"With what?" Salvatore answered without hesitation.

"I need an untraceable car and some ID delivered here tonight." A safeguard in place to escape with Celia in the morning, just in case his gut feeling played out. He'd learned to trust his gut.

"Not that I'm arguing, but just curious," Salvatore said drily. Nothing had gotten by the old guy when he'd been headmaster, either. "Why not have your personal detail take care of that? You've got a top-notch team."

In fact, some of them were former agents.

"This is too important." *Celia* was too important. "If it were just me, I could take care of myself. But with someone drawing a target on Celia's back…"

His fist thumped the railing, words choking on the dread in the back of his throat.

"Fair enough." The questions ended there. The two of them worked that tightly together with that kind of faith. "Whatever you need, it's yours."

"Thanks. I owe you." More than he could ever repay.

Colonel John Salvatore had become his father figure. The only real father figure he'd ever known, since his biological dad cut out on his family in the middle of the night, moving on to play his next honky-tonk gig. The bastard had sent a birthday card from the Florida Keys when Malcolm turned eleven. He never heard from him again.

"Malcolm," Salvatore continued, "I can put security in place for her here in the States so you can go ahead with your tour without worries."

"She's safer with me."

Salvatore's chuckle echoed over the line. "You don't

trust her to anyone else. Are you sure you trust yourself with her?"

God, he hated how easily Salvatore could read him.

"With all due respect, sir, the word games aren't necessary. I would do anything to keep her safe. Anything." His eyes scanned the small patio garden beside her carriage house with flowers blooming in splashes of purples and pinks. He recognized the lavender she used to love. His mother would have known the names of them all. Some were planted in the ground, others in pots. A fountain had been built into the stone wall, a wrought-iron chair and small table beside it. One chair. She sat there alone.

He didn't have any right to wonder about who she saw. But he couldn't deny he was glad she hadn't added a chair for her principal buddy yet.

Salvatore pressed, "What if I decide you're needed elsewhere?"

"Don't ask me to make the choice," he snapped.

"Apparently you've already decided."

"I have." Celia's safety would come first, even if it meant alienating Salvatore. Malcolm just hoped it wouldn't come to that. "Sir, I'm curious as to why the reports on Celia were incomplete."

"I don't know what you mean," he answered evasively.

"I respectfully disagree." Malcolm held his temper in check. Barely. "You're just trying to get me to say what I found out on my own in case I didn't learn everything. Then you can continue to hold back."

"We can play *this* game for a long time, Malcolm."

"Are you for or against me? Because I thought we were supposed to be on the same side."

"There are more people on your side than you know." When Malcolm kept his silence, Salvatore continued, "Celia's father did you a favor in getting you sent to my school. Without his intervention, you would have gone to a juvenile detention center."

Whoa. Hold on. He'd always thought the judge had pulled strings to get him out of Celia's life. The thought that her father had actually had a hand in helping Malcolm avoid jail time… He wasn't sure what to feel. He didn't want special favors. An important part of his life now consisted of helping to make people pay for their crimes.

After resenting Judge Patel for so long, this felt… strange. But then, because of his own dad, his gut made him naturally suspicious of other father figures. Which brought him right back around to the fact that Salvatore hadn't told him everything.

"What about this guy Celia's been seeing? The principal at the high school?"

"It didn't appear serious, so we didn't include it in the report. Apparently it *is* important to you, and that should tell you something."

"There are any number of ways that information could be important. What if he's the jealous type?" Um, crap, he could understand that too well. "Or if someone else is upset over the relationship. Details are important. Did you think I would go after him? You should know I'm not a headstrong idiot teenager anymore."

"You never were an idiot. Just young." Salvatore sighed, and Malcolm could envision the guy scratching a hand over his close-shorn salt-and-pepper hair. "I apologize for not including the principal in my report. If I find out anything else, I'll let you know. Meanwhile, whatever you need for protection, just ask and I'll make it happen."

Malcolm's temper inched down a degree. "Thank you, sir."

"Of course. Good night and be careful." The line disconnected.

Malcolm tucked his phone away but didn't go inside. Not yet. He couldn't avoid the truth staring him in the face. He'd just vowed he wasn't a headstrong idiot—yet he had acted like one in snapping at Salvatore, the man who had power and resources Malcolm needed. He'd all but proved the old man right, and all because he'd been knocked off balance by just the simple possibility of a kiss.

Except, nothing with Celia was simple.

It never had been.

His hands braced on the railing, he hung his head, staring down at that little garden grotto. He wanted to bring Celia down there and have a moonlit dinner together. The scent of those purple and pink flowers filled the air, while the music of the fountain filled the silence.

But he couldn't run the risk of someone seeing them. Not the bastard who'd been tormenting her. And not the press that hounded him.

Rather than regrets, he needed to focus on what he had. He had Celia to himself for the rest of the night. And by morning, he would have her rock-solid promise to come with him to Europe.

And he would keep his hands to himself.

Dinner together had been surprising.

Celia tucked the last of the dishes into the dishwasher while Malcolm checked the window for the umpteenth time. She'd expected him to press the issue of how close they'd come to kissing each other. She'd expected a big scene with oysters and wine and sexy almost-touches.

Instead he'd ordered shredded barbecue sandwiches that tasted like none she'd had before, served with Parmesan French fries and Southern sweet tea. There had even been pecan pie à la mode for dessert. The differences in their lifestyles didn't seem so big at moments like this.

She closed the dishwasher and pressed the start button. No busywork left to occupy herself, she had no choice but to face Malcolm—and the simmering awareness still humming inside her at the thought of kissing him again, touching him, taking things further. When they were teenagers, they'd spent hours exploring just how to make the other melt with desire.

Her face went hot at the memories.

"Thank you for ordering in dinner. That beat the dickens out of a warmed-over panino."

He turned away from the window, his deep blue eyes tracking her every move. "I hope you don't mind that I indulged myself in some selfish requests. I travel so much that I miss the tastes of home. Next meal, you choose. Anything you want, I'll make it happen."

Anything?

Best not to talk about exactly what she wanted right now. She'd already let her out-of-control attraction to him embarrass her once this evening.

"What a crazy concept to have whatever you want at your fingertips." She curled up in an overstuffed chair to make sure they weren't seated close on the sofa—or piano bench—again. "Are you one of those stars with strange, nitpicky requests, like wanting all the green M&M's picked out of the candy dish?"

"God, I hope not." He dropped back onto the piano bench, sitting an arm's reach away. "I like to think I'm still me, just with a helluva lot more money, so I get to call the shots in my life these days. Maybe I should take a Southern chef with me on tour."

She hugged a throw pillow. “You always did like pecan pie.”

“And blackberry cobbler. God, I miss that, and flaky buttermilk biscuits.”

“You must have picked up some new favorites from traveling the world.” Even in his jeans with a torn knee, he still had a more polished look with his Ferragamo loafers and…just something undefinable that spoke of how much he’d accomplished. “You must have changed. Eighteen years is a long time.”

“Of course I’m different in some ways. We all change. You’re certainly not exactly the same.”

“How so?” she asked warily.

“There. Just what you said now and how you said it.” He leaned back against the piano. “You’re more careful. More controlled.”

“Why is caution a bad thing?” Her impulsive nature, her spoiled determination to have everything—to have him—at any cost had nearly wrecked both their lives.

“Not bad. Just different. Plus, you don’t smile as much, and I’ve missed your laugh. You sound better than any music I’ve heard. I’ve tried to capture it in songs, but…” He shook his head. His blue eyes went darker with emotion, just the way they’d done all those years ago, and in that familiar moment, she felt his presence as deeply as she ever had from his kiss.

“That’s so…sad.” And incredibly touching.

One corner of his mouth kicked up in a wry smile. “Or sappy. But then, I make my living off writing and singing sappy love songs.”

“Off of making women fall in love with you.” She rolled her eyes, trying to make light of all the times the tabloid photos of him with other women had made her ache with what-ifs.

"Women aren't falling for me. It's all an image created by my manager. Everyone knows it's promo. None of it's real."

On a certain level, she got what he was saying, but something about his blasé attitude niggled at her. "You used to say the music was a part of you." She waved toward the antique upright behind him. "You were so passionate about your playing and your songs."

"I was an idealistic teenager. But I became a realist." He scooped up a stack of sheet music off the stand beside the piano. "I left this town determined to earn enough money to buy your father twice over, and music—" he rattled the pages in his hand "—was the only marketable skill I had."

"You achieved your financial goal. I truly am happy for you. Congratulations on succeeding in showing up my old man."

"More than succeeded." His eyes twinkled like stars lighting the night sky.

"So you can more than buy him out twice over. How many times over, five?"

He shrugged, his eyes still smiling.

Her jaw dropped. "Eight?"

He tossed the sheet music—scores she'd written for private students—back onto the side table.

"More than ten?" Holy crap.

"That's fairly close."

"Wow." She whistled softly. "Love songs pay well." A lot better than the little compositions she made for her students with dreams of putting them into an instruction book one day.

"People want to believe in the message," he said drily.

"You sound cynical." That made her sad when she thought of how deeply he'd cared about his music. "Why sing about something you don't accept as true? You obviously don't need the money anymore."

"You used to like it when I sang to you." He turned on the bench and placed his hands on the keyboard, his fingers starting a simple ballad, hauntingly familiar.

"I was one of those sappy women falling for you." When she'd been in Switzerland, his baby growing inside her, she'd dreamed of how they could repair their relationship when she got back and he finished his probation. Except, his letters to her grew fewer and fewer until she realized what everyone had told her was true. Theirs was just a high-school romance.

He tapped out another couple of bars of the melody line of one of the songs he'd written for her back when they'd dated. He'd said songs were all he had to offer her. This particular tune, one he'd called "Playing for Keeps," had always been her favorite. His fingers picked up speed, layering new intricacies into the simpler song he'd composed long ago. When he finished, the last note echoed in her tiny carriage house.

In her heart.

Her breath caught in her throat, her eyes stinging with tears that blurred the image of his broad shoulders as he sat at the piano. She ached with the urge to wrap her arms around him and rest her cheek on his back. She hurt from the lost dreams of what she'd let slip away. Apparently, he'd let a whole lot slip away from him, too. She didn't want to think about how cynical he'd grown.

Swallowing hard, she let herself dare to ask, "Was it real, what we felt then?"

He stayed silent, turned away from her for so long she thought he wouldn't answer. Finally, he shifted around again to face her. The raw emotion on his face squeezed at her heart.

A long sigh shuddered through him before he spoke. "Real enough that we went through a lot of pain for each other. Real enough that sitting here together isn't some easygoing reunion."

With that heavy sigh of his, she realized he'd suffered, too, more than she'd ever realized. Somehow, that made her feel less alone. Yes, they'd hurt each other, but maybe they could help each other, too. Maybe the time had come for a coda of sorts, to bring their song to an end.

"Malcolm, what's Europe going to be like if just sitting here together is this difficult?"

"So you've decided to come with me? No more maybes?"

She shoved to her feet and walked to him at the piano. "I think I have to."

"Because of the stalker?"

She cupped his handsome, beard-stubbled face in her hands. "Because it's time we put this to rest."

Before she could talk herself out of something she wanted—needed—more than air, Celia pressed her lips to his.

Five

Malcolm might not have planned on kissing Celia, but the second her mouth touched his, there wasn't a chance in hell he could pull away. She tasted like the sweet, syrupy insides of pecan pie and more—more than he remembered. Familiar and new all at once.

The tip of her tongue touched his, sending a bolt of desire straight through him until he went so hard at the thought of having her that he ached. His body surged with the need to take her, here, now. Because based on even this one kiss, he knew it would be even better for them than when they had been inexperienced, fumbling teens learning their way around…then learning the pleasure of drawing it out.

God, she was flipping his world upside down all over again.

Then the kiss was over before it barely started.

Celia touched her lips with a trembling hand, her

chewed nails hinting at how frayed her nerves had been lately. "Not the smartest thing I've ever done. I pride myself on being wiser these days."

No offers to make up the couch for him. Definitely no offer for him to come to her room. He hadn't expected otherwise…although a man could hope.

"We don't always want what's good for us."

"True enough. I got caught up in the memories from the music. The fact that you remembered the song from before… Well, I would have to be heartless not to be moved. Except, now reason has set in. If I follow through on that kiss, Europe is going to be very awkward—"

"Celia, it's okay. You don't need to explain or say anything more." He traced his thumb along her mouth. "I won't go psycho because you don't invite me into your bed after one kiss."

Still, his mind filled with the fantasy of tearing each other's clothes off, of carrying her over to the piano and sitting her on the keyboard, where he would step between her legs and bury himself deep inside this woman who'd always moved him in a way no other could.

Which had him wondering if perhaps they could indulge in more. If it was every bit as inevitable now as it had been eighteen years ago.

Indecision shifted in her dark brown eyes. Could she really be considering it? His pulse ratcheted up to never-before-tested speeds. Except, then she shook her head and turned away.

"I can't do this," she mumbled, backing away until his hand slid from her face. From the hall closet, she pulled out a stack of sheets and a pillow, then tugged a quilt from the back of the sofa. "Good night, Malcolm."

She thrust the linens against his chest and pivoted on her heels before he could say a word. No question, she was every bit as rattled as he was. Resisting the urge to go after her, he still allowed himself to savor watching the gentle sway of her hips as she left. His body throbbed in response, and he knew the feel of her would stay imprinted on him long after she closed her bedroom door.

Silence echoed after her, the scent of lavender wafting up from the sheets she'd given him. He hadn't slept on a sofa since his early days in the music industry, going to college on scholarship in the mornings, still half-asleep from playing late-night gigs. He'd gotten a degree in music with a minor in accounting because, by God, no manager was ever going to take advantage of his finances. He refused to be one of those musicians who made billions only to file for bankruptcy later. He knew what poverty was like and how it hurt the people around him—how he'd hurt the people around him because of his own dumb decisions.

He was in control these days.

Shrugging the tension out of his shoulders, he tossed aside the sheet and shook out the blanket. He stayed at five-star penthouse suites on a regular basis, but he'd never forgotten where he came from—and he damn well never would. The day a person got complacent was the day someone robbed them blind.

He refused to be caught flat-footed ever again. The lowest day of his life had been sitting in that police cell, arrested for drug possession. Wondering what Celia thought. Hating that he'd let his mother down.

The part that still stuck in his craw? For some twisted reason, his brush with the law made him all the more alluring to fans. The press had spun it into a "bad turned good" kind of story. He didn't want fans glorifying him or the things he'd done.

His mistakes were his own. He took responsibility for

his past. Atonement wasn't something to parade around for others to applaud. Receiving praise diminished the power of anything he might have done right.

Speaking of atonement…

He tugged the leather briefcase from beside the sofa. His driver had left the essentials. He pulled out his tablet computer to check for an update from Salvatore on Celia.

Because, with memories of that kiss still heating his blood, he sure as hell wasn't going to fall asleep anytime soon.

Celia kept her eyes closed even though she'd woken up at least ten minutes ago after a restless night's sleep. Her white-noise machine filled the room with the sound of soothing waves. She snuggled deeper under the covers, groggy and still so sexually strung tight her skin was oversensitive to the Egyptian cotton sheets. Just one kiss, and she was already burning up for Malcolm Douglas again.

The thought of facing him was mortifying—and a little scary. What if she walked out there, lost control and plastered herself all over him again?

Last night's kiss had rocked her to her toes. And the way Malcolm hadn't pressed her to hop right into bed together? That rattled her even more. But then, he hadn't pressured her as a teenager, either. She'd been the aggressor. She'd known him for years. They'd shared a music teacher, even performed at recitals together. But something had changed when they both came back from summer break, entering their sophomore year.

Her friend had gotten hot.

The other high-school girls had noticed, too. But she'd been determined. He was hers. No one had ever denied her anything, and she could see now how that had made her all the more determined to win him over. Her selfishness had played a part in how recklessly fast she'd pursued him.

She'd justified her actions by noting the interest in his eyes. Except, he'd insisted he didn't have the time or money for dating. He'd told her they couldn't be anything more than friends. She'd told him she didn't need fancy romancing. She just wanted him….

After they'd been dating for five months, she'd feared she was losing him. His mother had been filling out applications for scholarships for him to attend a special high school for the arts. Celia understood Terri Ann Douglas wanted the best for her son, but it seemed the push for him to attend school out of town had more to do with getting him away from Celia than obtaining a better music education.

Or at least that was how it had appeared in her self-centered teenage mind.

Already she'd felt as if she barely got to see him between his job and their music lessons and their eagle-eyed parents. Still, they'd stolen time alone together to make out, talk, dream—make out some more. Their make-out sessions had grown hotter, as hot as possible without going all the way.

She recalled every detail of that whole day, the day she'd lost her virginity. She remembered what she wore—pink jeans and a rock-band T-shirt. What she ate—cereal, an apple and not much else, because she wanted to keep fitting into those jeans.

Most of all, she remembered what it felt like stretched out on the backseat of her car with Malcolm, parked by the river at night. She'd already pitched her shirt and bra onto the floor, along with his shirt, too, because there was nothing like the feel of her breasts against his bare chest.

Her hand tunneled down his pants, and he was working the zipper on her pink jeans. They'd already learned how to give each other orgasms by stroking to take the edge off the gnawing need.

Except, that night she'd been selfish. Scared of losing him. And most of all, she'd been stupid.

They hadn't used a condom.

Although she'd still needed him to finish her with his hand afterward because it hadn't been anywhere near as earth-shattering as she'd expected. Not the first time.

But she hadn't gotten pregnant then, either. Which made them all the more reckless over the following weeks when Malcolm had been deliciously determined to figure out exactly how to bring her to that earth-shattering release while buried heart-deep inside her....

Celia snuggled deeper under the covers, cocooning herself in memories. The good—then the bad when everything had fallen apart. For years she'd told herself maybe he hadn't loved her as much as she'd loved him. That they'd only become a couple because she'd gone after him, and what red-blooded teenage boy said no to sex?

But last night, the way he'd played that song made her realize she'd only been trying to ease her guilt over how much she'd cost him, how much their breakup had hurt him, as well.

Now this new insight complicated the trip to Europe.

In the harsh light of the morning, leaving with him seemed like a reckless idea, and she didn't do "reckless" anymore. She'd left behind impulsiveness when she'd passed over her baby girl to parents who could give her all the things Celia couldn't. The pain of loss had pushed her over the edge.

She had to be smarter this time, to be careful for her

own sake, and for his. Just the thought of seeing him once she walked into the living room sent butterflies whirling in her stomach.

Damn it. He hadn't even been back in her life for twenty-four hours, and desire for him had flipped her world upside down. She hadn't helped matters with that impulsive kiss, brought on by nostalgia. She couldn't let sex cloud their judgment again. She wanted—she needed—her peaceful existence. To make that happen, she had to stay in control while facing her fears and guilt in order to move on with her life.

She flung aside the covers and clicked off her white-noise machine, the sound of waves ending abruptly, only to be replaced by a different buzz coming from outside. Frowning, she went to the window and parted the wood shutters.

Oh. My. God. Her breath caught in her throat. She stepped away fast.

Her lawn was absolutely packed.

Cars, media vans, even tents with clusters of people underneath filled her yard and beyond, overflowing onto the sidewalk. She slammed the shutters closed and locked them. Her home had been invaded, and she was damn certain it had nothing to do with her stalker.

Apparently, Malcolm had about a million of his own.

She snagged her cotton bathrobe from the foot of her bed. Sprinting for the door, she yanked on her robe and knotted the tie on her way to the living room.

Only to stop short again.

Malcolm was sprawled on the sofa wearing only his jeans, with the blanket twisted and draped over his waist. Her mouth dried up. The muscles she'd felt ripple beneath his shirt were all the more magnificent uncovered. Damn it all, why couldn't he have gone paunchy and bald? Or why couldn't he have at least become a totally arrogant jerk?

All right. He was a bit arrogant, but not at all a jerk. And the six-pack abs didn't show the least sign of paunch. His hair was so freakin' magnificent his fans named that signature lock of hair over the brow—calling it "The Malcolm." Men everywhere were letting their hair grow long over their foreheads because their girlfriends begged them to. Malcolm's fans.

His fans.

Damn. Not two minutes after vowing not to let the attraction derail her, she'd failed. She'd been so caught up in gawking at his naked chest that she'd forgotten about the sold-out audience on her lawn. Celia knelt by the sofa, her hand falling lightly on his shoulder.

His warm skin sent sparks shimmering through her.

She snatched back her hand. "Malcolm? Malcolm, you have to wake up now—"

He shot upright off the sofa. His arm whipped from under the blanket, a gun clasped in his hand and pointed at the ceiling.

A gun?

"Malcolm?" she squeaked. "Where did that come from?"

"It's mine, and it's registered. I keep it for protection, which seems appropriate given the threats against you. Probably a bit more daunting to an intruder than if I bash them over the head with a rolled-up music score." He placed the black weapon on the coffee table with a wry grin. "It's best you don't surprise me when I'm asleep."

"Do you get creepy fans waking you up often?" She rubbed her arms, suddenly chilled.

"When I first hit the charts, a fan managed to get past security into the house. But since then, no. That doesn't mean I'm letting down my guard, and my security detail is an impenetrable wall between me and overzealous fans."

"Then why sleep with the gun?"

"Because your life is too precious to trust to anyone else. I have to be sure."

Her heart squeezed in her chest, and it was all she could do not to caress his face, kiss him, claim that perfect mouth of his all over again.

Clearing her throat, she nodded to the living-room window covered with simple white shutters instead of curtains. "Check out the lawn."

His eyes narrowed, muscles along his chest bunching. He strode across the room and opened the shutters just a crack.

"Crap." He stepped to the side, out of the sight line. "Wish I could say I'm surprised, but I was afraid this might happen. I should have insisted we leave last night before they had time to rally."

Her misgivings churned again. "About leaving together for Europe. I'm…"

"Yeah, I agree." He snagged his button-down shirt off the back of the chair, tucking his feet back into his loafers. "We need to go right away."

She toyed with the tie of her bathrobe. "I'm not so sure about that."

He glanced up from buttoning his shirt. "We don't have a choice, thanks to the folks on the lawn with cameras."

"So you more than suspected this *might* happen?"

"I couldn't be certain." He tucked his tablet computer into a leather briefcase. "But I had to consider it and plan accordingly."

"What kind of plan?"

"A way for us to leave before it gets worse." He strapped his gun into a holster and stowed it in the briefcase, as well. "As soon as you get dressed."

"It can get worse than that? There's no more room on the lawn."

"There's always room," he said darkly. "Get dressed, and I'll pour some coffee into travel mugs. We'll have to eat on the road."

"What if I decide to stay here and let you leave on your own?" So much for her resolution to face her fears. *Chicken.*

He stood still. Waiting. Leaving her time to realize—she really didn't have a choice anymore. Once the press saw him leave, they would stay on her lawn until she walked out the door or until they somehow managed to break in. She needed to tuck her head and get out of here quickly.

"Right." She sighed. "I'm going with you. But why so soon? What about packing?"

"Arranged."

"Of course."

He could order anything now, thanks to his money and power. And at the moment, she wasn't in the position to turn that down. His guards had the crowd contained, but for how long?

"God, this is getting complicated." She scraped back her tangled hair in her hand. "I have an end-of-the-year concert tonight and grades to file."

Malcolm held a phone in his hand. "Tell me what you want, and I'll make it happen. I can have an army of guards around the entire school if that's what you need."

As much as it pained her, she knew there was only one solution. "That sounds frightening and dangerous. I'll call the high-school chorus teacher. She can conduct the concert if I send her the lineup, and I can file my grades online. Given the circus out there, I imagine the school will understand my decision to take a personal day."

He reached out a hand. "Celia, I'm so damn sorry about—"

"Uh, really, it's okay." The last thing she needed was his touch scrambling her thoughts again. "You were just trying to help."

Spinning on her heel, she raced back down the hall to her room. She yanked a sundress and sandals from her tiny closet before peeling off her pj's.

She couldn't help but wonder, if Malcolm suspected this kind of fan fallout, then why had he made such a public appearance? Had he been trying to force her to fall in line with his plan? If so, why? What did he have to gain from stepping in to protect her from the stalker?

None of this made sense.

She tugged out fresh underwear and didn't stop to think about why she bypassed simple white cotton for lemon-yellow lace. It shouldn't have mattered, and she shouldn't have noticed her choice.

But it did matter, and she had noticed. That made her angry with herself all over again. It had been tough enough tamping down her runaway attraction after a night spent dreaming about him and that dang kiss. Now she had the additional memory of chiseled abs and his formidable male chest etched in her brain.

She yanked on her clothes and jammed her feet into sandals while the scent of hazelnut drifted into the bedroom from her kitchen. She took a valuable thirty more seconds to brush her teeth and hair, before racing back into the living room, grabbing her floral tote bag along the way so she would have her wallet and computer. "I guess it's time to put your guards to work helping us run the gauntlet to your limo."

He passed her a travel mug of coffee. "We're not using the limo. We'll go down the inside stairs to the garage."

"My car is still at the school." She shrugged her bag over her shoulder, nerves singing freaking arias in her stomach at the thought of all those fans outside. "I really should give my dad a call. And damn it all, Malcolm, just because I'm going with you does not mean we will be sleeping together. You have to understand—"

"Celia, stop. It's okay. I hear you. Now hear me. I had a vehicle delivered last night in case we needed to make an escape—since the limo wouldn't fit in your garage. You can call your father and the other music teacher once we're on the road." He slipped his fingers down her arm in a shivery caress then clasped her hand. "Trust me. I will not let anyone—including myself—hurt you."

With a gentle tug, he guided her down the narrow enclosed staircase and opened the door to reveal…

A red Maserati.

Her jaw dropped and her feet grew roots. "Oh. Um, that's a, uh, nice car."

Sleek and sophisticated, not unlike the man beside her. The man she'd seen half-dressed this morning.

"Better yet, it's a *fast* car." He opened her door then sprinted around the front to the driver's side. He settled behind the wheel and reached into the glove compartment for a blue ball cap. "Are you ready?"

"Nope." Her fingers curled into the supple leather. All the better to prevent her from touching Malcolm. "I guess that doesn't matter, though."

"Sorry about that." He tugged on the cap, clicked the garage door opener and revved the finely tuned engine to life. She caught the scent of his aftershave in the close confines of the sports car.

Her stomach twittered at every growl of the engine. The garage door rumbled as it rolled up, revealing the clusters of people outside.

Somehow, her hand sought out his forearm and squeezed.

As he nosed out, fans pushed at the line of security guards, the high-pitched squeals and flashing bulbs piercing even the thick, tinted windows.

Only a slight flex of muscles along Malcolm's jaw showed any frustration on his part. This was, after all, everyday life to him now. And so totally alien to her.

The deeper they drove into the swarm of fans and paparazzi, the more and more she felt like Alice in Wonderland falling headfirst into the rabbit hole.

An hour later, Malcolm floored the Maserati on a deserted country road. The high-performance vehicle had given him the speed and maneuverability to dodge the paparazzi that had trailed him out of Celia's garage. Miles of empty farm fields rolled ahead of them, broken by the occasional sprawling oak or faded red barn.

Best of all, there was almost zero traffic. Tractors chewed up the land off to the side. So far, only two trucks had passed going the other direction. She'd made her calls to reassure her father and to detail the program requirements for the other music teacher.

Finally, he had Celia safely away and all to himself. He wasn't trusting the press not to find the distinctive car, so he had more change-ups planned. For now, he had a short window to be with Celia, alone on the open road. He needed to use this time wisely to help put her at ease around him again. If he expected to make a serious go at putting the past to rest, then she had to stop walking on eggshells all the time.

She'd showed signs of cold feet about coming to Europe with him when she'd seen the press and fans packing her lawn. Although, that paparazzi sit-in had also offered him the perfect excuse to whisk her away faster. Once he got her out of town and away from whoever was trying to scare the hell out of her, then he could…

What?

Somehow with that kiss, things had shifted between them. In spite of what she'd said about not sleeping together, the heat between them was still there, but matured. He'd spent most of the night thinking about her, wanting her. They were both adults. They both had settled into their lives and careers.

She hadn't been ready to see that attraction through to its conclusion last night. He could understand that. He meant it when he'd said he would not do anything to hurt her or abuse her trust. But he had to accept that the kiss changed everything. Though he'd meant to stay away, he now knew he couldn't leave this mission without having her one last time.

As for their past feelings for each other? Puppy love. The flowery notion of soul mates was a crock. Something created to sell music, movies and greeting cards. He was a more practical man these days. He and Celia could indulge in sex without risking their hearts.

Now he just needed to convince her.

He glanced over at Celia, his eyes drawn to the curve of her legs. Hell, he was even turned on by her cute feet with pink-painted toenails peeking out of her sandals.

Crap.

Focus on the road, idiot.

He downshifted around a curve on the two-lane highway. "I'm sorry to have made you miss out on the concert."

"I know you were just trying to help."

"Still, it sucks to lose something you've obviously worked hard on." He felt the weight of her stare and glanced over to find her forehead furrowed. "What?"

"Thank you for understanding how important this was to me—for not dismissing it. I know we're not a sold-out coliseum or a royal audience."

"Music isn't about the size or income of the audience."

She smiled for the first time since they'd left her home. "It's about touching the heart, the soul."

His grip tightened on the wheel as he thought of another time she'd said much the same thing. One night, he'd brought along his guitar to serenade her under the stars. He'd picked up fast food and a blanket and told himself someday he would give her better. Give her more. She'd quickly reassured him that money didn't matter to her, just the heart and the soul.

He should have listened to her. She hadn't wanted this kind of life then any more than now. Regardless of what she wanted, though, she did need him. At least for the moment.

Accelerating, he sped down the deserted two-lane road.

Celia smoothed the wrinkles from her gauzy dress. "That was quite an impressive getaway. I thought for sure someone would get hit or at the very least have their toes run over. But you got us out of there without anyone getting hurt. Where did you learn to drive like that?"

"Part of the job training." Except, it had more to do with his Interpol work than the music world, but he tried to stick to the truth as much as he could, as if that somehow made up for the huge lie of omission. But then it wasn't something he had leave to work into conversation. *Hey, I moonlight as a freelance agent for Interpol.*

She laughed lightly. "I must have missed the driving class in my music education."

"I have a friend who's a race-car driver." Another truth. "He gave me lessons."

"What friend is that?" She turned toward him, hitching her knee up so her whole body shifted.

For a second, his gaze drifted to the hem of her dress. The hint of skin the movement had exposed.

"Elliot Starc. We went to school together."

She gasped. "You went to school with Elliot Starc, the international race-car driver?"

"You know about Starc?" He stared at the road harder and told himself to keep his head on straight. "Most of the women I've met don't follow racing."

"Honey, this is the South, where people live and breathe NASCAR." Her soft drawl thickened a little as she laughed again. "Starc is, of course, more Formula One, but some of my father's friends take their racing interests further."

"Fair enough. So you've heard of Eric, then."

"There must have been a lot of lessons to get that good at maneuvering…the speed." She shook her head, her hair shifting over her shoulders. "I'm still dizzy."

He glanced at her sharply. "Are you okay? I didn't mean to scare you."

"You didn't. I'm all right." She laughed softly. "Goodness knows I got enough speeding tickets as a teenager. I'm a more sedate driver these days. I no longer expect Daddy to fix my tickets for me."

"A lot of time has passed."

"Yet you're here. *We're* here." The confusion in her voice reached out to him. But before he could figure out what the hell to say, she continued, "I just don't want you to get hurt protecting me."

"I'll be fine. I told you. I have this under control." Too bad he couldn't say the same about his resurrected feelings for Celia.

He was aware of her every movement beside him.

"Oh, right. Your plan." She straightened in her seat again. "Where are we going?"

To the one place he could be certain no one would find them. "To my mom's house."

Six

His mother's house?

Celia still couldn't wrap her brain around that nugget of information even a half hour after he'd spilled the beans. The press had reported in the past that he now supported his mother, declaring she deserved a life of luxury after all the sacrifices she'd made for him. But there were never any details about where Terri Ann Douglas had relocated after she'd left Azalea fourteen years ago.

Quite frankly, Celia hadn't been that interested in staying in touch with the woman who reminded her so deeply of all she'd lost. Terri Ann hadn't approved of Celia back then anyway, and with good reason. Celia was everything the woman had feared for her son—spoiled, selfish and more than willing to toss away her virginity if that tied Malcolm closer to her.

The thought of seeing Terri Ann again sent Celia's stomach into knots as they pulled up to a large scrolled gate covered by vines. Cameras moved ever so slightly, almost hidden in the foliage. Malcolm stopped by the security box and typed a code into the keypad. The gates swung wide, revealing a road that lead into…nothing but trees.

She couldn't see a house, and wouldn't be able to see people, even if they showed up. The security was… beyond crazy. As she began to grasp the depth of the protection here, she had to wonder, had he changed his mind about Europe and decided to stash her away here with his mother, where he'd obviously already lavished a good deal of effort to ensure privacy?

Disappointment gripped her, too much considering she'd been questioning the wisdom of going with him. But she couldn't deny a flickering wish deep inside her. Yes, her world had spun out of control since he'd returned, but she didn't want to step off the dizzying ride just yet. This was crazy and scary, out of character for the new, steadier path she'd chosen for herself.

Except, even if they didn't sleep together again—which they weren't going to do, she emphatically reminded herself—she finally had a chance for answers, for closure on her teenage years, a time in her life that had almost broken her. She didn't want to lose the opportunity.

"Malcolm, would you care to clue me in to what's going on?"

He drove the car deeper into the forest of towering oaks and pines, gravel crunching under the tires. "I needed to regain some control over the security. We're off the radar now, which gives us some breathing room."

Suddenly, he turned from the dusty path onto a paved road. The leafy branches parted to reveal—*oh, my God*—a compound.

A columned mansion was surrounded by every convenience from a pool to tennis courts. Even a pond sported a small dock with a gazebo picnic area by the shore.

The home was a magnificent getaway. But at the moment, it looked rather like a prison to her. "Do you plan for me to stay here instead?"

He looked at her quickly. "Not at all. We're still going to Europe. I told you my security would be taking care of you, and I meant that. We're simply leaving from here instead of from a public airport."

Too much relief zinged through her. Damn it, she was supposed to be gaining peace from this reunion, not wanting to spend more time with him. "Then I'm fuzzy on the details of how we're getting from this place to Europe. I don't see an airstrip."

He pointed in the distance.

A helicopter flew just over the treetops.

She shrank back in her seat even though she knew the tinted windows provided complete privacy. "The press found us already?"

"No, that's our ride." He put the Maserati in Park next to a large concrete pad.

A space large enough for that bird to land. Holy cow.

Her eyes stayed locked on the white helicopter flying closer, closer still, until it hovered. Roaring overhead, it landed a few feet away, blades stirring dust all around the car. "You're kidding."

"Nope. We'll fly in the chopper to another location, where we'll board a private jet and leave the country. Avoiding the press involves a lot more steps than going from point A to point B."

Wow, okay. He did have resources beyond anything she'd imagined. But…

"I thought you said we were visiting your mother."

"I said we were going to her house. She's not here." He pulled his briefcase from behind his seat. "She's at her vacation flat in London."

A vacation flat? "You're a good son. This amazing house. A place in England, too."

"What I give her is easy compared to all she did for me." His eyes went sober, pained even. "The house, the apartment, they don't even put a dent in my account. She worked two jobs just to put food on the table. She even cleaned my piano teacher's house in exchange for lessons. Mom deserves a retirement. Now, are you ready?"

She was running out of time to say what had been chewing at her gut since last night. "I don't want you to think that kiss meant more than it did."

"What did it mean?"

"That I'm still attracted to you, as well, that we share a very significant past. But that doesn't mean we have a future or that we should act on the attraction." Because honest to God, right now she wasn't sure how she would walk away from him a second time if they got even closer. They needed to use this trip together to talk through what happened when they were teenagers, to have the conversations they'd been denied because of immaturity—and the fact that he'd been locked away in a military school and she'd been sent to Switzerland. "It was more of a farewell to that past and a salute to friendship kind of kiss. Didn't you write a song once about goodbye kisses?"

"Someone else wrote that one." He smiled cynically. "My manager thought it would melt hearts."

"It melted hearts all the way to the top of the charts." She'd turned the radio station dozens of times to keep herself from crying over that damn song.

"Call me jaded—" he gripped the steering wheel so

tightly his knuckles went bloodless "—but sometimes I feel like I'm selling a flawed ideal to my fans."

"How can you deny there's love out there?" She turned toward him again, clenching her hands into fists to keep from reaching for him. "We felt it. I know we did. That song last night proved it. Even though it ended, what we had was real."

"Puppy love."

Her head snapped back, his words a splash of bitterly cold water. "Are you being a bastard on purpose?"

"Just helping you resist the urge to kiss me again." He reached across her and opened her door. "Our helicopter's waiting."

As her door swung wide, the biting wind blew grit and rocks inside the beautifully magnificent car, stinging her as tangibly as his angry words had. She grabbed her floral tote bag full of schoolwork and jumped out, slamming the door closed behind her. Helicopter blades whomp, whomp, whomped, slicing the air. Who traveled by helicopter besides the military and the country's president?

Apparently platinum-selling stars did.

He opened the door for her. "Sit up front."

Gingerly, she climbed inside the helicopter, the scent of leather and oil saturating the air as she settled in place. She eyed the empty copilot's seat, the thrill-seeking ways of her teenage years nowhere to be found. The thought of riding in a chopper—of actually going to Europe—made her chest grow tight. She forced herself to breathe in and out evenly, willing back the rising panic attack.

Damn it, she could do this—she had to do this. She would use this time to turn the page once and for all on the chapter of her life that included Malcolm Douglas.

She snapped her seat belt on and tugged it extra tight while glancing at the controls and the thin sides, the surrounding glass. Okay, so maybe she could do this in a different seat. She turned to ask the pilot if she could sit in back but he slid out before she could speak. He passed his headset to Malcolm and put Malcolm's ball cap on his head. The pilot sprinted toward the Maserati.

Malcolm slipped into the pilot's seat. He tugged on his headset and passed a second set to Celia. She pulled them on, her ears filling with chatter over the airwaves.

He leaned toward her. "If you want to speak privately, just tap this button."

And with that, he ran a check of the controls, his voice resonating in her ears as he called in to some tower for takeoff. How could the people on the other end of the radio not know they were speaking to Malcolm Douglas? His smooth baritone caressed her senses even when he just spoke, his voice utterly recognizable to her even without looking at him.

There was no denying he knew exactly what to do. "Um, Malcolm? Are you actually going to fly this—"

The helicopter lifted off. She bit down a yelp and grabbed her seat, terrified of touching something. It wasn't as if she was afraid to fly, but this was all happening so fast, with so little explanation. She looked out at the house growing smaller and smaller the higher they flew.

"I guess you really are flying the chopper. You have a license, right?"

"Yes, ma'am."

"You can't tell me Elliot Starc taught you to drive this, too."

"Not Elliot." He glanced at her and winked. "Private instructor."

She sagged back in her seat. "Of course. How could I not have known?"

Reservations about her decision were pointless now.

She was going to Europe with the man who'd stolen—and broken—her heart eighteen years ago.

Malcolm steered the helicopter through the sky.

He had to admit there were definite perks to having an unlimited bank account. He had the coolest toys. His work with Interpol had only expanded the scope.

Plowing through the sky in a helicopter, having the little bird at his disposal, beat the hell out of the days when he and his mom could barely afford to keep a rusted Chevy running. Vulnerable women were his weak spot, and he knew that. When it came to Celia and their history, his tendency to protect was all the more powerful.

He monitored the controls, his feet working in tandem with his hands—like playing the piano, it required two-handed coordination along with his feet. He played the chopper through the air, over tiny houses far below. Far above the threat to Celia, for now.

Because no matter how much he wanted her in his bed again—and he wanted that so much it gnawed at his gut—he could not lose sight of his primary goal here. He had to keep her safe. And that meant keeping his libido in check. A more restrained approach once he had her tucked far away from here seemed the better plan than pressing her on that kiss now.

Given her death grip on the seat, it appeared Celia had left her daredevil days behind. Her paling face sucker punched him, making him feel guilty as hell for being cranky with her when she talked about sappy emotions. Love hadn't pulled him out of his messed-up life. He'd put his world on track with practical determination and hard work.

Still, he couldn't stand to see her hurt…

He thumbed the private mic button. "It's going to be

all right, Celia. I swear. We're going to meet up with a school friend of mine at his vacation home in the Florida panhandle. He'll be able to help us slip out of the country without the fanfare, attention and danger of going through an airport."

At least he had her away from Azalea now. One step in the right direction.

She looked away from the windscreen and over at him. "A school friend?"

"Yeah, a few of us have kept in touch." A few? A select few. The ones who worked for Salvatore, a group of pals from school who'd dubbed themselves The Alpha Brotherhood.

"Close friends?"

"Definitely," he said simply. "There were two types of people at that boarding school. Those who wanted a life in the military. And those of us who needed the regimen of a military education."

"You were already incredibly regimented and motivated." Her soft voice caressed his ear, the hum of the helicopter engine fading until he only heard her. "You didn't need that."

"Apparently I did." He couldn't deny it. "Hanging out at bars underage, knocking up my girlfriend. I wouldn't call that succeeding at life."

"I played a part in that." Her voice held so much regret it reached across to him.

"I'm damn lucky I ended up there, where they could straighten me out."

"How bad was the school they sent you to?" Her hands slid from the seat to twist in her lap. "I worried about you."

"Not as bad as jail would have been. I know I was lucky. Like I said, I got a top-notch education, music lessons and discipline." It wasn't what he would have chosen for himself, but he'd made the most of the opportunity, determined to prove himself to all the doubters. "And the major bonus? My mother didn't have to work double shifts anymore."

"Ahhh." Her melodic voice hummed softly. "So you really stayed at the school for your mother."

"You always did see right through me." He checked the controls again, refusing to let the tension knotting his gut affect his skills. "I was so angry back then that I wanted to tell the judge where he could stick his 'deal.' I was innocent and no one was going to label me a drug user. But one look at my mother's face, and I knew I had to accept."

"So you left town."

"I did." He'd left her. That had been the toughest part, knowing she was carrying his child and he'd failed to provide a future for them. "Chances of me walking away from that trial with a clean slate were slim."

She'd already told him she planned to give up the baby, and as wounded as he was by her decision, he had nothing to offer to change her mind. He'd left town. There'd been no reason to stay.

"Tell me about these close friends who are going to help us out?"

A safe enough subject. Most of the press knew who his friends were; they just didn't know the details of what bonded them to each other. "Troy Donavan will be meeting us when we land."

"The Robin Hood Hacker… I didn't expect that."

Troy had hacked into the Department of Defense's computer system as a teen to expose corruption. He'd done the crime and proudly served his time at the military school. If anything, Troy had griped about *not* being sent to jail.

He continued naming. "Conrad Hughes will meet us along the way."

"A casino magnate with questionable ties? And Elliot Starc, as well, playboy race-car driver?" She laughed, but she also sank deeper in her seat. "I'm not feeling all that safe here."

If only she knew…

He explained what he could. "Yes, we landed at that school for a reason and came out better men. If it makes you feel any better, our Alpha Brotherhood includes Dr. Rowan Boothe."

"The philanthropist doctor featured in *People* magazine's 100 Sexiest Men issue? He invented some kind of revolutionary computerized surgical technique…"

"With our computer-expert buddy Troy. Do you trust my friends now?" He glanced over at her and found a twinkle in her eyes.

Damn. She'd played him, getting him to share more than he'd intended. He'd always been susceptible to this woman. She might appear less impulsive, more steady.

But she was every bit as seductive.

Why did everything she learned about Malcolm have to be so blasted appealing?

Celia had worked during the whole helicopter ride to find a flaw in him, and the more he shared about how he'd spent his life since he left Azalea, the more she found to admire about him.

She pulled her eyes off his handsome profile as the helicopter began landing at his friend Troy Donavan's beach house on the Florida Gulf Coast. Apparently the

Robin Hood Hacker allowed choppers to land on his lawn, as well.

What an unexpected friendship. Malcolm had been so straitlaced as a teenager. Although the tabloids certainly painted him as a partying Romeo now.

But she couldn't stop thinking about his saying he'd chosen the reform-school option for his mom rather than fighting the charge. Without question, Celia knew he'd never touched drugs. And she also knew him to be very prideful of how hard he'd worked. To swallow his pride and accept a plea bargain had to have been horribly difficult for him.

This decision to go with Malcolm to Europe grew more complicated by the second—and more enticing. What other secrets might she discover about him? What other nuances were there to the adult man he'd become?

A man who flew a helicopter as adeptly as he played the piano.

The chopper touched down lightly on the lawn with a simple kiss to the earth. The blades rotated overhead, sea grass bending with the rotor gusts. A uniformed guard opened her door and offered a hand to help her out. She snagged her floral tote bag and stepped free, the ground buzzing beneath her feet.

Before she could blink, Malcolm was at her side. His arm looped around her waist, warm and muscular, guiding her not toward the stucco beach mansion but toward a small private airstrip with a Learjet parked and waiting.

She felt as if Alice had just slipped a little farther down the rabbit hole. Her father traveled first-class, and even periodically rented a Cessna, but nothing on as grand a scale as this.

Seconds later, Malcolm palmed her waist as she

stepped inside the luxury aircraft, where another couple waited in the cabin of white leather and polished brass.

A red-haired woman with freckles stood, her hand extended. "You must be Celia. I'm Hillary, Troy's wife."

The wife of the Robin Hood Hacker.

Hillary appeared down-to-earth, blessedly normal, wearing jeans and a T-shirt—no doubt designer given how perfectly they fit. But still, no fake boobs or platinum-bleached hair. Just genuine red hair and freckles with a natural smile.

Already, Malcolm had moved past her to shake hands with a man she recognized from newspaper articles—Troy Donavan, quirky computer mogul who'd once used those skills to breach the cyber walls of the Department of Defense.

She overheard Malcolm's familiar Southern drawl. "Sorry we're late. The drive out took us longer than we expected."

"No worries, brother." Troy led him to a row of computer screens at a corner-office console in the tricked-out jet. "I'll give you a quick update while my wife keeps our lovely guest occupied."

Her eyes lingered on the broad expanse of Malcolm's shoulders, the strong column of his neck exposed as he leaned over the computer.

Hillary touched her lightly on the arm to regain her attention and gestured to a seat. "You look shell-shocked. I'm guessing he didn't take much time to explain. But covering his trail from the press, the fans and whoever has been bothering you had to happen fast."

Celia sank onto the leather sofa and patted along the seat for the belt. They were leaving now? No packing, no passports? No telling her friends… What the hell had she agreed to?

Her gaze tracked back to Malcolm. Who was this man she'd just agreed to leave the country with?

Hillary sat beside her. "We've heard a lot about you from Malcolm."

She looked up quickly, warily. "What did he say?"

"That you're old friends and you're having trouble with a stalker. So he's helping you out."

"He is. I'm lucky," she conceded to Hillary and herself just as the Learjet engines buzzed to life.

The captain's voice piped over the intercom, welcoming them all. All four of them. Not just Malcolm's friend, but Donavan's wife, as well. She hadn't expected Hillary to come along. Did the woman's presence here—the whole "group" outing—mean the romantic signals she'd been getting from Malcolm were wrong?

No wonder he hadn't acted on the kiss.

She should be grateful. The pressure was off since he wouldn't be tempting her. She could tamp down the crazy desire to jump his bones and just chalk it up to nostalgia. She kept right on repeating that to herself as they climbed into the sky, heading for the first stop on Malcolm's European tour.

Except, no matter how many times she told herself otherwise, she couldn't deny the truth. She wanted more, more of Malcolm's kisses. More of *him*.

And there wasn't a chance in hell she could afford to act on that desire.

Seven

The trip across the Atlantic to France passed in a blur for Celia as the time change plunged them into the night. But then her flights usually consisted of delayed connections, long layovers and lost baggage, followed by finding a cab in the heat, rain or snow.

Thanks to Malcolm's influence, she'd experienced superstar posh luxury and speed. Even sending in her grades had seemed surreal as she'd sat at a decked-out business center on the plane, with a cabin steward bringing her tea and fruit.

Now the Learjet was parking at the terminal at the Paris–Charles de Gaulle Airport, the first stop on Malcolm's European tour—with his friends along.

Surprisingly, though, she'd enjoyed getting to know Hillary during the flight, and bottom line, she should be grateful for the distraction. Distraction? Okay, the *chaperone* who would help Celia hold strong in her resolve *not* to plaster herself against Malcolm again in some impulsive moment.

And there were at least a few hundred other chaperones outside waiting under the halo of halogen lights. She glided her fingers down the glass of the window, showcasing legions of fans waving signs that were both handmade and professional.

I heart Malcolm.

Marry me.

Je t'aime.

Police and airport guards formed a human wall between the fans and the carpet being rolled out to the Learjet. Screaming, crying females threw flowers and…

Panties? Ew. Gross.

The gentle hum of the plane stopped, and everyone unbuckled as the steward opened the door. Noise swelled inward, high-pitched cheers, squeals and screams. The words jumbled together, but their adoring enthusiasm for Malcolm Douglas was unmistakable. He was this generation's Harry Connick Jr. and Michael Bublé—times ten.

Chuckling, Troy scooped up a fedora and dropped it on his head. "Dude, I think there's a woman out there who wants you to autograph her breasts."

Malcolm scowled, shrugging on a blue jacket with his jeans and button-down. "We'll just have to tell her I forgot my marker."

Hillary held up her leather portfolio and said with a wicked glint in her eyes, "I'm sure I have one in here you could borrow."

"Not funny." Malcolm smiled tightly.

Celia agreed. The thought of women climbing all over him made her ill.

Troy clapped him on the back. "Where's your sense

of humor, man? You're always quick with the sarcasm when somebody else is stressed."

A joker? He hadn't been that way back in high school. He'd been intense and driven, but never sarcastic or jaded. The fact that his achieving his life's dream hadn't left him unscathed niggled at her.

"I'll be a lot less stressed after we reach the hotel. So let's get moving." Malcolm picked up Celia's floral bag and started to pass it to her.

Troy choked on a cough.

Malcolm looked at him sharply. "What now, Donavan?"

"I just never thought I'd see the day when you carried a woman's purse for her."

Celia snatched it from his hands. "It's not a purse. It's a tote bag for my computer and my wallet. My favorite bag, for that matter. I bought it from the Vera Bradley Collection—" She stopped short, wincing. "I'm not helping you, am I, Malcolm?"

"No worries," he reassured her, planting his hand between her shoulder blades with unsettling ease. "I'm confident enough in my manhood I could carry that pink flowery bag like a man purse straight into that crowd."

"Photo, please?" Troy asked. "I'd pay good money."

Celia watched them joke and laugh together as they made their way to the door, and she realized she'd never seen Malcolm with friends before. Not even eighteen years ago. He'd never had time for recreation then. Between school, work and music lessons, he'd been driven to succeed, to make his mother's hard work pay off even at the expense of any social life most teens expected as their due. What other changes were there in his life now?

They stopped in the open hatch, and the crowd roared to a fever pitch of squeals and screams. He'd earned this, fame and adulation, yet he was still a man at ease with carrying her bag. He waved to the crowd, stirring the cheers even louder.

His hand slid along her spine until his arm went around her waist, cutting her thoughts short with the shock of his solid hold.

"Malcolm?" Halting in the open hatchway, she glanced at him, confused. "What are you doing?"

"This," he warned her a second before sealing his mouth to hers.

So much for worrying about holding strong against kissing him again. He planted a lip-lock on her to end all lip-locks. The familiarity of his mouth on hers tempted Celia, and before she could think, her hand gravitated to his chest. Her fingers curled into the crisp linen of his jacket.

The crowd roared. Or was that her pulse?

Malcolm dipped her ever so slightly back, stroking her face and along her hair before guiding her upright again. Thank goodness he kept his arm around her waist, because her knees were less than steady as he ended the kiss. Her blood pounded in her ears, her fist still clenched along the lapel of his jacket.

"What the hell was that all about?" she hissed softly, trying not to look at his friends grinning behind him.

Malcolm covered her hand with his, his blue eyes holding hers with an intensity she couldn't mistake. "Making sure the world knows you're mine and anyone who touches you will have hell to pay."

He peeled her hand free then locked arms with her, starting down the metal steps onto the concrete. She held on tightly, her legs still wobbly from his kiss in front of a crowd of people and camera lenses. What about him warning her about the possibility of the press seeing them at a B and B? Had he just said that before because he wanted her to go with him?

Her skin chilled in spite of the warm summer breeze, carrying the scent of flowers tossed by fans. A sleek white limousine waited a few strides away.

Desperate to regain her balance, she angled toward Malcolm to whisper, "I thought we were giving off the impression of friends traveling. Casual companions. What about how you worried the press would see us at a hotel?"

"I didn't want to claim you until you were safe."

Safe? Her feelings for him were anything but safe. "Weren't you the one who made fun of puppy love in the limo?"

His cerulean-blue eyes slid over her, soothing like cool water on overheated flesh. "Darlin', this has nothing to do with puppy love and everything to with adult passion. With cameras in our face 24/7, it'll be impossible to carry off a lie. Those photographers will pick up on the fact that I want you so badly my damn teeth hurt."

Her breath hitched in her throat. "I don't know what to say."

He stopped at the limo, waving to the crowds once before he looked at her adoringly again. Totally an act. Right? He waved her into the stretch limousine before following her inside.

"Celia," he said quickly while Troy and Hillary were still outside, "rather than lie about our attraction and make the press all the more desperate to prove what they already sense, it's better just to be honest about this. So be forewarned. I'll be kissing you and touching you and romancing you very publically and very often."

A shiver of anticipation skittered up her spine. How would she ever withstand that kind of romantic assault?

"But I already told you. We can't do this. We can't go back. I'm not climbing into bed with you again."

She willed herself to believe it.

"It won't matter." He kissed the tip of her nose, then whispered against her skin, "Your eyes are crystal clear. The camera will pick up the truth."

She couldn't catch her breath, and her skin flushed where he touched her. Kissed her.

"Do tell, Malcolm. What truth might that be?"

"Darlin', you want me every bit as much as I want you." He stretched an arm along the back of the seat, going silent as Troy and Hillary settled in across from them.

Hillary grinned from ear to ear. "Welcome to Paris, the city of love."

Malcolm stood alone on the hotel balcony overlooking the Eiffel Tower. Celia and the Donavans had already settled into their rooms for the night, turning in now to combat jet lag.

He, however, was too restless to sleep, too caught up in the need to take Celia into his room, his bed. He used to fantasize about bringing Celia to France, taking her to concerts and proposing to her in a place with a view just like this one. Yet another dream that hadn't panned out the way he'd planned.

The whole flight, he'd found his eyes drawn to her again and again. Taking in the waves of her hair draping along her shoulder, even how she chewed her thumbnail while poring over grades, trying to decide whether or not to give a student an extra point for a better letter grade.

Everything about Celia entranced him. It always had. Even when they were kids on a playground, he'd known she was special, a dynamo with an electric personality that people wanted to be around. Other kids gravitated to her open smile, melodic laugh and her willingness to try anything. Even come to stick up for the new kid in the middle of an embarrassing-as-hell asthma attack.

Yet even then, as she'd helped him fish his inhaler out of his backpack, he'd been aware of their differences. For class parties, her mom brought a clown to set up an ice-cream bar, and his mom made cupcakes in their tiny kitchen. Such a strange thing to remember now, especially when money was no longer an issue.

He felt the weight of eyes on him and turned sharply, then relaxed.

Colonel John Salvatore stood in the open doorway, wearing his standard gray suit and red tie. The colonel worked at Interpol headquarters in Lyon, France, so it shouldn't be surprising he'd shown up here. Only surprising he'd arrived in the middle of the night.

"Good evening, sir." Malcolm didn't bother asking how Salvatore had gotten into his suite. "You could have called, you know. Anything new to report?"

"Nothing new." The retired headmaster stepped up beside him at the rail. "Just in town for your concert. Thought I would say hello, Mozart."

Mozart… Back in the day, his classmates had called him by the name of just about every composer out there since he spent so many hours playing classical music. Mostly, he played the classical stuff because it tended to chase off the other students, allowing him some peace in the crowded school.

"I appreciate the extra security, Salvatore. I mean that. I'll rest a lot easier knowing Celia's safe until the authorities can sort out the mess back home."

The colonel loosened his tie and tucked it into his pocket. "Are you sure you know what you're doing?"

With the simple discarding of his tie, Salvatore went from distant boss to caring mentor.

Malcolm shook his head, his eyes locked on the Eiffel Tower glowing in the night. "Hell, no, but I can't back away."

"Do you have some kind of vendetta against her?"

"What?" Malcolm looked back sharply, surprised the man even had to ask. "I would hope you know me better than that."

"I know how troubled you were when you showed up at the school."

"We all were." Angry. Defiant. Wanting to have a normal high-school experience but knowing damn well it was too late to go back.

"You tried to run away three times."

"I didn't want to be locked up," he said, dodging the real reason for why he'd risked everything, even jeopardizing the peace he'd brought his mother.

"You risked jail time leaving." Salvatore leaned his elbows on the railing, the ground seven floors below. Sparse traffic drove by, late-night partiers stepping into the hotel next door.

"But you never reported me." Malcolm still didn't know why, any more than he could figure out why they were discussing this now.

"Because I knew you were one of the few kids sent to that school who were actually innocent."

Malcolm straightened in surprise. He'd never once proclaimed his innocence, and everyone had assumed he was guilty. Everyone except Celia, but even she had pulled away from him in the end. Not that he could blame her. Still, hearing the colonel's unconditional confidence… It meant a lot, then and now. "How can you be so sure?"

"I'd seen enough users and dealers come through that

school to recognize one when he crossed my path. You weren't involved in drugs in any way, shape or form," he said with unmistakable certainty in his voice. "Besides, if you had a drug problem, this lifestyle would have wrecked you long ago." As if to lend weight to his words, drunken laughter drifted up from the street.

"So you believe in me because of your proof."

"The facts merely reinforced my gut. I also know that a man will do anything for his child. I understand. I would die for my kid," he said, offering a rare glimpse into himself. "I figured you took that job at the bar hoping to make enough money to support Celia and your child. You didn't want her to give up the baby, and I'm guessing you wanted to keep the child because your father abandoned you."

"Damn, Colonel." Malcolm stepped back, looking for an escape from the truth. "I thought your doctorate was in history, not psychology."

He'd relived enough of the past since seeing Celia again. He wasn't prepared for this kind of walk down memory lane, especially when the trip was a rough ride that always left him raw.

"Doesn't take a shrink to know you're protective of your mother, and you have reason to resent your biological father. So? Do you have a vendetta to fulfill? Some revenge plan in having Celia close to you?"

"No—hell, no." Malcolm denied it and meant it. The last thing he wanted was to see Celia hurt. "Celia and I are both adults now. And as for our kid, she's almost an adult, as well. So there's no going back. The notion of a redo or revenge is moot."

"Nothing's ever moot. Remember that."

He'd had enough of these pointless jabs at old wounds.

"Why don't we talk about your kid, then? Don't you have a ball game to go to or something?"

"Fine." Salvatore held up his hands. "I'll just spell it out for you. It's all well and good that you want to protect Celia. But you need to accept your feelings for that woman aren't moot if you're ever going to move forward with your life."

And with that parting shot, Salvatore disappeared as silently as he'd appeared, leaving Malcolm alone on the balcony. God, he needed to go inside and sleep, charge up for the performance, protect his voice from the night air.

Instead, he kept right on staring at the Eiffel Tower, battling a bellyful of regrets. Given what Salvatore had said, it didn't sound as if he had much chance of ever putting the past to rest. Try as he might to move on, he still carried a whole lot of guilt about what had happened. More than that, he still had feelings for Celia. Feelings that weren't going to go away just because he tried to ignore them.

In which case, maybe ignoring them was a piss-poor idea. He wasn't getting anywhere like this. So why the hell was he denying himself what he wanted most right now? There was nothing stopping him from persuading Celia to let him back into her bed.

And the concert tomorrow would be the perfect place to begin.

Toying with the twisted seed-pearl necklace, Celia stood backstage at the concert with Hillary as Malcolm gripped the mic, walking along the edge of the stage and serenading the swarms of females reaching up. Their screams combatted with the sound system pumping out his voice and the band. She'd spent a large portion of her life performing, so the lights, the parade of backup instruments and techies didn't faze her. Still, she couldn't help but be awed by the intensity of it all, the energy radiating off the thousands of people who'd come to hear Malcolm Douglas.

He'd been emphatic about her staying backstage. He didn't trust her safety out in the audience, even sitting in one of the exclusive boxes. So she watched from the sidelines, enjoying the sight of him in profile. He wore a black suit and shirt without a tie, his songs a mix of current soft-rock tunes and retro remixes of old classics.

And oh, God, his voice was stirring her every bit as much as his kiss at the airport.

At least she had Hillary to keep her company, along with another friend of theirs, Jayne Hughes. Jayne was apparently married to another reform-school buddy of Malcolm's. They'd all come out in force with their husbands to see him perform—and keep watch over her. Malcolm's friends and their wives were rock-solid loyal, no question.

While Hillary was fresh-faced, freckled and approachable in her jeans and sequined tank top, Jayne was so darn elegant and poised in her simple sheath dress that Celia resisted the urge to check her makeup. She smoothed her damp hands down the loose, silky dress she'd chosen from the racks of clothes Malcolm had ordered sent to her room. He'd been gone all day for sound checks.

The chic, blonde Jayne leaned toward her. "It's a little overwhelming."

Hillary arched up onto her toes for a better view. "And incredible."

Jayne continued, "And overwhelming."

Celia reevaluated her image of Jayne Hughes as a cool socialite as she realized the woman genuinely was worried for her. "You can go ahead and ask."

"Ask what?" Jayne answered.

"Why I'm here. Why I'm with Malcolm." She glanced at him onstage as he took his place behind a grand piano. So many times she'd sat beside him to play in tandem, or accompanied him on the guitar. Their shared appreciation of music had added layers to their relationship back then. "Or maybe you already know the story."

"Only that you and Malcolm grew up in the same town, and you've come here to get away from a stalker at home." Jayne smoothed her already perfectly immaculate hair, shoulder-length and bluntly cut. She looked every bit the casino magnate's wife, adored and pampered. Loved.

Celia shifted her attention back to the stage. Malcolm's smooth baritone washed over her, so familiar even with the richness of maturity adding more flavor to the tone. "We've known each other since we were kids, dated in high school."

Jayne tipped her head to the side. "You're different from the other women he's seen."

She wondered if they referred to the women he'd really dated or the ladies he'd been photographed with for—as he insisted—strictly publicity purposes. Still, she couldn't resist asking, "Different how?"

"You're smart," Jayne answered without hesitation.

Hillary chimed in, "Serious."

"Not clingy," Jayne continued.

Hillary added, "Literate."

They made her sound utterly boring. "Thank you for the…uh…"

"Compliment," Hillary said. "Totally. Malcolm's a lot deeper than he likes to let on."

He was. Or at least, he had been back then. And now? It was tough not to appear too hungry for these nuggets of information about Malcolm's life since they'd been apart.

Jayne tapped her foot lightly to the music, one of Malcolm's more upbeat songs. "I met Malcolm just over seven years ago. In all the time I've known him, he's never made friends beyond his school buddies. Even his manager went to the military academy with him."

Hillary held up a finger. "And he's close to his mother, of course."

Yeah, she knew that and respected him for it even though Terri Lynn had disapproved of her. Okay, more than disapproved. His mother had hated her. Celia smiled tightly, staying quiet.

Jayne's blue eyes slit with sympathy. "You must have been important to him."

"We share a lot of history." Understatement of the year.

"And we're nosy. Just ignore us both, and let's enjoy the concert."

Grateful to have the spotlight off her for now at least, she turned her attention to the stage, where the focus narrowed to a true spotlight on a lone bar stool with a guitar propped against it.

Malcolm sat, his foot on the lowest rung, and settled the guitar on his knee. "I have a new song to share with you tonight, a simple song straight from the heart…."

The heart? She resisted the urge to roll her eyes as she thought of how he'd vowed he didn't believe the love songs he sang. She watched with a new, more jaded perspective.

With the first stroke of his fingers along the strings, Celia gasped. Her stomach knotted in recognition.

Each strum of the acoustic, unplugged moment confirmed her fears, touched her soul and rattled her to her core. A completely low blow, unfair—and designed to bring her to her knees. She didn't know whether to cry or scream as he sang the first notes of the song he'd written for her years ago.

He sang "Playing for Keeps."

Eight

The strains of "Playing for Keeps" echoed in his head even after he'd finished the last encore, reminding him of a time when he'd actually believed that idea. The audience ate up the simple melody and sappy premise.

Exiting stage right, he began to doubt the wisdom of rolling out that old tune to soften up Celia. He couldn't read her face in the shadowy wings, but he damn well knew his insides were a raw mess. Thank God his Alpha Brotherhood buddies were backstage with her, a wall of protection behind her while a couple of the wives kept her company. So his pals had her back—and his—until he could get himself on level ground.

This whole trip down memory lane was a double-edged sword, but he wouldn't lose sight of the goal. He and Celia needed to see this through. To settle the past before they could move forward with the future. The applause and cheers swelling behind him meant nothing if he couldn't find some resolution with Celia.

God, she was gorgeous in a silky sapphire dress with a hint of ruffle teasing her knees. And the plunging neckline—he couldn't look away, especially as throughout the concert she'd toyed with those tiny strands of pearls twisted together. Her feminine curves had always driven him to his knees and drained him of the ability to think. But holy hell, he could feel.

Turned on and turned inside out.

He wanted to have her naked in his arms again more than he wanted air. More than he wanted another concert or even another assignment. Getting into her bed again had become his mission of the moment. She was, and always had been, the woman he wanted more than any other.

As he drew closer to her, though, he realized he'd made a big, big mistake with the song. Her lips were tight, her eyes sparking with anger and something even worse.

Pain.

Crap. The sight of her distress sucker punched him. He'd meant to tap into her emotions, not hurt her.

Stepping into the backstage shadows, he reached out to her. "Celia—"

She held up both hands, keeping an arm's distance between them. "Great concert. Fans adored that new *love* song of yours. Congratulations. Now, if you'll excuse me, I'm ready to turn in for the night. Looks like I have plenty of guards, so you're officially absolved of protective detail."

With a brittle smile, she pivoted on her heel and walked away, pushing through the crowd double-time.

Hillary Donavan studied him with perceptive eyes before nudging Jayne to join her in racing to catch up with

Celia. Bodyguards melted from the backstage melee, encircling the women in an almost-imperceptible bubble of protection.

Malcolm slumped against a pallet of backup amps. How could he win over stadiums full of people yet still be clueless when it came to this one woman?

A hand clapped him on the shoulder, and he damn near jumped out of his skin. Troy Donavan stood beside him to his left, Conrad Hughes to his right. The international casino magnate was a lot less brooding these days since he'd reconciled with his wife.

Troy thumped Malcolm between the shoulder blades again. "Woman troubles?"

"Always," Malcolm said simply.

Troy charged alongside. "My advice? Give her space—"

Conrad interrupted, "But not so long that she thinks you're avoiding her."

Troy continued, "Enough time to cool down about whatever lame-ass thing you did."

Fair enough and true enough, except, "I can't afford to give her space, not with—"

"A stalker." Troy finished his sentence. "Right. She has guards. We'll be in the room next to hers playing cards. Meanwhile, smile your way through the reporters and let's get back to the penthouse."

An offer his stressed-out brain could not resist.

The limo ride through the night streets of Paris with the Arc de Triomphe glowing in the distance was as awkward as hell. With Celia looking anywhere but at him, the others in the vehicle made small talk to fill the empty air.

Finally—thank God, finally—they reached their historic hotel. The women smiled their way past reporters as they charged up the steps between stone lions. And before Malcolm could say "What the hell?" he found himself staring at Celia's closed door in the penthouse suite.

He turned back to the spacious living room connecting all the bedrooms. While he tried not to take the wealth for granted, the carved antiques and gilded wood were wasted on him tonight. His longtime buddies were all doing a piss-poor job of covering their grins.

"Gentlemen." Malcolm scrubbed a hand over his bristled jaw. "There's no reason for the rest of you to hang out here in the doghouse with me. Granted, it's a luxurious doghouse. So enjoy your cards and order up whatever you want on my tab. But I'm done for the night."

Troy straddled a chair at the table in the suite's dining area. "Like hell. We're not letting you check out on us any more than you would let us leave. The rest of our party should be arriving right about—"

The private elevator to the penthouse dinged with the arrival of…

The rest of the party? Crap.

The brass doors slid open in the hall to reveal three men, each one an alumni of the North Carolina Prep School. Alpha Brotherhood comrades. And recruits of Salvatore for Interpol.

Malcolm's concerts gave them the perfect excuse for reunions. First out of the elevator, Elliot Starc, a Formula One driver who'd just been dumped by his fiancée for playing as hard and fast as he drove. Behind him, Dr. Rowan Boothe, the golden-boy saint of the bunch who devoted his life to saving AIDS/HIV orphans in Africa. And lastly, Malcolm's manager, Adam Logan, aka The Shark, who would do anything to keep his clients booked and in the news.

Shoving away from the window, Malcolm shrugged

off his jacket, which still bore the hint of sweat from the concert. "We're gonna need a bigger table."

His manager grinned. "Food and drinks are on the way up." He took his chair at the far side. "There are going to be a lot of brokenhearted fans out there once they realize this thing with Celia isn't just a new fling."

There was no escaping his pals, who knew him so well. Better to meet their questions head-on—and bluff. "Logan, I don't have a clue what you're talking about."

Conrad shuffled the cards smoothly. "Seriously, brother, you're going to play it that way?"

The saintly doctor dropped into a seat. "I thought you were over her."

"Clearly, I'm not," he said tightly and too damn truthfully. Everywhere he looked in the room, he already saw reminders of her—and it was just a hotel room, for God's sake.

Elliot poured himself a drink at the fully stocked bar. "Then why the hell did you stay away for eighteen years? It's all I can do to stay away from Gianna since she gave me my walking papers."

When had his brothers started ganging up on him? "That's the way Celia wanted things then. Now our lives are very different. We've moved on."

His manager tapped his temple. "Two musicians who're obviously attracted to each other. Hmm...still not tracking your logic on being wrong for each other."

"Breaking up was best for her," Malcolm answered, irritation chewing his already churning gut. "I wrecked her life once. I owe it to her not to do that again."

Logan kept right on pressing. "So even though you let her go, you've been making billions to show up her old man."

"Or maybe I enjoy nice toys."

Troy tipped back in his chair, smoothing a hand down his designer tie. "You're sure as hell not spending it on clothes."

"Who appointed you the fashion police?" Malcolm unbuttoned his cuffs and rolled up his sleeves. "Start dealing. I'll be back."

He strode over to the bulletproof window for a better signal and pulled out his phone to check for messages from Salvatore. He'd seen his old mentor in a private box at the performance, a glamorous woman at his side. But even when he socialized, the colonel was never off the clock. Malcolm's email filled with data from Salvatore's intelligence on the principal Celia had been "sort of seeing." His references, his awards and a dozen other ways he was an all-around great guy.

So why didn't he have even partial custody of his kids? Strange, especially for a principal. Malcolm typed an answer to Salvatore then shut down his phone.

He turned, finding the saintly doc lounging in the doorway.

"Damn, Rowan," Malcolm barked, "you could have spoken or something to let me know you were there."

"You sound a little hoarse there, buddy. Is the concert tour already wearing on your vocal cords? I can check you over if you're having trouble."

"I'm fine, thanks." He clipped his phone to his belt, and still Elliot didn't move. "Anything else?"

"As a matter of fact, yes, there is," the golden boy pressed, but then he never gave up trying to fix the world. "Why are you tearing yourself up this way by being with her again?"

"You're the good guy. I would think you'd understand. I let her down once." Malcolm started toward his bedroom door to ditch his sweaty coat and give himself a chance to regain his footing. "I need to make up for that. I have to see this through."

"And you'll just walk away when you figure out who's after her?" he asked, his sarcasm making it all too clear he didn't believe it for a second.

"She doesn't want the kind of life I lead, and no way do I fit into hers now." The last thing he wanted was to go back to Azalea, Mississippi. "I promised myself I wouldn't get involved. What she and I had was just puppy love."

"What happens if someone breaks into her house next month? Or a student lets the air out of her tires? Are you going to come running to her side?"

Rowan's logic set Malcolm's teeth on edge.

"Quit being an ass." He charged past, back into the living room.

His manager leaned back in his chair and called over to him, "Quit being delusional. Either claim the woman or don't. But time to commit to a course."

"Damn it, Adam," Malcolm growled, closing in on the round table. "Do you think you could speak a little softer? I don't think they heard you over in Russia."

He looked down the hallway toward Celia's room. Once he was confident the door wouldn't open with an angry Celia, he sat as Conrad dealt the cards.

"Claim her?" the casino magnate repeated. "I can almost hear my wife laughing at you if she heard that. Brother, they claim us. Body and soul."

Elliot grimaced, "You're sounding like one of those sappy songs of Malcolm's… 'Playing for Keeps'? Really, dude? Be straight with us. You wrote that one to get some action."

Malcolm bit back the urge to haul him out of the chair and punch him the way he'd done when Elliot ran off at the mouth in school. Only the image of Celia's pained face made him hold back, humbling him with how much he'd screwed up somehow. "Hope you're going to be happy growing old alone with your race cars and a cat." He gathered his cards. "Now, are we playing poker or what?"

Even as he pretended to shrug off what his friends had said, he couldn't deny their words had taken root. For tonight, he would let her cool down. But come morning, he needed to quit thinking about seducing Celia and actually get down to the business of romancing his way back into her bed. Romancing her, seducing her, was not the same as falling for her. He could make the distinction and so could Celia.

And by learning that, they could both quit glorifying what they'd shared in the past and move on.

Celia tipped her face toward the morning sun, the boat rolling gently under her feet as it chugged along the Seine River. Hillary Donavan told her they'd set up a private ride for their group to see some of the city before they flew out for the next stop on the tour. Such a large group of friends and their wives. While she understood their school connection, she wondered why Malcom's entourage included such luminaries. Usually artists traveled with lesser folk, always remaining the star of their circle. But Malcolm traveled with very high-placed friends from an array of backgrounds. His lack of ego was…appealing.

Gusts channeled down the canal, fluttering her gauzy blouse against her oversensitive skin. She needed this breather before she saw Malcolm again. He hadn't been in the limo with them this morning, and she'd pushed down the kick of disappointment. No doubt he must be sleeping in, exhausted after the performance.

Taking in the image of the Eiffel Tower set against the

backdrop of the historic city, she appreciated the thoughtfulness, as well as the chance to escape the hotel suite. She needed this opportunity to air out her mind before they climbed onto the claustrophobic luxury jet again.

The restless night's sleep hadn't done much to settle her tumultuous nerves over how Malcolm had used that piece of their history—onstage, no less—to play with her emotions. He'd always been driven, but she'd never expected him to be ruthless. Her hair lifting in the breeze, she gripped the brass railing of the boat powering along the canal.

"Why are you ignoring me?" a male voice rumbled behind her.

Malcolm's voice.

Rich, intoxicating tones that sent a shiver down her spine.

Her toes curled in her sandals.

Celia turned on her heel to face him, leaning back against the rail. How much longer before his voice stopped making her knees go shaky? Plus the sight of him? Equally dreamy. The past and present blended in his look of faded jeans with designer loafers and a jacket. He wore a ball cap and sunglasses, likely to hide his identity, but she would have known him anywhere.

And just her luck, all of his buddies were making tracks to the other side of the boat, leaving her here. Alone. With Malcolm.

She blinked back the sparks of the morning sun behind his broad shoulders. "I thought you were still at the hotel asleep when I left."

"I came to the boat ahead of the rest of you, slipped on board with the boat captain to reduce the chances of the press finding me." He captured a lock of her hair trailing in the wind and tucked it behind her ear. "Back to my question. Why did you avoid me *last night,* after the concert?"

"Ignoring you?" She angled her head away from his stirring touch. "Why would I do that? We're not in junior high school."

"You haven't spoken to me since those few brief—vague—words after the concert last night." He frowned, shoving his hands into the pockets of his jeans. "Are you pissed because I kissed you on the plane?"

"Should I be upset that you kissed me without asking?" A kiss that still made the roots of her hair tingle. "Or should I be angry about the photos of us together plastered all over tabloids and magazines? Oh, and let's not forget TV gossip shows. We're—and I quote—'The Toast of Paris.'"

"So that is why you've refused to talk to me." He pressed a thumb against his temple, just below the ball cap.

"Actually, I got over that. But the way you mocked me by playing a song you wrote about us in high school—" her anger gained steam "—a song you recently called a puppy-love joke? Now, *that* made me mad."

"Damn it, Celia." He hooked a finger in a belt loop on her jeans and tugged her toward him. "That wasn't my intention."

"Then what did you intend?" she asked, unable to read his eyes behind those sunglasses. She flattened her palms on his chest to keep from landing flush against him, body to body. Still, with their faces a breath apart, her heart skipped a beat.

"Hell, I just wanted to pay tribute to what we shared as teenagers. Not to glorify it, but certainly not to mock it," he said with unmistakable sincerity. "We did share something special back then. I think we can share that again."

Air wooshed from her lungs, making it almost impossible to talk. The sound of the flowing water alongside the boat echoed the roar of blood rushing through her veins. Her fingers curled in the warmth of his jacket. "You missed the mark big-time in getting your meaning across on the stage, Malcolm."

"Let me make it up to you." Pulling off the shades, he rested his forehead against hers, the power of his deep blue gaze bathing her senses.

"You don't have to do anything. You're protecting me from a stalker. If anything, I owe you." She squeezed his jacket tighter. "But that's all I owe you."

His hand slid around her. "I don't want you feeling indebted to me."

Her face tipped to his, so close to kissing, so close to bliss. Her mouth tingled in anticipation. It was getting tougher and tougher to remember why this was a bad idea. The roaring of the water and her pulse grew louder and louder until she realized it wasn't the river or her heartbeat.

"Damn it, the press," Malcolm barked softly, stepping back and sliding his sunglasses on again.

Paparazzi ran along the shore with cameras in hand. Shouts carried on the wind, disjointed phrases.

"—Douglas."

"Kiss her—"

Celia raced alongside him toward the captain's cabin. "I thought you intended for us to kiss for the camera."

"Changed my mind," he called, pulling open the door. "Keeping you happy suddenly became a higher priority."

He tucked her inside, the boat captain glancing over in surprise. Malcolm waved for him to carry on. Apparently Elliot Starc hadn't him given boat-driving lessons, too, she thought, hysterical laughter starting to bubble inside her. Her nerves were seriously fraying.

"What now?" she asked.

Malcolm nodded to the floral bag dangling from her arm. "You could answer your phone."

She looked down fast, the chiming surprising her until she almost jumped out of her skin. "I didn't even hear it."

Fishing inside, she dug through until her hand closed around the phone. She pulled it out and saw her father's number blinking on the screen.

"Hello, Dad. What do you need?"

"Just checking on my baby girl," he said, concern coating every word, "making sure you're all right. I, uh, saw the newspapers this morning."

She grimaced, avoiding Malcolm's eyes. "I'm fine. The pictures were...staged. It's all a part of making sure everyone knows I'm very well protected here in Malcolm's entourage."

"Staged, huh?" her father answered skeptically. "I never knew you were a theater person, because that was some mighty fine acting in the photo."

Her chest tightened with every word from her father. "I don't know what more I can tell you."

"Well, I've been fielding calls all day."

"From the press?" The thought of them hounding her dad made her swallow hard—not easy to do when she was finding it tougher and tougher to breathe.

"My number's unlisted. You know that. The calls are from your friends at school, even that high-school principal you went out with a couple of times."

"I didn't go out with him." She glanced at Malcolm quickly as the enormity of this washed over her. Being with Malcolm now had changed her life in ways she could never undo. Her ordered existence was falling apart. She was losing control—but for once, that didn't seem to be such a bad thing. "We just happened to sit together at events we both attended for work."

"Who drove?"

"Stop it, Dad," she snapped, then backtracked, guilt pinching her. She started pacing restlessly in the small cabin. "I love you, and I appreciate your concern, but I'm an adult."

"Malcolm's standing there with you, isn't he?"

"Why does that matter?" And why couldn't she bring herself to just end the call? God, she hated being caught between them again.

Her father sighed through the phone lines. "Just protect yourself, Celia. You'll always be my baby girl."

His voice stirred more guilt as she thought of his pain over losing his oldest daughter. She pressed a hand to her head, dizzy from lack of breakfast and, yes, pangs of guilt. She thought of her own ache for the baby she'd given up, but at least she knew her child was alive somewhere, growing up loved. Worrying for her father heaped on top of her nerves, which were already stretched to the max by trying to sort through her feelings for Malcolm.

"Dad, I promise I'm being very careful." She measured her words carefully, trying not to let her perceptive father hear the quaver in her voice. "And you? Are you okay? Have you gotten any threatening messages?"

"I'm fine. Blood pressure is in the good zone, and there hasn't been so much as a peep of a threat."

"Thank God," she said, praying that wouldn't change. "I really do appreciate the call. Love you, Dad."

Her heartbeat sped up, new worries crowding her head and making her chest feel tight. Oh, no. She knew the old symptoms. Knew what might happen next if she didn't pull it together.

She thumbed the off button and dropped her phone back into her Vera Bradley bag with shaky hands. "Well, your plan is working. The whole world—even my father—thinks we're having an affair." She gasped for air, trying to fight down the encroaching panic and not succeeding all that well. "Do you think we could just go back to the hotel?"

"Are you okay?" Malcolm asked, just before she could have sworn the boat began listing to the side.

Ah, hell. She reached for Malcolm's hand just before she blacked out.

Nine

Disoriented, Celia pushed through the fog back to consciousness, confusion wrapping around her. Was it morning? Was she at home? No… She was in a *car*.

With each deep breath she inhaled, she drew in the essence of Malcolm. She knew he was beside her.

The past merged with the present, bringing memories of another time she'd fainted. When she was sixteen, she'd snuck out of her room at midnight to meet Malcolm when he finished at the burger joint where he worked after school. She'd been skipping meals because of nausea, and it had been all she could do to stay awake to meet him as promised. But talking to him had been so important. She'd needed to tell him before her parents saw the signs. Before she started to show. But before she could finish telling him, she'd passed out.

Malcolm had rushed her to the emergency room, where of course the doctor called her parents. She squeezed her eyes closed tighter even now over the explosion of anger that had erupted in that E.R. over her pregnancy. Malcolm had insisted they get married. Her father had lunged at Malcolm. Her mother had sobbed.

Celia had wanted to die....

Well, at least she knew for damn sure she wasn't pregnant now. She'd blacked out for an entirely different reason.

Slowly, she took in the feel of the leather seat of the limousine. She must have been carried and put inside. The sounds of the voices around her steadied and the cause of this fainting spell gelled in her mind. She'd been freaking out and gasping for air until she passed out on the boat. Her eyes snapped open. She was inside a limousine with Malcolm and his entire entourage of alumni pals.

He leaned over her, stroking back her hair. His buddy Dr. Rowan Boothe had her wrist in his hand, taking her pulse. The rest of their friends loomed behind them, her world narrowing to this stretch limo with tinted windows and a lot of curious, concerned faces.

How incredibly embarrassing.

She pushed up onto her elbow, sitting. "What time is it? How long have I been—"

"Whoa, whoa, hold on..." Malcolm touched her shoulders and glanced at Rowan. "Doc?"

"Her pulse is normal." Rowan set her hand aside and tucked himself back onto a seat. "I don't see any reason to go to the E.R. I can check her over more thoroughly once we're on the plane to Germany."

Malcolm moved closer again, looking unconvinced. "Are you sure you're okay? What happened back there?"

"I'm fine." She sat up straighter, blinking fast as she tried to regain equilibrium. "Probably just low blood sugar from skipping breakfast."

The lie tasted bad on her tongue. But admitting the truth? Explaining her lingering battle with panic attacks? She wasn't ready to share that.

Malcolm seemed to accept her explanation, though. His shoulders relaxed a little as he opened the mini-fridge. He passed her a bottle of orange juice and a protein bar. "No offense, beautiful, but you don't look okay."

She twisted off the cap and sipped, just to appease him and make her story more believable. What she really needed were some breathing exercises or her emergency meds. Or a way to distance herself from all the feelings Malcolm was stirring up.

She looked out the window as they drove along the shore of the Seine River.

He eyed her for five long heartbeats. "We used to understand each other well, from the second on the playground when you threw sand at that kid for making fun of my asthma attack. Now, though, I want the chance to fight back for you."

Without another word, he gave her the space she'd requested and took a seat at the far end of the stretch limo. Quite a long way. Especially with all of his friends, plus Hillary and Jayne, sitting between them and trying to pretend there wasn't a thick, awkward silence all the way to the airport.

Once the Learjet was airborne to fly them to Berlin, Malcolm continued to honor her request for space, which was actually the best way to get closer to her again. Did he remember that from their past? She fished in her floral bag for her eReader to pass the time and calm her nerves, still jangled from the incident on the boat. She had to steady herself before she ran the gauntlet for the next concert. She pulled the reader case out, her fingers fumbling with the zipper.

Dr. Boothe knelt in front of her, taking the case from her hand and opening it before setting the eReader beside her. "Want to tell me what's wrong?"

She glanced around the plane. Everyone else seemed occupied with the business station or talking in the next cabin. Hillary, an event planner, was in deep conversation with Jayne about a fundraiser in the works for Dr. Boothe's clinic—where apparently Jayne worked, as well. Even the steward was busy readying lunch in the galley.

Turning back to the fair-haired doctor, she said carefully, "I already told Malcolm. I forgot to eat breakfast, but I'm feeling better now," but he still didn't move away. "I'm just going to read until lunch. Thank you."

He picked up her wrist. "Your pulse is still racing and you're struggling for breath."

"You said back at the limo that my pulse rate was fine." She tugged her hand away.

"It wasn't Malcolm's business unless you chose to tell him."

"Thank you." She picked up her eReader pointedly. "I'll let you know if I have a heart attack. I promise."

He shifted to sit beside her. "I don't think that's what's going on here, medically speaking."

Of course it wasn't, but she didn't particularly want to trot out the details of how she'd screwed up and left her medicine at home. She didn't need it all the time, and it had been so long since she'd reached for an antianxiety pill, she'd hoped…

Dr. Boothe stretched out his legs, as if in the middle of some casual conversation. "We can make this a patient/doctor thing, and then I can't say a word to anyone else. The whole confidentiality issue."

She shot a quick look at him, and he seemed…nonjudgmental.

Weighing her options, she decided it was better to trust him and hope he could help her rather than risk another embarrassing incident. "I'm fighting down a panic attack. I left home so quickly I didn't have a chance to get my, uh, medicine. I don't have to take anything regularly anymore, but I do have a prescription for antianxiety medication. The bottle just happens to be sitting in my bathroom cabinet."

A big oversight given that she had a stalker on her tail. But oddly, the thought of being in danger like that wasn't half as scary as the resurrection of her old feelings for Malcolm. The memories of what they'd given up. She hadn't realized how deeply this time with him might affect her.

She hadn't *wanted* to admit it.

Rowan nodded slowly. "That's problematic. But not insurmountable. Your doctor can call in the prescription."

She had already thought of that. "Malcolm is so worried about the stalker back home that I can't make a move without him noticing. It's not that I'm ashamed or anything. I'm just not ready to tell him yet."

"Understood," he said simply, the window behind him revealing a small and distant Paris below. "If you'll give your doctor permission to speak with me, I can take care of a prescription."

"Thank you." The tightness in her chest began to ease at the notion of help on the horizon.

"If you don't mind my asking, when did these attacks begin?"

She recognized his question for what it was, an attempt to help talk her down. "After I broke up with Malcolm. I've had some trouble with depression and anxiety. It's not a constant, but under times of extreme stress..."

She blew out a slow breath, searching for level ground and some control over her racing pulse.

"This sure qualifies as a time of stress, with the threats back home and all the insanity of Malcolm's life."

As the engine hummed through the sky, she thought about the patients he saw on a regular basis in Africa, of their problems, and felt so darn small right now. "You treat people with such huge problems. I probably seem whiny to you, the poor little rich girl who can't handle her emotions."

"Hold on." He raised a hand. "This isn't a competition. And as I'm sure your own doctor has told you, depression and anxiety disorders are medical conditions like diabetes. Serotonin or insulin, all chemicals your body needs. And you're wise to keep watch over your health."

"But your patients—" She stopped short as Malcolm stepped away from the business center. She picked up her eReader. "Thanks, Dr. Boothe, for checking on me. I appreciate your help."

She powered up her book and pretended to read the most recent download from her book club. If only she could act her way through the rest of her problems.

But when it came to Malcolm, she'd never been all that adept at hiding her feelings—feelings that were escalating with him in such close proximity. No question, the man disrupted her well-ordered world, and she feared where that could lead.

Yet, she couldn't bring herself to say goodbye.

His suite in downtown Berlin looked much the same as their digs in Paris, except with less gild to the antiques. But then his tours usually became a blur of hotel rooms and concert halls. God knew his attempt at a bit of sightseeing for Celia in Paris hadn't played out that well. He needed to step back and rethink how to win her over.

Starting with clearing out his well-meaning, advice-peddling pals. They interfered with his plans to get Celia alone. He'd thanked them for gathering around him when he'd called them to help build a wall of protection around Celia as the concert tour started, and he appreciated their ready turnout. But the need for their help had passed. Once they left Germany, his friends would be peeling off, returning to their lives.

At least his concert in Berlin tonight had gone off without a hitch since he'd left "Playing for Keeps" off the playlist. He scanned the living room full of his friends until his eyes landed on Celia curled in a chair, her head resting on her arm as she listened to Troy turn storyteller about their school days, sharing a tale about Elliot Starc since the race-car driver had left earlier.

Not much longer and Malcolm would have Celia all to himself. Finally, they would be alone, aside from his manager. Logan knew how to make himself scarce, though, probably keeping busy working the next angle for his client. Malcolm felt like a jerk for wishing they would all hit the road now.

Part of his impatience could have something to do with what great buddies Celia and Rowan had become. More than once today, they'd sat in a corner, their heads tucked close in conversation. The good doc had even brought her a bag of pastries to make sure she ate enough.

Hell, yes, Malcolm was jealous. The guy had pastries, and Malcolm didn't even have a hint of a plan for what to do next as far as Celia was concerned. His other plans had backfired—kissing for the press, singing "Playing for Keeps." So he did what he did best. He lost himself in music, while staring at Celia's beautiful face. He hitched his guitar more securely on his knee and plucked strings softly while Troy continued his story.

"My senior year—" Troy twirled his fedora on one finger as he talked "—Elliot was new to the school and wanted to impress us, so he hot-wired one of the laundry trucks and smuggled us all out for the night. We snuck into a strip club."

Hillary snagged her husband's spinning hat from his finger. "Strip club? Seriously? This is the story you choose to tell?"

Jayne laughed softly, snuggling into the crook of her husband's arm. "Someone's sleeping alone tonight."

Troy spread his hands wide. "Let me finish. We quickly figured out the club wasn't anything like we'd seen in the movies. The women looked…weary. A couple of the guys wanted to stay but most of us left and went to a pancake house that stayed open all night."

Malcolm remembered the night well. He'd opted to stay in the truck, in a crummy mood because it was Celia's birthday and he resented like hell that he remembered. He'd been aching for her.

Not much had changed.

Hillary dropped her husband's hat onto her head. "I'm not sure I believe you."

Troy kissed his wife's head. "I would never lie to you, babe."

Hillary rolled her eyes. "I'm assuming Elliot went with them to the pancake house since otherwise how would you have gotten the truck started?"

Conrad raised his hand. "Me, too, for the record. I did not stay at the strip club, just so we're clear. I had pancakes with blueberry syrup, extra bacon on the side. Waitresses fully clothed."

Jayne thunked him in the stomach. "Enough already."

Their ease with each other reminded Malcolm of what he and Celia once had—and lost.

Celia hugged a throw pillow. "Why did Elliot end up at the school?" She glanced at Malcolm. "Is that okay to ask?"

"It's in his public bio, so it's no secret." Malcolm sat in the wingback chair beside her—before Rowan could claim the seat—and continued to strum the guitar idly, playing improvised riffs and breathing in the praline-sweet scent of her. "His Wikipedia page states that Elliot was sent to the school for stealing cars. In reality, he took his stepfather's caddy out for a spin and smashed it into a guardrail."

The calm seeped from Celia's face. "Seems like a rather extreme punishment for a joyride."

Malcolm slowed his song, searching for a way to steer the conversation in another direction so she would smile again.

Troy answered, "Multiple joyrides. Multiple wrecks. His stepfather was beating the crap out of him. He wanted to get caught or die. Either way, he was out of his house."

Celia leaned forward. "Why wasn't his stepfather stopped and prosecuted?"

"Connections, a family member on the police force. Lots of warnings, but nothing happened."

Her lips went tight, and she shook her head. "His mother should have protected him."

"Damn straight," Troy agreed. "But I'm sliding off my path here. Let's get back to more entertaining brotherhood tales, like the time a few of us were stuck staying at school over Christmas break. So we broke into Salvatore's office, spread dirt on the floor and tossed quick-grow grass seed. He had a lawn when he returned. He knew we did it, but the look on his face was priceless…"

Malcolm started strumming again, adding his own impromptu score to Troy's tales, but his brain was still stuck on the moment Celia asked why Elliot's mother hadn't protected him. Her reaction was so swift, so instinctive he couldn't avoid the image blaring in his brain. An image of Celia as the mother of his child, fiercely doing everything in her power to protect their baby. He'd been so frustrated—hell, angry—for so long over losing the chance to see his kid that he hadn't fully appreciated how much she'd been hurt.

And damn it all, that touched him deep in his gut in a way that had nothing to do with sex. Right now, he had less of a clue about what to do with this woman than he had eighteen years ago.

The next night, after Malcolm's concert in the Netherlands, Celia put together a late-night snack in their suite. Foraging through the mini-fridge, she found bottles of juice, water and soda, along with four kinds of cheese. She snagged the Gouda and Frisian clove to go with the crackers and grapes on the counter.

Yes, she was full of nervous energy since Malcolm's friends had all gone home. Now she was finally alone with him. How strange that she'd resented their presence at first and now she felt antsy without the buffer they'd provided. Malcolm's manager had stood backstage with her at the concert tonight in Amsterdam. But Logan had his own room here on another floor.

Not that Malcolm had pressured her since they'd checked into the posh hotel. In fact, since her panic attack during the Seine River tour, he'd backed off. On the one hand, she'd wanted him to quit tempting her, but on the other it hurt to think he was turned off by her anxiety.

They had a two-bedroom suite with a connecting sitting room. He was showering, the lights having been particularly powerful—and hot—tonight at yet another sold-out show.

As she heard the shower in the next room stop, she arranged the food on a glazed pottery tray to keep her hands busy and her thoughts occupied with something other than wondering how different the adult, naked Malcolm looked. And what he thought of the "adult" her. She smoothed her hands down her little black dress, lacy, with a scalloped hem that ended just above the knee. Should she rush and change?

She shook off vanity as quickly as she kicked off her heels and loosened her topknot. Lifting the tray with food and a pot of tea, she angled around the bar, past the baby grand piano and into the living area.

Overall the room was brighter, lighter than the other places they'd stayed, the Dutch decor closer to her personal style. On her way past, she dipped her head to sniff the blue floral pitcher full of tulips. She placed the tray on top of the coffee table and curled up on the sofa with her tea. She'd made a pot with lemon and honey to soothe Malcolm's throat after three straight nights of concerts. He had to be feeling the effects.

The door to his bedroom opened, and her eyes were drawn directly to him. So drawn. Held. He stood barefoot, wearing a pair of jeans and T-shirt that clung to his damp skin. His hair was wet and slicked back. And God, did her hands ache to smooth over those damp strands.

What else did she want?

Silly question. She wanted to sleep with Malcolm again, to experience how it would feel to be with him as a woman. All the tantalizing snippets his friends had shared of his past and present drew her in, seducing her with both the Malcolm he'd been and the Malcolm he'd become. She burned to sleep with him, and she couldn't come up with one good reason why she shouldn't.

Would she have the courage to throw caution to the wind and act on what she wanted? "I made us something to eat—as well as tea with lemon and honey to soothe your throat."

"Thanks, but you don't have to wait on me," he answered, his voice more gravelly than usual, punctuating her point about the need for tea. He walked deeper into the room, his hand grazing a miniature wooden windmill, tapping the blades until they spun in a lazy circle.

"Direct orders from your manager," Celia said. "You're to have something to eat and drink, protect your health for the tour."

"What about you? Any more dizzy spells today?" He sliced off a sliver of Gouda. "Here…have some cheese."

She rested her fingers on his wrist, a small move, just a test run to see how he would react. "I'm good. I promise. Your pal the doctor gave me two thumbs up."

Malcolm eyes narrowed before he tossed the cheese into his mouth and paced restlessly around the room, past the baby grand piano, a guitar propped against the side. "You two seemed to hit it off."

Wondering where he was going with the discussion of Rowan, she poured another cup of steaming-hot tea. "What exactly did he invent?"

Malcolm dropped onto the other end of the sofa and reluctantly took the tea. "He devised a new computerized diagnostic model with Troy. They patented it, and they both made a bundle. Essentially, Rowan can afford to retire if he wishes."

Interesting, but not surprising given what she'd gleaned about Malcolm and all his friends. "And he chose to work in a West African clinic instead. That's very altruistic of him."

"You can join the Rowan Boothe fan club. It's large."

She lifted an eyebrow in shock. "You don't like him?"

"Of course I do. He's one of my best friends. I would do anything for him. I'm acting like a jealous idiot because you two seemed to hit it off." He tossed back the tea, then cursed over the heat. He set the cup down fast and charged over to the mini-fridge for bottled water.

He was jealous? Of her and Rowan? Hope fluttered.

She set her cup down carefully. "Your charitable donations have been widely reported. Every time I saw you at an orphanage or children's hospital… I admire what you've done with your success, Malcolm, and yes, I have kept up with you the way you've kept up with me."

Malcolm downed the bottle of water before turning back to her. "Rowan's the stable, settle-down sort you keep swearing you want now. But damn it all, I still want you. So if you want him or someone like him, you'd better speak up now, because I'm about five seconds away from kissing you senseless."

"You silly, silly man." She pushed to her feet and walked toward him. "You have nothing to be jealous of. I was asking for his medical help."

"What did you say?" He pinned her with a laser stare. "Are you ill? God, and I've been hauling you from country to country."

"Malcolm, stop. Listen. I have something I need to tell you." She drew in a bracing breath and willed her fluttering pulse to steady. Before they got to the kissing-senseless part, she needed to be sure he was okay with what had happened during the boat ride. Trusting him—anyone—with this subject was tough. But she hoped she could have faith in the genuine, good man she'd seen earlier with his friends. "I was having a regular, old-fashioned panic attack."

He blinked uncomprehendingly for a few seconds before clasping her shoulders. "Damn it, Celia, why didn't you tell me, instead of—"

She rested a hip against the baby grand piano. "Because you would have acted just like this, freaking out, making a huge deal out of it, and believe me, that's the last thing I could have handled yesterday."

Comprehension slid across his leanly handsome face. "Rowan helped you. As a doctor." He plowed his fingers through his hair. "God, I'm such an idiot."

"Not an idiot. Just a man." She sighed with relief to finally have crossed this hurdle without a drawn-out ordeal. "I left my medicine at home. He helped connect with my doctor and get my prescription refilled."

"You've had panic attacks before?"

"Not as often as I used to, but yes, every now and again."

His shoulders rolled forward as he rubbed his forehead. "The concert tour was probably a bad idea. What was I thinking?"

"You had no way of knowing because I didn't tell you." She couldn't let him blame himself. She stroked his forehead for him, nudging aside his hand. Just a brief touch, but one that sent tingles down her arm. "Staying home with some criminal leaving dead roses in my car wasn't particularly pleasant, either. For all we know, I would have had more anxiety back home. You've taken on a major upheaval in your life to help me."

"Are you okay now?" He reached for her, stopping just short of touching her as if afraid she would break.

"Please don't go hypercautious with me." She eased back to sit on the piano bench. "I felt much better after a good night's sleep. The medicine isn't an everyday thing. Not anymore. The prescription is just on an as-needed basis. And while I needed help yesterday, today's been a good day."

He sat beside her, his warm, hard thigh pressing against her. "When did the panic attacks start? Is that okay to ask?"

Gathering her thoughts grew tougher with the brush of his leg against hers. "I had trouble with postpartum depression after… The doctor said it was hormonal, and while the stress didn't help, it wasn't the sole cause—" she pointed at him "—so don't start blaming yourself."

He clasped a hand around her finger, enfolding her hand in his. "Easier said than done."

"You are absolved." She squeezed gently, her heart softening the rest of the way for this man. She'd never had any luck resisting him, and she wondered why she'd ever assumed now would be different. "And I mean that."

"After what happened yesterday, I'm not so sure I can buy into that." Guilt dug deep furrows in his lean face.

"You have to." She cupped his cheek in her palm, the bristle of his late-day beard a seductive abrasion against her palm. Until, finally, she surrendered to the inevitable they'd been racing toward since the minute he'd walked back into her life again. "Because I desperately want to make love with you, and that's not going to happen if you're feeling guilty or sorry for me."

Ten

Malcolm wondered what the hell had just happened.

He'd been turning himself inside out to come up with a plan to romance Celia back into his bed, except then he'd been derailed by thoughts that Rowan was a better man for her, then by concerns for her health and how best to approach her in light of all she'd just told him.

Instead, she propositioned him when he was doing… absolutely nothing.

God, he would never understand Celia Patel. He'd also never been able to turn her down. "Are you sure this is what you want? It's been a stressful couple of days and I want you to be certain."

"I may have had a panic attack yesterday, but I am completely calm and certain of this." Her fingers curved around the back of his neck, her touch cool, steady… seductive. "You and I need to stop fighting the inevitable. I could have sworn you felt the same."

"I do." His answer came out hoarse and ragged, and that had nothing to do with hours of singing. No second thoughts, he reached for her. He gathered her against him. Finally, he had her in his arms again.

Kissing her was as natural as breathing. She sighed her pleasure and agreement, her lips parting for him. A hint of lemon and honey clung to her tongue. His body went harder, his need for her razor-sharp after so damn long without her. No matter how many years had passed, he'd never forgotten her or how perfect she felt in his arms. Better yet, how perfect she felt coming apart in his arms.

Pulling her closer, he stood, guiding her to her feet, as well. Her fingers plowed through his hair, tugging lightly, just hard enough to increase the pleasure. She took his mouth as fully as he took hers. Owning. Stamping possession of each other.

The press of her body against him, the roll of her hips against his, the soft give of her full breasts against his chest ramped up his pulse rate. The heat of her reached through their clothes, tempting him with how much hotter they would feel skin to skin.

His hands roved up her back, into her hair—this woman had the most amazing mass of hair. The curls tangled around his fingers as if every part of her held him, caressed him. He swept the tangled mass over her shoulder and found the top of her zipper. He tugged the tab down the back of her lacy black dress, stroking along her spine as he revealed inch after inch of the softest skin. The scent of her soap, her light fragrance, teased him, and he dragged in a deep breath to take it in.

Hungry to feel more of her, he tucked his hands in the open V of her dress and palmed the satin-covered globes of her bottom. He guided her hips closer as she rocked against him in response, the perfect fit sending his pulse throbbing louder in his ears. The sound of her ragged breathing stoked the heat in him higher, hotter as he kissed along her jaw, the delicate shell of her ear. She whispered her need for more, faster, and damned if he could scrounge the restraint to hold back.

Later, once they'd both taken the edge off, he would go slower. Oh, so much slower, taking his time rediscovering her all night long with his hands and his mouth.

He stroked up her back again, enjoying the goose bumps of pleasure rising on her skin. Cupping her shoulders, he slid the sleeves of her gown to the side, baring her skin and the satin straps of her bra. She was even more damn beautiful than he remembered, with pinup-girl curves that all but sent him to his knees from aching to be inside her again.

A growl of possessiveness rolled up his throat as he peeled the lacy dress down her body, revealing those curves that had threatened to drive him to his knees. He nipped and tasted along her satin bra, kneeling and taking the center clasp between his teeth for a sensual instant before releasing it again, leaving it in place. For now. He skimmed the dress farther down. Fabric hitched on her hips. Pressing his face to her stomach, he inhaled more of her floral scent.

"Cecelia Marie." He sighed her whole name against her, repeating again and again.

Her fingers tangled in his hair, a flush of desire spreading over her skin, encouraging him to continue. He swept her gown down to pool around her bare feet, and ah, she wore black thigh-highs that just begged for him to peel one, then the other, down her smooth legs. He gathered the shimmery hose in his hand, soaking in the residual heat of her before he set them reverently aside.

He rocked back on his heels and took in the sight of

her in black satin panties and a bra. His fantasies didn't look this good, and he'd fantasized about this woman many, many times.

"Malcolm?" A quaver threaded through her voice before she steadied it. "Are you going to sit there all night? Because I have urgent plans for you."

"Plans?" He laughed softly, grateful she didn't intend to roll out questions or doubts. She was keeping things light. "Tell me more."

"Plans for us on the sofa, in the shower and, eventually, in the bed. But the more I talk, the more time we waste. So come back up here and I'll start showing you instead." She tugged him to his feet again to kiss her.

Not that he needed much persuasion to claim her plump mouth. To claim her.

Her tongue met his in bold, familiar touches and strokes. She tugged at his T-shirt, easing back only long enough to yank it over his head. The gust of the air conditioner cooled his overheated flesh, and then she touched him. The feel of her hands against his stomach, along the fastening of his jeans, threatened to send him over the edge. He'd never been good at self-control with her. That thought alone offered enough of a splash of cold water for him to think rationally.

To be smart.

To protect her in the way he hadn't before.

"One second. Wait." He stepped back, his breathing ragged.

"Are you kidding me?" She sagged against the baby grand, and the sight of her in that pose gave him even more ideas about how he planned to spend this night.

Once he took care of one very important detail.

"Birth control," he called as he backed toward his

room, holding up a hand. “Stay right where you are. As you are. Don’t move.” He smiled. “Please.

A quick sprint to his suitcase, and he returned with a condom in hand. Only to halt in his tracks, mesmerized to his core. Celia had been beautiful and sexy as a teenager. She was a gorgeous, sensual woman now.

She still leaned against the baby grand as he’d requested, her satin underwear a bold contrast to her skin. Her long, dark wavy hair draped over her shoulder, skimming her skin the way he intended to very, very soon.

He tore off his jeans and boxers on the way over to her, but not nearly fast enough. Her mouth curved into a sultry smile as she eye-stroked the erection straining against his stomach. She stretched out an arm and stopped him from pressing flush against her.

Holding his gaze deliberately, seductively, she thumbed open the center clasp of her bra and let the straps slide the rest of the way off until the scrap of satin dropped to the floor. She swept away her panties and kicked them to the side.

“Celia,” he groaned, “you’re absolutely slaying me.”

Her smile wavered. “I assure you, the feeling is entirely mutual. It always has been.”

His mouth dried up, and he reached out to skim the back of his knuckles along the curve of her breasts. His body throbbed impossibly harder at just one touch to her naked flesh. And then both her palms flattened against his chest, her nails grazing him lightly—down, then up again to curl around his shoulders. She urged him toward her, body to body, his hard length flat against her stomach, and he almost came undone right then. He needed to regain control, and soon. That fantasy he’d envisioned when he’d seen her posed against the piano came blazing through his mind again, an image he could make a reality now.

He eased his body from her, still holding her face, kissing her until the very last second. And once more. Her hands grappled to hold on to him, and he almost gave in. But he had a mission.

Trailing a hand along her stomach, he walked around to the side of the piano, removed the prop and closed the sleek ebony lid.

Celia tipped her head to the side. "Care to clue me in on what you're doing?"

He clasped her waist and lifted her onto the piano. "I'm doing this. Any objections?"

Her eyes lit with approval. "None whatsoever."

He stepped closer, parting her legs with his body. Her ankles hooked around his back, and she drew him in with the press of her heels. Her arms looped around his neck. She kissed him fully, with a maturity and passion that made their teenage affair fade in his memory. This moment with her, now, the passion combusting between them, burned away everything else.

She was his again.

The impact of that reality thrummed through his veins. He kissed along her jaw, down the vulnerable curve of her neck. He took his time with her breasts even though he ached with the need to be inside her.

But he needed to be certain she was every bit as absolutely on fire for him as he was for her. He took one pebbled nipple in his mouth, tempting her with his tongue and his teeth until her head fell back and her hips rolled against him. He held on to control by a thread, such a thin edge he knew he needed to bring her to completion now, because once he buried himself deeply inside her, restraint would be damn difficult to scavenge.

His hands glided down her spine, lowering her back as he kissed lower and lower still until she reclined along the piano. Her beautiful naked body sprawled on top of the sleek ebony grand took his breath away. Her hair trailed over the side of the piano in silken waves. He would never forget this picture of her as long as he lived. She was burned in his memory, on his soul.

He trekked along her body until he reached the core of her, damp and needy for him. He nudged her legs farther apart and nuzzled her essence, tasted her and teased her until her head thrashed back and forth. Her breathy moans of pleasure filled the air with a music that had seduced him then and now.

Her sighs grew to a crescendo that flowed through him, her back arching with the power of her release. He pressed a final kiss to her, then another against her stomach before he stood again.

And as the final ripples of aftershocks shivered through her, he scooped the condom from the corner of the piano and sheathed himself. Clasping her knees, he leaned over her and nudged inside, fully, deeply. He groaned at the total bliss of being exactly where he belonged. The warm clamp of her body gripping, pulsing around him nearly finished him before he could move, and oh, how much he wanted to move inside her. And move again, and again, filling her with each rocking thrust.

Her arms splayed, she gripped the sides of the piano to anchor herself to meet him, locking him more firmly with her legs around his waist. Guiding him. Holding him. With him every second of the way as she came undone with him all over again, their shouts of completion twining together.

Gasping with the power of what they'd shared, he leaned over her, blanketed her. He buried his face in her hair, their naked bodies slick and sealed with perspiration. With each steadying inhale of her sweet, floral scent, he knew.

Even if those threats against her evaporated in the morning, there wasn't a chance in hell he could let her go.

Celia sat naked on the silk sheets in Malcolm's bedroom, her body flushed and languid from making love on the piano. Against the wall. In the bed. In the shower.

Now they were in bed again. Or rather, she was. He'd stepped into the living area for the tray of cheese and fruit.

They'd stayed up most of the night, and not just making love. He'd brought his guitar into the room about halfway through the night and sang her the silliest made-up songs. She'd laughed until her sides ached, then taunted him by taking the guitar and composing her own ditties in return.

They would leave for London in the morning. She could sleep on the plane. For now, she intended to make the most of this night with Malcolm, because thinking about the future felt too uncertain, and she refused—absolutely refused—to do anything that would risk triggering a panic attack.

Angling to the side, she grasped the neck of his guitar and lifted it from the chair by the bed. She tucked it in place, scooped a pick from the bedside table and plucked through a riff of her own, not as intricate as his by any stretch, but she loved music. Loved that they shared this between them.

Their night together had been too perfect. Too special. She didn't want to think about threats at home or what the future held.

Malcolm strode through the door, gloriously naked and

all man. Muscles filled out his lean lines, sandy-brown hair dusting along his bronzed skin. He set a large silver tray in the middle of the bed, having added bottles of sparkling water to go with the food.

"What are you playing? An ode to my masterful… pick?"

"Ha, you're a comedian *and* a rock star. Imagine that." Laughing, she started to set aside the guitar.

He stopped her with a touch to the wrist. "Don't let me keep you from playing. I'm enjoying the music and the view."

"We can 'play' more later." She set aside the guitar and plucked free a handful of grapes. "Right now, I'm starving."

He settled beside her, careful not to tip the tray on the thick, downy comforter. "I'm sorry you didn't get to see more of Amsterdam. After we arrive in London tomorrow, we'll have an evening to ourselves, a day's break before two nights of concerts, then on to Madrid." He twisted open one of the chilled bottles and poured water into the two crystal glasses. "I feel bad that you haven't had much sightseeing or relaxation while we were in some of the most beautiful cities in the world. Choose whatever you want to do on the day off."

"More of what we're doing right now." She pressed a grape to his lips.

"No arguments from me." He bit free the fruit, nipping her fingers lightly.

Purring, she leaned forward to kiss him quickly, the sweet taste lingering on his mouth. "We'll lock ourselves in the hotel—"

"Actually, I have personal accommodations in London." He toyed with a lock of her hair, still damp from the shower they'd shared.

"Oh, that's right. Your mother has a flat there." She rocked back, taking her water glass, avoiding his eyes. Would Terri Ann be more open to her presence in Malcolm's life this go-round? If not, it could be quite awkward staying in an apartment together.

"I have a house in London, as well. I bought it to spend time with her when she's in town. We don't step on each other's toes." He grinned reassuringly. "Don't worry. I'm not taking you to my mother's place, where I would have to sneak into your room in the middle of the night."

Might as well meet this head-on. She didn't play games anymore. She wasn't an immature, spoiled teen. "Your mom has never been my biggest fan, and I get it. She was protective of you. And honestly, I admire how hard she worked to give you the best life possible." The town had never been short on gossip about the way Malcolm's father—a musician in a band—played a gig in Azalea, then cut out on his family. "The past and present can't help but be entwined."

"Remember how in fourth grade we had music class together? You were like magic at the piano, so happy when you played. You made the music come alive." He caressed down her arm to link fingers with her.

She laughed, squeezing his hand. "You played right alongside me, faster, trying to show me up. I recall that day well."

"No, I wanted you to notice me, so I figured I'd better step up my game. I'd mastered the technical side, but I missed the boat when it came to understanding music the way you did." He leaned back against the headboard, his glass resting on his bent knee.

"I never guessed." She blinked in surprise. "I thought you needed a duet partner for the talent show."

"You accomplished what all those music teachers had

been pounding their heads against the keyboard to make happen. I appreciate what my mother sacrificed for me, but all of this, the concerts, none of it would have happened without you."

A stint in reform school wouldn't have happened without her relentless pursuit of him, either, she thought wryly. She'd worked hard to change, but that didn't alter the past. He'd been so angry with her for insisting the baby be put up for adoption. Had he let that anger go? Or was it just set aside for now while the adrenaline and hormones worked to keep them both sated, relaxed?

She wondered if she could bring herself to ask him about it when their reunion was still so fresh, when only heaven knew how long it would last.

Instead, she drew circles on Malcolm's muscular chest. "You would have gotten there on your own. I was just in the right place when you were on the brink of understanding the music."

She remembered those days when Malcolm had catapulted from a skilled player to a talent to be reckoned with. She could almost see the music coming from his heart instead of his head when he'd been at the piano.

"Tell yourself whatever you want." He set aside his glass and hers, then gathered her against his chest.

In spite of all her good intentions five seconds ago, she couldn't stop herself from asking, "Why didn't you contact me after you got out? It's not like I was tough to find, hanging around our old hometown."

He rested his chin on top of her head. "I'd already wrecked your life once." His voice rumbled in his chest against her. "I was mature enough not to do an encore."

"But you're with me now because my life's in danger." Instead of shying away from the tough questions, she decided she deserved real answers. "Would you have stayed away forever?"

"Would *you?*" he countered.

Ouch. Good point. "You're a world-famous singer. I wouldn't have been able to get past your first line of body-guards. That security is why I'm here now, remember?"

"I wouldn't have turned you away." His arms wrapped tighter around her.

"It's not like we can even blame evil parents for keeping us apart. We did this to ourselves." She understood her reasons, if not his. "I've been punishing myself. Atoning for every mean-girl thing I ever did."

"Where the hell do you come up with this mean-girl notion?"

"I was a brat."

He tipped her chin up and stared at her with intensely blue eyes. "You were rebellious, funny, spoiled and absolutely magnificent. You still are."

"Spoiled?"

"Magnificent." He sealed the word with a kiss, nipping her bottom lip then nuzzling her ear. "I don't want this to end when the tour ends or even if all your father's enemies are locked up."

Stunned, she arched back, staring into his eyes. "You're serious."

She'd just managed to think about being with him tomorrow and now he was talking about longer.

"Absolutely serious," he answered. "Let's spend the summer together, explore what we're feeling and see where it takes us."

What about after the concert tour ended in four weeks? Where would they spend the rest of the summer? He'd avoided his hometown for nearly eighteen years. But the life she'd built there was a part of her, a part of who she was and the peace she'd found. She could enjoy this part of his life, but could he enjoy hers? Or did he only want the impulsive, bold girl she'd once been?

"What if I said I want to spend the rest of the summer in Azalea after your tour ends?" Why was she pushing when just that one question made her chest go tight? She didn't have to have the answers today.

"If that's where you want to be—" pausing, he cricked his neck from side to side "—I can stomach a few weeks there."

Stomach? Not a ringing endorsement for the safe life she embraced. "And in the fall?"

They were only delaying the inevitable crash, delaying the confrontation of the things that had made both of them choose to stay apart all these years. Her guilt over how she'd ruined their lives. His anger over her decisions. Her need for the stability of Azalea. His preference for luxury and travel.

Her feelings of betrayal because yes, damn it all, she'd expected him to come back for her a long time ago, but he'd chosen this life over her.

He moved the tray aside and took her hands. "This isn't going the way I intended. Do you need some kind of commitment from me? Some sign that you mean more to me than just a fling? I can do that."

That wasn't what she'd meant at all. Her heart fluttered in her chest, and it wasn't panic, but it was fear. What if he proposed and she said yes? Could she let go of the past and be with him? Could she live with the uncertainty and lavishness of his lifestyle after working so hard to create a stable existence? What if he was genuinely willing to live a regular, boring life with her when he wasn't on tour?

Was that even possible with his notoriety?

"Celia, I'm not just a musician."

"I know. You're also a gifted composer." She thought of the songs he'd written for her when they were younger, and even beyond that to the dozens of award-winning tunes he'd sent soaring up the charts over the years.

"That's not what I meant."

"Oh…" Disappointment and confusion swirled inside her. "What did you mean, then?"

He drew in a deep breath. "What I'm about to tell you can go no further, but I want you to know I trust you. That I'm committed."

There was that *commitment* word again.

"I work for Colonel Salvatore—" he paused "—and John Salvatore works for Interpol."

Eleven

Celia struggled to grasp what Malcolm had just told her, but what he'd shared seemed so unbelievable, so unexpected. He couldn't be serious. Except, as she looked at him, she saw he was completely sincere. He was some kind of secret agent.

"Interpol?" she asked, needing more details, needing some frame of reference for how this could be possible. "I'm really not tracking with what you're saying. You're going to need to help me understand."

"I'm trusting you with very sensitive information here. Salvatore manages a group of freelance operatives for Interpol. People he taps maybe once or twice a year for undercover help gathering evidence in an international criminal investigation. Because of my job, I move in some influential circles—some of them with shady ties. Having someone like me on the Interpol roll saves having to spend months building a cover."

As he explained, pieces shuffled in her mind. Other things began to make sense.

"That's how you knew about the threats against me. You have connections, intelligence connections." Her skin prickled with icy realization. "You've been watching me."

"Just keeping track of your life to make sure you're all right." He frowned. "That didn't sound right. Not in a stalking sort of way. More like a request to my boss that I be notified if you had a problem. The truth about my job isn't something I've told anyone other than you."

"Not even your manager? Or your friends?" All of his high-profile friends who had gone to Colonel Salvatore's school. Had they all gathered around to guard her? Or did they connect because they could discuss their common job? "Are they also freelance agents with high-profile lives—"

He kissed her silent. "Don't ask questions I'm not allowed to answer. I shared with you as much as I can to let you know I'm not taking what happened between us here lightly. This meant something to me. You mean something to me. I'm trusting you. Can you offer me some trust in exchange?"

His words so closely echoed ones they'd said to each other before, a replay of their past. He'd wanted her to trust that he could carve out a future for them. She'd needed him to trust her decision to give the baby up for adoption. In the end, they'd both gone their separate ways rather than risk being hurt.

They were older now, wiser. But they didn't seem to have a helluva lot more answers. As much as she wanted to lose herself in this time away from Azalea, it seemed her home and past just kept right on following her.

In fact, a huge part of that past waited for her in London when she saw his mother again.

* * *

After the flight to London, Malcolm drove his Aston Martin deeper in the rolling English countryside. He'd trusted Celia with a lot in Amsterdam, but that revelation hadn't gone as he'd expected. He'd hoped she would feel safer, that she would understand he was trying to welcome her into his world. Sharing the truth about his Interpol world had been a big step for him. Hell, admitting he still had feelings for her had been a giant leap.

And she'd reacted with silence and more silence. He could see the wheels turning but didn't have a clue what she was thinking. He could only hazard a guess. Was she upset over his hidden job? Worried? She didn't look as if she was having an anxiety attack.

He glanced at her sitting beside him in the silver sports car. "You've been quiet since we left Amsterdam."

She smiled over at him, her hair carrying on the breeze through the open window. "I thought men liked peace."

"Maybe I'm getting intuitive in my old age." He draped his wrist over the steering wheel, guiding the finely tuned machine along the curving two-lane road past an apple orchard.

"Or maybe you got those intuitive skills from your second job," she said as if joking, but not quite hitting the note.

"Freelancing for Interpol isn't nearly as intriguing as it sounds."

"Can you tell me anything about the cases?"

He weighed his words, wanting to give her what he could to bring her peace so they could move forward. He'd told her to make things easier between them, not more complicated. "Think of the corruption that goes on in the entertainment industry."

"Drugs?"

"I already have a built-in backstory on that one," he said darkly, thinking of his brush with the law as a teenager.

"Your partying lifestyle is a cover?"

"That's not what I meant." He took her palm in his, her dress silky against the back of his hand. "I haven't been a saint since I left home, but I do *not* touch drugs. I never would, especially not after what my father put my mother through."

"Your father was into drugs?" she asked, surprise lacing her voice.

"He was a meth addict." The admission burned, along with anger and betrayal. "He was the stereotypical stoned musician in a going-nowhere band. He blew through everything he and my mother had worked for. He would have sold his soul—or his family—for his next fix."

"Your mother's been through a lot." Celia's fingers gripped his tighter. "I'm sorry I put you in a position where you were forced to hurt her."

"Stop blaming yourself for everything that happened. I take responsibility for my own actions." He lifted her hand, kissing her knuckles. "You make me sound like I had no say in things. I wanted you. I would have done anything to have you in my life."

"Not anything…" she said softly, turning her head toward the open window as if the cottages and sheep were infinitely interesting.

"Hey." He tugged her hand until she turned back to him again. "What do you mean?"

"Nothing. Forget I said anything. So how much farther to this home of yours?"

He started to press her on the point, but then he noticed the nervous way she chewed at her thumbnail. She wasn't as calm as she pretended. He thought of her issues with anxiety and pulled back, saving the question for a better time.

"Not much farther. The gate's just beyond those trees." He crested the hill, revealing his home away from home for the past two years.

Celia gasped. "You leased a castle?"

He laughed. "Not a castle, actually—a manor house." A very large, brick manor house, restored but dating back to the seventeenth century. He wanted somewhere to escape the chaos around his L.A. home, and this small village called to him. "And, uh, it's not leased. I own it."

"And your mother has a flat in London. What would that be? Quarters in Buckingham Palace?"

"Not *in* the royal palace, but with a nice view of it." His mother had followed his father around for ten years while his dad played in bars and honky-tonks, dragging her son along, as well. When they reached Azalea, Mississippi, his mother had woken up the next morning to a note on the pillow. Apparently dragging a woman and kid around was killing the band. For a long time, Malcolm wondered if his mother would have left him behind if she'd been given the choice.

But she hadn't. And there was no denying she'd sacrificed everything for him and for his talent, even though his love of music had to be a hard pill for her to swallow given his father's proclivities. She'd made peace with it when she'd decided he would achieve the star power his father never had reached. He'd practiced to make her happy, to pay her back for costing her security.

He took his foot off the accelerator, coasting down the hill toward the gates covered with ivy. "My mother and I need our space after living in that crappy two-bedroom apartment for so many years."

"This is definitely...spacious."

"You disapprove?" He stopped outside the heavy iron gates, letting the security scan his irises.

She shook her head. "Your money is yours to spend. I'm just a bit overwhelmed by the scope of what you have."

He drove through, her reaction to the house he'd chosen far too important to him. "This is what I wanted to give you, a fairy-tale home."

"The sort of happily ever after you sing about." She grinned at him impishly.

He winced, downshifting around a curve on the winding driveway. "Not fair, turning my cynicism back on me, you know."

"Actually, I was being honest." She leaned out of the window, inhaling. "And oh, my goodness, there are flowers everywhere. It's truly a beautiful home."

Apparently she approved of the sculpted gardens he'd ordered with her in mind. He didn't know the names of most of the flowers. When he'd overseen the renovations, he'd just pointed to pictures in the landscaper's book, but he'd specifically requested climbing roses and lavender.

"I'm glad you like it." Pride kicked through him over pleasing her, having finally found the right way to romance this complex woman.

"Who wouldn't? The place is magnificent."

He wanted to press for more. Hell, when hadn't he wanted to push for more from Celia? He wasn't the most perceptive man on the planet, but something in her tone was still...off.

And opening some deep discussion right now didn't seem wise since his mother had just stepped out onto the lanai to greet them.

* * *

Celia dried her palms along her whispery red dress, sitting on the lanai beside Terri Ann Douglas and feeling the woman's eyes boring into her. Malcolm was parking the car and putting away their minimal luggage. Apparently, he'd had his mother arrange for everything else they would need here. Terri Ann had ordered the kitchen stocked, the beds fluffed. She'd given the main staff the weekend off, with only a catering service making very brief—discreet—stops by for meals.

"Um, Mrs. Douglas—"

"Terri Ann, please," his mother said nicely enough.

"Okay, Terri Ann, um…" She forgot what she was going to say.

God, this was awkward. She'd been semi-prepared to talk to the woman when she'd thought Malcolm was going to try to dump her on his mother back in the States. But she was totally unprepared for this visit now.

Perhaps because the memory of their night together was still so fresh in her mind and she was wondering how soon they could distract themselves with sex again. She trailed her fingers along the waist-high wall between her and those magnificent gardens with an angel fountain glistening in the late-afternoon sun. The scent carried on the air, and she couldn't even enjoy it because her stomach was in knots over this confrontation she should have seen coming. Malcolm's mother was here, serving up tea and sandwiches, for heaven's sake, as if the past didn't exist. As if they could erase the last time this woman had spoken to her.

Screamed, actually.

Crying and accusing her of wrecking Malcolm's life.

So long ago.

Time had been kind to Terri Ann, smoothing the

edges. Her dark blond hair may have grayed somewhat, but her blue eyes were no longer tired with dark circles. She still favored cowboy boots and jean skirts. Did she also hold on to grudges?

Celia tried to smile, waving to the table of pretty little sandwiches, cakes and tea. "Thank you for going to so much trouble for me."

"No trouble at all. After all Malcolm does for me, the least I can do is help him out whenever he asks." She sat on one side of the stone table and served up a plate. "And he doesn't ask often."

Celia nibbled the edge of a cucumber sandwich. "Uh, thank you."

Damn, she sounded like a broken record.

"Malcolm will want something heartier from the pantry, but these seemed more ladylike for you."

Terri Ann thought she needed some kind of special airs put on? She just wanted to have an adult, comfortable conversation with the woman.

"I'm sorry." Celia set aside the delicate china plate carefully. "Would you mind if we use this time to clear the air before Malcolm arrives?

"I don't know what you mean." Terri Ann folded the napkin on her lap once and over again.

"You made it very clear eighteen years ago that you didn't approve of me." Celia pleated the hem of her dress between her fingers and hated that she betrayed her nerves this way. Hated even more how this woman made her feel sixteen and awful again. "I don't expect us to be best friends now just because Malcolm brought me here."

"That's good to know," Terri Ann said, giving little away. "I don't want to upset my son."

"And I don't intend to run telling tales to stir trouble. I

know you don't have any reason to trust me, but I'm not the same self-centered girl I was in those days."

"If we're being honest, then yes, you were spoiled, but my son made his own choices," Terri Ann conceded—surprisingly generous. "In the long run, you didn't ruin his life. Getting sent to that military boarding school was the best thing that ever happened to him. He got opportunities there I could never give him, no matter how many second jobs I took cleaning a salon or waiting tables."

Celia had certainly never thought of it that way. His sentence had seemed like just that…a sentence for a crime he didn't commit. She kept her silence as Terri Ann continued.

"Your father made that chance happen. He pulled strings with one of his judge cronies for Malcolm to go to that school rather than to jail or some crime-riddled reform school."

Celia wrestled with the shifting image of her past and the secrets her father had kept from her. Why hadn't he told her what he'd done for Malcolm? "My dad never told me. But then I was dealing with some pretty serious issues in those days."

She'd sunk into a depression during her pregnancy that had only deepened after the baby was born. The postpartum blues had spun out of control into a full-out breakdown. Putting the pieces of her life—of her sanity—together again had been a long, painful process.

Had her father just not wanted to risk her revisiting that time, even in memories? She might not have been strong enough to discuss the subject in the beginning, but she was now. And wow, how strange if felt to realize that about herself. To accept it. To let that confidence settle deep inside her.

Terri Ann smiled, thumbing a smudge of bright pink

lipstick from the corner of her mouth. "I won't deny I was glad you were no longer in my son's life. I know what it's like to be a parent too young, and I wanted him to have better than I was able to give him."

"But Malcolm turned out amazing. He's built an incredible life for himself." Did his mother know about the Interpol angle and just how far her son took being a good guy? "You did a good job bringing him up on your own."

"It was tough as hell, but I owed him for bringing him into this world. Do you think I wanted him to go through those same struggles, even younger than I was when I had him? At least I was nineteen when I had him." Terri Ann stared at her pointedly. "But then you certainly understand what I mean about making the best choice you can for your child. We can only do what we can with the resources we are given."

And here Malcolm's mother had shocked her all over again with support from an unexpected corner.

Terri Ann's smile faded. "Now, that doesn't mean we have to be best friends, like you said. I don't know you, the adult you. So as far as I'm concerned, let's both just start with a clean slate." Standing, she smoothed her denim skirt, picked up two sandwiches, carefully wrapping them in her napkin. "I'm going to leave you and Malcolm alone. Please tell my son I put some of his favorite barbecue in the fridge and a pecan pie on the counter."

Giving Celia the tour of his home had been satisfying and nerve-racking as hell. But so far, she liked the place. She'd sighed in appreciation over the antiques in the dining room. Spun a circle in the sunlight streaming through the domed conservatory. Sighed in bliss over the music room.

And he still wasn't any closer to finding out what had set her on edge after talking to his mother.

Perhaps it was time for a more direct approach."What did you and my mom talk about?" he asked, leading her through the kitchen toward the steps to the cellar, where his favorite feature of the house waited.

"We talked about you, of course. She left you some of your favorite foods in the kitchen," she said, skimming her fingers along the cool stone walls of the narrowing corridor. Sconces lit the way with bulbs that resembled flickering flames. "And we discussed how you ended up at the military boarding school. How she felt like my dad did you a favor sending you there."

"Ohh-kay." That stunned him for at least two quick heartbeats before he said, "Not your average light chit-chat."

"Does she know about your Interpol work?" Her foot-steps echoed behind him.

"No, I don't want to worry her." He glanced over his shoulder. "I meant it when I said telling you was a big commitment."

Her deep brown eyes stared back, still a little wary, confused even. Maybe he was moving too fast and should focus on how they communicated best. With sex. Really, really spectacular sex. Later, when she was ready, he could tell Celia that his feelings for her were about more than just the physical.

He stepped aside to reveal his latest treat for a woman he wanted to pamper with everything he'd earned over the years.

The old cellar enclosed a bubbling hot spring in the far corner. Except, it was more than a cellar. He'd reno-vated the space into a luxurious spa with modern conve-niences while preserving the historical feel. Weathered bricks, tan and ancient, lined the walls of the sprawling space. The natural spring had a deck of slick stones with steps leading down into the inviting waters. Steam rose toward fans hidden in the ceiling, the wafting heat attesting to the muscle-soothing promise those springs held.

Lounge chairs filled a corner by a wooden bar refurbished from an old pub. The bar had been outfitted with a refrigerator. On top, candles glowed alongside vases of flowers and a silver wine bucket holding a bottle of champagne—he'd placed that there himself. Some things, a man simply could not ask his mother to do.

The space provided the ultimate escape from the world for a man who had one helluva time finding peace and solitude. Intricately carved screens shielded a corner for changing, with fluffy robes and towels hanging on hooks buried into the walls.

Celia's gasp of pleasure mingled with the sound of trickling water. "This place is incredible."

"I looked at quite a few manor houses, even a couple of castles. But the minute I walked down here and saw the hot springs, I knew. This place would be mine." He knew this was the home he'd once dreamed of buying for Celia. And even thinking he would never be with her again, he'd still bought the place to remind himself of what they'd had. To remind him of the mission he had to make up for past mistakes.

"You renovated it, though, didn't you?" She eyed the sconces flickering on the wall and casting shadowy illumination.

"I had some help from a professional, but yes, I gave substantive input on what I wanted the place to look like. How did you know?" He pulled out the magnum of champagne and uncorked the bottle.

"I didn't know for sure until you just confirmed it. You have a great eye."

He filled a crystal champagne flute, then a second. "One of my friends recommended this guy who does great work renovating historic homes, blending the old with the new while still listening to the owner. I didn't want this to be some showplace for magazines that no real person would ever enjoy. I wanted this for me…for you."

"But you didn't know we would see each other again when you bought this home."

"And still, every decision I've ever made has been somehow tied to you." He passed the crystal flute to her, tiny bubbles fizzing to the top. "While we were dating, I used to make lists of all the things I would give you someday."

"I'm sorry I made you feel like I needed more." She sipped the champagne. "That wasn't fair to you."

"You were a teenager with parents—very wealthy parents—who loved you."

"Parents who spoiled me, you mean."

"I was a defensive teenager, full of pride and resenting like hell that I couldn't even drive you to the movies in my mom's old rust bucket of a car because she worked nights and needed it."

She tapped the edge of her glass to his. "What else was on that list?"

"Jewels. Houses. A car to make out in, a car that wasn't bought by your dad. And flowers." His slid his hand around a vase of fresh-cut roses on the bar. "An endless supply of fresh flowers."

"I love the flowers, outdoors and here."

"I had plans for those flowers over there." He pulled a creamy-white rose free from the vase.

"Like what?"

"Bed of petals upstairs. Bath with petals down here." He plucked a handful of petals from the heavy bloom, sprinkling them into the bubbling springs. "And always with you naked."

"You, too, of course." She set her glass down along the edge of the pool.

"That can be arranged."

Celia couldn't remember a time she'd peeled off her clothes so quickly. Not since she and Malcolm had gone skinny-dipping in the river near where they liked to park and make out. Luckily, he was pitching aside his clothing just as speedily before refilling their champagne glasses.

And placing a row of condoms along the ledge.

Smiling over her shoulder seductively, she walked down the steps. The water was a hint too hot, then completely perfect for melting tensed muscles. Her quick acclimation made her wonder if perhaps she'd been overthinking things. Maybe they could take this romance one day at a time. Simply enjoy each other and unlimited sex, making up for all the lost years when no one else came close to touching her in that very special way.

The steaming water wrapped around her waist, lapping higher and then teasing along her breasts until her nipples beaded. The slick stone floor under her feet was warm and therapeutic, as well. She hadn't expected even her toes to feel pampered by the experience. Bubbles flowed around her and under her, caressing her between her legs and along her breasts erotically. Deliciously.

"Oh, my God, this is…just beyond what I could have needed. Did you dump Xanax into the water?" She winced at her own word choice, glancing at him sharply. "Okay, that was a weak attempt at a joke."

"Was it some kind of Freudian slip?" His handsome face creased with concern.

She waded through the steam and over to him, standing toe to toe, needing to read his eyes as she spoke. "I have to know that you're not freaked out by the fact that I've had a breakdown. I have to know you're not going to handle me with kid gloves for fear I'll have a panic attack."

His hands fell on her shoulders, curving around to her back. "The urge to protect you is strong, and it was there long before you told me anything about medications or the stress after…the baby was born. I can't promise I won't go Cro-Magnon if someone threatens you. But I can promise I would have reacted the same way regardless."

With those few words, he wiped away her concern. "Good enough for me."

He walked backward, guiding her with him until he sat on a stone seat cut into the pool and pulled her into his lap. "When we were together before, I hated that I didn't have the cash to take you on real dates. I planned all the ways I would romance you when I had money."

"I treasured our time together. You put so much thought into what we did, just like you have here." She sipped her champagne, enjoying the tickle to her nose almost as much as she enjoyed the feel of Malcolm's muscular legs under her. "Even back then I knew what you did was tougher than tossing money around. Like the way you planted a sunflower at the spot where we first kissed."

"I stole a sunflower from the side of the road."

"It was sweet." She stroked back his stubborn lock of hair, teasing the familiar texture between her fingers. "Don't wreck the memory."

His hands slid up to cup her breasts, his thumbs teasing lazy circles until she beaded even harder against his touch. “I wanted to buy you flowers and take you to the homecoming.”

“I don’t care for football anyway. I just wanted to be with you.” Sparks of pleasure shimmered from her breasts, gathering between her thighs. Wriggling to face him, she straddled Malcolm’s lap, his hot, thick erection pressed between them. “Amazing, but I want that exact same thing from you now. More specifically, I want you to be inside me.”

“You won’t get an argument from me.”

She reached past him for a condom, then slid her breasts along him, the bristle of his chest hair a tantalizing abrasion against her nipples. She sighed her pleasure, the head of his erection nudging against her, rubbing against the tight bundle of nerves aching for release.

With deliberate attention to detail, she sheathed him underwater, stroking the length of him and cradling his weight in her hands until his head fell back with a groan. She knew his body well again after their time in Amsterdam, but he’d been the one orchestrating their experience there. She savored being in control now.

“Celia, darlin’, you’re killing me…” His jaw flexed with restraint, muscles bunching and twitching. “Celia…”

“How much do you want me?” She angled closer, digging her fingers into the corded biceps bulging under her touch and rubbing their bodies against each other. Rubbing his erection between her cleft and against her stomach. But still she held herself back from giving them both what they wanted.

He growled, nipping her shoulder. “You know I want you more than I’ve ever wanted anyone.”

“Do you know how many nights I laid awake thinking of you, your memory making me ache from wanting you? The sound of your voice over the radio in the morning would catch me unawares, leaving me needing you. Needing this."

She sank down, taking him deep inside her, fully and quickly. A raw groan of pleasure burst from his mouth, and she reveled in knowing he was every bit as helpless when it came to this attraction. She rolled her hips against his, arched her back for his attentive mouth on her breasts. Each flick of his tongue, every suckle followed by a puff of air drew the tension tighter inside her. He knew just how to play her body, strum her most sensitive spots, stroke and pluck just so until the need to come apart in his arms was almost painfully intense.

Water sluiced around them as they moved together, her arms locked tightly around him. The wall scones flickered shadows over the hard planes of his face, teasing her with glimpses of his pleasure. His hands cupped her bottom, lifting and guiding her as he thrust upward. And her body answered, gripping him, holding him as pleasure built, higher until…

Fulfillment showered through her, sparkling through every fiber of her being. Gasping again and again with aftershocks rocking her, she scored Malcolm's shoulders, sinking in her nails as she held on. Her arms trembled. His grip tightened as he thrust faster and faster until, yes, he joined her.

And she held him close as his pleasure rocked through him, his breath hot on her neck, his beard a delicious abrasion against her temple as they clung to each other.

Even afterward, she stayed tangled with him, her legs wrapped around his waist now as she sat with him still inside her. Her skin cooled, even with the water steaming all around them. The lap of the bubbling tide stroking over her.

She gasped against the damp skin of his neck. She

wanted him, and God help her, she loved him, too. She always had.

But could she see this through with Malcolm, sign on for more? Could she live this out-of-control life with a man who played to sold-out arenas and royalty? Even if she could find her way around the anxiety of that lifestyle, there was the whole Interpol bombshell and his disdain for spending time in Azalea.

Desperately, she wanted to find a way through this crazy maze of a life he'd built for himself. An amazing life, without question, but it wasn't hers. It wasn't even close to what she wanted for herself… Well, maybe the spa part could stay….

God, she was a mess. She needed to find a path they could walk together.

Because if she didn't, staying with him only prolonged the inevitable, increasing the pain of losing Malcolm all over again.

Twelve

Malcolm sprawled in a chair on the lanai, brunch having been set up by a service his mother had arranged to make discreet appearances and speedy exits throughout their brief stay. He scrolled through his email while waiting for Celia to finish her shower.

Celia.

His hand slowed on the tablet, his eyes scanning the elaborate garden he'd had planted for her, not even knowing if she would ever see it. His gaze settled on a rose bush climbing along an archway over a bench. How many times over the past couple of years had he envisioned her there reading or singing? She'd been with him in his every thought over the years, every decision he made guided by what he'd wanted to give her.

Whatever it took, wherever his manager told him he needed to be to advance his career, he'd done it. He realized now that he'd done all this for her. He'd been keeping track of her because he wanted her back in his life. Protecting her had just been an excuse. He was so close to having what he'd dreamed of as a heartbroken kid. But he refused to let the surge of victory distract him from remembering his duty—making sure she stayed out of harm's way until Salvatore could get a lock on who'd left those threatening notes.

"Good morning." Celia smiled in the open French doors, the sun shining on her dusky beauty. Her hair glided over her shoulder in a side ponytail.

She strolled through the door. Her simple sundress, long and vibrantly blue, caressed her legs as she walked closer. Her hand glided over his chest as she dipped to kiss him, a hint of rose-petal perfume still clinging to her skin with reminders of how they'd made love in the spa for hours. If only they could block out the world awhile longer.

Protective urges surged through him, and he wondered why the hell it was proving so difficult to track down the person responsible for threatening Celia. He forced his fists to unclench and then stroked her ponytail. "Good morning to you, too, beautiful. Brunch? There's plenty."

He pulled out a chair for her at the table set with a full English fry-up of eggs, bacon, sausages, fried bread and mushrooms.

Celia bypassed it all, picking up a scone and a small pot of lemon curd as she took her seat. She swept the hem of her dress to the side as she settled in a move so utterly feminine it had him wanting to carry her out into the garden and make love to her all over again.

Except, then he noticed her brow was furrowed.

"What's wrong?" he asked, returning to his side of the table.

She slathered lemon curd on a corner of her scone.

"I'm still trying to piece together all the new things I'm learning about you, fill in the gaps of those years we missed."

"Such as?" he asked warily. He wanted to let her into his world, yet he wasn't a man used to talking about himself. He'd grown accustomed to keeping people at arm's length.

"I know you can't tell me about your friends and details about Interpol, but what about your time at school? Those early days when we were apart?"

He wasn't sure why she wanted to know, but he couldn't see the harm in sharing. "We weren't the typical button-up types who planned to go into the military. We banded together to get through, formed a new family since ours had been taken away. We broke rules, pushed boundaries. We called ourselves The Alpha Brotherhood, and in the confines of those prisonlike walls, we kept each other from losing our minds."

"You said you broke the rules—like when Elliot Starc hot-wired the truck?"

"Exactly." He speared food onto his plate. "One night, Troy broke into the security system, rewired the whole thing so Conrad's ankle monitor wouldn't register. We left school grounds, bought pizza and came back."

Laughing, she thumbed a crumb from the corner of her mouth, reminding him of all the ways she'd driven him crazy with those lips the night before. "Real rebels."

He cleared his throat. "It's like counting coup."

"Counting coup?" She broke off another bite of the scone, her attention to his words so intent it was as if the world hinged on what he would share.

"Mental games, war games—sneak into the enemy camp and leave a sign that you were there. Show your enemy their security is worthless." His mind filled with memories of how sweet those victories had tasted then as he'd lashed out at the world. "No need to destroy anything. Just let them know you're able to come and go as you please, that you can dismantle the whole system if you choose. Makes sticking around a lot easier."

"And your headmaster, this man who now works for Interpol, Colonel Salvatore. He was the enemy?"

"Back then he was, yes. And sneaking one past him was the ultimate victory for a group of teens who were feeling they'd been kicked in the teeth by the world." Little had they known then it was all a part of Salvatore's strategy to get them to work together as a unified team.

"What made you change your mind and join him?" Cradling a china teacup in her hands, she eyed him over the rim.

Malcolm set aside his silver fork with a clatter. "Turns out he was better at war games than we were. He found my weakness and he used it."

"I'm not sure I understand." She set her cup back on the saucer carefully and reached for her scone. "What did he do?"

His mind filled with memories of that fateful meeting when John Salvatore had approached him with the Interpol offer, when he'd revealed all the power that could be his if he just said yes, the power to keep track of Celia. The power to know…everything. A mixed blessing.

"He showed me pictures of our daughter."

Celia's scone crumbled in her hands, her fingers clenching too hard as shock sliced clean through her at Malcolm's words. At what he'd known all this time and never said a word about. He'd never offered her the consolation such information could have given her.

Her hands shaking, she dusted the crumbs from her

fingers and willed herself not to jump to conclusions, to be logical and hear him out.

"You had access to…things like that?"

He looked down at his uneaten food. "I haven't seen her in person or made contact. I honored the decision we made to leave that up to her."

The old ache inside her swelled. So painful. So empty.

She squeezed her eyes closed and blurted out, "I know you blame me for giving her up for adoption."

So much for the calm, logical approach.

"Celia? Celia," he insisted, taking her hand until she opened her eyes. "I signed the paperwork. I accept responsibility for my own decisions. I was in no position to be a parent stuck states away in a boarding school for misfits. It would have been selfish of me to put her life on hold waiting for me to get out."

"Then why haven't you forgiven me? Why can't we just be happy?"

"I have regrets. That's not the same as holding a grudge." He squeezed her hand in a reassurance that didn't quite warm the chill spreading inside her. "Do I wish things had turned out differently? Of course. I wanted to be the man who could take care of you both."

A whisper of suspicion curled through her like steam from the teapot. "Is that what all of this has been about? Coming to my rescue now to make up for what you think you should have done eighteen years ago?"

"In part, yes," he said, confirming her fear that things could never be simple for them, not after everything that came before. A fresh start for them wasn't an option. Malcolm leaned forward on his elbows. "What did she look like when she was born?"

"Didn't your Interpol connection give you photos from the nursery?" she snapped, then paused, holding up a hand. "Sorry for being defensive. She looked... wrinkled with her face scrunched up. She had dark hair and the softest skin. I wanted her." Her breath caught in her throat, every word slicing her like razor cuts on an ache that had never fully healed.

She shoved back from the table, needing air, space. "I really wanted her, and all my life I'd gotten everything I wanted. But something changed inside me when I looked in her eyes. I knew that as much as I wanted to keep her, I couldn't give her what she needed on any level."

She shot to her feet, desperate to escape the painful memories and the accusation she knew she would find in Malcolm's eyes. "I can't do this. Not now."

Tears blurring her view of the two roses on the table, she started toward the French doors.

"Her name is Melody," he said, his voice raw.

She stopped in her tracks, hardly daring to believe what she'd heard. Bracing her hand on the open door, her back to him, she said, "Her adoptive parents asked me what I'd been calling her. I didn't expect they would keep the name."

"They did. The photo I saw of her was taken when she was seven years old—the only photo I saw—but even then, she looked like you."

She clapped her hands over her ears. "Stop. If she wants to find us, she will. That's her choice. We agreed."

"I can make this happen, though." He shoved to his feet, closed the space between them in two strides and clasped her shoulders. "We're a couple now. We can get married and reach out to her."

"I meant it when I said that has to be her decision. I owe her that choice." She blinked fast, her head whirling as her heart squeezed tight. She didn't want him to ask for old times' sake or some need to make up for the past. "And that proposal of yours was every bit as abrupt as when you asked me before when we were teenagers."

His eyes snapped with frustration. "And you're shutting me down just as fast."

"You're changing my life." She eased his hands from her shoulders. "You have to accept I'm not a reckless, impulsive teenager anymore. I have a life I'm proud of and have no interest in abandoning. I'm not cut out for this high-octane lifestyle of yours—the concert tour or the Interpol implications. God, Malcolm, think. We can't jump into this."

"Admit it. This isn't about where we live or what we do. It's about making a commitment to me." He took a step back, face stony with disillusionment, a replay of the way he'd looked at her so long ago. "You don't want to try now any more than you did then."

Why couldn't he understand she wasn't pushing him away, just looking for a compromise? "That's not true. You aren't even trying to see my side of this. And damn it, Malcolm, I am different now. I refuse to let you tear my heart out again."

Her chin high, her pride all she had left, she spun away and almost slammed into his mother in the doorway. Could this humiliating, heartrending moment get any worse? To hell with pride. She needed to get out of here.

Celia angled past with a mumbled "Excuse me," then ran. Her sandals slapped against the sleek wooden floors as she raced into the restored manor house. She ran up the curved staircase and into the bedroom full of antiques, florals and stripes. She slammed the door closed and sagged back against the panel only to realize…

She wasn't alone in the room.

A broad-backed male spun away from her suitcase, her tote bag in one hand, a piece of paper in the other.

"Adam Logan?" She walked toward Malcolm's manager. "What are you doing in my room?"

Her eyes went to the paper in his hand, a typed note with big block letters she'd seen on threatening notes over the past couple of weeks. Block letters that even from here she could read.

WATCH YOUR BACK, BITCH.

Malcolm scrubbed a hand over his face, trying to pull himself together before he spoke to his mother. God only knew how much of that train wreck of an argument she'd overheard. "Mom? What are you doing back here? Did you need something?"

"Actually, I was hoping to talk to you and Celia, but maybe this isn't the best time." His mother hovered uncertainly in the doorway.

"No, Mom, it's fine. Celia and I both could use some time to cool off." Although eighteen years of cooling off hadn't helped them. "Come sit down. Have a scone."

"If you're sure." She cleared the door, her yellow leather boots clicking across the tile lanai.

He moved Celia's plate aside as his mother sat. "What's on your mind?"

"I've been letting you support me for long enough," she said in a rush, as if she'd been holding the words inside.

What the hell? Who tipped the world upside down while he wasn't looking? "Mom, that's ridiculous. I owe you. I *want* to give you these things—anything you need."

"You're my son." She patted his arm. "It was my job to take care of you. You don't owe me anything."

"Damn it, Mother, the money doesn't even make a

dent in my portfolio. I don't miss it." He could have retired from the concert scene years ago.

"That's beside the point," she said primly, folding her hands in her lap.

"To you maybe. But not to me. I can't watch you work that hard ever again." Years of guilt piled on top of him, so much he didn't know how he would ever dig out. "I just can't."

"Well, I'm not looking to embrace abject poverty." She laughed lightly. "I've gotten used to the softer side of life. But maybe a little too used to it."

"What do you mean?" He tried to sort through her words, really tried, because apparently he'd been missing the mark with both of the women in his life.

She took a deep breath, as if bracing herself, then said, "Do you think that monstrously large bank account of yours could handle sending your old mother to school? I'd like to become a professional caterer, one who specializes in entertaining on a budget. When I said I've become accustomed to the softer side of life, I meant it. I'd like to bring those treats and delicacies to others who never thought they could afford them."

He was stunned, to say the least. But the plan she'd spelled out made perfect sense. The pieces fit, and he was happy for her. "Mom, I think that's a great idea. But I'm still curious. What brought this big turnaround?"

"Seeing you with Celia in the news, hearing all the reports about what she's been doing with her life. She could have relied on her father's money, but she carved out a place for herself in the world. That's admirable, son."

His mother was right. Celia had. And she was clearly stronger for that, more confident. She'd been telling him she wasn't the selfish, spoiled girl he'd once known, but had he actually understood? Accepted? He forced himself to focus on his mother's words. Apparently a man never got too old to learn something from his mom.

"Malcolm, those pictures the press has been running of her with students showed how much she loves her profession. This may sound strange, but I never considered that work could be fulfilling. The jobs I did before, I took pride in them, sure, but they were just a means to put food in your mouth. And there weren't a lot of choices. I have a choice now, thanks to you—"

A scream split the air.

Celia's voice.

What the hell?

Malcolm shot from his chair, toppling it as he sprinted for the stairs. Celia's screams continued, mixed with masculine shouts. His gut clenched with fear. Where were the guards? Why hadn't security been triggered? What the hell had he been thinking lowering his own guard with her just because he had her an ocean away from the threat?

He raced through the door and barely had time to register what he was seeing. Celia held a huge vase of flowers high and crashed it down on the head of…

Adam Logan?

His manager?

Logan's knees buckled, and he fell to the ground.

Malcolm barked, "What the hell's going on here? Celia, are you okay?"

She backed away, pointing at his manager, now kneeling in a puddle of water, shattered glass and roses on the thick Persian rug. "He was in my room, going through my things. He had a threatening note and a dead rose. He was putting it in my bag."

Malcolm turned to Logan, a man he'd called his friend,

his brother. "Adam? You were the one behind the threats on Celia? Why the hell would you do that?"

Logan sagged back on his heels, his shoulders slumping forward. "I just wanted to get the two of you together again."

It made no sense. Malcolm looked to Celia, who appeared just as confused. He wanted to drape an arm around her, tuck her close, but she stood quietly on the other side of the room.

"You'd better explain. And fast." His pulse pounded beneath his eye, anger roiling.

Logan leaned forward, his eyes gleaming with the cutthroat, ambitious light that had helped push Malcolm's career to the limit. "Your bad-boy image was starting to drag on your numbers. And you have to admit, we got a lot of good press out of the high-school-sweethearts-reunited angle. It was easy enough to pull off, then make sure Salvatore heard." He shrugged. "It's actually sort of funny when you think about it, pulling off a prank on the old colonel again."

Malcolm wasn't laughing. This bastard had terrified Celia for absolutely no good reason. Already brimming with frustration from his fight with Celia, Malcolm couldn't stem the anger for a second longer. He hauled back his fist and punched Logan square in the jaw.

His manager crumpled back onto the rug, out cold. A formality, actually, since Celia had clearly handled things on her own. She stood strong and magnificent, in control of the situation.

His thoughts synched up in that moment as the truth truly sank in. Celia could take care of herself. As his mother had said, Celia had built the life that she wanted. He was the one still chasing the past, trying to change the outcome or hide from the tougher parts. Like how he'd stayed away from Azalea and Celia rather than face up to his feelings. Rather than risk putting his heart on the line again.

She had every reason to be angry with him. He'd failed to acknowledge the strong and incredible woman she'd become, the completion of the dazzling young girl he first fell for. The woman he still loved.

If he didn't figure out how to get his priorities in order, he didn't stand a chance of winning her back. And losing wasn't an option. He loved this woman with every fiber of his being. Every note he played, every breath he took was for her. Always for Celia.

Whatever it took, he would be the man worthy of spending his life with her.

As Celia stood in the back of the concert hall that night, her mind was still reeling from the shock of finding Malcolm's manager in her room. Of learning he'd been behind those threats all along. Adam Logan had orchestrated everything as a way to get Malcolm some extra publicity. Her life had been horribly manipulated.

But the frustration and anger she experienced had to be nothing compared to the disillusionment Malcolm felt over his friend's betrayal. There hadn't been time to talk after the attack. Malcolm had been so focused on dealing with the crisis at hand that she'd been shut out as the mess in front of her was "handled." He'd made the decision to contact Salvatore and let him wade through the legal ramifications. The press from this, however, would be rough on Malcolm—betrayed by his own manager.

For that reason, she'd been unable to leave right away. In honor of all she and Malcolm had shared, in the past and in the present, she would stay for tonight's concert. If Adam Logan had been correct, that she'd been good press for Malcolm, she would at least give him this night to help smooth over the rough patch he was bound to face with the media. And after he sang that last encore?

She honestly didn't know. She just wished she had some kind of sign as to what she should do next. Marry Malcolm and change her life? Or return to what she'd had?

From the back of the auditorium, she watched him perform, her eyes riveted by his mesmerizing charisma. The audience hung on his every note, his every word. His performance was as smooth as ever, even though he couldn't play the piano or guitar tonight. He'd broken two fingers punching out his manager. Sometime during the chaotic day, a doctor had been called to splint Malcolm's fingers just before he left for the sound check.

In fact, his concert was beyond phenomenal tonight. She couldn't put her finger on the difference. Her eyes scanned the sold-out historic theater. The space resembled the Amsterdam venue. The acoustics of the old building were formidable, but not the best she'd heard. Nothing had changed with the lighting. Yet, still…tonight *was* different. Exponentially better in some undefinable way.

Perhaps the fact that this was a charity benefit added something to his performance? She smoothed her hands down her floor-length red satin gown, feeling a bit like Cinderella at the ball with midnight only seconds away. Certainly, Malcolm looked heart-stoppingly handsome in his tuxedo. As the concert rolled to a close, she realized he didn't intend to sing "Playing for Keeps." Although, how could she blame him after the grief she'd given him the last time he'd performed it? She'd chewed him out for selling fans a fake bill of goods, crooning to them with lyrics he didn't believe in.

And then, as he finished the final ballad of the night,

sitting on a bar stool and singing directly to the audience, she grasped the difference in tonight's show. The difference in Malcolm.

He *wasn't* performing.

Tonight when he sang about love won and lost, love's pain and joy, she would swear he really believed the words. That had to be it. He felt the emotion, believed in love and happily ever after. The feelings were so real they shone from his eyes. His proposal earlier hadn't sprung from some gut reaction or need to protect her. Somehow Malcolm's faith in happily ever after had been restored. He'd come to believe in it again. This was the sign she'd been waiting for. She'd thought his proposal was for old times' sake or to make up for the past.

And she'd thrown his proposal back in his face.

Her heart squeezed tight with emotion as she realized how very badly she'd messed up, and how every second that passed was filled with pain neither of them should have to endure. They'd both been through enough. They'd sacrificed and lost too much because of their mistakes. They'd made amends.

They deserved to be happy.

Hitching up the hem of her floor-length gown, she sprinted back out into the lobby, searching for the backstage entrance and regretting like hell that she'd refused the backstage pass earlier out of fear. Out of some contrary need to put up walls between them.

She ran toward the guards at the doors, and thank God, one of them remembered her and waved her through with a wink and a smile. He even pointed the way. High heels clicking along the concrete floors, she dashed past crates and music stands, endless equipment crowding her path. Finally, she made it to the wings, stopping beside the stage manager, who held up a finger to his lips.

Although with the loud applause as Malcolm bowed, it wasn't as if anyone could hear her.

Celia nodded anyway, breathless from her mad dash. Her heart pounded in her ears with anticipation and hope. Malcolm had already started to exit the stage, walking toward her. Although he hadn't seen her yet since he still waved to the audience, already on their feet clapping.

Malcolm stepped out of the lights and into the darkened wings, his hand already out for the customary bottled water the backstage assistants would pass him before he returned for an encore.

Celia thrust out her hand with a water bottle, their fingers brushing.

Sparks flying as always.

Malcolm halted in his tracks. "You're here."

"Where else would I be?" she said simply. She didn't bother weighing her words to preserve her pride. What a silly emotion anyway. "I love you, so I'm here."

The stage manager covered his grin.

Malcolm clasped her arm and guided her away—the stage manager's smile quickly shifting to panic as Malcolm tucked her in a private corner of storage containers.

"Celia, did I hear you right?" He set the water aside, his focus solely on her.

"I meant every word, and I'm sorry I didn't say it earlier instead of running."

He hauled her close and held her tightly. "Oh, God, Celia, I love you, too," he whispered in her hair. "I always have."

Although she knew that already. She'd heard it in his voice with every word he sang. Still, it was so very good to hear him say it plainly.

He angled back, cupping her face. "I'm sorry I let so many years go by without reaching out to you. I let pride get in the way of us having a chance at fixing the past, of building a future. And most of all, I apologize for not trusting you now, for not listening to what you want for your life. For not believing what's right in front of me."

"What might that be?" She skimmed the overlong lock away from his forehead.

"You fascinated the hell out of me eighteen years ago. But you absolutely mesmerize me now. You are an incredible woman, stunning, independent. And so damn giving I can't figure out what I did to deserve this second chance with you."

The pounding of the audience stomping the floor for another song was nothing compared to her heartbeat in her ears. "It's time we both believe and trust that we deserve to be happy. We deserve a future together."

"Darlin', I do like the way you think." He sealed his mouth to hers, a sure and perfect fit. He finished with a kiss on her nose before he rested his forehead against hers. "What would you say to my retiring?"

The stage manager hovered, but Malcolm waved him off.

"From Interpol? I know what Adam Logan did hurt you—"

He shook his head. "That's not what I meant. What if, after this tour, I retired from the stage."

"I'm…stunned."

He searched her eyes. "Good stunned or bad stunned?"

"I'm just surprised. I thought you lived for your music." She pointed toward the stage, the audience still on their feet applauding for their encore. "They live for your music. And tonight, the heart you put into your songs propelled you to another level."

"Celia, it's about you. It's always been about you. I've been chasing success to prove something to your father, to you—to myself—that really doesn't matter. I've learned so much from you these past several days… I want to compose music, and I have the financial luxury of never working again if I choose."

Wow, he really meant it. This wasn't some half-baked idea. He'd found his direction. And the fact that he attributed that to her meant more than she could say.

"Malcolm, your fans are going to grieve."

"There are plenty of singers more than ready to step into any void I might leave on the charts."

"You're really serious."

"Absolutely. I was approached not too long ago about writing a score for a movie, a sprawling postapocalyptic saga with an edgy vibe of modern-day meets classical—Adam advised me not to…" He hung his head briefly, then drew in a deep breath, meeting her eyes again. "I can do that anywhere, even in Azalea."

"Or there and here," she offered in compromise. "We could live in Azalea and London. I could still teach privately, work on a series of music books for students."

"That sheet music I saw in your office the first day…"

"Sounds like we're building a plan, together. And we can fine-tune the details later, because right now, you have a concert to finish."

His eyes glinted with an idea. "What do you say we give them their encore?"

Laughing, she rolled her eyes. "They're calling for you."

"Crazy, I know, but I don't want to let you go." He reached for a guitar. "Maybe you could play since I can't. We could sing together, like we used to. We can be a team, you and I."

Without hesitation, she hooked her arm in his and let him escort her out onto the stage. The crowd went wild at the sight of her. And when Malcolm took her hand as she settled on the bar stool, the crowd held their breath in anticipation. Celia looked out at the audience and saw his mother beaming from the front row. Celia smiled back before settling the guitar in her lap and turning to Malcolm.

Sharing a microphone with him, her heart in her eyes, she strummed the opening chords to "Playing for Keeps," the notes committed to memory years before. The melody was already a part of her heart.

* * * * *

He couldn't let his guard down and think of her as a woman.

He had an investigation to run and involvement with Lucy Royall would compromise his objectivity. Compromise him. He was ethically bound to keep emotional distance between them.

"Hayden?" she asked breathlessly.

He gripped the steering wheel until his fingers hurt, trying to anchor himself to something. "Yes?"

"Were you about to kiss me?"

His heart stuttered to a stop. He should have known Lucy wasn't the type of woman to let things lie, to choose the sensible path. "There was a moment, before I thought better of it," he admitted.

"I wish you had."

NO STRANGER TO SCANDAL

BY
RACHEL BAILEY

Published in Great Britain 2013
by Mills & Boon, an imprint of Harlequin (UK) Limited,
Eton House, 18-24 Paradise Road, Richmond, Surrey TW9 1SR

Special thanks and acknowledgement to Rachel Bailey for her contribution to the DAUGHTERS OF POWER miniseries.

ISBN: 978 0 263 90475 8
ebook ISBN: 978 1 472 00609 7

51-0613

Harlequin (UK) policy is to use papers that are natural, renewable and recyclable products and made from wood grown in sustainable forests. The logging and manufacturing processes conform to the legal environmental regulations of the country of origin.

Printed and bound in Spain
by Blackprint CPI, Barcelona

Rachel Bailey developed a serious book addiction at a young age (via Peter Rabbit and Jemima Puddleduck) and has never recovered. Just how she likes it. She went on to earn degrees in psychology and social work, but is now living her dream—writing romance for a living.

She lives on a piece of paradise on Australia's Sunshine Coast with her hero and four dogs, where she loves to sit with a dog or two, overlooking the trees and reading books from her evergrowing to-be-read pile.

Rachel would love to hear from you and can be contacted through her website, www.rachelbailey.com.

For my father, Colin.

You didn't live to see my name on a book cover, but I know you'd have been proud. I miss you.

Acknowledgments:

Thanks to Barbara DeLeo and Sharon Archer for reading early drafts of this book and your insightful comments. And to Bron and Heather for the cheer squad.

Thanks to the other authors in the Daughters of Power continuity—it's been a pleasure working with you. And to Charles Griemsman, the editor for the series—as always, your guidance was invaluable.

One

Hayden Black flicked through the documents and photos scattered across his D.C. hotel suite desk until he found the one he needed. Hauntingly beautiful hazel eyes; shoulder-length blond hair that shone as if polished; designer-red lips. Lucy Royall. The key to his investigation for Congress that would bring down her stepfather, Graham Boyle.

After his preliminary research from his New York base, he'd decided the twenty-two-year-old heiress who'd been handed life on a silver platter was the weak link he'd target to gather all the information on Graham Boyle's criminal activities. His first appointment this morning had been to get a colleague's take on Ms. Royall so he would be prepped when he met her.

He flicked the photo to the side and picked up another—this one her publicity shot from Boyle's news network, American News Service, where Lucy worked as a junior reporter. Even with the professional tone and her eyes heavily made up with expertly applied gray smudges and mascara, she looked far too young, too innocent, to be mixed up in the dirty business of ANS illegally hacking into the phones of the president's friends and family. But looks could be deceiving, especially when it came to pampered princesses. No one knew that better than he did.

Lucy Royall had been billionaire Graham Boyle's stepdaughter since she was twelve, and her own deceased father had left her a vast fortune. She hadn't been born with a plain old silver spoon in her mouth—hers had been pure platinum and diamond-encrusted.

He dropped the photo and picked up one of another blonde journalist—ANS senior reporter Angelica Pierce. Only ten minutes ago he'd completed an interview with Ms. Pierce, so he could vouch for both the perfectly white, straight teeth in her plastic broadcast news journalist smile and her aqua eyes. There was something strange about that shade of blue—it looked more like colored contacts than natural. But she spent half her life in front of a TV camera. Angelica Pierce wouldn't be alone in the industry if she was trying to make the most of what she had to look good for the viewers.

Angelica had been eager to help, saying the phone hacking scandal tainted all journalists. And she'd been especially eager to help on the subject of Lucy Royall. Apparently, when Lucy had graduated from college, Boyle had handed her the job of junior reporter over many more qualified applicants, and now, according to Angelica, Lucy could be found "swanning around the office like she's on a movie set, refusing assignments she doesn't like and expecting privileges."

Hayden glanced back at Lucy's photo, with her silk shirt and modest diamond earrings—all tastefully understated yet subtly conveying wealth and class. He could believe she had a sense of entitlement.

But during the interview, Angelica had done something particularly interesting. She'd lied to him about Lucy threatening her. The signs in her body language had been almost imperceptible, but he'd interviewed countless people over the years and was used to picking up what other people missed.

Of course, there were reasons she might lie—a star reporter watching a young, pretty journalist who happened to be related to the network's owner coming up through the ranks would be nervous. People lied for less every day.

But something told him there was more to the story. Admittedly, his first instinct was always to distrust journalists—they were too used to manipulating facts to make a good story. But this whole investigation centered around journalists, so for objectivity's sake, he'd have to put that aside and take them as they came for now.

He shuffled the photos till he found one of Graham Boyle. Hayden's background research for the congressional committee's investigation into phone hacking and other illegal activities kept leading him back to Boyle.

And his stepdaughter.

Angelica Pierce might have lied about Lucy Royall threatening her, perhaps to protect her job. But he had no trouble believing that Ms. Royall was a spoiled princess playing at being a journalist. Which suited him just fine. Coaxing an admission from her about Boyle's dirty dealings would be a piece of cake—he'd had enough experience with pampered heiresses to know exactly how to handle them.

Lucy Royall was going down, and taking her stepfather with her.

* * *

Lucy wedged the phone between her shoulder and ear and kept typing up the questions for Mitch Davis, the anchor of one of ANS's nightly news shows. He was interviewing a Florida senator in four hours and wanted the list by midday to give himself a chance to familiarize himself with it. Which gave her exactly ten more minutes, and she had an appointment with the congressional committee's criminal investigator, Hayden Black, at one. So the call from Marnie Salloway, one of the news producers, was bad timing. Though that was exactly how this job always seemed to work—too many tasks, too many bosses.

"Marnie, can I call you back in fifteen?"

"I'll be in a meeting then. I need to talk to you now," Marnie snapped.

"Okay, sure." Lucy smiled so her voice sounded pleasant despite her frantic mood. "What do you need?"

"What I need is a list of locations to send the cameraman this afternoon to get the background footage for the story on the president's daughter tonight."

Lucy frowned and kept typing. "I emailed that this morning."

"You sent a list of ten options. Not enough. Have twenty in my inbox by twelve-thirty."

Lucy glanced at the glowing red digital clock on the wall. Nine minutes to twelve. She held back a sigh. "All right, you'll have it."

She replaced the receiver and wasted a precious twenty seconds by dropping her aching head to her desk. When she'd graduated, Graham had offered her a job as a full-fledged reporter. She'd refused, so he'd offered her the spot as a weekend anchor. He was just trying to help her, as he'd done since she was twelve, but she didn't want a top job.

No, that wasn't true—she definitely wanted a top reporting job. But she wanted to earn it, to be *good.* To be respected for her journalistic ability. And the only way to develop that expertise was to work under the great journalists, to learn the skills.

But days like today had her questioning that decision, or at least questioning the decision to take a junior-reporter role at ANS. She wasn't the only junior here, but she was the only one treated like an indentured servant. And the person who'd treated her the worst had been her former hero, Angelica Pierce. Drawing in a deep breath, she went back to typing the last questions for Mitch Davis's interview and emailed them to him with three minutes to spare, then called up the list of locations she'd emailed Marnie for the background footage and opened her web browser to look for alternatives.

It had been made very clear to her on her first day that the other ANS staff resented having Graham's stepdaughter in their newsroom. Rumors had made it back to her that they suspected she was a spy for Graham. Lucy was pretty sure their antagonism was misplaced resentment for authority—people always loved to dig the boot into the boss, and she represented the boss to them. In some ways she couldn't blame them, but she wouldn't let them get to her. Her policy had been to keep her head down and do every menial task the more senior staff asked of her, ridiculous or not.

She sent the extended list to Marnie, grabbed her bag and ran out the door for her meeting with Hayden Black. If she caught a cab and there wasn't too much traffic, she'd make it with a few minutes to spare. On the street, she grabbed a coffee and raspberry muffin, stuffed the muffin in her scarlet hold-all handbag and took a long sip of the coffee before hailing a cab. This was one meeting she didn't want to arrive at late—Congress was wasting time and money on a wild-goose chase, investigating her stepfather for illegal phone-hacking practices at ANS despite already having the culprits in custody. Today was her turn to be interviewed, to defend Graham. He'd been there for whatever she needed for almost half her life; now she would be there for him.

The cab dropped her at the Sterling Hotel, where Hayden Black was staying and conducting his interviews. Apparently he'd been offered an office for his investigation but he preferred neutral territory—an interesting move. Most investigators liked the extra authority afforded by an official office. She sipped the last of her coffee in the elevator and checked her reflection in the mirrored wall—the wind had blown her hair all over the place. The doors slid open as she combed her fingers through the disheveled mess to make it more presentable. First impressions counted, and Graham was depending on her.

She checked the number on the hotel suite door, then knocked with the hand holding the empty paper cup, straightening her skirt with her other. She looked around for a trash can, but turned back when she heard the door open and started to smile in an I've-got-nothing-to-hide way.

And froze, the smile only half-formed.

A tall man in a crisp white shirt, crimson tie and neatly pressed dark trousers filled the doorway—Hayden Black. The air shifted around her, became heavier, uneven. She'd met a lot of powerful men in her job, in her life, yet none had had the *presence* of this man before her, as if his energy somehow flowed out and charged the space around him. The thicker air was difficult to draw into her lungs and she had to struggle to fill them.

Frown lines formed across his forehead. Dark brown

eyes stared at her from a lightly weathered face, and they didn't seem to like what they saw. Her skin cooled. He was judging her already and the interview hadn't even begun. All her resilience coalesced, snapping her out of whatever flight of fancy had overtaken her for those moments, and she straightened her spine. That was more than fine—she was used to people judging her based on preconceived ideas about her wealth, her lifestyle and her upbringing. An investigator for Congress was just one more to add to the list. She lifted her chin and waited.

He cleared his throat. "Ms. Royall. Thank you for coming."

"My pleasure, Mr. Black," she said using the polite voice her mother had taught her to always start with when she wanted to win something. *You catch more flies with honey than vinegar, Lucy.*

He extended an arm to show her through the door. "Can I get you anything before we start?" His voice was gruff, unwelcoming.

"I'm fine, thank you." She took a seat and put the hold-all bag on the floor beside her.

He lowered himself into the chair opposite and granted her a condescending glance. "We'll run through some simple questions about ANS and your stepfather. If you keep your answers to the truth, we shouldn't experience any trouble."

A surge of heat rushed across her skin. The patronizing jerk. If she kept her answers to the truth, they shouldn't experience any trouble? She was twenty-two, had a degree from Georgetown University and owned one-sixth of the biggest department-store chain in the country. Did he think she would accept being treated like a child?

She gave him her best guileless smile, reached for her large red bag and deposited it on the desk in front of her.

Then she combined the sweet voice of her mother with the rapid-fire manner she'd learned from Graham, laying on her North Carolina accent extra thick for good measure. "You know, I think I will have a glass of water, if that's okay. I've got a muffin here I'd like to eat—you don't mind, do you?—I skipped lunch to make this meeting and I'll think more clearly with some food in my stomach."

He hesitated, then murmured, "Of course," and rose to get her water.

She took a satisfied breath—she'd thrown him off balance. When he put the glass in front of her, she handed him her paper coffee cup. "And could you throw this away for me while you're up? I didn't want to put it in my bag in case any residual moisture leaked out, and there wasn't a trash can in the hallway." He took the cup, but seemed far from happy about it. She smiled at him again. "Thank you. You'd be surprised how many people refuse a simple request, but then again, you're a criminal investigator. Maybe you wouldn't." She broke off a piece of muffin and popped it into her mouth.

He sat back in his chair and stared at her, hard. Seemed he'd regained his balance. "Ms. Royall—"

Swallowing, she reached into her bag and came out with a notepad. "I'm going to take notes on what we talk about. I always find it's best if everyone remembers exactly what's said in interviews, whatever kind they are. Helps everyone keep their answers to the truth and that way we shouldn't run into trouble." She broke off another piece of her muffin and held it out to him. "Raspberry muffin?"

His eyes narrowed and she wondered if she'd pushed too far. But he simply said, "No." Albeit with a stern finality.

"It's a very good muffin." She slipped the piece into her mouth and reached into her bag again for a pen.

"Are you ready?" he asked in a tight voice.

She looked down at her pen and clicked it. "Just give me one more moment. I'd rather be fully prepared for an important conversation like this." She put her bag on the floor again, and wrote at the top of her page,

Hayden Black interview. April 2, 2013.

Then she beamed up at him. "I'm ready."

Hayden resisted the impulse to groan and instead called up the neutral expression that was normally easy to find in an interview. Lucy Royall was exactly like her photo, yet nothing like it. Her hair was shiny and blond, but sitting haphazardly around her shoulders, as if she'd stood in a gust of D.C. wind. Her lips were the same as the photo, but were bronze today, and full, sensual, as they moved while she ate the muffin. Despite his intentions, his breath hitched. Her eyes were the same shade of hazel, but in person they shone with intelligence. He knew she was trying to play him, and damned if she wasn't having some success. And he was unsure if that irritated or amused him.

But one thing that didn't amuse him was his unexpected reaction when he'd first opened the door. He'd been thunderstruck. She wasn't merely beautiful, she was breathtaking. There was a light around her, inside her. A glow that was so appealing, he'd had to focus hard so his hand wouldn't reach out. And was there a more inappropriate woman on the planet for him to have a reaction this strong to? The daughter of the man he was investigating on behalf of a congressional committee. A woman who, if his guess was correct, was complicit in her stepfather's illegal activities.

The woman herself raised her brows, either because

his face had contorted with self-disgust or because she was sitting there, pen poised, waiting for him to start the interview while he merely stared.

Clearing his throat, he thumbed the button to start the recording equipment. "Tell me about your relationship with Graham Boyle."

She didn't hesitate. "Graham has been my stepfather since I was twelve years old. He's a sweet man with a good heart."

Sweet? In another setting he may have laughed. The man owned a national cable-news network and was feared by competitors and allies alike. For Graham Boyle, the ends justified the means—he demanded that his reporters do anything to get a story.

And someone who'd been part of Graham Boyle's immediate family for ten years couldn't be completely unaware of his ruthless nature.

"That's not the common perception," he said mildly.

"Do your parents see you the same way your friends do, Mr. Black? Your girlfriends? Employees? Bosses?" She drew in a breath and seemed to grow taller in her seat. "My stepfather has the type of job where he has to make tough decisions, and people who disagree with those decisions might see him as hard-hearted. But he has been nothing but kind and generous to me."

"I'm glad to hear it. But he hasn't been accused of making tough decisions, Ms. Royall. He's been accused of authorizing or at least condoning illegal phone hacking to obtain information about the president's illegitimate daughter."

She stilled. The only movement was the rapid rise and fall of her chest. Then she leaned forward, slowly, deliberately. "Let me tell you what sort of man he is. When my mother died three years ago, Graham was devastated. He could barely walk away from the graveside service—he had to be supported by two family friends, he was that riddled with grief. Then, despite the hours his job demands, and his own grief, he made a point of calling me, visiting, bringing me gifts. Making sure I was okay." She sat back again, but her body remained tense. "He's a good man."

There was something deeply attractive about her impassioned defense of her stepfather. The way her eyes sparked made his breath catch. Made his pulse that much faster—a far from ideal response to an interviewee. Determinedly, he ignored it. He was a professional.

"Al Capone was good to his family," he said.

Her cheeks flushed red. "I resent the heck out of your implication."

He flicked his pen between the fingers of his right hand and arched a brow. "I wasn't implying anything beyond pointing out that being good to his family doesn't automatically exclude a person from engaging in illegal activities."

Lucy held his gaze across the table for long, challenging seconds. He let the silence lengthen. In situations like this, patience was his friend.

She dropped her gaze to the pad of paper in front of her and her blond hair swung forward a little. An image rose in his mind of threading his fingers through her hair, of tilting her face up to him, of lowering his own until his mouth gently touched hers, of feeling the softness of her plump lips, the passion she—

Suddenly his shirt collar was too tight. Damn it, what was he doing? In an important investigation like this, he couldn't afford to be attracted to a witness.

Get ahold of yourself, Black.

He drew in a breath and stared at her until all he saw was a woman covering up for a criminal.

"Have you participated in any instances of illegal surveillance at ANS?" he asked, more harshly than he'd intended.

"No," she said, lacing her fingers together on the table in front of her.

Without missing a beat, he continued. "Are you aware of any instances of illegal surveillance at ANS?"

"No, I'm not." Her voice was measured, even.

"Have you participated in or been aware of any instances of any illegal activity at ANS?"

"No."

"Did you work with former ANS journalists Brandon Ames and Troy Hall when they used illegal phone hacking to uncover the story about the president's illegitimate daughter?"

"No."

"Were they carrying out orders from your stepfather?"

"Of course not."

"They initially blamed the phone hacking on a temporary researcher, but the researcher was clean. Do you know who it was at ANS who helped them?"

"As far as I know, no one."

"What's your take on why the accusations have been made against ANS and Graham Boyle?"

She let out a long breath. "Those who make something of their lives always attract those who want to tear them down."

Unfortunately, he knew that wasn't where the accusations had originated. Graham Boyle might have a good point or two, might treat his stepdaughter well, but he was still a ruthless jerk who'd hurt many.

"How do you think ANS came up with the leads that uncovered President Morrow's daughter? He was a Montana senator before his presidential campaign—it's not as if no one's looked into his background before."

For the first time, an uncertain line appeared between her brows. “I don’t know. I wasn’t working on that story.”

He knew he had to push further, but God help him, with that look on her face, he wanted to reassure her instead. To take her hand across the table and tell her everything would be okay. Despite that, the cynical part of his brain knew it was probably an act. He needed to listen to that side of himself more.

“But you talk to other journalists, surely,” he said, thankfully hitting the skeptical note he’d aimed for. “And this story and its methods are very high profile. You’re telling me you’ve heard nothing about how they got the lead?”

“Good old investigative journalism—it’s hard to beat.” Her perkiness was forced, but he didn’t get the sense she was lying in an underhanded way. Not like the last woman who’d sat in that chair. This was a woman who didn’t get on with her colleagues, felt excluded from them and was covering up for that. A shaft of unwanted tenderness hit him squarely in the chest.

But Angelica Pierce had made it clear whose fault that lack of integration was. Feeling sorry for Lucy Royall was a dangerous trap. He rubbed a hand over his face. This interview wasn’t working, wasn’t getting him anywhere. Perhaps the lack of sleep over the past few months was finally affecting his investigative edge.

Hayden glanced at his watch. Maybe it’d be better to finish early today, pick up his son from the nanny next door and go for a walk in one of D.C.’s parks. He could interview Lucy Royall again when his focus was stronger.

“Thanks for your time,” he said, his voice almost a growl. “I’ll be in touch when I need to speak with you again.”

She tucked her notebook and pen into her bag and

stood. "Mr. Black, I understand that you're just doing your job. But I hope you haven't already discounted the possibility that Graham Boyle might be innocent."

Hayden pushed to his feet and rested his hands low on his hips. "If the evidence shows he's innocent, Ms. Royall, that's what I'll report back to Congress."

But his gut instinct never lead him astray, and his gut told him that Lucy Royall's stepfather was as guilty as they came. It was up to him to prove it.

He held the door open for her then watched her walk down the hall, her hips subtly swaying. Beauty and a glorious accent had covered surprising strength and determination in his interviewee—and had caught him off guard.

Luckily, he was even more determined.

Next time he met Lucy Royall, he'd be ready for her.

Two

Lucy quietly slipped through the door to her stepfather's office—his secretary had told her he was on the phone but to go through anyway. Graham nodded when he saw her, then barked more orders at whoever was on the other end of the line.

Used to being in the background while he worked, Lucy took the chance to look through his top-floor window at the panoramic view of D.C. She loved this city. She'd moved here from Charlotte, North Carolina, when she was twelve and her mother had married Graham. The town—and Graham—had been good to her.

From a basket under the desk, Rosebud, his bulldog, lifted her head and, recognizing Lucy, lumbered out to greet her. Lucy dropped her bag beside the chair and crouched down to rub the dog's velvety, wrinkled face.

"How's it going, Rosie?" she whispered and was rewarded with a wide doggie smile, complete with a pink tongue almost curled back on itself.

With a final terse comment, Graham ended the call and crossed the room.

"Lucy!" he boomed and held out his arms. She stood and leaned into his bear hug, letting go of all her worries for a few precious seconds. He was the one person she could always count on. Her only family.

"Hang on," he said, pulling back. "I've got something here for you."

She couldn't help the smile at the familiar words. "You didn't have to."

"Of course I did." And she knew he was right—it was the way he showed love. In the same way he was her only family, she was all Graham had. They made an odd couple in some ways, but their unusual little family worked for them.

He opened a door in the sleek cabinets that lined one wall and pulled out a deep blue velvet box. He handed it to her, his grin proud. She opened the lid and took out an exquisite crystal bulldog the size of her palm.

"It's Rosebud." At the sound of her name, the real Rosebud thumped her curly tail on the carpet. "Thank you," Lucy said and kissed Graham's cheek.

Graham smiled with his heart in his eyes, as he always did in these moments, then he cleared his throat and strode back to his desk. He'd never been particularly comfortable with emotions, so the moments, although heartfelt, were always short. "Tell me how the interview with Black went."

She sank into an upholstered armchair in front of Graham's heavy desk. "Shorter than I expected." She'd puzzled over that on the cab ride back. "He only asked a few questions, really."

He flicked his wrist dismissively. "That means he was just taking your temperature. There will be more."

"He said he'd be in touch when he needed to speak to me again." Remembering Hayden's words—and his deep voice saying them—sent a shiver across her skin. If she wasn't careful, she'd develop a crush on the investigator, which would be bad on more levels than she could count. But, oh, that man had been delicious. So tall and broad, with a dark, brooding demeanor to accompany his looks. Even his hands had fascinated her—he'd flicked his pen over and under his fingers as he'd considered a point and she'd been mesmerized. They were long fingers with blunt ends, dexterous, lightly tanned. Instead of paying attention to the questions, for one sublime, stolen moment she had imagined his palm cupping the side of her face, those fingers stroking her cheek.

Graham leaned back in his chair and laced his own fingers behind his head, bringing her attention back to the present. And to the gravity of the issue on the table.

"Our biggest risk here," he said, eyes narrowed and aimed at a point on the wall, "is that someone with an ax to grind will falsify testimony. Feed Black lies and say they saw something." He glanced back to her. "Did you get a sense from him that he's got anything like that?"

"He played his cards close to his chest. But one thing was obvious," she said gently, as if she could soften the blow. "He thinks you're guilty."

Graham swore under his breath. "I refuse to sit back and wait for an investigator who's not objective to 'find' evidence to support his theory. We need to expose Black before he does too much damage."

She tilted her head to the side. "What do you have in mind?"

"I want you to start your own investigation," he said in his trademark firecracker rhythm. "I'm taking you off all other duties. You'll run this on your own. No word to anyone else. You're the only one I can trust one hundred percent not to stab me in the back for the notoriety, or whatever-the-hell reason people frame other people for."

None of it was a question, but he was waiting for her response. She reached over and clasped one of his cold hands between hers. "I'll start right away."

"You're a good girl." He patted her hands, then released them. "Congress will have vetted him for the job, dug into his past, but we're better. Find the skeletons in his closet and bring them out to play. We'll air an exposé as soon as you have enough."

Her insides fluttered. This wasn't a style of journalism that she liked or particularly wanted to be involved in. And Hayden Black being the target made her even less comfortable. She shifted in her chair. The discomfort could have been a result of the stirrings of attraction, but she still didn't like the idea of targeting him.

Then she remembered his closed-off expression when she'd left his suite less than an hour ago—he was going after Graham, already convinced of his guilt. Doing an exposé might leave a bad taste in her mouth, but Hayden Black's own actions made it necessary. Besides, if he had no skeletons hidden away, there'd be nothing to find.

She nodded, decision made. "You can't have me on air with this. Everyone knows I'm your stepdaughter. We'll need someone with a good reputation and a bit more distance from you."

"We'll worry about that when we have the content ready to go. You do the research, get the story, and I'll bring someone in to host then."

Her mind clicked over into journalist mode and she took out a notebook from her hold-all bag. "Who's our source at the Sterling Hotel?"

Graham picked up the phone on his desk, dialed,

barked an order, then after he had his information, disconnected and looked at Lucy again. “Concierge named Jerry Freethy.”

“Okay.” She dropped the notebook back in her bag and stood. “I’ll keep you up to date.” She blew Rosebud an air kiss and headed for the door.

“Lucy,” Graham said gruffly, and she turned. “Thank you.”

Emotion clogged her throat but she found her voice. “Don’t worry about it. I’ve got your back, Graham.”

The next day, at half past one, Lucy saw her target. The concierge had told her Hayden Black liked to take a walk in the park across from the Sterling Hotel with his son on his lunch break, but that the time of the break varied. So Lucy and Rosebud had been wandering the park since just after eleven. Rosebud was panting from the exertion, but thoroughly enjoying her day out meeting random people who stopped to pat her.

Hayden was striding along a paved path about twenty feet away, talking to an infant he carried in one arm, holding a brown paper bag in the other. The sight of him trapped her breath in her lungs. Wide, strong shoulders that tapered to narrow hips. Long legs that walked with confidence and purpose. The masculine grace in the way he held his son.

She swallowed hard. “Come on, Rosie, I have a little boy I want you to meet.” Rosebud looked up, her curled tongue poking out as she smiled.

Lucy had spent the afternoon and evening before gathering as much information as she could on Hayden Black. There wasn’t a whole lot available on the web, but then, he was a professional investigator, so it made sense that he protected his own information. She’d found New York newspaper articles about his wife's death a few months earlier in a car crash, leaving Hayden the single father of a nine-month-old baby, Joshua, who would now be one year old. And currently wearing denim overalls, a bright-blue hat and a cheeky grin.

As they came closer, Lucy gazed at the trees, their branches heavy with spring flowers, but kept man and child in her peripheral vision. Hayden had his head bent, talking to his son, not paying a lot of attention to where they were, the people rollerblading past or the joggers making their way along the wide path. The hitch in her lungs had smoothed out and now her breaths were coming a little too fast for comfort, which she told herself was excitement about the story, but she suspected had more to do with seeing Hayden Black again.

When they were only ten feet apart, she heard a squeal, followed by, "Goggie!" Lucy finally glanced up to see Hayden had stopped midstep, and probably midsentence, given the way his mouth was open, as if forming a word he'd since forgotten.

She'd never paid much attention to men's mouths—shoulders and biceps had usually caught her attention first—but Hayden's mouth was a thing of beauty. Sensual lips that she could almost feel tracing a path along the side of her neck. Her skin heated and prickled.

Before becoming too carried away, she found a smile and walked Rosie over. A gentle breeze blew her hair around her face, and she tucked it behind her ears as she stopped in front of father and son.

"Ms. Royall," he said. His voice was pleasant, probably for his son's benefit, but his face told a different story—eyebrows slashed down, jaw tight. He was annoyed at running into her. Just because he didn't want to mix work and family? Or was there something more...?

"Lovely day, isn't it?" she said, leaning down to give Rosie a scratch behind the ears. "Little birds in the trees, the flowers are out, the weather's warm—everything is just so perfect. Rosebud and I love April."

A speculative gleam appeared in Hayden's eye. He'd know everything there was to know about Graham from his shoe size to what he liked for breakfast, so knowing Rosie belonged to one of the targets of his investigation was guaranteed. And he'd just realized he could use Rosie to engage Lucy in conversation about Graham, and hope the casual setting caused her to slip up. Precisely what she was doing to him.

Although that didn't explain why he'd been annoyed when he first saw her—he was renowned for his investigative acumen, so that should have been the first thing that occurred to him. Perhaps he hadn't wanted his time with his son to be interrupted. Entirely possible, but it had felt like more than that….

Perhaps he disliked her personally and was annoyed at running into her away from work? Her belly hollowed out before she gave herself a mental shake. Just because her hormones went haywire when she saw him didn't mean the chemistry was mutual. Besides, the man had lost his wife only a few months ago.

She should be pleased that at least one of them wouldn't be carried away by flights of fancy. Getting involved with the man she was investigating, and worse, who was investigating ANS for Congress, would be unthinkable.

"Goggie!" Josh squealed again, apparently impatient to be getting to the dog-patting action.

Hayden looked from Rosie to her. "Is it okay for Josh to pet her?"

"Sure," she said, laying on her Southern accent thick and smiling innocently. "She's as gentle as a lamb."

Hayden crouched down beside her and supported Josh as he found his feet and reached out to touch Rosie's ear.

"Her name's Rosebud," Lucy said to the toddler.

As they watched Josh and Rosie interact, Hayden asked, "How long have you had her?"

"She's Graham's dog," she replied, as if she hadn't worked out that he'd know that. "He's had her for six years. Since she was a puppy."

Hayden leaned forward and joined Josh in petting her. "Nice dog."

His shoulder was only a couple of inches from hers—if she moved a little she'd bump against him. A mischievous impulse urged her to lean into him, knowing he'd be solid and warm, and it took all her willpower to resist. The scent of clean, masculine skin surrounded her, made everything else fade into the background, made a hum resound through her bloodstream.

Rosie rolled over onto her back, producing her tummy for rubs with no shame at her brazen request for attention. Lucy blinked down at the dog, fully aware she walked a knife's edge of being just as obvious. She squared her shoulders. Time to move away from temptation and remember she was a journalist working on a story.

Hayden rubbed the dog, barely able to concentrate on anything but Lucy at his side. Within touching distance. If he wanted to, he could reach out a hand and trail it down her arm. Or wrap his fingers under her curtain of silky blond hair and discover if the skin on her neck was as soft as it appeared. His heart thudded like a bass drum. The jolt of attraction when he'd first seen her in the park had thrown him off balance and part of him was still scrambling to find his equilibrium.

Lucy stood, breaking the spell. "I was just about to give

Rosebud a drink." She took out a bottle of water and a rolled-up waterproof canvas bowl from her bag. "Would Josh like to help?"

Hayden looked down at his son and, for the briefest of moments, was at a loss, uncertain what Josh would or wouldn't like. His gut twisted tight. He hated not instinctively knowing these things. Then he gave himself a mental shake. Of course Josh would like to help—it was a dog and water, both of which spelled fun.

"He'd love to," he finally said.

Lucy gave Josh the bottle of water and explained how to fill the canvas bowl in terms a one-year-old could understand. Josh sloshed more water on the ground and on Lucy than in the bowl, but no one seemed to mind, and soon the dog was enthusiastically drinking and Josh was trying to catch her wagging, curly tail. Hayden's heart expanded to see his son smiling and so obviously filled with joy.

Lucy screwed the top back on the water and slid it into the same large red bag she'd had yesterday at the interview. Seemed she had all contingencies covered inside that bag—yesterday a muffin, notebook and pen; today a water bottle and a dog bowl. He wouldn't be surprised if she pulled out a picnic blanket and folding chairs next.

He sat back on his haunches. "I read somewhere that Graham had a dog that he takes to work each day," he said conversationally.

"This is her." She didn't look up, but gave Rosebud an extra rub on the neck.

"So you spend a bit of time in Graham's office to see Rosebud?"

She smiled, obviously aware of where his questions were leading. The dog finished her drink and Josh, looking for the next interesting adventure, held his arms out to Lucy. Without hesitation, she bundled him in.

"How's it going, Josh?" she said, charming his son, then looked at Hayden over his son's head and said, "I see Graham and Rosie a few times a week."

Instead of following the line of questioning he'd planned in his head, Hayden couldn't draw his eyes from the easy way Lucy interacted with his little boy. Josh had only just met her, but was already happy in her arms. And Lucy was relaxed, as if she knew just what to do with a toddler. Lord above, Hayden wished *he* knew what to do with one. Sure, he had the basics covered, like sleeping, bathing and feeding, but he was still getting used to being the primary caregiver to a child, and most of the time he felt he was swimming out of his depth.

Why did it seem so natural for her? From his research, he knew she had no siblings, no young cousins around, yet she seemed supremely confident where he often felt awkward and unsure. Maybe because he wanted to be a good father so damn much and Lucy had nothing riding on it at all.

He blew out a slow breath and stood—he was losing his focus with Lucy Royall again. This time he'd almost recovered from the force of her allure and managed to steer the conversation toward Graham Boyle, but now he'd become distracted again by her natural way with his son. He rubbed his fingers over his eyes and refocused on his new plan—build rapport and see what else he could discover in the casual setting.

"We're walking this way, how about you?" he said, sinking a hand into his pocket. "Josh and I have just come out for our lunch break."

Lucy beamed over at him. "We'd love to join you for a walk, wouldn't we, Rosie?"

Hayden hoisted Josh up onto his shoulder, but the boy leaned toward Lucy with his arms out. Hayden arched an eyebrow. Josh didn't normally go to new people this easily—why did he have to overcome his trust issues with someone Hayden was investigating?

Lucy laughed and held up Rosebud's lead. "How about we swap?"

Still, he didn't move. Building rapport while taking a walk was one thing, but letting her carry his son, crossing personal lines, was dangerous, and something he'd never done before.

"Daddy," Josh said, pointing to Lucy. "Up."

And right there was his Achilles' heel. Josh wanted Lucy, and Hayden wanted Josh to be happy. Complex ethical issues boiled down to pure simplicity.

"Sure," he said. He took the dog's lead and handed over his son, trying to minimize touching Lucy in both tasks since he was in enough trouble as it was. "I'll take that bag while you have Josh."

"It's fine." She tickled Josh's side and was rewarded with giggles. "I'm used to having it over my shoulder."

He nodded and they started along the paved path that wound alongside the sparkling river, Hayden busy trying not to physically smack himself over the head. He'd been brought in by a congressional committee to investigate ANS, and Graham Boyle in particular. And now here he was, in a D.C. park, talking a stroll with the man's stepdaughter, allowing her to cuddle his son, offering to carry her bag and walking the wretched man's dog.

Not to mention that his pulse was pounding too hard for a casual walk, which had less to do with the exercise than with the woman whose elbow was mere inches from his own. So close he could practically feel all her vibrant energy radiating out and filling the air around her.

He cleared his throat. "Ms. Royall—"

"Lucy." With his son's fist wrapped around her fingers, she glanced up at him. "We're walking in a park on a lunch break. I think you can call me Lucy."

"Lucy, then." The name felt unusual as his mouth moved around the word. He'd only said it aloud together with her surname before, but alone it seemed special, prettier. More intimate.

"Yes?"

He looked down at her, frowning. "Yes, what?"

"You were about to say something when I told you to call me Lucy."

Good point. But he had no idea what it had been. He thrust the fingers of his free hand into his hair. He'd called their interview to a halt because he was getting distracted. Seemed the extra twenty-four hours to regroup hadn't helped any.

He searched his brain for a way to informally find a path to the information he wanted. "Did you always want to be a journalist?"

They waited while Rosebud sniffed the base of a tree, and Lucy shrugged one shoulder. "Maybe not always. But since I interned with Graham when I was sixteen."

"What did you want to be before that?"

"My father's family is in department stores," she said casually. "When he died I inherited his stock. I always thought I'd do a business degree and work there."

Her family was "in department stores"? He almost laughed. In his preliminary research he'd found that Lucy was one of the Royall Department Stores Royalls. A family of old money that stood alongside the Rockefellers, Vanderbilts and Gettys in stature. The woman had pedigree coming out her ears.

Genuine curiosity nibbled. "Have you stayed in touch with that side of your family?"

"Occasionally I see Aunt Judith and her family," she

said softly, with just a tinge of regret. "She has a gorgeous lodge in Fields, Montana, where we sometimes gather for birthdays and Christmases."

"Fields is a nice place," he said. Great ski fields and snowboarding, although now just as famous for being the birthplace of President Morrow as its natural charms.

"We've had some good family times there. Plus, a couple of times a year I go to a board meeting, and occasionally talk to them about charity events."

As she tapped a finger on his son's nose, Hayden watched her and tried to get it all to make sense. Her choices didn't quite add up with the image he had of a pampered princess.

"Wouldn't it have been an easier path to work in the Royall family business? You already own significant stock there. You wouldn't have had to start out at the bottom like you did at ANS." That was what his wife, Brooke, had done—worked in her family's banking empire. But in effect, it had only been role-playing. She'd had a big corner office and taken a lot of long lunches.

Lucy arched a challenging eyebrow. "What makes you think I'd want to take the easier path?"

"Human nature." He didn't try to hide the cynicism in his voice. "Who wouldn't want the easier option?"

She was silent and the moment stretched out; the only sound was Josh's gurgling baby talk. Then she looked up at him with eyes that seemed far too insightful. "Tell me, Hayden, did you take the easiest career option available to you?"

"No," he admitted. But then, he hadn't been brought up an heiress like Lucy or Brooke. Completely different situation.

"How long have you been a criminal investigator?" she asked.

"A few years now." But he wasn't here to talk about himself. He rolled his shoulders back and changed the conversation's direction. "What story are you working on now?"

She moved Josh onto her other hip and adjusted his blue hat. "Are you officially asking me?"

He could sense her reluctance, but that wasn't unusual with journalists trying to keep their scoop under wraps. And since his investigation was about past practices, her current story was irrelevant. He shrugged. "No, just conversation."

"Then I'll pass on the question." She looked up at him and unleashed a dazzling smile. "Did you come out just to walk, or do you have lunch in that bag?"

He held up the brown paper bag. "Lunch. I can offer you half a room-service cheese and tomato on rye." He'd found that when dealing with hotels, the plainer the order, the less likely they were to ruin it with some embellishment meant to impress but usually falling short. He was a man of simple tastes—he'd take sandwiches on fresh bread from the deli near his office over a fancy restaurant lunch any day.

"You can keep your sandwich," she said. "I have mine in my bag."

"Tell me you don't have a picnic blanket in that bag," he said, one corner of his mouth turning up.

Her forehead crinkled into a confused frown. "A picnic blanket wouldn't fit in here."

"You seem to pull out all sorts of things, so a blanket wouldn't have surprised me," he said dryly.

They found a patch of grass under a weeping willow a little farther back from the path. He pulled out a sealed plastic bag with a wet washcloth inside and wiped off Josh's hands before passing him a banana.

"That's pretty organized," Lucy said, watching him with those huge hazel eyes.

His hackles went up. "For a dad, you mean?"

"For anyone." Her head tipped to the side, as if puzzling him out. "I didn't mean it as an insult."

He nodded. Just because he was prickly about his parenting skills didn't mean she'd taken a swipe at him. He offered a self-deprecating smile as compensation for his overreaction. "The nanny packed it all. I wouldn't have thought of a washcloth, so you weren't far off the mark."

She broke off a piece of her granola bar and popped it in her mouth. They ate in silence for a couple of minutes, watching Josh with his banana.

Lucy leaned back, propping one hand on the grass behind her for support. "Is that where Josh is during your interviews?"

"I hired the nanny for while we're in D.C. She comes nine to five." He hadn't been sure how the arrangement would work out, but it was fine. The biggest adjustment had been not having his sister close by—he was flying solo as a parent for the first time, and he was determined to make it work.

"What does Josh normally do during the day?" she asked as she fed a piece of granola to Rosebud.

"When we're in New York, a couple of days a week he goes to my sister—she has a three-year-old boy, and the cousins enjoy their time together. The other three days a week he goes to a day-care center at my office. There are five kids of staff members there, and I can see him at lunchtime."

She smiled over at Josh. "Sounds ideal."

No, ideal would have been Josh having two parents to spend time with him, love him and make him the center of their world. But even before Brooke's death, Josh hadn't had that. The weight of needing to make things perfect for his son crashed down on him, as it did regularly. His gut contracted and clenched. He was all Josh had and he'd do his damned best to make his childhood as close to ideal as he could.

He looked up and saw Lucy was still watching him. This had become far too personal. What was it about Lucy Royall that made him forget everything that was important? What he needed to do was schedule another interview, and this time he'd write a complete list of questions—something he hadn't done in years—to make sure he stayed on topic.

He grabbed the remnants of his lunch and stuffed them back into the brown paper bag. "Josh is getting sleepy. I need to get him back for his nap."

"This was nice," she said, picking up the washcloth and wiping the banana from Josh's fingers. "Maybe Rosie and I could join you again sometime."

Join him again sometime? He coughed out an incredulous laugh. Out in the forest, this was a woman who'd poke a hungry bear until it ate her. He stood and picked Josh up. Thankfully, the little boy curled into his neck, as if supporting Hayden's prediction that he was ready for a nap.

"Look, Lucy," he said, more gruffly than he intended. "I'm not sure what you think is going on here, but this investigation is serious. I'm not here to make friends." Her eyes widened and he immediately regretted his tone. He blew out a breath, and said more softly, "Even if I wanted to, I can't."

Lucy stood, as well. "You'd like to be my friend, Hayden?" She arched an eyebrow, her eyes glimmering with something he couldn't read.

"Under *different circumstances,*" he emphasized, "it's possible that we would have been friends."

Her chin lifted. "I know how important this is. I take Graham's future very seriously. But just so we're clear—" she fixed him with sultry hazel eyes, and her voice slid deeper into the accent of a Southern belle who took no prisoners "—under different circumstances, I wouldn't want to be your friend, Hayden. I'd make one heck of a pass at you."

She turned and walked off, blond hair glinting in the sunshine, Rosie at her heels, leaving Hayden poleaxed.

Three

At four o'clock the next day, Lucy knocked on the door to Hayden's suite, then rolled her shoulders one at a time to try and ease the bunching tension in them.

Hayden had called her cell an hour ago and asked if she could come by to answer a few more questions, and she'd jumped at the chance to see him again in his suite, maybe find a few more clues for her story. The only other time she'd been to his hotel was before Graham had handed her the assignment of the exposé, so this time she'd pay more attention to the little things. The clues.

But now that she was here, her knees quivered—in fact her whole body was unsteady. She wiped damp palms down her calf-length skirt. This was the first time she'd seen him after saying that if things were different, she'd make a pass at him. And she had no idea how things had changed between them, or if she'd ruined the fragile rapport she'd been building with the man who was her target.

After she'd turned a corner yesterday at the park and was safely out of his line of sight, she'd called herself every type of crazy. Rosie had looked up, worried, and Lucy had explained to the dog that she'd probably just uttered the most reckless, foolish words of her life.

Even if they were true.

But she had to be careful. It wasn't just that they were in the midst of a congressional investigation. Hayden Black was the last man on the planet she could afford to be involved with. People already judged her for being the daughter of Jonathon Royall and the stepdaughter of Graham Boyle—two wealthy, high-profile, well-connected men. The common opinion was that she'd been handed everything she wanted on a silver platter. That she hadn't had to work for her own achievements. If she were to be seen with another wealthy, high-profile, well-connected man like Hayden Black, especially given that he was a few years older than she, people would write her off as a woman who was dependent on strong men. Her achievements would again be discounted as not coming from hard work. At just thirteen she'd realized what people assumed about her and it had made her determined to prove to the world that she could achieve anything she wanted on her own.

No, Hayden Black was not for her. She needed an average guy, maybe one just starting out in his career, like her.

With a heavy whoosh, the door swung open and there stood the far-from-average man himself, as broodingly gorgeous as she remembered. "Thank you for coming," he said, his voice like gravel, as if he hadn't used it all day.

And there was something new in his expression—his dark coffee eyes were wary as they assessed her. Seemed she'd thrown the great criminal investigator a curveball yesterday. Her taut shoulders relaxed a little. Perhaps, despite it being a crazy thing to say, it had worked in her favor.

"You're welcome…." She paused as she stepped into the room. "Do I call you Hayden or Mr. Black, since this is an official interview?"

"Hayden is fine." He closed the door behind her and led her to the desk and chairs where they'd spoken two days ago.

She glanced around, taking note of details that might be useful later. Besides the papers on the wooden desk and the coffee cup on the kitchenette counter, the room was neat, nothing out of place, as if he'd just moved in. Hotel housekeeping would have had something to do with that, but there was more to it—as if he was keeping a firm line between Hayden the father and widower and Hayden the tough, take-no-prisoners investigator. She also spied the recorder sitting on the desk again and approved. Recordings were less likely to be misinterpreted than notes.

"Would you like a drink?" he asked.

She took her seat and lifted her bag onto the desk. "I'm fine."

"You're sure?" he asked with a raised eyebrow, and she remembered that last time she'd made him go back for water after they'd sat down, then to throw away her paper coffee cup. Her mouth began to curve at the memory, but as their gazes held, heat shimmered between them. Time seemed to stretch; goose bumps erupted across her skin. Then Hayden looked away and gave his head a quick shake.

"I have a bottle of water in my bag," she said in a voice that was more of a husky whisper.

He folded himself into his chair, as if nothing had just passed between them, and muttered something that sounded suspiciously like, "Of course you do."

She took out her water, notepad and pen and lined them up beside each other, using the extra moments to find her equilibrium.

"Let me know when you're ready," he said, opening the laptop that sat on the desk in front of him.

She picked up her pen, wrote the date at the top of a clean page, then pasted a smile on her face. "Ready."

He nodded, switched the recording equipment on and gave the date, time and her name. "Do you understand what illegal phone hacking entails?" he asked bluntly.

Seemed they were jumping right in. She straightened her spine. That suited her just fine. "Yes, I do."

"So you're confident you'd recognize phone hacking if you came across evidence that it had happened," he asked without hesitation and looking directly at her as if daring her to lie. If she wasn't mistaken, he was working from a list of questions on his laptop today. Perhaps this interview was more important than the first?

She leaned forward in her chair, her hands laced together and resting on the desk. "I believe I would."

"We already have evidence that ANS has been involved in illegal phone hacking. The evidence against former reporters Brandon Ames and Troy Hall is indisputable—they were caught on camera hiring hackers to record the phone and computer activity of Ted Morrow's and Eleanor Albert's families and friends. The only questions that remain are who else was involved, and who knew about it." There was something vaguely intimidating about the intelligence in his eyes, the determined jut of his chin, the perfect Windsor knot of his pale blue tie. This man would be a formidable adversary.

She arched an eyebrow. "Assuming someone else *was* involved or knew about it."

Not acknowledging her comment, his eyes flicked back to the laptop. "Do you work much with Angelica Pierce?"

Lucy kept her face neutral despite the distaste that rolled through her. *There* was a woman who was capable of something immoral, like phone hacking, if her treatment of her underlings was any gauge of her moral character. Angelica was mean, vain and selfish. But she wasn't here to talk about whom she personally did and didn't like, so she simply said, "I do a fair bit of background and preparation work for her."

"What about Mitch Davis?" Hayden flicked his pen over and under his fingers as he watched her. The man had an intensity in his gaze that was mesmerizing.

"Mitch has his own show, and he's a star at ANS. I rarely have a chance to speak to him directly." Mitch had been the one to announce the news of the president's illegitimate daughter at an inauguration gala, but Brandon and Troy had uncovered the information and given it to Mitch to reveal in a very public toast that put the new president on the spot. Those guys had given ambition a bad name with their slimy tactics, and they deserved the full force of the law—which they were now receiving. But as far as she was aware, they'd acted alone—other than blaming a casual researcher who'd already left ANS—and this witch hunt to try to implicate others in the pair's crimes was dangerous for everybody.

"Did you work with Brandon Ames or Troy Hall on their story about the president's daughter?"

She unscrewed the cap on her water bottle and took a sip, putting the cap back on before replying. He may have been asking the questions, but she was retaining a smidgeon of control over the process. "As I said when you asked the question two days ago, no, I didn't."

Barely acknowledging her reply, he pushed forward. "What about Marnie Salloway?"

"Marnie is an ANS producer and has the authority to assign me tasks," she said, making a list in her notebook of the names he was asking about. She wanted the record for when she reported back to Graham, but also to gain a little power in this meeting.

"Has she ever asked you to do anything illegal?"

"No."

"Anything involving phone hacking?"

"That would be illegal—" she smiled sweetly "—so my reply stands. No."

"Did you know that your stepfather and the president attended the same college at the same time?"

"Yes," she said. It was hardly a secret.

"Are you aware of any bad blood between them?"

Not apart from Graham thinking Ted Morrow had strutted around campus as if he owned it. "They didn't move in the same circles."

For another twenty minutes he grilled her, trying to trip her up, asking questions in different ways, expertly circling back over the line of questioning again and again. She had to admire his technique, but since she had nothing to hide, it was easy not to stumble.

When he paused to take a sip of water, she asked, "Hayden, do you honestly think someone else at ANS was involved in the hacking with Brandon and Troy, or are you fishing?"

"Someone else was involved," he said, his voice dropping a notch. His dark brown eyes burned with the intensity of his conviction.

Her fingers tightened around her pen. "Why are you so sure?"

"To start with, neither of them understood the process

well enough to have masterminded it. They were pawns, used by someone bigger."

She frowned as she followed his investigative reasoning. "I'm not someone bigger."

"No," he said slowly. His gaze locked on hers, taking on a speculative gleam and, as she understood his meaning, her stomach fell away.

"You're using me to get to Graham." She swallowed past an uncomfortable constriction in her throat. "I'm not here for routine questioning like the others. You think Graham ordered those goofballs to do it and that I know something that will implicate him."

One broad shoulder lifted, then dropped, as if this was a casual conversation, yet the intensity in his eyes didn't waver. "It's one theory."

A shiver ran down her spine. She'd known there was suspicion, of course. They all had. But if it was certain that someone else was involved, then ANS was in more trouble than she'd thought. They still had a bad seed in the company, and if Congress couldn't find who it was, they'd keep their focus on Graham. The exposé alone wouldn't save her stepfather. She had to do more.

She tapped a beat with the end of her pen on the desk as fragments of ideas flitted through her mind until one coherent plan formed.

She rested her forearms on the desk and leaned forward. "Hayden, I have a proposal for you."

He stilled. "I'm listening."

"If there truly is someone else in ANS who was involved in the hacking, and they were pulling Brandon and Troy's strings, then I want to know who they are, too. I can tell you now, it's not Graham. I know that man, and I know what he's capable of—he's not your guy. But the only way to prove that is to find the real culprit."

Hayden leaned back and folded his arms over his wide chest. "What exactly are you suggesting?"

"I'm going to help you with your investigation," she said, mind made up. "I can be your person on the inside. But I won't be involved in a witch hunt—this has to be evidence-based." She wouldn't be manipulated into finding circumstantial or misleading evidence against Graham.

"So you'll gather information for me?" He spoke slowly, as if testing the idea as he said it.

"Within reason. We have agree to some parameters first."

He cocked his head, brown eyes curious. "Your stepfather will be okay with you doing this?"

"I won't tell him just yet. It's possible he trusts someone he shouldn't, so for the time being, no one at ANS will know I'm assisting you." She felt a little queasy at the thought of keeping something of this magnitude from Graham, but in this case, the ends justified the means. The most important thing was that she was working in Graham's best interests.

Hayden rubbed a hand across a jaw darkened by five-o'clock shadow. "You believe in Boyle that much?"

"More."

He tapped one finger heavily on the desk three times, then blew out a breath. "Okay, I'm willing to give it a go and see how it pans out. But I have to warn you that I still think Boyle was involved, and I won't be dropping that line of inquiry just because you're helping."

"Noted." As soon as she found the person behind Troy and Brandon's crimes, Hayden's theory about Graham would be moot.

There was a sharp knock at the door. Hayden glanced

down at his watch. “Excuse me,” he said, closing his laptop and striding across the room.

A neatly dressed woman in her thirties stood in the doorway behind a stroller containing a squirming Josh. Lucy felt her mouth curve into an unstoppable grin at the sight of the boy. He was gorgeous—Hayden’s mini-me—and his expression was full of joy and delight.

“Daddy!” Josh squealed and reached out to his father.

“I’m sorry,” the woman said. “I didn’t realize you were still busy. Would you like me to keep him longer?”

Hayden reached down and lifted his son high, planting a kiss on top of his head. “No, we’re almost done. I’ll take him.”

“Okay.” The nanny leaned forward and said goodbye to her charge. The image of the three of them was so beautiful in that moment that Lucy felt an aching hollowness spread through her middle. They looked like a family.

After closing the door behind the nanny, Hayden wheeled the empty stroller across the room with Josh in one arm. When Josh saw Lucy, his face lit up, then he looked frantically around the room. “Goggie!” he demanded.

“Hello, Josh,” she said on a laugh. “Rosebud is asleep in her basket at home.”

Josh’s little bottom lip pushed out for a split second—until he noticed how close his father’s face was, and began to pat his cheeks. Despite flinching at one of the pats that hit his eye, Hayden pushed the stroller into a corner. “If you can give me five minutes, I’ll set Josh up in his playpen with a few toys and we can continue,” he called over his shoulder.

“Sure,” she said. He opened the door to one of the suite’s bedrooms and Lucy slipped out of her chair to follow—partly because it was a great chance to look for more clues for the assignment Graham had given her on Hayden, and partly out of curiosity.

At the park yesterday, she'd carried Josh most of the time and played with him, so she hadn't had much of a chance to observe father and son together. This evening, with Hayden setting his son up in the playpen, asking him which toys he'd like, she could see more clearly. And there was something a little…awkward about the interaction. Her gaze drifted around the room. Sitting on top of an end table was a haphazard pile of baby manuals, one thick tome perched on the top, open and spine up, its pages dog-eared. Perhaps Hayden was floundering now that he was a single father? She glanced back to man and son, her heart clenching tight for them both, for all they'd lost. For all they were dealing with now.

"He's a beautiful boy, Hayden." An acknowledgment of that truth wasn't much, but it was all she could offer him. "So precious."

Hayden looked down at Josh, who chose that moment to give a wide, toothless grin. "Yeah, he is," he said softly.

A bright, sparkling idea formed in her mind—a way to get more time with Hayden and his son. She squeezed her hands together and told herself she needed that time because Hayden had his guard down more when his son was there, so her subtle digging for information for the exposé was easier. But she was uneasily aware that she wanted to spend more time with the males in the Black family. She just hoped to high heaven that it wouldn't influence her professional judgment.

"I know a park that's the best place to feed the ducks," she said. "I was thinking, since you're not from D.C., you might be looking for places to take Josh. Rosebud and I could show you on the weekend if you want."

His fingers stilled against the top of the playpen, where they'd been tapping. "Lucy, I don't—"

"No problem if you'd rather not. I just thought Josh might get a kick out of seeing the ducks. There's a great playground there, too. And I'll be taking Rosie on the weekend anyway, so it's no bother," she said, aware she was babbling now.

He wrapped a hand around the back of his neck as he watched his son for endless moments. The expression on his face was so tender, so filled with love, it was heart-breaking. Eyelashes of darkest brown lay in a fan, almost resting on his cheeks as he gazed down.

He shook his head slowly. "Lucy, it's inappropriate to socialize with you."

"What if we use the time to plan what I'll be looking for at ANS?" she said as she tucked her hair behind her ear. "A briefing for your spy, so to speak, and Josh gets an outing as a bonus."

He scrubbed his hands through his hair, then let them rest low on his hips. "Okay, sure. But bring pen and paper, because we will be working."

A burst of nervous anticipation skittered up her spine. He'd agreed. Part of her hadn't believed he would—the same part that wondered now if she'd bitten off more than she could chew. Wondered if spending a day in a social setting with Hayden—and all his brooding testosterone—was akin to playing with fire.

She bit down on her lip. No, this would be fine. It was still a good plan. The best plan she had. Plan A.

She drew in a full breath and tried to calm her racing heart. "You can pick me up Sunday morning. Say, ten?"

"Ten's fine." A faint frown line formed between his brows, showing he wasn't convinced he should have accepted. He wasn't alone.

She glanced around for a piece of paper. "I'll write down my address for you. It's not far from—"

"I know where you live," he said, his voice a low, solemn rumble.

"Of course you do," she said wryly—he probably knew more about her than many of her friends did. Having spent her first eleven years living with her media magnet of a father in something of a fishbowl, she preferred now to be the one controlling the news story—the journalist instead of the target. So it was surprising that Hayden doing background research on her didn't worry her as much as she would have predicted. There was something strangely safe, something honorable and decent about Hayden Black, despite his investigation's potential for disaster for her family.

He guided her out of the bedroom with its playpen, toward the desk where he'd been grilling her just a few minutes ago. "We'll wrap it up here for today."

She gathered her things and tucked them in her bag, glad to have a task to hide how restless her hands suddenly were. "I'll see you Sunday," she said and looked back at Hayden. His forehead was lined and she felt cold apprehension filling her veins. She hesitated, and he opened his mouth to say something, but before he could cancel, she turned and slipped out the door.

Two days later, Lucy sat with Hayden on the shady banks of the Potomac River, a sleeping boy on a blanket between them. They'd fed the ducks, strolled around and now, as Josh was recouping his energy, Lucy and Hayden had fallen into an *almost* comfortable silence. From the moment he'd picked her up, it was as if they'd both been warily circling the social component of the day. Hayden had been unfailingly polite, if distant, and she'd followed suit. In the past, her social skills had been strong enough to cope with conversing with the rich, the royal, the famous and the powerful. But those same social skills faltered with Hayden Black. They'd mainly talked to, or about, Josh.

It wasn't just the investigation—though that was enough to make things less than comfortable between them—it was the unfailing awareness she had of him as a man. She could *feel* where he was, and when he'd been close she could smell the masculine musk of his skin. She'd lost the trail of something Josh had been saying more than once because she was paying more attention to his father at her side. And there were still those unguarded words she'd said the last time they'd been in a park together that were hanging between them—she was no closer to knowing what he thought about them.

Though there were a few things she did know more about now. The digging she'd done for the exposé in the past two days had focused on his company—it seemed working in the security business was lucrative. Or it was if you were as good as Hayden Black. The company he'd started only a few years ago now took in several million dollars in fees a year, and his personal wealth was estimated to be in the millions and growing. He'd come a long way from the boy who'd put himself through law school on a military scholarship and worked as an investigative lawyer in the military police until his time in the armed forces was up. Now he was a wealthy single father of a one-year-old.

She looked down at the sleeping boy, his face flushed a faint pink, remembering the trace of awkwardness she'd seen the night Hayden had set him up in the playpen. That image had worried at the edges of her mind. She moistened her lips and dared a personal question. "Has it been hard becoming his sole parent?"

Hayden's head snapped up, surprise in his eyes. Then he leaned back on his hands and nodded wearily. "The hardest thing I've ever done."

If they were going to get into a deeper conversation, she should be looking for clues to skeletons in his professional career for her exposé, or evidence of bias, yet she couldn't help prodding a little further into his relationship with Josh. "Did your wife do most of the care before she died?"

He coughed out a bitter laugh. "Brooke didn't do much with him at all. Besides buy him designer clothes and show him off when she thought it would grant her social cachet." He pulled a cotton cover over his son and placed a hand protectively on the sleeping boy's back.

"So you looked after him?" She folded her legs up beneath her, turning to face Hayden more. This was the most personal information he'd disclosed and she was hungry for every detail, every expression.

"No," he said, wincing. "Brooke had staff for everything, including Josh. She—" He hesitated, obviously weighing how much information to share. She waited, letting the decision be completely his, though wishing she could ease the tension that bound his body tight. "She was a socialite from a very wealthy family who expected to be pampered. When we were first together, I was happy to oblige, but it turned out that she needed more pampering than a husband alone could give." His expression was wry, but it obviously veiled deeper emotions. "She had staff to clean the house, a chef, a personal trainer and from the day he was born, two live-in nannies for Josh, so they could work round the clock. He rarely saw his mother."

"Oh, Hayden." One of her father's sisters, Evelyn, lived

like that, but she could imagine nothing worse than outsourcing her life, her son, so completely.

"I should have done something, been more involved." His voice was thick with self-recrimination, his face twisted with regret. "But Brooke said that children were her domain and she'd handle them the way she wanted. The way she'd been raised. And I hate to admit it, but I was sick of the arguments, so I let her have her way for some peace. For all our sakes, including Josh's. Besides, I was out of my depth—I'd never been a father before—how did I know the way she'd been raised was wrong?"

"I'm assuming that was quite different from the way you were raised," she said gently.

"You can say that again." He gazed down at Josh for a long moment before reaching out to smooth the hair back from his son's face. "I spent time with him when I could. Played with him at night, did things when I had a day off, but I guess part of me must have been okay with the way Brooke wanted things done or I would have changed them. Insisted." He rubbed two fingers across the deep lines on his forehead. "I was stupid."

"You seem to be making up for it now," she said.

He shook his head dismissively. "There's a long way to go before I become the type of father I want to be."

"I don't think you should be so hard on yourself." She reached over and laid a hand on the warm cotton covering his forearm, wanting to bring any comfort she could. "Josh clearly loves you, and he's happy. You're doing something right."

"Thanks," he said with a half smile and glanced away. His expression was usually so serious that even a half smile seemed bright, drew her in till all she could see was him. His gaze dropped to the hand that still lay on his arm. When he looked back up to her, his coffee-brown eyes darkened, and his chest rose and fell too fast. She knew how he felt—suddenly this open park didn't contain enough oxygen. The strong muscles under her fingers burned with heat and held her hand trapped as if by magnetic force.

From what felt like miles away, Josh sighed in his sleep and curled his teddy in closer. Hayden stiffened and looked down at his son before jerking his arm away from her. Lucy blinked and blinked again, trying to reorient herself to the world around them. To the park. To the reality that she'd almost fallen under the spell of a man she needed to keep at arm's length. Of a man who would likely feel betrayed if he knew her real agenda in meeting him today.

Hayden cleared his throat. "Tell me why you're so good with Josh. You don't have any brothers or sisters, no young cousins or nieces or nephews. Is it just a natural thing with babies for you?"

She looked down at Josh, still holding his teddy close as he slept. If Hayden didn't already know her involvement with babies, his research would soon unearth it, especially as he already knew about the lack of children in her family. There was no reason not to tell him—it wasn't a secret, it was just something she normally didn't discuss. Yet…something deep inside her wanted him to understand this part of her.

"Before my father died," she began, still watching Josh, "he used to take me to volunteer at a residential home for people with disabilities that he'd established. He believed strongly that the wealth we'd been born to was a privilege, and it was our responsibility to help others. He also wanted me to stay in touch with how other people live."

"Sounds like he was a wise man."

She looked up to see if there was any other meaning behind his words—people occasionally grabbed the opportunity to take a sarcastic swipe about her father and his family, a consequence of their wealth and high profile. But Hayden's eyes held only interest in the story she was telling, and she was more grateful for that simple acceptance than she would have expected. She stretched her legs out in front of her, relaxing a fraction.

"After he died, my mother wanted to continue his mission with me. But she said I could choose my own charity—the residential home had been my father's passion."

"And being a typical ten-year-old girl, you chose babies," he said, stretching his legs out beside hers.

She bit down on her smile. "It was almost kittens."

He chuckled. "What did you do?"

"We set up a free clinic in North Carolina for mothers who are having a hard time with their new babies. It's staffed mainly by professionals—nurses, social workers and consulting doctors—and the moms and babies can stay a few nights, up to a week, to get help with feeding or getting their babies to sleep or whatever the problem is."

He tilted his head to the side as he regarded her. "That sounds like a great service."

"It is," she said, feeling a soft glow of pride filling her chest—those midwives were doing fabulous work. "When we moved to D.C., we set up another one here. I go in and hang around most weekends, just being an extra pair of hands. Sometimes it's babysitting while the new mom gets some rest, sometimes it's manning the phones."

Though helping out in person wasn't an act of charity—she loved those times. Being part of a team and helping to make a real difference in people's lives. She'd always thought of journalism as making a difference, too, but since the phone-hacking scandal had broken, she'd started to wonder.

Hayden reached into the picnic basket and offered her a strawberry. "Do you fund it on your own?"

She took the shiny red berry—her fingers practically sparking when they grazed Hayden's—and twirled it on its small stem. "It started with just me, but I'm working on getting Royall Department Stores involved and building more clinics throughout the country. Aunt Judith is already eager to help—I went to see her in Montana last year to discuss it, and we'll take the plan to the whole board soon."

"That's amazing," he said with simple but genuine respect in his voice, in his eyes. "You've created something that's made the world a better place."

A warm flush spread across her skin, and she smiled at him, basking in his approval, letting it soak through her. Then, with a start, she realized she'd let his opinion matter more than it should. She forced herself to look away. A harmless flirtation with Hayden was one thing. Melting inside because he'd approved of her charity work was quite another. This man was still running an investigation into ANS, and believed Graham was guilty. The last thing she needed was to become emotionally involved with Hayden Black.

She pulled her legs up and tucked them underneath her, and reminded herself of the rules.

Flirting, okay.

Emotional attachment, not okay.

She would just have to try harder to keep the line where it needed to be. Still, if she didn't remember, then Hayden probably would. He seemed to have a very firm grasp on where the lines should be.

And why did that thought rankle so much?

Four

Lucy dropped the strawberry back into the container and dusted her hands on her skirt. "So, about this investigation. What do you want me to do?"

Hayden didn't answer right away; he regarded her with that intense, steady gaze, as if he could see inside her soul and knew exactly what she was doing by changing the subject away from herself. Then he nodded once. "I'll be speaking to Marnie Salloway next, since she was the producer on the story that aired."

Lucy let out a relieved breath. They were back on solid ground instead of the slippery slope of potential emotional entanglement. "What about Angelica Pierce? Seeing as she was the journalist who fronted all the follow-up stories, she could be the one." She said the word *one* carefully—she might have accepted the probability that someone had helped Troy Hall and Brandon Ames, but there was no way there was a chain of people leading up to her stepfather. The sooner this investigation proved that, the better. But Hayden either didn't notice, or was choosing to ignore her inflection and its meaning.

"I'm not as worried about Angelica at this stage," he said, absently laying a hand on Josh as he slept on the blanket. "Or Mitch Davis for that matter, since both were handed the scripts—Mitch for the announcement at the inaugural ball and Angelica for the stories that followed. But Marnie is different. She could easily be the person who ordered the phone hacking, or filtered the order down from higher."

The gentle breeze from the river blew a strand of Lucy's hair across her face and she tucked it behind her ear as she watched him. "You're not worried I'll tip Marnie off?"

"Will you?" he asked, with only curiosity in his eyes—no trace of concern.

"No." She was on board with this project, believed in its goal to find the rat in ANS so she could protect Graham. Undermining it wasn't on the agenda.

"Even if you do, she'll find out in the morning when I call to make a time with her. And she has to be expecting that she's under suspicion, so I'm not telling you anything that's a state secret." His broad shoulders lifted then dropped in a casual shrug. "What's your take on Marnie?"

"This is off the record, right? Just background." Marnie would love an excuse to complain about her to Graham, to dig the knife in as deep as it would go, and Lucy would rather not give her the ammunition if she could avoid it.

"Off the record," he agreed.

She could say this directly or sugarcoat it, and she had a feeling Hayden would prefer plain speaking. "Marnie is rude and self-important."

His expression didn't alter, as if he'd been expecting as much. "She treats you badly?"

"She doesn't treat anyone below her well," she said, trying to be as balanced in her assessment as she could. "But she makes a special effort to make my life unbearable."

Something in his eyes changed, sharpened. "Is she the only one?"

"There's a club. They have T-shirts," she said with a half smile to cover the faint sting of rejection. It wasn't the first time in her life she'd found herself the target of others' thinly veiled jealousy or venom, and she knew it wouldn't be the last. She'd learned to not let it get to her a long time ago. Mostly she was successful at that.

"Have you told Graham?" he asked quietly.

Tell Graham? She almost laughed. Oh, yeah, that would go down well at the office. "Just because I'm related to the owner doesn't mean I can run to him when I have problems."

"Sounds to me like the opposite is happening. You're being treated worse because you're related to the owner." Deep frown lines appeared on his forehead. "Any other employee would have the right to complain about being harassed, so if you don't feel you can make that complaint, you're suffering discrimination."

"I'll be fine," she said and found a carefree smile. She didn't need his sympathy, or to have someone stand up for her. She was a big girl, in charge of her own life. Being a target of people like Marnie and Angelica was part and parcel of the privilege she'd been born to, nothing more, and she could handle it.

Hayden's head tilted to the side as he regarded her. "Did Graham offer you the junior reporter role?"

"He offered me a full-fledged reporter role. Then, when I turned it down, the weekend anchor job." Graham had just been trying to help, to give her a leg up in the industry.

The dear man had been baffled when she'd turned down the offers, but he'd grudgingly respected her decision.

"You'd make a good weekend anchor."

"No, I'd be okay as one." Being okay wasn't part of her career plan. "I want the role, sure. But when I get there, I want to be truly good."

"You're not what I expected," he said with the ghost of a smile on his lips.

"Neither are you," she admitted, though she wasn't sure what she had expected. Perhaps her experience with Angelica, Troy and Brandon had skewed her perception of investigators, but she hadn't been expecting Hayden to be as considered in his approach, as quietly perceptive. And she certainly hadn't expected the simmering chemistry between them. Even now, in the midst of a discussion about a congressional investigation, she could feel the almost visible haze of heat that filled the air whenever she was near him.

He cleared his throat. "So. Marnie. Could she have been involved?"

"Well, yes, she *could* have been involved." She'd tossed the same thought around a few times herself. "But just because she's horrible, and had the opportunity, that doesn't mean she *did* break the law."

He rubbed a hand across his chin. "From your insider's perspective, could Ames and Hall have obtained their information from phone hacking without Marnie knowing?"

"Sure, it's possible."

"Possible but unlikely?" he prompted.

She shrugged. "Unless you were suspicious that someone had illegal sources, it wouldn't be hard to be blindsided. Things happen in broadcast news so quickly that not everyone can be on top of everything."

He nodded slowly and she could almost see the cogs

turning in his mind. "It would be good if you could get me something on Marnie before I meet with her. Something that rattles her enough to admit to knowing."

She arched an eyebrow. "Assuming she was involved."

"Naturally," he said, one corner of his mouth quirking up.

She looked across at him, the investigator for Congress, the man who was haunting her dreams. And she started to wonder if she could say no to him about much at all. She held up her hands. "I'll see what I can do."

Dark had closed in when they pulled up in front of Lucy's row house, the only light coming from a nearby streetlamp that bathed them in a gentle glow. Her home had been something of a surprise—he would have guessed she'd live in a penthouse apartment within walking distance of cafés, not a place large enough for a family, painted in a rich cream. Every time he thought he had Lucy Royall pegged, she did something else to surprise him.

He shouldn't like that so much.

He shouldn't like *her* so much. No denying that he did, though. Couldn't wait to hear what she'd say next, what she'd do. When she was near, he found it hard to look at anything else—it was as if she had a golden glow about her, an aura of stardust. And that mouth—a generous cupid's bow that had driven him to distraction all day—every time she moistened those lips or pursed them in thought, heat had stroked down his spine. Keeping a professional distance was becoming more challenging by the hour.

He switched the car off and pulled on the hand brake. "Just let me get Josh out of the car seat and I'll walk you to your door."

"Don't disturb him. He's sleeping so peacefully," she said softly, turning to look at his son in the baby seat. "And don't lock him in either—just stay with him. It's about eight feet to my front door. Honestly, I'll be fine. I do it all the time."

Chivalry fought with fathering instincts—could he let a woman walk to her door alone, even if it was only a few steps away? But he looked at Josh in the rearview mirror, and fatherhood won. And perhaps avoiding a doorstep scene was wise—this might not be a date, but would he be able to resist kissing her?

He turned back to Lucy. "Once you're inside with the door locked, call my cell. I'll wait right here till I hear from you."

"That's very sweet," she said.

Sweet? He almost laughed. She wouldn't be saying that if she knew the thoughts that were currently bombarding him. Thoughts about the things he'd like to do with her, starting with peeling those clothes off her body, piece by piece. Underneath he knew she'd be luscious and petal-soft….

He cleared his throat and tried to clear his mind of its impure thoughts at the same time. It didn't work. Distraction, that was the key. He needed to say something, preferably about a neutral topic. "Thank you for today—Josh had a great time."

"I had a good time, too," she said, her voice barely more than a breath. Her mouth suddenly seemed so close, and he began to lean in before summoning his control and pausing. As she realized his intent, her pupils dilated. The pulse at the base of her throat fluttered like crazy. Still, he held—not leaning in farther, but not able to move away. Her moist, full lips were slightly parted, inviting him. A groan worked its way up from deep in his chest. Desire like this, that consumed, engulfed, had been absent from his life for a long time. He wanted nothing more than to give in to it, grasp it with both hands, to grasp *Lucy* with both hands and sink into the sensations she evoked in him.

But he couldn't let his guard down and think of her as a woman. He had an investigation to run and involvement with Lucy Royall would compromise his objectivity. Compromise him. He was ethically bound to keep emotional distance between them.

He clenched his jaw tight and leaned slow, excruciating inches back.

"Hayden?" she asked breathlessly.

He gripped the steering wheel until his fingers hurt, trying to anchor himself to something. "Yes?"

"Were you about to kiss me?"

His heart stuttered to a stop. He should have known Lucy wasn't the type of woman to let things lie, to choose the sensible path. "There was a moment, before I thought better of it," he admitted.

"I wish you had." She said the words softly, but there was no flirtation in them—they were honestly delivered and all the more powerful for it. Desire still tugged hard in the pit of his belly, demanding that he follow through and kiss her, but he couldn't give in. Wouldn't.

He muttered a curse and closed his eyes to limit the number of senses being assaulted at once. "Don't say that."

"But it's the truth," she said, her Southern accent thick. He opened his eyes in time to see her pink tongue peek out and moisten those lips that drove him crazy. "I've been wondering what kissing you would be like."

"Lucy, don't." There was a harshness in his voice that he hated, but was powerless to help. He was on the edge; every muscle vibrated with the effort of holding them still. If she pushed much further, he'd consign his ethics to hell and reach for her.

"What sort of kisser are you, Hayden?" She turned in the seat, facing him, pupils large in the dim light. "Soft and gentle? Strong and demanding?"

He groaned and banged his head back on the headrest. Was she trying to kill him? "This can't happen," he growled. "I can't compromise my objectivity."

"What if I never tell?" Her voice was pure temptation, full of invitation and delicious promise, making his thundering heart thump even harder in his chest. For a moment, he wondered…could he? A shudder ripped through him. *Could he?* He glanced out the window, seeking a sign, maybe permission.

Instead he saw a fashionable D.C. street, and it struck him with the force of a blow.

D.C.

He was in this town to do a job. He'd been employed by *Congress,* damn it.

He scrubbed his hands down his face and refocused on what was important, then turned to Lucy to make sure she understood, as well. "*I'd* still know. And things would be different between us."

One corner of her mouth curved up into a half smile. "You don't think they'll be different after this conversation?"

"You'll notice I tried to stop this conversation before it started."

"Oops," she said and bit down on her lip, looking anything but sorry. "What should we do now?"

"Pretend it never happened." It was the only option left.

There was silence for long seconds as she watched him with a small line between her eyebrows. "And if I can't?"

"We don't talk about it." He slashed a hand down to

rest on his thigh, hoping he appeared more decisive than he felt. "Never let the topic come up again."

"Can you do that?"

"Yes." Sure, he could avoid *mentioning* it, but the look on her face now in the dim light of the car interior would be burned into his memory, and there was nothing he could do to avoid *thinking* about kissing her. Dreaming about it.

She picked up her hold-all handbag from the floor and held it close to her chest. "I should probably go inside."

"Yes," he croaked. Then he cleared his throat and tried again. "Yes, that would be best all around."

"Okay, then." She opened the car door with only a brief glance over her shoulder.

By sheer force of will, he let her walk up the three concrete stairs to her front door instead of drawing her back, keeping her beside him for even a few moments longer. Once she'd let herself in, he dropped his head to the steering wheel and cursed. He'd been stupid, *stupid* to let his guard down and consider kissing a key witness. What kind of investigator was he?

His cell phone rang and Lucy's number flashed on the screen. He drew in a fortifying breath and thumbed the talk button. "You're in?"

"Safe inside, with the door locked." Her voice was smooth velvet, enfolding him in the dim lamplight. His eyes drifted closed, shrinking his world down to just the cell at his ear and Lucy's voice.

"Good," he said, which was about all he could manage.

"Hayden, about that conversation we shouldn't have had…"

He knew he should hang up the phone now, knew he would regret this, but he couldn't stop himself from replying. "Yes?"

"I'm glad we did." He could just imagine her biting down on her luscious bottom lip as she paused, and his pulse spiked. "Though I would have been even happier if you had kissed me."

His head swam. *Hang up the cell, Black.*

He pinched the bridge of his nose and summoned his willpower. "Good night, Lucy."

"Night, Hayden."

He disconnected, threw the phone on the passenger seat and started the car. If he wasn't careful, this investigation might just kill him.

Three nights later, Lucy was in Hayden's suite, sitting cross-legged on one of the sofas, reams of paper, scribbled notes and printed photos spread around her. Hayden sat on the other sofa a few feet away, his long legs stretched in front of him, ankles crossed on the coffee table, going through a different pile of evidence.

Hayden glanced up at her, his hair haphazard from dragging his fingers through it. "Did you talk to the receptionists?"

Over the past three days, Lucy had spent time with everyone she could corner who worked in support roles at ANS—people who might have had the opportunity to notice things that didn't add up, and would have been treated badly by Marnie and her friends. Today she'd asked Graham's secretary, Jessica, to have lunch with her and the other executive assistants, after telling her that being Graham's daughter was making it hard to make friends.

"I heard a lot of gossip about who's sleeping with whom—I had no idea it was that much like a college dorm."

His eyebrow quirked. "Any interesting connections?"

"Why? Fancy someone at ANS?" she asked with as much innocence as she could muster.

The heat that had been lurking in his eyes for three days blazed to life, but his voice was even. "I was thinking in terms of the investigation. Which you knew."

She did know, but flirting with Hayden Black was dangerously alluring. Like touching a naked flame.

"If we're talking about the investigation, then apparently Marnie had a fling with Mitch Davis. Since we don't think Mitch had anything to do with the story besides being handed the toast to give at the inauguration ball, it's probably not relevant."

"Ames or Hall sleeping with anyone?"

"Brandon Ames was seeing one of the accountants, but she dumped him when she found out what he'd done. And I'm not sure if an accountant would have been much use with phone hacking, so I doubt she was involved."

"Hall?" he asked, leaning forward.

"No one had heard anything. If he was seeing someone, it was probably outside ANS."

Hayden swore under his breath. "Maybe it was too much to hope for a sexual link to lead us to the other perpetrators. But thanks for trying."

"I've made friends with one of the custodians—or rather, Rosebud has—and I'm hoping to run into her tomorrow night again. She might know something about any late-night meetings that other people wouldn't notice."

"Rosebud comes in handy," he said dryly, and she wondered if he realized she'd used Rosie to start a conversation that first day in the park.

She smiled noncommittally. "She sure does."

Connections with other journalists came in handy, too—she'd heard back this morning from a friend she'd graduated with who'd gone on to work for a New York newspaper. Lucy had asked him to poke around and see if he could find any secrets in Hayden's past for Graham's exposé. Her friend had dug up someone who knew Hayden's in-laws. Seemed they weren't his biggest fans. They'd wanted their daughter to marry someone of her own class, not a boy—then in the military—who'd come from nowhere. The only thing they were happy about was that he'd put the money he'd inherited from his deceased wife into a trust fund for Josh. Nothing particularly explosive for the story, but her background research folder was growing.

Lucy sifted through more of the papers around her, documents she'd already read, searching for an evasive clue, until Hayden looked up sharply.

"Did you know Angelica wears contacts?"

"Doesn't surprise me, but no." And now that she thought about it, Angelica's eyes were an unusual shade of blue—almost aqua.

He laid down the papers in his hand and picked up his coffee mug. "Why doesn't it surprise you?"

"She's vain, and very careful about letting anyone see her unless she's wearing a full face of makeup. The other on-air journalists are always immaculately presented when they go on camera, but off air they're more casual."

He returned the mug to the coffee table. "It probably doesn't mean anything. I just don't trust her."

"Well, I sure don't trust her," Lucy said. She'd seen her being nasty and vindictive—experienced it herself—far too many times for that. "Do you think she could be involved?"

"Could be, but it's unlikely." There was a definite note of frustration in his voice. "If she'd found the leads, would she let Ames and Hall take the credit? She's ambitious and it was the biggest story of the year—surely she'd want her name attached."

He was right, which left them back at square one. Well, not exactly square one, because they'd eliminated some leads. Putting her hands in the small of her back, she stretched, trying to get rid of some of the kinks that sitting on the sofa had created. From the corner of her eye she noticed Hayden subtly watching and her pulse picked up speed. She turned her head a fraction, just enough to let him know she'd noticed. He didn't look away. If anything, his gaze intensified. Her mouth dried and she moistened her lips—he watched that, too. Then, oh, so slowly, he drew in a breath and looked away, dissolving the tension that had risen. She steadied herself and followed his lead. Falling under Hayden Black's thrall was a bad, bad idea for her sanity.

What was she supposed to be doing? The investigation. Who else could have been helping Troy and Brandon if it wasn't Angelica. Right.

She rubbed her hands over her face, hoping it would help her focus. "If someone else is involved, it makes more sense that they're more senior, not just another reporter."

He riffled through a pile of reports until he found a chart she'd drawn two nights ago. "Tell me again about who was supposed to be managing Ames and Hall."

She scooted over to his sofa and looked at the chart illuminated in soft lamplight. Heat emanated from his body. "This is the line of responsibility." She reached across and touched a fingertip to the paper he held, and as she did, the sensitive underside of her wrist grazed lightly over crisp hairs on his forearm. A shiver ran up her spine.

She heard a sharply indrawn breath and looked to see his gaze locked on her, his eyes darkened with the same need she felt. For a charged moment, neither of them moved, and the only sound she heard was the pounding of her heart. He was so close—a whisper away.

"Lucy, we can't." His voice was torn from his throat.

Hearing he was as close to the edge as she was had the opposite effect from what he'd intended. She'd never been good at following rules, or doing what she was told. The day's stubble on his cheeks beckoned, and she ran her fingertips across it to see what it felt like, what *he* felt like. His jaw was clenched so hard that a muscle in the corner jumped.

"I've been wondering what it would feel like to touch you," she said, watching the path her fingers traveled over his jaw. "In fact, I wished for it."

He winced as if in pain. "You should be more careful about what you wish for."

"I was careful," she murmured. Her fingertips feathered along the strong column of his throat. "I'm wishing for it again right now."

He stilled, his only movement the rapid rise and fall of his chest. "I swear, Lucy, you'd try the patience of a saint." His gaze fell to her lips. "And I hate to admit it, but I'm no saint." Finally, his hands crept under her hair to cradle the nape of her neck, lightly massaging, sending a spray of fireworks across her skin.

"No regrets yet," she said, though she wasn't sure her voice was strong enough for him to hear. He leaned in, his body tense, and his lips brushed across hers, the softest of caresses, yet enough to leave her trembling.

"Hayden," she whispered with all the need inside her. A shudder ripped through his body. He pulled her flush against him and kissed her, the warm pressure of his mouth like nothing she'd ever felt. When his tongue moved against hers, the shimmering heat exploded inside her, and she crawled onto his lap. It still wasn't close enough. At last, after all these days of hoping and nights of dreaming, Hayden was kissing her. Hungrily. Gloriously. And she was melting.

On a groan, he wrenched his mouth away and they both gasped to find their breath again, but she didn't stop touching. Couldn't. The skin on his neck, below where the stubble ended, was surprisingly smooth and oh, so warm. She pushed her fingers down past the collar of his shirt, wanting nothing more than to feel the strength of his shoulders, to know how they'd taste. But before she could make much headway, he brought her mouth back to his.

"This is a bad idea," he murmured, lightly kissing the edges of her lips, lingering at the corner of her mouth.

He ironed a hand down her back and her pulse jerked erratically. "A very bad idea," she agreed with a catch in her voice.

"But damned if I don't want to do it anyway." He cupped her face and the fine tremor that ran through his hands created an answering shiver that spread through her whole body.

"Oh, yes. Me, too," she moaned.

He cursed under his breath, then gave a rueful half laugh. "I was hoping you'd be the sensible one."

She caught his earlobe between her teeth and gently nipped. "There's no fun in being sensible all the time."

"I'm beginning to see that," he said as he laid her down on the sofa, pressing her into the cushions with his body. He kissed along her throat. "But if we do this—"

"If?" she said incredulously, desire scorching along her skin at every point Hayden's body touched hers.

He lifted his weight on hands that rested at either side of her head. "If we do this, we have to agree on a couple of ground rules first."

"Anything." She reached for him, trying to get him to bring his delicious heat back.

He didn't move. "I'm serious, Lucy."

"I can see that," she conceded on a sigh and wriggled to sit up. Seemed they were having a conversation whether she wanted to or not.

Five

"So, ground rules," Lucy said, her hands pressing against Hayden's chest as they sat entwined on the sofa. For the moment, ignoring her body's insistent straining toward him was her best option so they could get the talking part of the night over as quickly as possible. Then they could get back to the part where he was kissing her. She went a little dizzy just thinking about it.

He swallowed hard and she watched the progress of his Adam's apple, up then down. "This can only be a one-time deal."

She slid the first button of his shirt through the buttonhole. "Sure." She wasn't thinking ahead; she was too busy being smack-dab in the middle of the moment, so if he thought she'd put up an argument about some future possibility, he was wrong.

His hands were motionless on her hips, but his fingers dug in, his heart thumping so hard she could feel it through his shirt. "No one can know."

"I won't breathe a word." She released a second and third button. A fourth. A whorl of dark hair peeked through the opening she'd made, teasing her. Daring her.

"And," he rasped, "we both promise not to use it against the other if things get sticky with the investigation."

She paused a beat and met his gaze. "We wouldn't do that."

His dark brows drew together until they almost met. "You don't know I wouldn't use it to my advantage."

"I know." Hayden Black was a man made of honor. And *heat.* The burning imprints of his hands held her hips in place beside him on the sofa, much too far away. Why didn't he pull her closer?

"Agreed?" His voice was tight, his gaze locked intently on her.

"Agreed," she said, barely caring what she agreed to, as long as it led to more of his bone-melting kisses.

He pulled her against him and his mouth met hers, giving all that heat to her at last. Her throat hummed with a sound of sheer pleasure and she twined her arms around his neck, unwilling to give him the chance to break away again. She'd wanted him in this exact position for days, and the reality was living up to every single fantasy. The hunger. The solid muscle under her hands, the taste of his lips. Sizzling energy rushed through her veins, melting her from within.

When they broke apart for air, there was a flare of satisfaction in his eyes, and it sent a shiver skating across her skin.

"Lucy," he said, his voice almost reverential, yet thick with need. "I've wanted you so badly, I thought I'd go crazy with it."

She smiled, glad she wasn't the only one who'd been

stuck in that place of torment. "I haven't been able to think straight since I met you."

Groaning, he pulled her onto his lap and she wrapped around him, knees on either side of his thighs, pressing as close as she could with layers of fabric between them. She found the thick ridge of his need and pressed into him even more.

Swiftly, he undid her buttons and peeled her top back, kissing the tops of her shoulders as he exposed them and sliding the fabric down her arms before wadding it into a ball and throwing it across the room.

"Your skin is like cream," he said against the curve of her neck. "Smooth and delectable."

In one fluid move, he unhooked her bra and threw it in the direction of her top. The cool air nipped at her naked breasts, but the simmering intensity in his eyes more than compensated. Hot fingers trailing her collarbone slipped lower, and his mouth followed them down. She arched back, her mind full of him; nothing could penetrate her thoughts but Hayden and his exquisite torture of her senses. When his lips closed over the peak of her breast, she speared her fingers across his scalp, loving the slide of his hair over the sensitive skin between her fingers. Loving what his mouth was doing even more.

One of his large palms encircled her breast, squeezing ever so gently, and her eyes drifted closed to absorb the full effect of the magic he was wreaking.

"They're some impressive skills you have there," she said on a ragged breath.

"All driven by desperate need for you," he growled.

His shirt was hanging open, yet concealing far too much of him. She pushed the open sides over his shoulders and down his arms until he flicked the shirt off completely. With a ragged moan, she spread her hand over the planes of his chest, reveling in the feel of crisp dark hair under her fingertips, greedy for as much of him as she could touch. She scraped her teeth across his biceps, feeling his shudder as it ripped through his body. It was too much, but not enough.

His hand snaked down between their bodies and released her trouser button and zipper, and when his fingers slid over the exposed satin, she bucked her hips to meet them. She'd never been this crazed with desire before. Being with Hayden was beyond her wildest dreams.

He twisted and laid her back onto the sofa, the fabric smooth and luxurious against her bare skin, and he loomed over her, breathing heavily. Time slowed as she took in the sight of him, of the masculine beauty that was all hers tonight. She'd never forget the way he looked in this moment, the way he'd made her feel. A ripple seemed to run through the air and she knew this was a memory that would last her entire life—a defining moment, a turning point. Nothing would ever be the same again. Nothing.

"Hayden," she whispered, and suddenly the world started again as he leaned down to capture her lips, kissing her deeply, hungrily, sliding his tongue against hers. She wrapped her legs around his waist and arched up into him, savoring the feel of his body pressed against her. He ground into her and every cell in her body came alive with an electric current, vibrating and sparking.

Then Hayden stilled and heaved in a breath. "That bottomless bag of yours has got to have condoms."

Delicious sensation came to a screeching halt and she blinked up at him. Protection? "No," she said slowly, mentally running through the contents of her bag. "You don't have any?"

He swore under his breath and wrenched himself away. "No idea, but I'm hoping like crazy." He ditched his jeans and strode to the bathroom, disappearing through the door, leaving Lucy to run through the options. One of them could sprint to the drugstore. A possibility, but it was a long time to be separated in their current state. She glanced at the lights of the city twinkling through the window across the room—she didn't want to leave this suite alone for anything less than a fire. They could both make a mad dash to her place—she had some condoms in a drawer. No, Josh was asleep, they couldn't leave. They could ring the concierge and see if he kept a supply—

Hayden reappeared—fully sheathed—with a predator's grin and prowled across the room. She managed to ditch her trousers and panties by the time he reached her, anticipation singing through her entire body.

"Thank goodness," she said as he climbed back on the sofa and covered her with all that heat. "I was making contingency plans and they were getting more ridiculous by the second."

"I look forward to hearing about those plans," he said, nipping at her earlobe. "Later."

"Much later," she said. "I have other plans for our mouths right now."

Never slow on the uptake, Hayden kissed her, nipping, sucking, stroking until her head swam and she was writhing underneath him.

"Now," she begged. "Please, now."

After drawing out the moment for several more agonizing seconds, he captured her gaze and slid into her in one smooth, deep stroke. The world swirled around her and came alive. *She* came alive. She tightened her grip on his waist with her legs, holding him there, savoring the sensation. Then, despite her hold, he began to move, and she was lost to the dance of their bodies, helpless to do anything but match his rhythm and give in to the sensations.

She soared higher than the stars, and Hayden's voice at her ear telling her she was beautiful, that she felt incredible, sent her higher still. The rhythm they created together was pure magic; her body was sparkling with bright, pulsing energy. His deep murmurs at her ear became more intense, edgier, pushing her to the brink, and she dug her fingers into his back, holding on, wanting the moment to last. His thrusts became faster, more urgent, and a wave of pleasure rose within her, too big to be contained, and she cried out his name as it burst in an explosion of color and light and intensity, dimly aware that Hayden followed her soon after.

Hayden stared at the ceiling from his position on the sofa, Lucy wedged beside him, his stomach slowly hollowing out. That had to be the stupidest thing he'd ever done, which was saying something, because he'd done a lot of stupid things in his life.

Making love to Lucy had been earth-shattering, yes. Bone-melting, definitely—he might not be able to stand again for a week. But still stupid.

What exactly were those rules beforehand meant to achieve, other than to give him a false sense of security and permission to sleep with her? He liked Lucy—maybe too much—but she was still lying to cover for her stepfather, and had pretty much admitted she'd do anything to save Graham Boyle.

Hayden had no doubt Lucy had genuinely wanted him tonight—the need in her eyes had been a thing of beauty. But would she use what had happened between them against him to protect Boyle, if she felt she had no other choice? His gut clenched tighter. He'd like to think not, but obviously his judgment was seriously impaired when it came to her.

Even if she wasn't lying to protect her stepfather, she was ten years younger, for Pete's sake. He'd been twenty-two once, with all the fun and experimentation that entailed. But he was thirty-two now, with a son. Lucy and he were in completely different places in their lives. He winced and called himself a few more versions of idiot.

The wisest move was probably to step down from the investigation and hand it over to someone else in his company. He now had a conflict of interest. But he was so close to finding the key to this case, and a new investigator would take time to get up to speed. That time could be the difference in catching Boyle and letting him slip through a hole in the net. No, as long as he kept his distance from Lucy now and didn't let it affect his integrity as an investigator, then staying on was the best thing for the case.

Lucy stirred beside him and leaned up on one elbow, a drowsily satisfied smile on her face. "Under different circumstances—" she said, and he cut her off.

"Under different circumstances it still would have been a one-time deal." He said it as gently as he could—despite it being the truth, it wasn't the best etiquette to reject a woman right after making love to her.

Undeterred, Lucy tilted her head to the side. "I thought it went well. Granted, it might have been better had we made it to the bed, and things did get a little carried away toward the end there, but you have to admit that parts of it were glorious."

His skin shivered with the memory of how good it had been. "Lucy, all of it was glorious." He cupped the side of her face in his palm. "There wasn't a millisecond that wasn't glorious."

She laid a hand over his as he stroked her cheek, confusion in her hazel eyes. "But you wouldn't want me again if things were different."

Wouldn't want her? "Oh, sweetheart, I'd have to be dead not to want you again." He withdrew his hand, feeling the loss of her warm skin. "But my life is a mess. I'm all Josh has now—he deserves a parent who's focused on him. And any attention I have free needs to be on my business. I've let things slide a little since becoming a single father, so this investigation is important to my career. I just don't have time to experiment with relationships."

One dark blond eyebrow jumped up. "I haven't asked you for forever."

"I know." He scrubbed a hand through his hair and tried to regroup—he was making a mess of this, as well. "I'm sorry. This is my fault—I should never have let it happen."

"There were two of us on this sofa, Hayden," she said with a touch of impatience and sat up.

"But one of us thinks being sensible is overrated," he pointed out. "I thought so, too, at your age. Which is why I needed to be the one who was thinking about consequences tonight."

She stilled and her eyes turned to ice. "That won't be a problem again." She stood and began collecting her clothes.

He thumped his head back on the armrest—hard. He'd basically called her a child. Could he have created a bigger disaster of the night if he'd tried? "Lucy—"

"No, you're right," she said as she threw on her blouse, then stepped into her trousers. "We were irresponsible. It won't happen again."

She was at the door before he'd gathered enough wits—or pants—to respond. He strode across the room, still buttoning his jeans, and laid a palm on the door above her head, shutting it. She leaned her forehead against the door, her fingers still gripping the handle.

"Lucy, I've botched this." Understatement of the year, but his brain still wasn't working at full capacity after the best sex he could remember.

She didn't lift her head. "Yes."

"No, don't spare my feelings," he said wryly.

A soft, reluctant laugh floated up from where her face was hidden against the door, followed by a sigh. "What do you want me to say, Hayden? You wanted it to be a one-time deal. Well, I'm on my way out the door, with no intention of allowing a repeat. You got your wish. So why are you stopping me?"

"I want things to be right between us. I don't want you to leave now with things this screwed up." He was normally good at smoothing things over with people, at allaying their concerns. It was a skill that came in handy during investigations. Yet after crossing boundaries he'd set for himself and sleeping with Lucy Royall, he'd managed to insult her. Things had now veered outside his area of expertise. His temples throbbed. In truth, things had left his area of expertise some time ago.

He looked down at her blond head leaning against the white door and cursed himself. He liked Lucy and he'd never forgive himself if he let her walk out of here hurt.

"You said you'd help with the investigation," he said slowly. "That won't happen if you walk out that door now."

She tucked her hair behind her ears then turned to look up at him with a wobbly smile. "Things are fine between us."

Cupping her shoulders to steady them both, he peered into her eyes, seeking evidence that she was telling the truth. "You're sure?"

She shot him a rueful look. "One hundred percent."

"Prove it." He stepped back, letting her go if she

wanted, hoping like all hell she didn't. If she slipped through that door, she'd take all the warmth from the room with her.

She didn't leave, instead eyeing him warily. "How do you suppose I prove it?"

"Have a normal conversation with me. You have to give evidence to Congress tomorrow—you need to be in top form for that. We should discuss it."

"Thanks for the offer, but I'll be all right. I'll stick to the truth and we won't have any trouble," she said, repeating his words from their first meeting with a small smile.

He let out a relieved breath. "That's always a good policy."

"Will you be there?"

"At the back of the room, so you probably won't see me. I'll give you a call in the afternoon."

"Talk to you then," she said, and this time when she opened the door and slipped out, he let her go despite the pressure in his chest.

Lucy stepped into a cab and gave the driver the address of the ANS offices. She'd just finished giving evidence to the congressional hearing and was exhausted and needed a muffin, preferably chocolate chip, but Graham would be waiting to hear how it went. She sat back in the seat and leaned her head back, the questions they'd asked and her answers rolling around in her head.

One question in particular kept repeating.

"Have you heard the name Nancy Marlin?"

She'd said no, but the name kept coming back into her mind, as if there was a memory just out of reach. She closed her eyes, let out a long breath and tried to clear her mind of everything except the name.

It hovered, she could almost see it…then she plucked it from her memory. Her eyes popped open and she grabbed her cell, dialing Hayden's number on instinct.

"You did well," he said when he picked up.

She almost smiled at the warm approval in his voice but stopped herself in time—the time had come for emotional distance from Hayden Black. It should have been a priority last night—no, from day one—but it was even more important since they'd made love. Sleeping with him while she was working on Graham's exposé had been a monumental mistake. It was likely that Hayden would find the person behind the phone hacking before Graham set an air date on the exposé, but if Hayden found out in the meantime that she'd worked on it even after they made love, he'd have a right to feel betrayed. He'd find the culprit in time, she had no doubt. And in the meantime, emotional distance was the key. She set her shoulders.

"Where are you now?" she asked as she checked out the window for her own location.

"In the corridor outside Senator Tate's office."

"I've remembered something else."

His voice immediately changed, became 100-percent business. "I'll meet you at my hotel in fifteen."

She pictured his hotel room as it had been last night—strewn with their clothes, their naked bodies sprawled on the sofa. The blood in her veins began to heat. Then she remembered how she'd left and her blood went ice-cold. Maybe she shouldn't have called him now.

"Lucy?"

No, she'd done the right thing to call. Hayden was the investigator for Congress—the exact person she should tell. They just had to meet somewhere private that wasn't his hotel.

"My place has muffins, let's meet there," she said.

"My hotel. I'll pick up muffins on the way," he said and disconnected.

When Hayden arrived at his suite, Lucy was already there, looking as she had on the screen when he'd watched her give evidence—conservative mint-green dress, her hair scraped back and pinned at the nape of her neck. And now, as then when he'd seen her, his pulse galloped along like a wild horse with no intention of being tamed.

He tossed her a paper bag that was fragrant with the scent of freshly baked muffins, and unlocked the door. "As promised."

"You're a prince among men, Hayden Black."

He threw his keys and wallet on a side table and turned to find her already making headway with the first muffin. She seemed comfortable enough given the nature of their meeting, and it filled him with relief. After the way things had ended last night, he'd feared she might not return his calls, or agree to see him with anything short of a subpoena. But thankfully things appeared to be okay between them, if a little awkward. Now all he had to do was not cross any lines with her again. Never let his guard down.

He grabbed his notebook and sat at the desk. "First, tell me you didn't remember this when you were in front of Congress and keep it from them."

"No, in the cab afterward," she said, taking the other chair at the desk. "But it was their question that made me remember."

"Which question?"

"They asked if I'd heard of Nancy Marlin."

"And you said no." He'd been taking notes through all the hearings, but he didn't need to check the notes from Lucy's testimony—he remembered every word.

She nodded, she was practically vibrating with restless energy. "But the name bugged me and I remembered in the cab on the way back to work. I overheard a conversation months ago where the name came up."

"Who was talking?"

"Marnie Salloway and Angelica Pierce."

The wheels in his mind began to turn. This could be the piece of the puzzle that made all the others fit together.

"Who is Nancy Marlin?" she asked.

"A friend of Barbara Jessup." When the president was young, his family had employed Barbara Jessup as a maid—the list of questions for the hearing had included random names of people connected to the president, even by two or three degrees of separation. There was only one reason journalists could have to be talking about a maid's friend.

Lucy's eyes widened. "This is it."

Part of him agreed with her—this *could* be it—but he didn't want to count his chickens and jinx it. He drew in a measured breath. "Do they know you overheard them?"

"I doubt it. I was in the supply closet and they stopped just outside the door. Once I had what I wanted, I waited for them to finish—with Marnie and Angelica, keeping a low profile is essential to survival."

Having met Angelica, he understood. "I want you to repeat word for word what they said."

"At first they were complaining about one of the other producers, then Angelica asked, 'Is there any progress with Nancy Marlin?' Marnie said, 'Not yet, but we're still trying.' And Angelica said, 'Keep me up to date.' After that, they went their separate ways and I sneaked out and back to my desk."

A buzz of excitement was growing in his blood. He'd finally found it. "They're both involved," he said, staring down at the conversation he'd just copied onto paper. "They've hacked into Barbara Jessup's phones."

"Do you want to tell Congress to call me back?"

"We might have to, but I'll try with Ames and Hall first. One overheard conversation isn't much to go on, but if I can get them to give Marnie and Angelica up, they might be able to give me more evidence so the charges will stick."

She put the remains of her second muffin back in the bag and brushed the crumbs from her fingers. "Wouldn't they have given them up already if they were going to?"

"If they think we're onto Marnie and Angelica anyway and it's only a matter of time before we gather enough evidence, then they might try to negotiate with whatever they have on them. I can also interview Marnie and Angelica again, telling them that this conversation was overheard. It might be enough for one of them to panic or slip up."

With a restless move of her shoulders, she glanced out his window. "I wish I'd remembered earlier."

"Remembering at all is great." Gently, he turned her back to face him. "I'll try and keep your name out of it if I can."

Her eyes flashed fire. "Our ground rules said we wouldn't let our involvement interfere with the investigation. Don't try to protect me."

"I'd do what I could to protect any witness. If I can get stronger evidence, then we won't need yours and there's no point putting you in the line of fire. If we need you, don't worry," he said, cupping the side of her face, "I'll put you back before Congress without blinking."

As he'd hoped, his words had coaxed a reluctant smile from her.

"As long as you had more of these muffins, I'd be okay." Her smile faded and she picked up her red hold-all bag. "I have to get back to the office. Graham's waiting to hear how it went."

He handed her the leftover muffins. "Are you going to tell him about Marnie and Angelica?"

"I'll have to. They're his employees," she said, her gaze on the paper bag she'd accepted from him.

The cynical part of his brain was still sure she was covering for her stepfather. Graham Boyle was at the top of this chain of deceit, Hayden had no doubt. What he wasn't sure about was whether Lucy's willingness to help with the investigation was part of her plan to ensure she was on the scene once he found the evidence on Graham. Perhaps she even hoped to influence him into discarding that evidence.

He hated thinking that way, wished he could just be open with her, but he had to be realistic. Her information had been invaluable so far, but she was an employee of ANS and Graham Boyle's stepdaughter. Her loyalty would always be with him. Hayden understood that. Didn't mean he couldn't protect his investigation where he could.

"Don't tell him yet. Come back tonight after work and we'll make a plan for interviewing Marnie and Angelica again. I'll see what I can do with Ames and Hall in the meantime. Tell Boyle when we know more."

She bit down on her lip as her gaze swept the room, probably remembering the last time she had been in this room at night, and he thought she was going to say no. His gut clenched. Then she said, "Okay, tonight," and everything inside him leaped as much as it had when they'd made the breakthrough on the case just moments earlier. He cursed under his breath. Seemed working on Ames and Hall wasn't the only work he needed to do today—he also needed to shut his body into lockdown before Lucy knocked on his door again.

* * *

When he opened the door to Lucy that evening, there was an awful formality between them. Only his son seemed to make her relax. Josh squealed from his place on the lounge and reached his arms out, and Hayden felt a stab of envy—he wanted to hold his arms out to Lucy, too.

As he watched her with Josh—both of them talking and laughing—he couldn't tear his gaze away.

Then Hayden's cell rang and he was almost relieved by the distraction. When he picked it up, the number that flashed on the screen was unfamiliar.

"Hayden Black," he said.

"Mr. Black, this is Rowena Tate. I'm Senator Tate's daughter."

The senator had mentioned today that his daughter was in town, but Hayden hadn't met her, so the call was something of a surprise. "Good evening, Ms. Tate."

"I've been following the congressional committee's investigation," Rowena said. "As you know, my fiancé has an interest in the proceedings."

The senator had also mentioned Rowena's engagement to Colin Middlebury, a British diplomat who'd worked with Senator Tate to have Congress ratify a privacy treaty, and had helped the senator form the committee looking into the phone hacking in the first place.

"What can I do for you?" he asked as he tracked Lucy's progress across to his kitchenette to get a glass of water, Josh on her hip.

"I have a suspicion about one of the key players at ANS that you might be interested in."

His attention snapped back to the phone in his hand. "I'm listening."

"Any chance you can meet me tonight at the airport? I'm flying back to L.A. in a couple of hours."

"Tonight?" he repeated, wrapping a hand around the back of his neck. It was almost Josh's bedtime and he hated the idea of dragging a sleepy boy out in the dark of night. "Tonight might be difficult."

Lucy moved into his field of vision. "If you have to go out," she whispered, "I can stay with Josh."

"Hang on a minute, Rowena," he said, not taking his gaze from Lucy. Then he put his hand over the receiver. "I can't ask you to do that."

"Is it about the investigation?"

"Yes."

"I'm helping you with the investigation," she said, sweeping an arm toward the piles of documents they'd been sorting through. "Staying with Josh is simply part of that."

"But it's his bedtime in about an hour."

"He's had dinner, hasn't he?"

"Yes," he said, running a finger around the inside collar of his shirt, "but—"

"I'll handle the rest. I've helped out at my charity enough to handle one bedtime. You can show me where things are before you go. We'll be fine."

He glanced down at his son—who was gazing adoringly at Lucy—wondering if a good father would leave his son with someone else this way. His gaze flicked back to Lucy. He might not trust her about Graham, but he trusted her implicitly with his son. "Are you sure?"

"One hundred percent." She nodded decisively. "Go."

"Thanks," he said, then removed his hand from the phone to speak to Rowena. "I'll be there."

Six

Hayden scanned the crowd in the airport terminal until he caught sight of Colin Middlebury in a café. He headed over and held out his hand. Colin and the woman at his side pushed their chairs back and stood.

"Thanks for coming, Black," Colin said, shaking Hayden's extended hand.

"Good to see you again, Middlebury." He'd met the British diplomat when he'd first taken on this job, but hadn't met Rowena before.

"This is my fiancée, Rowena Tate." Colin put an arm around Rowena's shoulders and beamed at her.

The willowy blonde smiled first at the man beside her, then across at Hayden. "Thanks for coming on such short notice."

"It's no problem," Hayden said, trying not to think about Lucy looking luscious on the sofa back at his hotel suite.

Colin indicated a third chair at their table, and they all sat, both men turning to Rowena and waiting.

"We won't take much of your time, Mr. Black. I asked you to come because I didn't want to discuss this over the phone, given the nature of the investigation."

"Sensible." He knew his cell was safe from hacking, but he couldn't be sure about anyone else's. He glanced around—no one was sitting close enough to overhear. "So what's your suspicion?"

"It has to do with Angelica Pierce." She leaned closer over the table, and lowered her voice. "She's always seemed oddly familiar, but I saw her on the TV reporting a story and the camera caught her at an unusual angle, just off to the side. And I was suddenly struck by her similarity to a girl I went to boarding school with, Madeline Burch. Different-colored hair and eyes, and, if it's her, she's had a nose job and some other work. While she was still on the screen, I called a friend who went to Woodlawn Academy with us, and she thinks it could be Madeline, too."

Interest piqued, Hayden took a small notebook out of his shirt pocket and wrote the name Madeleine Burch. "Any reason a reporter changing her name to something more appealing is suspicious?"

"Madeline was…*unbalanced* is probably the best word. Always bragging that her father was someone big, but she never said who. Apparently he'd paid her mother some hush money so they couldn't mention his name. And if anyone challenged her on it, she'd lose it."

"Define *lose it,*" he said, suddenly very interested.

"One time she'd had argument with another girl. I can't remember what it was over. And that night when we went back to our rooms, the other girl's clothes were all over the floor, cut into pieces."

He arched an eyebrow. "Anything done about it?"

"They had no evidence." Rowena shrugged one shoulder in a gesture of helpless frustration. "Madeline told the teachers she saw a younger girl sneak into the dorm room, which was a lie. That girl wouldn't have hurt a mouse."

He rubbed his chin as he considered the woman before him. Rowena was showing no signs of lying—she seemed confident and open. On the current evidence, he was inclined to believe her.

"Was that an isolated incident?" he asked, taking notes on what she'd said so far.

"Unfortunately, no. She was unpredictable and vindictive. And even though we always knew it was her, she'd try to blame her crimes on someone else. Even conning younger girls to confess a couple of times. We pretty much gave her a wide berth whenever we could. Until the day she was arguing with another student about her 'secret father' and the other student called her a liar and a freak. Madeline attacked the girl and was finally expelled."

His pulse picked up speed as bits of information fitted together like interlocking puzzle pieces. "Did you see her again?"

She shook her head. "When all this came up recently, my friend Cara Summers and I searched the internet and couldn't find a trace of Madeline after she was expelled. And, oddly enough, Angelica Pierce doesn't have much of a trail before then. I'm not sure if it will help, but I decided it was better to tell you than not."

He nodded at the couple, his poker face in place despite the way his mind was racing. "I'm glad you did."

Rowena handed over an envelope. "These are the results of our research, such as it is. Mainly basic information, and we suspect that much of it is falsified. I'm sure you have other channels to go deeper. But there is one photo of Madeline that Cara managed to track down from another old school friend." Hayden thanked both Rowena and Colin, said goodbye and made his way out through the airport. If Angelica was Madeline Burch, she could have set up Troy Hall and Brandon Ames to carry out the plan then take the fall—that would fit the pattern of Madeline's school days. His blood pumped faster as his investigator's senses twitched. Something about this felt *right.*

Variations of possible scenarios played out in his mind on the trip back to the hotel and, as he used his key card to open the door, he was still buzzing with the new directions his investigation could take. This was a lead that could break the case wide open and point the way to solid answers.

Everything in the suite was silent, so he quietly walked behind the sofas to peek into Josh's room. His little boy was sleeping peacefully. Relieved, Hayden smiled as he shut the door. He'd have to thank Lucy later—

Then he saw her curled up asleep on the sofa and his breath stilled. Despite the temperature-controlled room, his skin heated.

She was so achingly beautiful, with her blond hair falling over the creamy curve of her cheek. Memories of touching her bare skin assaulted his senses, of the fragrance of her hair, the shape of her hip. Of her fingers touching him, feather-soft at first, then urgently when she needed him. Without realizing he'd moved, he was beside her, crouching down, close enough to feel her breath fan gently over his face.

His heart frantically battered at his rib cage, and a distant part of his brain screamed to move away before she woke, but he didn't pull back. Couldn't. He swallowed hard. Her skin was porcelain smooth, her lips slightly parted as she dreamed. Would he be in those dreams? She'd certainly been in his.

He leaned forward just a few inches and kissed her lightly. Sweet torture. His eyes drifted closed. He'd pull back any second now. He would. Just as soon as he committed this moment to memory.

With the softest of moans, Lucy moved her lips languorously under his and her eyes fluttered open. Now was the time to move away, *now,* but she smiled against his mouth and threaded her fingers through his hair and he couldn't summon the will to allow any space between them.

"Hayden," she murmured, then kissed him again. As she lifted herself up on an elbow, he slid an arm around her, dragging her against his chest, silently cursing the fabric between them. He was lost, drowning in her. The musky scent of warm skin surrounded him, curled through his mind, luring him to the edge of sanity, to a place where the reasons this was wrong didn't exist.

Yet a tendril of awareness remained, a slow-blinking warning light in the peripheries of his mind. He tried to push it away, to give himself over completely to the lushness of the woman in his arms, but deep down he knew…

Thrusting a hand up to cradle the back of her head, he kissed her one more time, a kiss tinged with desperation, before wrenching his mouth away and sitting back on his heels.

"Lucy," he said, his voice barely audible through a tight jaw. "I'm at breaking point." He dropped his forehead to rest on hers, holding her more tightly. "I want you—I can't tell you how much I want you—but making love again would be wrong on so many levels."

She pulled back and moistened her lips, unknowingly daring him to throw caution to the wind again. She blinked up at him, as if she was only now truly waking up, then she relaxed and smiled sleepily. "It'll be fine. Come down here. After last time I know there's enough room for two."

Frustration clawing through his veins, he speared the fingers of both hands through his hair, then tangled them together behind his head. "There's nothing I want more in this moment, but you know we can't."

She pushed herself up to a sitting position and rubbed her eyes. The movement just made him want to draw her into his arms even more, so he forced himself to go over to the other sofa, creating something of a safety barrier. Though if her pink tongue peeked out and wet her lips one more damn time, that distance would provide no obstacle at all.

She tucked her legs up beneath her and nodded. "Okay. Let me make a proposal."

"Sure," he said. It would need to involve a suit of body armor for one of them if it had any chance of effectiveness. Or perhaps separate cities.

"Here's how things stand." She held up a closed hand, ticking the points off by raising a finger for each one as she went. "We have some undeniable chemistry. You're only in D.C. for a short time. You don't have space in your life for a relationship. Your work won't allow for a relationship with me in particular."

He winced. Said aloud like that, their situation sounded even more hopeless than it did in his head. But he nodded slowly, prepared to hear her out. "I'm with you so far."

"Then we'll have a secret fling," she said, smiling, seeming pleased with herself.

Everything inside him tightened, ready to accept her offer, but he frowned. "What is that? Just sleeping together?"

"Purely physical," she confirmed. "Completely under the radar."

Was she serious? His body might already be on board, but the idea was insane. However, Lucy didn't seem to be joking. "The investigation—"

"We're both already compromised—this will hardly make it worse. Tell me," she said, tucking strands of blond hair behind her ear, "has sleeping with me convinced you of Graham's innocence?"

"No." Graham was guilty, he had no doubt, and nothing but irrefutable evidence to the contrary would change his mind about that.

She tilted her head in acknowledgment of his point. "Are you at all likely to alter your findings because of our intimacy?"

"Not a chance." It was inconceivable that he'd ever alter his findings. Integrity was everything in this business, to say nothing of his own sense of right and wrong.

"Then we're good," she said and nodded. "We can have a fling."

"A fling," he repeated. He really didn't have enough blood in his brain for this conversation. It had all headed south at the first touch of her lips, and now he was struggling to follow Lucy's reasoning.

"It solves everything. It's a great plan," she said, holding upturned palms out as if this was obvious.

He stood and stalked to the window, hoping the movement and view of nighttime D.C. would bring clarity. It didn't.

"You're okay with this?" he finally said. "A purely physical arrangement." He might want her more than he wanted any woman, but he wouldn't use her. It went against everything inside him.

Her blond brows drew together and she glanced down at her hands, as if deciding how much to confide. "I don't want anything serious right now. You say that your focus is on your son and your business—well, my focus is on my career." She paused and the skin around her eyes pulled taut. "Because of who my father and stepfather are, I have to work twice as hard as anyone else to prove my independence, prove myself. And to be honest, after the work I've already put in, the last thing I need is a relationship with a rich older man who has a high profile and connections."

He drew in a long breath, suddenly struck by her meaning. He'd been worried about his reasons for not getting involved, but hadn't thought about it from her side before. She had as much to lose as he did. Yet she still wanted him enough to propose this plan.

He crossed to the sofa she was perched on and sat on the armrest, taking her hands in his. "We'll have an affair with an end date of when I leave town, both of us going in with our eyes open." He managed to keep his voice even, but his entire body was straining forward at the thought.

"So you want to?" she asked, her voice surprisingly uncertain.

"Lucy, I want to more than I can say. But I have conditions." He released her hands and stood again before he consigned his own conditions to hell and took her there on the sofa. "First, we keep the rule we already made about secrecy. No one can know we're doing this. And the rule about us not letting our involvement influence us."

"Done," she said simply.

An electric shiver raced down his spine. This was really going to happen. He cleared his throat before continuing. "Also, no making love here in my suite. It's the center of my investigation, I keep research here and I meet people here. We only sleep together at your place, and only during the day when Josh is with his nanny. The geographical distinction will keep a firm boundary in our minds so we don't compromise the investigation."

"Makes sense," she said, her face serious but voice breathless. "I'm good with that one."

He knelt down in front of her, wanting there to be no misunderstandings on the next point. "And if it becomes awkward or too much for you, promise me you'll say so."

Nodding, she laid her hands on either side of his face. "I'll promise, if you will."

"Sure," he said, barely able to form the word when she was so close and touching him.

"I can work from home tomorrow."

Blood sparking as if it carried an electric current, he mentally ran through his schedule. "I don't have any appointments in the morning. I'll be over at nine-thirty." She moistened her lips and he groaned. "Though if you don't leave this second, we'll start right this minute."

With a look of mischief, she grabbed her bag and practically scurried out the door, and Hayden was left alone and wondering how he'd make it till nine-thirty.

At ten past nine, Hayden answered a knock at his hotel-suite door. The only appointment he had this morning was to see Lucy in twenty minutes…to begin their fling. His skin heated. He'd been dressed and ready for the day—for Lucy—since eight. The nanny had come for Josh at nine, and for ten minutes Hayden had been restlessly shuffling papers, willing the hands on his watch to move faster.

When he pulled the door open, Angelica Pierce stood there in a figure-hugging red dress, pulling her Botoxed lips into a plastic smile. "Hayden, darling," she said brightly.

"Good morning, Angelica." His training came to his aid, allowing him to smile and be pleasant without betraying either his annoyance at being delayed from seeing Lucy or his increased suspicions about Angelica after meeting Rowena last night. "Did we have an appointment?"

"No, no," she said as she brushed past him and into the room. "I was in the area and I thought I'd touch base. See if there's anything I can do to help."

"You want to help?" he asked mildly, digging his hands into his pockets.

"Of course I do! These awful crimes tar all journalists with the same brush in the public's mind. The sooner it's all cleared up, the better for news broadcasters everywhere." She sat on the sofa and patted the cushion beside her. "Come and sit next to me, Hayden, so we can talk about it."

The sight of Angelica on the sofa where he'd kissed Lucy less than twelve hours ago was jarring. "I'm sorry, but I need to leave for a meeting."

"Oh, *darling,* I think you'll make time for me." She stretched her neck to one side and lowered her shoulder, and the sleeve of her blouse fell down her arm, revealing a perfectly tan shoulder, unencumbered by a bra strap.

Despite his urge to throw her out, Hayden regarded her pose analytically. It was a clear invitation, and from what he knew of Angelica already, if he handled this badly she might overreact. And if she did, that might make her slip up and reveal something...

"Angelica," he said, finding a polite but firm tone. "I really do have to leave."

She pushed herself up from the sofa and slinked over to his side, standing too close. His skin crawled. When he stepped away to create a little distance, she followed.

"Hayden, let's not waste words." Her smile was part sex kitten, part great white shark. "I know you're interested in me, and I'm attracted to you, too."

"Angelica," he said bluntly, crossing his arms over his chest. "It's not going to happen. Not now, not ever."

There was silence for a long beat. Then, as if a switch had been flicked, she roughly grabbed her sleeve and tugged it up, her aqua eyes sparking with rage.

"This is because of *her,* isn't it?" A finger with a fire-engine-red nail jabbed the air in the direction of the door.

Hayden stilled. "Who?"

"Lucy Royall," she spat with more venom than a rattlesnake. "She was all you wanted to talk about the other day. You have a little crush on her, don't you?"

A trickle of unease seeped down his spine. He'd thought she'd turn her anger on him, not Lucy. Had he put Lucy in the line of fire?

Angelica must have seen something on his face that gave him away, because she smiled, satisfied.

"Don't worry, darling, all the men do. It's the princess act she's perfected. But let me give you a friendly word of advice." She paused, a devilish gleam in her eyes. "Your little crush is doing an investigation into you. Gathering material for an exposé that will air soon on ANS. I heard it directly from Graham Boyle last night."

An icy hand crept over his heart and squeezed. Lucy had played him? Was working on an exposé when she'd told him she wanted to help his own investigation? No, he refused to believe she could be that manipulative. Although…how well did he really know her? Nausea roiled in his stomach, leaving a bitter taste in his mouth. Maybe she was capable of planning this. And, if so, was her idea of a *fling* all part of the scheme?

Whatever was going on, he wasn't sharing a thing with the woman in front of him. "I think it's time you left, Angelica," he said and strode over to the door.

"Sure." She'd morphed again—this time into a sincere

confidante. "When you're ready to talk, let me know. I'm the one who can help you, remember that. And in the meantime," she said, slinging her bag over her shoulder and heading out the door, "don't give that Royall actress anything you don't want to see on prime-time news."

Three minutes later, Hayden was in the rental car on his way to Lucy's place. This morning's visit might have been planned as a romantic liaison, but now they'd use the time for Lucy to give him some information. The truth would be a good place to start.

Seven

It was almost ten o'clock when Lucy saw Hayden's car pull up. With butterflies in her belly, she looked down at her soft cream wraparound dress—easy to remove—which covered lacy lavender lingerie. The ensemble had seemed appropriate for the start of a fling, though she'd changed outfits twice already, and had been having second thoughts about this one for about ten minutes. If he hadn't arrived now, she would have darted back upstairs and changed again.

Pulse jittery, she opened the door to him. "You're late, Mr. Black," she said in her best saucy voice, then registered his thunderous expression. Her heart skipped a beat. "What's wrong?"

He pushed past her, strode into her living room, then turned to face her with hands low on his hips. "You're doing an exposé on me?"

All the air rushed from her lungs. "How do you know?" she asked in a raspy whisper.

"Rules about secrecy, rules about a fling." His coffee-brown eyes flashed fire. "One we forgot to add was a rule about not gathering material for an exposé while we were *sleeping* together."

Her knees wobbled, but she stepped forward. "Hayden—"

Ignoring her attempt to explain, he walked across the room and leaned a hand over the window frame, looking down on the small courtyard at the back. "At least I was up-front about my investigation. You knew what I was doing from the start, and I told you I suspected Graham and that you were covering for him." He swiveled to face her again, eyes narrowed. "Apparently I don't deserve the same courtesy."

"Okay, you're angry," she said, slowly crossing the room toward him. "I get that. And I'll allow that you have a right to be."

He coughed out an incredulous laugh. "Generous of you."

"But your investigation could ruin a man's life. An innocent man." Her stepfather, who'd been nothing but kind and generous to her for ten years. "Graham could lose his company, his reputation, even his freedom. And there are people in ANS who would set him up to ensure that happens. You don't think we'd have a plan B in this situation?"

"That Boyle and ANS would have a plan? Sure. That you'd be leading it?" He ran a hand through his hair, his gaze pinning her to the spot. "It's a rotten way to treat a man you're sleeping with, Lucy."

"You're right. I'm sorry." She sank down into the overstuffed sofa and pulled a cushion into her lap, suddenly bone-weary from all the different directions she was being pulled. "But you have to understand that when Graham asked me to do the piece, I'd only met you once. I didn't know if I could trust you."

He held up a hand. "Do you trust me now?"

"Yes." She sighed. "I'm not sure when that happened, but I do."

"So why not tell me yesterday? Last week? After we slept together?"

It was a fair question, one she'd been asking herself. "I guess I was hoping you'd uncover the ringleader of the phone hacking and your investigation would be over before the exposé was ever needed."

"And what if the timing didn't work like that, if I took longer?" He paced across the room, then turned on a heel to face her again. "Were you going to tell me before the show aired? Or let me find out along with everyone else?"

"I would have warned you, I swear. And for what it's worth, I'm sorry, Hayden. But put yourself in my shoes for a moment. My boss—my stepfather, a man I love—tells me to work on a secret project that could save him. I only met you a few weeks ago. Are you saying I should just switch my loyalties like changing socks?"

He winced as the point hit home. "You were stuck between your family and your lover."

Her shoulders dropped a fraction of an inch. "This thing between us is crossing boundaries left and right, isn't it?"

Hayden blew out a breath, seeming to deflate somewhat, and came over to sit on the coffee table in front of her, their knees brushing. "Yeah, it is. I've been thinking I should hand the case to someone else in the company."

"No," she said, grabbing his hands. "Please don't."

He tilted his head to the side. "But I think Graham is guilty. It could be better for you to try your luck with someone else."

"You might think he's guilty, but you're honest and honorable. As soon as we find the evidence that exonerates Graham, you'll respect that. You're our best hope, Hayden." Every word she'd said was true, but there was something else, something even stronger pulling at her insides, demanding she not let him go. Not yet. *Please, not yet.*

He looked at her for a long moment and she held her breath, waiting for his decision. Finally, he nodded once and relief flooded her veins. Even as she smiled her gratitude and released the tight grip she had on his hands, somewhere in the back of her mind was a niggling voice saying her reaction was too strong for simply having an investigator stay on the case, but she brushed it aside.

Hayden rubbed a palm over his closely shaved jaw. "You said before that people in ANS are setting him up. Why would you think that?"

This was better—stick to the investigation and Graham. Safer. She rose and padded on bare feet across the carpets to the kitchen, filled two glasses with sparkling water and handed one to Hayden. When she saw him leaning against the island counter, her mouth dried. His dark, masculine beauty was emphasized by the pale marble countertops and white cupboards. She didn't tend to have people at her place very often—she usually met friends out—so Graham was the only person who'd spent much time in her kitchen. Maybe if she'd had more men here, she wouldn't feel so overwhelmed by Hayden's presence. He wouldn't seem to dominate it so much. But she doubted it—that was Hayden's effect wherever he was.

She took a sip of the sparkling water to moisten her throat so she could speak. "You said yourself that someone was pulling the strings. Whoever that is, they don't plan on going down for this. Passing the buck up the ladder is the perfect alibi." She took another sip, thinking back over the clues they had, then stilled. "Who told you about the exposé?"

"Angelica," he said, distaste clear in his voice. "She just came to my room, tried to seduce me then gave me a friendly warning not to trust you."

Lucy's heart skipped a beat at the *tried to seduce me* comment, but she managed not to let her personal reaction affect her professional interest in the development. "It's Angelica behind this whole thing. I know it is."

"I think you're probably right." He put his empty glass in the sink, then leaned back against the counter again.

I think you're probably right? Had he seen the truth? "So you think Graham is innocent."

"No," he said, shaking his head. "He still must have known what was going on, perhaps worked with her on it, but I suspect Angelica masterminded it."

She crossed her arms under her breasts. "You'll see about Graham. By the end of the investigation, we'll have the evidence that he's innocent." Graham's nature was to push as far as he could go, but once he hit the edge of legality, he'd stop. He wasn't the first man to believe in an employee who turned out to be bad.

"Listen," he said taking her hand and interlacing their fingers. "Something else about Angelica's announcement bothered me."

"The attempted-seduction part?" She grinned, inordinately pleased at the thought of Hayden rebuffing another woman's advances.

He shook his head as if that was inconsequential. "No, that was easy to fend off. It was the venom she has for you. She didn't even try to hide it."

"She's always hated me." Lucy shrugged. It was something she'd accepted within a week of joining ANS. Angelica treated everyone below her badly and seemed to take special pleasure in targeting the boss's stepdaughter. She wasn't the only one—Marnie and Mitch had been the same way. Par for the course with a last name like Royall and a stepfather who owned the network.

Hayden tugged her closer with their joined hands. "This was something beyond hate. Way beyond."

His gaze was intent, and this wasn't a man who spooked easily. She swallowed. "Oh."

"Why would she hate you specifically?" He traced a pattern over her hands with his thumbs. "You've never had a run-in?"

"I don't know. I always thought it was because I was the stepdaughter of the network's owner. They resent having me in their workspace."

"Could be. But why is she more vindictive than the others? And if she's capable of manipulating at least two people in a complicated scheme of illegal phone hacking—and having them cover for her even after their arrests—then she's not a person to underestimate."

"She wouldn't do anything to me," Lucy said, but even to her own ears her voice sounded unconvinced.

"Lucy, this is my area of expertise. Angelica Pierce would hurt you if she got the chance. I want you to stay close to me, where I can protect you. Tell ANS that you need to stick near me while you're working on the damn exposé."

Something inside her chilled. Angelica would hurt her if she had the chance? What sort of person operated that way? She'd known about Angelica's complete lack of ethics in her reporting and information gathering, but this was something else altogether….

She withdrew her hands from Hayden's clasp and wrapped them around her waist. Journalism had once seemed a shining light of truth-seeking and integrity. Seeing the tape of Troy Hall and Brandon Ames hiring hackers to illegally invade people's privacy hadn't affected her too much, because she'd figured the pair were rogue elements. But Angelica Pierce was a star reporter, and even though Lucy had known she was nasty, before she'd worked at ANS she'd idolized Angelica's reporting. What was the saying about never meeting your idols…?

She lifted her chin. One thing was for sure—Angelica wouldn't get the better of her. "I'm not a child in need of protection. I'll be fine."

"Believe me, I know you're not a child." He ran his fingers down her arm and then drew her against him. "Let me protect you," he murmured in her ear.

At every point of contact, her skin heated until champagne sparkles fizzed through her bloodstream. But she tried not to lose herself in her body's reaction to him.

"It's not your job," she said against the cotton shirt covering his chest.

He smoothed fingertips down her sides till he reached the curve of her hips and drew her even closer. "I want to protect you. I want you safe."

She winced. The last thing she needed in her older lover was for him to think of her as a damsel who needed rescuing—couldn't he see that?

Laying her palms flat on his chest, she eased away so she could see his eyes, so he could understand this was important to her. "Hayden, I don't want you to see me as someone you need to look after."

His gaze softened, then blazed. "There are many things I see in you. Your courage and determination. Your lush curves. That someone who's possibly crazy has it in for you. That I can't stop thinking about making love to you again. That—"

"Stop there." She moistened her lips. "Go back to that one."

"That someone who's possibly crazy has it in for you?" he drawled with a knowing smile.

She shimmied against him. "The one after that."

He lifted her hand to his lips and kissed one fingertip after the other. "I can't stop thinking about making love to you again?"

Her breath caught high in her throat. "That's the one. Tell me more about that."

"There are the waking thoughts and the dreams at night," he said, turning them so she was trapped between his solid body and the counter behind her.

"Start with the dreams."

He gave her a slow, sensual smile full of promise. "In my favorite one, I was in bed at home in New York, and you slipped through the door and climbed under the covers with me."

She shivered as the image formed in her mind. "What was I wearing in this dream?"

"Nothing." His voice dropped to a seductive whisper. "That's why it's one of my favorites."

Her eyes drifted closed and a dull throb pulsated at her core. "What happened once I was under the covers with you?"

His freshly shaved jaw scraped over her cheek as he pressed his lips to her ear. "I spent the rest of the night making sure you had a good time."

Her heart skipped a beat. "And did I?"

"Oh, yes," he said, teeth nipping at the side of her throat. "You were very enthusiastic in your appreciation. When I woke, I was surprised you weren't still there."

Such a simple fantasy, but it aroused her to the tips of

her tingling toes—thinking about what they'd done, but also just that Hayden Black had dreamed about her.

She wound her arms around his neck. "Sounds like a dream that was meant to come true."

"I'm working on it." He glanced around. "You got a bedroom in this place?"

"Down the hall. Tell me about the waking thoughts," she said, and bit down on her lip.

He swung her up into his arms and headed out of the room. "They mainly center on regrets."

"Regrets?" She placed a hand on the side of his face, bringing his gaze back to her as he carried her along the hall. "About making love to me?"

"Yep. I've got a list." He indicated the open door to her bedroom with a tilt of his head and she nodded.

"Such as?"

"It happened too fast," he murmured in her ear, his mouth hot. "I didn't get to do some things I wanted."

He eased her down on the pale blue coverlet, then climbed onto the bed, prowling over her, filling her vision. "To taste the skin just where your diamond pendant hides." Slowly, he undid the tie holding her wraparound dress together and pulled it open. She held her breath as one hand firmly cupped the lavender lace he'd uncovered and his head dipped to the hollow between her breasts. The heat of his mouth and tongue sent a shower of sparks through her bloodstream, and when his teeth gently bit at the slope of her breast she arched up, offering more, wanting more.

When he lifted his head, his eyes were as dark as night, and filled with banked desire. "Or to feel the satin smoothness of your inner thigh," he said as a hand snaked down her body and drew one knee up. He kissed a trail down her belly, around her hip, to her leg and up to her raised knee while his fingertips traced circles on her inner thigh near the edge of her panties.

"I didn't get to linger in places I wanted to." His tongue joined his fingers and she came close to dissolving on the spot. "I'm a man who hates having regrets, so if it's all the same to you, I'll be rectifying the situation right now."

"Be my guest," she said breathlessly.

For what seemed like hours, Hayden drove her slowly out of her mind, bringing her close to the edge then ruthlessly turning his attention to yet another sweet zone, removing pieces of clothing as he went. All the while, she explored the ridges of his abdomen, the powerful muscles of his shoulders and arms, the rough hair covering his thighs, every part of him she could reach, peeling his clothes away until there were no barriers between their skin except the protection. They didn't have forever, she knew that, but for now he belonged to her. Today and for a few days she laid claim to his body; here in her bed, his attention was focused on her. And there wasn't another place in the world she'd rather be in this moment. Maybe there never would be again.

Hayden paused, looking deep into her eyes, then his lips came down to meet hers, all his passion and hunger coalescing into one perfect kiss. She practically floated off the bed, but Hayden's weight pressing down on her kept her anchored.

"Lucy," he rasped when he broke away. "I've never wanted anyone this much." He shook his head, as if having trouble believing it himself. *"Anyone."*

He lifted her knee and, without losing eye contact, entered her. Air hissed out from between his clenched teeth, and, unable to restrain herself, she called his name. His eyes flared and he began to move, slowly at first, then faster. She arched her back, wanting everything he could give her, wishing this could last forever, needing him more than she'd thought possible. When she reached the edge, he captured her mouth, pushing her right over the brink, not slowing, keeping her soaring high, then followed, her name wrenched from his throat. As she drifted back to earth, Hayden eased up, then pulled her along the length of his body. She'd never felt as safe, as cherished. Never felt as much herself. Would anything—any man—be enough again?

Later that afternoon, Lucy sat in Graham's office, a large lump of panting bulldog at her feet. She fingered the framed photo still sitting in a box on her lap, surrounded by tissue paper—her fifteen-year-old self, standing between Graham and her mother, beamed up at her. Her stepfather had arranged for it to be reproduced and framed and had given it to her when she'd walked in a few minutes ago.

"Thank you for this," she said through a ball of emotion in her throat.

"I know you still miss her." His voice sounded a little affected, as well.

She touched a fingertip to her mother's face in the photo. "I do." Graham gave her presents regularly, but this one was priceless.

"So how's the research for the exposé going?" he asked as he leaned back in his chair, changing the subject as he always did once it became too emotional. "We almost ready to start production?"

She tucked her hair behind her ears in an effort to stop a guilty blush from creeping up her cheeks. "Not so much."

"You haven't found anything?" Deep frown lines appeared across his forehead.

A barrage of images filled her mind of all the things she

had found out about Hayden Black—the ridges of muscle that crossed his abdomen, the way the dark hairs covering his chest felt against her cheek, the expression on his face when he found release inside her….

She picked at a spot of lint on her skirt, then shrugged a shoulder. "There don't seem to be any skeletons in his closet. He's a good man, a newly single parent and straight up and down in his job." Her research had found evidence of minor issues, such as an uncomfortable relationship with his deceased wife's parents, and some hard partying when he was a student, but nothing that would fill an exposé. It wasn't even worth mentioning now.

Graham waved her assessment away with a sharp slashing motion. "There must be something you can find."

"Actually, I've hit a slight snag." She rubbed Rosie's chest with the toe of her shoe as she formed the question she needed to ask. "How far do you trust Angelica Pierce?"

Graham didn't hesitate. "Good journalist. Solid instincts."

"She told Hayden that I was doing an exposé on him."

His eyes widened. "Damn."

"I thought you didn't trust anyone else to know that plan." That was the part that had surprised her the most about the whole situation.

"She came to me last night, worried about what damage Black's investigation might do to the network. I told her we had it covered. I was going to use her to front the piece, so she would have found out soon enough anyway." He picked up a pen and began tapping a furious beat on his desk. "She went straight to Black?"

Straight to him with the information, plus a bonus attempted seduction. "She dropped in on him this morning."

"She must've thought she could use it to get some leverage. Get him to back off, or give up his sources."

Lucy bit down on her lip, amazed he was already explaining away Angelica's actions. Making excuses for her. Couldn't he see what was under his nose?

"Until this is over," she said carefully, "I don't think you should trust her."

"Rubbish. Angelica won't bite the hand that feeds her. She'll put ANS's interests first." He threw the pen he'd been tapping across the desk and scrounged in a drawer till he found his ever-present antacid tablets. "How did Black take the news? Is he going to be difficult?"

Given the things Hayden's mouth had done to her this morning, she'd say he'd taken the news very well, all things considered. "No, he'll still let me help with his investigation. I convinced him I'd be ethical about it."

Graham grinned as if he thought she'd lied to Hayden, and something inside her withered. Angelica's ruthlessness had given Lucy pause. But Graham seemed to respect that about his star journalist. And now he'd shown approval at the possibility his own stepdaughter would lie and double-cross someone. She'd known Graham was a hard-nosed businessman, but she'd—probably naively—thought that there were different expectations of the journalists at ANS.

Where did that leave her plans for her own career? If she refused to be like them, to play in a sandbox with loose rules, did she have a future in broadcast journalism? Her stomach hollowed out. She had no answers.

"I need to get back to Hayden," she said, reaching for her hold-all bag and pushing up out of her chair. "I said I'd help him with some research this afternoon."

Graham's brow folded into deep wrinkles, making him resemble Rosie. "You're not getting too close to Black, are you? Don't be fooled into sympathizing with your target. Rookie mistake."

She thought of Hayden stretched naked across her sheets only a few hours ago, smiling lazily at her as she brought them a tray with toast and coffee.

Her hand fluttered up to circle her throat. "No, we're not too close."

"Good," he said with a decisive nod. "I knew I could count on you."

But Lucy had begun to wonder—just who really could count on her? And just as important, who could she count on? She looked down at the photo of her with Graham and her mother for long moments, then slipped it into her red bag. She rolled her shoulders back and pushed the disloyal thoughts away. Graham could count on her and she could count on him. They were family.

She gave Rosie a final scratch under the chin, hugged Graham quickly and left.

Hayden stared at the two photos side by side on his laptop screen, a triumphant rush filling his veins. The resemblance was unmistakable. Without taking his eyes from the computer, he reached for his cell and dialed Lucy's number.

"Can you come over?" he asked when she answered. They'd fallen into a routine over the past few days of taking personal time at her house each day—but at varying times, for discretion's sake—and her dropping over to his hotel either in the afternoon or evening to touch base on the investigation. But now it was only 7:00 a.m.; Lucy would be on her way to ANS soon and his discovery couldn't wait a full day.

She didn't hesitate. "Sure. What's up?"

Unwilling to say too much on the phone, he simply said, "I've found some things you'll want to see."

"I'll be there as soon as I can."

By the time Lucy arrived, Hayden had put together a slideshow of the images his office had sent him and strapped Josh into his high chair for breakfast. As he opened the door, he stole one lingering kiss, then before he drowned in her floral scent and broke their rules by dragging her off to his bed, he led her over to share his discovery.

"What have you got?" she asked, her hazel eyes bright with curiosity. She kissed Josh on the top of his head and slipped into the chair Hayden had pulled over on the other side of his, laying a hand proprietarily over his thigh. At the simple gesture, something moved in his chest.

He froze. This was supposed to be a fling—was he becoming emotionally entangled? No, he wouldn't let himself. There was no future for a single father from New York with a twenty-two-year-old heiress from D.C. Ignoring her hand and any deeper implications it represented, he turned the laptop screen so she could see the images and gave Josh a spoonful of stewed fruit.

"After a bit of digging, I found a photo of a girl called Madeline Burch." He clicked the mouse and a picture of a teenager with mousy brown hair, plain features and dishwater-brown eyes appeared. "When I met with Rowena Tate that night at the airport, she said that she and a friend had suspicions about Madeline Burch. She gave me a photo of Madeline from their school days, but the resolution was too low. So I found a better one and sent it to the tech guys at my office. They did some imaging work and came up with these projections."

He gave Josh another spoonful with one hand and clicked the mouse with the other. The same girl now appeared with straight blond hair. On the next click, she had aqua-blue irises. Then lips that were plumper.

"If Madeline colored her hair, wore contacts, had her lips done and had a nose job—" he clicked the mouse again and the same girl now had a different nose "—then she becomes more recognizable."

"Angelica," Lucy murmured. She took the baby spoon from him and stood, seamlessly taking over feeding Josh while watching the screen over his shoulder.

"Bingo. Angelica Pierce started life as Madeline Burch. I've also tracked Madeline's records, and she disappears a couple of years after graduation. Angelica's records go back to school years, but the tech guys in the office looked deeper and found they're all plants. She's tried to cover her tracks, and it's worked, to an extent."

Lucy tapped a fingernail against the bowl she held. "That's a pretty thorough makeover."

"No doubt about it." He flicked through the slideshow again as he spoke. "My main question now is, did she do this for a new start, maybe to increase her chances of scoring an on-camera job…"

"Or is she hiding something?" Lucy finished for him.

He nodded. "I've made a few calls, and no one from her school has stayed in contact with Madeline. She was brought up by a single mother who's passed on, and doesn't seem to have any other family. Several women remember that Madeline was always bragging about having a rich father whom she couldn't or wouldn't name, but other than that, no one knew much. I had my staff trace her birth certificate, but her father wasn't named."

"And I'm betting we won't be able to find anyone who knew Angelica Pierce as a child."

"Not that I've found so far." He flicked his pen over and under his fingers as his mind ticked through the facts.

"In fact, besides you, I can't find a single person who will say a bad word against Angelica. Troy Hall and Brandon Ames will only sing her praises, even though I'm pretty sure she set them up."

When Josh finished eating the stewed fruit, Hayden wiped his face with the washcloth and Lucy took the bowl to the sink.

"She's got to be blackmailing them with something," she said over her shoulder.

"Agreed." He unbuckled a clapping Josh and lifted him free of the high chair before giving him a quick hug and depositing him on the sofa with his toys. "If she's gone to this much trouble to reinvent herself, I can't see her setting someone up and leaving a loose thread. She would have had the blackmail material before choosing Ames and Hall to take the fall."

"You know," she said slowly, as if she was uncomfortable with what she was saying. "I talked to my stepfather and mentioned that Angelica had told you about the exposé. But he still trusts her."

Hayden scanned her face, looking for signs that there were layers to what she was saying, but couldn't find any. She was honestly telling him that she was surprised Graham Boyle still trusted Angelica Pierce after Angelica had betrayed him. It hit him then that Lucy truly believed her stepfather was innocent. She wasn't covering for him—she really had no idea that Boyle was behind the illegal activities at ANS. Anger simmered that Boyle could have someone with a pure heart like Lucy in his life and risk dragging her into his sordid work. He should have kept Lucy away from ANS, away from a company that would likely leave her tarnished. Lucy deserved better.

He sank back into his chair at the desk. If he shared his thoughts with her, she wouldn't believe him. She'd continue defending Boyle with more loyalty than the creep deserved, so instead he simply said, "Angelica's ability to make people trust her is what's gotten her this far."

She reached into her hold-all bag and came out with a pale yellow muffin. She broke a large chunk off and handed it to him. "Lemon and poppy seed. I bought it on the way over."

He took the chunk and bit in as he looked back at the images on his laptop. Angelica seemed to be holding all the cards. Everything came down to her, but they didn't have one shred of evidence. Yet.

Brushing her hands, Lucy turned to him. "So what do we do next? We can't just wait for her to slip up."

"I'm heading to Fields, Montana. The president's birthplace is where this whole debacle started, and I'd lay down money that it's where Angelica started her hacking on this story. If I can get the evidence that she did, I can catch her." Fields had been the place where Ted Morrow had gotten Eleanor Albert pregnant, the place from which Eleanor and their baby, Ariella, had disappeared. Journalists had been crawling over the town since Morrow declared his bid for the presidency, and since the story about Ariella Winthrop had broken, investigators and police had joined in, and their discovery of phone taps had sparked the congressional investigation. But they had focused on Ted Morrow's and Eleanor Albert's friends and families. Hayden had been through all that evidence and one thing still bugged him—why were all the hackers looking for a baby in the first place?

In the video that captured Hall and Ames hiring the hackers, they'd specifically asked for confirmation there had been a baby. What had sparked the idea to search for that? And who had found those first glimmers of the story? It was time to widen the circle of his investigation to cover more residents of Fields. Lucy's overheard conversation about Nancy Marlin, friends of Barbara Jessup, was his strongest lead, and the place he'd start.

"How long will you be gone?" Lucy asked.

"A couple of days." Which was a couple of days too many to leave Lucy alone in D.C. unprotected. He'd been serious about Angelica being a potential threat, and he wasn't willing to take a single chance. He cupped her shoulders with his hands and found her gaze. "Come with me."

Eight

Lucy looked at Hayden, her head and heart at war. Now that he'd shared her bed, a couple of days apart seemed an eternity, so going with him to Montana was tempting on that factor alone. But there were unspoken words in his tone that made her think there was something else behind the invitation.

She stood to give herself some distance and took a few steps away. "Why do you want me to come?"

"We've been working together, so it makes sense." He casually shrugged his broad shoulders and leaned back in his chair. "Can you get the time away from work?"

She was sure she could, since Graham wanted her to focus on the exposé, so the more time with Hayden, the better. Still, Hayden's expression was too serious, too concerned.

"A few days ago you were angry at me for not being honest about doing the exposé. You said you'd been upfront. So, do it again now—be straight with me." She crossed her arms under her breasts. "Why do you want me to come to Montana?"

He pushed his chair away from the desk and stood, but he didn't come closer, as if respecting the distance she needed for this conversation. "I don't want to leave you in the same town as Angelica when I'm not around. I don't trust her, and she's fixated on you."

"I'd been in the same town as Angelica for years before you came along."

He shook his head. "That was before. Her visit here a few days ago showed she's on edge. She knows the walls are closing in."

"You think you need to protect me," she said, voice flat.

"Of course I should protect you." He rubbed the back of his neck. "It's my investigation that's pushed her. It's my responsibility to make sure you're safe."

Responsibility? There was that word again. Her stomach hollowed out. The last thing she wanted her lover to see when he looked at her was someone to be responsible for. Would he think that if they didn't have a ten-year age difference? Would he see a woman his own age as able to look after herself?

She straightened her spine. "I can take care of myself."

"I know you can, Lucy. But if I'm right about Angelica, she's capable of things worse than we already suspect her of." With hands around her shoulders, he pulled her close and whispered in her ear. "Did I mention Josh will be staying in D.C. with the nanny? And that I'd book two suites in a new spa hotel—one for us and one for appearances. The one for us would have a hot tub built for two." He placed several damp kisses on the shell of her ear, then pulled her lobe into his mouth, making her blood sizzle.

"Hayden..." she said on a sigh as she melted into him.

"I could make you very glad you agreed to come."

Oh, yes, she knew he could. That fact wasn't in question. What she needed to decide was whether she *should* go. Hayden's hands slipped down to her waist and, nudging the edge of her blouse up, found bare skin just above her skirt. The delicious heat started to rise, and all reservations about going away with him evaporated.

"Okay," she said, swaying against him. "But no more telling me what you think I want to hear. Promise you'll just say what you mean."

"Promise." His lips moved across her cheek and captured hers in a kiss that was as much a vow as his word had been.

As the check-in receptionist at the Fields Chalet handed over the keys to her suite, Lucy smiled and thanked him, then moved aside so Hayden could check in to his suite. A buzz of excitement had been building deep in her belly since they'd left D.C. On the flight, and at both airports, she and Hayden had acted as if they had only a professional relationship, a charade they were keeping up for now.

She glanced around the foyer, all thick wooden poles and soaring glass panes showing the spectacular mountain view beyond. She'd been to Fields to ski in the past, but had always stayed in her aunt's villa on the mountainside, which was kept fully stocked, so she hadn't strayed into town. Since Hayden needed to interview people in the old township, they'd booked into this high-end chalet on the main street. Its grand opulence could have seemed out of place a few doors down from the feed store and across the road from a sawdust-and-peanut-shells tavern, but the chalet had landscaped the area between the road and the front door to create a buffer between the two worlds of Fields.

In the years the president had gone to school here, it

had been a sleepy town of ranching families and local businesses, but over time that had changed. The rest of the country, including Lucy's own aunt Judith, had discovered the stunning skiing and snowboarding location and development had soon followed. Now Fields was a hybrid of the charming old town and shiny new developments.

Hayden came up behind her and she could feel the warmth emanating from his body. Not touching him during the trip had been a special kind of torture.

"Would you like me to help you to your room?" he asked politely, taking her carry-on suitcase.

"Thank you," she said in the calmest voice she could muster. "That's very kind."

They set off for the elevators, her body vibrating with the need to feel his skin under her fingertips, his mouth on hers. Hayden hit the button for the elevator, and in the partly secluded alcove, he dared to let the desire in his gaze flare to life.

"I hope you don't have plans once you reach your room, Ms. Royall," he said, his voice low.

A shiver raced across her skin. "Something in mind?"

"Hell, yes," he said as the doors whooshed open.

As soon as they'd entered and the doors closed out the world, she turned to him. "Hayden—"

Before she could get any other words out, he'd pushed her against the wall, his hips pressed against hers, and claimed her mouth. Everything inside her melted and she dropped her handbag to the floor so she could use her hands to touch him—shoulders, biceps, neck, wherever she could reach. Under her fingers, his body shuddered, which only made her belly tighten even more, made her want him more. She arched her back, bringing her hips into closer contact with his, and was just considering pulling his shirt from his trousers when a chirpy bell sounded and the doors opened.

Hayden groaned as he pulled away. "I couldn't wait another second." He thrust a hand in front of the closing door to keep it waiting for them. "That trip was far too long—being so close, but not being able to kiss you."

She swallowed, trying to get her voice to work. "And now there's the walk from this elevator to our rooms. Yours or mine?"

"Your room, my room, I don't care." He cupped her chin and gave her bottom lip a butterfly-light caress with his thumb. "As long as it's a room with a bed."

She trembled with anticipation. "Then my vote is for the closest one."

The corner of his mouth quirked. "Race you."

He stepped out of the elevator, holding the doors open until she'd picked up her handbag and followed, then he strode down the hall, carrying both the bags, faster than her legs could keep up with. She caught him as he stopped to open the door with the key card. He grabbed her around the waist, pulling her through the door with him and nudging his carry-on bag through with a shoe.

The heavy door shut behind them and she had a few seconds' glimpse of the opulent room with a gas fireplace and a majestic view of the mountain before Hayden dropped her bag and took up their kiss where they'd left off in the elevator. This time she wasn't wasting any time and, as his tongue moved in her mouth, she undid his belt and slid it out of the loops on his trousers before throwing it as far across the room as she could.

When she reached for his zipper, Hayden pulled her hands back and wrenched her shirt over her head. "I need to feel your skin, to taste it." His mouth came down on her shoulder, his tongue moving, teeth scraping across to her collarbone.

She moaned and felt for the wall behind her, taking a small step back, using it to help her stay upright. Hayden followed, pinning her against the cool wall as he found her mouth again. She pulled his shirt from his trousers as she'd wanted to do in the elevator, and he broke away for the seconds it took to grab it from the back and yank it over his head. When he came back to her, the feel of his bare chest on her sensitized skin made a sob rise in her throat. The dark, crisp hair brushed against her cheek while she tried to catch her breath, the muscles moving under her fingers as he kept moving, unzipping his trousers and kicking them away, divesting himself of his boxers, then sliding her skirt up her thighs and moving on to her panties.

"Condom?" she asked with what was probably her only remaining brain cell.

He held a foil packet up between his fingers. "I threw a couple in my pocket in case of an emergency."

"This certainly qualifies as an emergency," she said and took it from him, ripped it open and rolled it down his length, luxuriating in the solid feel of him.

The instant she was finished, he lifted her and brought her legs around his waist. She pushed against the wall at her back to give her traction and slid down onto him, all the breath leaving her body in a ragged sigh as she did.

He stilled and looked at her with such hunger, such raw need, that her pulse spiked even higher. "You know there's a bed about ten feet away," she whispered.

"Too far," he said as he moved inside her, and all thought stopped. All she could do was feel—feel his hot mouth on her throat, the building wave inside, the frantic need that grew with every touch, every movement, until it was too big to contain and it reared up and crashed down over her, through her, and she was helpless to do anything but hold on to Hayden with every last bit of strength she had. Within moments, he rasped her name and shuddered, and she gripped him even tighter, panting, never wanting to let him go. Never.

Never.

Her skin turned cold. *Never?* This was a fling. Of limited duration and purely physical. She unwound her legs and slid down his body, and let him lead her over to the bed. Had she left her heart unguarded? Hayden pulled her down and under the covers, then wrapped her in his arms. Squeezing her eyes tight, she ignored the fluttering in her belly and let herself enjoy him for the time she had left. She'd deal with the fallout of a bruised heart when—*if*—it happened.

A couple of hours later, Hayden pulled the rental car up in front of a little cottage with bright pots of flowers and plants clustered on the porch and the paved walkway that led from the front gate. A little painted sign on the mailbox proclaiming "Jessup" showed they'd found the house of the former maid to the president's family. His gut told him this was where Angelica Pierce's phone-hacking odyssey had begun.

Lucy undid her seat belt and turned to him. "What are we looking for?"

Hayden straightened his tie, reconsidering the wisdom of bringing Lucy. His main thoughts had been about getting her out of D.C. while he was away, and keeping her safe from Angelica, but when he'd been trying to convince her to come, he'd implied she'd be helping with the investigation. Unfortunately, he hadn't thought much past her safety till this morning.

"Hayden?"

"Tell me I'll be able to trust you in there," he said gruffly.

Her cheeks flushed pink. "You're doubting me?"

"I'm acknowledging your split loyalties."

"I've already proved you can trust me several times, including not telling Graham about Nancy Marlin when you asked me not to." Her gaze was unwavering. "I'm on the side of truth, Hayden."

His shoulders relaxed a fraction as he accepted her words. "Okay. But just so we're clear, this interview is confidential."

"Not a problem. I'm actually looking forward to seeing you interview someone else."

"I usually run interviews alone, but if you have something to ask, let me know."

"Which one am I—good cop or bad cop?" Her eyes twinkled with humor and suddenly he had to clench his hands on the wheel to stop himself reaching for her and feeling that curving mouth under his own.

"Barbara Jessup hasn't done anything wrong, so we can probably dispense with the bad-cop role this time. Though if you're still in the role-playing mood when we get back to the chalet—"

She laughed as she opened her door and said over her shoulder, "Let's just deal with this meeting first."

Barbara Jessup was an older woman with neatly pinned-back white hair and a welcoming smile. Hayden made the introductions when she met them at the door, and explained that Lucy was an ANS employee who was working as a consultant on this case. When she brought them into her living room, there was a plate of homemade cookies and a pot each of coffee and tea. He'd already spoken to her on the phone and she'd been keen to help, so after only a few minutes of small talk, they were able to jump to the heart of the matter.

Hayden placed his small recorder on the table and turned it on, then picked up his notebook and pen. "You spoke to Angelica Pierce, a journalist at ANS?"

"Oh, yes. A couple of times. The first time was back when President Morrow was just a senator. I always knew that boy would go far," she said, pride filling her features.

"Then you spoke to her again more recently?"

Barbara picked up the plate of cookies and offered them around as she spoke. "About the time he was elected. Ms. Pierce said she had a few more questions."

Hayden took a raisin-and-nut cookie but put it on his plate, keeping his hands free for taking notes. "Did you tell her about Eleanor Albert and the baby?"

The older woman squirmed a little in her seat. "In the first interview, she was asking about his school days and his friends, wanting to know if there were any left living here she could talk to. I gave her a few names, and when we came to dear Eleanor, I said I didn't know where she was now and hadn't seen her since she moved towns after giving up her baby."

Just as he'd suspected, Angelica had stumbled over the information that had started the story. "Did you mention the baby might be the president's?"

"Of course not!" Her teacup clattered into its saucer. "I'd never betray the family that way, even if I did know the truth."

"I'm sure they appreciate that," he said with a genuine smile. He liked Barbara Jessup. "When Angelica Pierce came the second time, did she ask about the baby again?"

Barbara sniffed. "She certainly did. But I told her I didn't know anything."

"And did you know more than you told her?"

"I know a lot of things about a lot of people, including about that baby. That doesn't mean I'll tell a journalist." She looked pointedly at Lucy.

Lucy's brows drew together and Hayden smothered a smile. "As I said, Lucy is helping with this investigation—you can trust her. Do you have friends or family who know the same things about Eleanor and the baby as you? People you might have talked to on the phone after Angelica left?"

Her face crinkled up in thought for a moment. "I did phone my friend Nancy Marlin and told her how the interview went."

"Nancy knew about the baby?" He'd been planning to ask about Nancy Marlin since Lucy had overheard Angelica and Marnie discussing her, but it was even better that it had arisen naturally in the conversation.

"She worked for the Morrows for one summer, the one when Eleanor left, so she knew—or suspected—as much as me."

He caught Lucy's gaze. There was a faint flicker in her eyes that most people would have missed, but he'd come to be able to read Lucy—her investigator's senses had perked up the same time his had.

He looked back to Barbara Jessup and gave her a warm smile. "This is very important, Mrs. Jessup. Think back to that phone call for me. Did either one of you mention in that conversation that you thought the baby might have been Ted Morrow's?"

Her hand flew to cover her mouth, her eyes wide. "Is it all my fault?" she said from between her fingers. "Has that boy got all this trouble falling on his head because of me? I wasn't even sure the baby was his. Oh, sweet Jesus, what have I done?"

Lucy moved over to the sofa beside Barbara and put a comforting hand on her arm. "No, Mrs. Jessup. This is not your fault. You did really well when you were interviewed. You kept the Morrows' secrets."

He'd bet money that after Ted Morrow was elected president, Angelica, like hundreds of other journalists across the country, had gone looking for a new angle. Something different to put on TV. She would have gone back over the footage and interviews from her first trip to Fields, looking for tidbits. When she saw the baby mentioned again, she would have done a simple internet search, as Hayden had done, and found Eleanor Albert was Ted Morrow's prom date. There was no record of Eleanor Albert having a baby, or even of Eleanor herself after high school, so Angelica would have had no idea if she'd gotten pregnant within a time frame that could implicate the president.

So, hoping for a scoop, she would have gone back to Fields, interviewed the same people again, stirred up memories, and planted the taps on the phones. She'd lucked out when she overheard Barbara and her friend Nancy discuss the baby and their theory that Ted Morrow had been the father. Then she would have had Ames and Hall hire the hackers that focused on Ted Morrow's and Eleanor Albert's friends and families—the infamous scene that had been caught on tape—and they found enough information to run the story that had aired after the president's inauguration. It was all clicking into place.

"I'm sorry to tell you, Mrs. Jessup," Hayden said as gently as he could, "it's very likely there's a tap on your phone and some of the conversations you thought were private have been overheard."

Her face twisted in disgust. "That's plain wrong, that's what that is."

Lucy's gaze met his again, just briefly, but in that moment he knew their thoughts were completely in sync. He felt somehow warmer.

"We agree," he said, nodding. "And I'll be working hard to make sure those responsible face justice. In the meantime, I can take care of your phone for you. And if you give me a list of your friends Angelica or her team spoke to, I can check their phones, as well."

"You're a good man, Mr. Black." She turned to Lucy and patted her hand. "You hold on to this one real tight."

Lucy's mouth opened, startled. Hayden hesitated with his coffee mug halfway to his mouth. If Barbara Jessup had suspected their connection, they'd have to be more careful of betraying it, become more circumspect when they were together.

And even if he could admit there was something between him and Lucy, neither of them would be holding on to the other one tight. What they had was temporary. Physical and temporary.

Before Lucy could reply, Hayden stood and headed for the phone in the corner of the room. "I'll start with this one."

They stopped at a deli in town for lunch after their interview with Barbara Jessup. While Hayden waited for their sandwiches to be made, Lucy found a pretty table on the sidewalk. The town had an interesting vibe with the mix of traditional and new and she soon lost herself to people watching—a lifelong pastime that came in handy now that she was a journalist on the lookout for stories.

"Lucy? Is that you?"

She twisted in her seat to see her aunt—a tall woman dressed in understated elegance—emerging from the ski shop next door. Within moments, Lucy was off her feet and finding herself wrapped in a warm embrace.

"Aunt Judith," Lucy said, hugging her tightly.

Judith stepped back, pulling a tissue from her bag and

dabbing at her eyes. "I didn't know you were in Fields, sweetie. You should have let me know."

Lucy felt her own eyes mist over and blinked the moisture away. She should make more of an effort to see her father's family—a couple of times a year was nowhere near enough. Being busy might be true, and it definitely had been easier to spend time with them when her father was alive and able to be the conduit, but family was important.

"I'm here for work," she said, promising herself she'd visit again, soon. "Otherwise I absolutely would have called."

Judith's face brightened. "How long?"

"Just tonight."

"You'll have to come up to the villa for dinner."

She glanced back to the deli, where Hayden was waiting for their order. "I'm traveling with a colleague."

"Bring them," Judith said with a generous sweep of her arms. "Philip and Rose are here, too, so we'll make a cozy group."

From the corner of her eye, she saw Hayden approaching their table. How would he react to the invitation? He'd made his feelings about his ex-wife's family clear—inherited money didn't impress him. In fact, he'd been disdainful of their lavish lifestyle. Aunt Judith was her father's sister—a Royall through and through—and had expensive tastes to go along with her wealth.

She stepped away from her aunt and turned to Hayden, who'd placed the sandwiches and drinks on the table. "Judith, this is Hayden Black. Hayden, this is my aunt, Judith Royall-Jones."

Hayden reached out a hand. "A pleasure to meet you."

"And you, Mr. Black. I was just telling Lucy to bring you up for dinner tonight at the villa."

Hayden turned to her and raised an eyebrow. She started to shake her head, wanting to save him from a situation he might find uncomfortable.

"We don't get to see enough of our Lucy, so I won't take no for an answer." Judith linked her elbow though Lucy's and grinned, obviously certain of Hayden's answer.

He looked from her aunt back to her, then a charming smile spread across his face. "In that case, I'd love to come."

Nine

That night, Hayden drove the rental car up the mountainside to Lucy's aunt's lodge. They'd spent the afternoon visiting Barbara Jessup's friends whom Angelica had interviewed and checking the phones at each house. Most had taps. There were a few more people he wanted to interview in the morning, then he and Lucy would catch a lunchtime flight back to D.C. But before that, there was dinner with some of Lucy's family to contend with.

He cast a quick glance over to the passenger seat. Lucy was staring out the window, seemingly lost in thought.

"So who will be there tonight?" he asked.

She turned to him, tucking a few strands of shiny blond hair behind one ear. "Aunt Judith and Uncle Piers—it's their lodge. My cousin Philip and his wife, Rose. She didn't mention anyone else, but with Judith, nothing surprises me." She reached over and laid a hand on his thigh. "Hayden, I'm sorry you were dragged into this."

"It's no trouble. Besides, maybe I'd like to meet some of your family." It was true—his curiosity was piqued about the Royalls. During his marriage, he'd thought Brooke's family wealth had been the cause of her pampered-princess ways. But Lucy's family was much richer than Brooke's, and Lucy hadn't shown a sign of the high-and-mighty or petulant behavior that Brooke had wielded like a weapon. Lucy had obviously been raised very differently.

He covered her hand on his thigh with his palm. "But if you're really sorry, how about you make it up to me later?"

She laughed. "Deal."

Lucy directed him to the house and when he turned into the drive, he gave a low whistle. "When you said lodge, I was expecting, I don't know, a lodge. Not a mansion." The place was huge—four stories built into the side of the mountain so each level was stepped in as it went up. Glass and wood everywhere, a soft golden glow coming from many windows, and a carpet of spring flowers that wove around paths. It looked like it belonged in some kind of fairy tale.

"Aunt Judith likes her little comforts," Lucy said with an ironic twist to her mouth.

He chuckled. Going by what he could see of the house, that was something of an understatement.

Judith met them at the door, taking Lucy's hands and squeezing. "Lucy, dear. I can't tell you how thrilled I was to see you in town today."

"Me, too," Lucy said with genuine warmth.

"And Mr. Black." She turned a welcoming smile to him. "I'm glad you could come."

He shook her hand. She was tall, with glossy silver hair that came to just under her chin and hazel eyes that reminded him of Lucy's. He liked her already. "Call me Hayden."

"Then you must call me Judith. Please, come in."

She led them through a house that was all soaring glass and warm wood tones. Fires crackled in grates as they went past, and thick wall-to-wall carpets kept the rooms toasty from the spring-night air in the mountains.

They emerged from a hallway into a large library with soft yellow walls, fresh flowers on small tables and built-in bookshelves on each wall. Three people were already standing in the room, each holding a sparkling crystal glass—he recognized them from Lucy's descriptions as Piers, Philip and Rose. Piers and Philip came over to give Lucy hugs, and Judith performed the introductions.

Within minutes, Hayden had a martini in his hand and was ensconced in small talk with Philip that mainly revolved around skiing and red wine. Every so often he met Lucy's eyes across the room and lost his place in the conversation, but he seemed to cover well enough for Philip not to notice.

Partway through a discussion on the finer points of choosing a good merlot, Judith interrupted them to lead the group into the dining room—a room with spectacular views of the town below. Hayden found himself seated with Lucy on one side and Rose on the other and served stuffed mushrooms that appeared to be a traditional family favorite. The main course followed and conversation flowed smoothly among the group.

"So, Hayden," Judith said in a deceptively sweet voice once the plates were cleared. "Are you married? Single?"

Hayden cleared his throat. "Widowed."

"Oh, I'm sorry to hear that." Judith's tone was sympathetic, but she clearly intended to pursue the topic. He shifted in his chair and prepared to redirect the conversation.

"Hayden has a little boy," Lucy said from beside him.

He held back a smile—she'd dived in to protect him from her family. She was a good woman, that Lucy.

"How old is he?" Judith asked.

Hayden took a sip of his wine. "He just turned one."

"Such a lovely age," Judith said. "I remember when Philip was that little. He was so sweet, always rushing up with flowers he'd picked for me."

Hayden saw Philip look across the table at Lucy and share a glance of amused exasperation. Either not noticing or not minding, Judith continued. "And Philip was always being carried around by one of his sisters when he was one. He milked it for all he was worth."

"Smart boy," Hayden said to Philip and grinned.

Philip tilted his head in acknowledgment. "What's your boy's name?"

"Joshua. Josh." His chest hurt, missing his little boy—he hadn't been away from him overnight since Brooke died and he'd taken complete parental responsibility. He was already looking forward to seeing him again the next afternoon.

Judith leaned forward. "Do you have a photo of him?"

Hayden found one in his wallet and passed it across to Rose, sitting to his side, just indulging in a quick look himself first. "It's a couple of months old now, but he looks much the same. Just bigger."

"He's gorgeous," Rose said, and passed the photo along the table. Hayden's chest expanded an inch or two. Josh was the best son a man could hope for.

"So you'll be on the lookout for a new mother for him?" Judith asked, smiling to cover for her complete lack of tact.

"Mom," Philip interjected good-naturedly. "The man lost his wife not long ago. Give him a little peace."

"It's okay," Hayden said. "It has only been three months, but, no, I won't be looking for a new mother. I won't marry again." He resisted the impulse to glance over at Lucy and gauge her reaction, but she'd known their relationship was only temporary. This shouldn't be too big a shock for her.

"Maybe with time..." Judith began but let her words trail off when Hayden shook his head.

"It's not about time, or healing. It's about parenting. This might sound selfish, but I'm not prepared to share decision making about Josh ever again."

Judith's brows shot up with unbridled interest. "You didn't agree with your wife's philosophy on child raising?"

"Not even close to agreeing with it," Hayden said with blunt honesty, which seemed to please Judith. "In fact, I was locked out of most of the decisions. Obviously, I should have challenged it at the time, but I didn't. I won't risk a situation where I don't have a say about my own son again."

"What about love?" Judith asked, leaning back in her chair, wineglass in hand. "You can't control that."

"Love isn't the most important thing. Josh is," Hayden said. There was nothing he was more certain about in his life. "I know I'm not a perfect father. I'm still learning as I go, but I have a clear vision of what I want for him, and I won't compromise. Even for someone I loved."

"Aunt Judith," Lucy said, "I was thinking I might show Hayden your garden before dessert. Even at night, it's gorgeous. Besides, I think Hayden's put up with enough of the Royall inquisition for one night."

The others laughed, including Judith. "Go ahead," she said, waving an arm in the direction of the door.

"C'mon," Lucy whispered.

Hayden followed her down a hallway into a small room full of boots, coats and paraphernalia, glad for the chance to be alone with her for a few minutes. Her family seemed nice enough, but he'd choose time with Lucy outside in the dark without question.

She took two coats down from hooks and handed him one. "It's quite cool at night."

He held her coat for her to thread her arms through, then pulled the larger one on before following her outside. The landscaped side yard was terraced and bursting full of spring flowers, most of which had closed their buds for the night, yet still looked magical in the moonlight.

"I'm sorry about Judith's questioning," Lucy said as they walked along a winding paved pathway. "She means well, but she's used to being the matriarch and pretty much being able to do and say as she pleases."

He found her hand and intertwined their fingers, loving the slide of her skin against his. "I didn't mind. She reminds me of my mother. A bit nosy, but good people."

They walked farther along, then Lucy stopped and pointed up to the sky. "There's the moon. I wonder if it's waxing or waning—living in the city I lose track."

"It's nice," he whispered. "But it's not the prettiest thing out here." Cupping her cheek in his palm, he brushed a thumb over her lip. She was so beautiful. Incandescent. And when she looked at him with those hazel eyes filled with rich desire for him, he was lost. He dipped his head and found her mouth, waiting and ready for him. With excruciating patience—he couldn't afford to get carried away in her aunt's garden—he kissed her, just lightly, a gentle sweep across that landed at the corner of her mouth, a hint of teeth as he nibbled on her lush bottom lip. She shuddered and moved in closer. Her lips were beguilingly soft as they moved beneath his, but still he held himself in check. Then she sighed and her tongue slid against his and suddenly the kiss was carnal and he was helpless to pull it back. He tightened his hold on her and she pushed her hands under his coat, to move across his chest.

They were seconds away from being completely undone, so he wrenched his mouth away but stood, chest heaving, for long minutes before he could get his throat to work.

"Lucy," he finally said. "Unless you're ready to go back to the chalet right now, we need to stop doing that."

"You're right." She squeezed her eyes shut, but didn't let her hold on him loosen.

"And if we go inside now, with the way you look, all rosy cheeks and puffed lips, they'll have no trouble guessing what we've been doing." He said the words calmly enough, but he hated the need for secrecy. If he could walk back into that room and have everyone know he'd kissed Lucy senseless out in the moonlight, he'd be the proudest man in the state. She was the sort of woman a man was proud to have by his side. Instead, they had this mess of rules and secrets that sat more uncomfortably inside him each day. He rubbed a hand through his hair. "How about we talk for a couple of minutes? Till we lose that just-kissed look."

She dug her hands deep in the pockets of the coat and looked up at him. "You really believe what you said to Judith about not sharing Josh again? That you'll always be a single father to him?"

"I do." He'd given it a lot of thought over the past three months. It was the best arrangement for everyone, no question.

"That's kinda sad," she said softly. "I don't want to think about you being alone for the rest of your life."

Her sympathy didn't sit well. This was his choice and he was happy with it. "It's not the rest of my life. Only until Josh is older. And I wouldn't always be alone. Just never married again."

She looked out at the view of the town below. "That's still sad."

With a finger, he turned her face back to him. "You only think it's sad because you have such a good heart."

"You have a good heart, too," she said, but there seemed to be more behind her words. Was she having second thoughts about ending their arrangement? Perhaps this sympathy was Lucy's way of telling him he didn't have to be alone, that she wanted things to continue. His chest constricted painfully. He couldn't let her start thinking that way, let her be set up for disappointment.

"Maybe once I had a good heart," he said carefully, needing her to understand this. "But it's jaded now. Yours is fresh and pure—" he laid a hand over her chest and could feel her heartbeat "—far too pure to be polluted by someone like me. I hate to admit it, but the sooner I'm out of your life, the better for you. Though I can't deny I'll miss you like crazy once I'm gone."

"I'll miss you, too." She drew in a long breath. "Maybe if I'm up in New York—"

"No." Though he flinched as he said it. "The cleaner the cut, the better. Remember our rules? No emotional entanglement, just physical. If we let it linger, it'll turn into something neither of us wanted. Something that might become bitter, and I don't want anything to tarnish the memories I'm taking of you."

"I'll cherish these memories forever," she said, and he could see her eyes glistening in the moonlight.

Unable to help himself, he kissed her again, pulling her flush along his body in the moonlight, wanting to create as many memories as he could before the inevitable moment their time expired.

* * *

Lucy and Judith carried the dessert plates into the kitchen an hour later. “Thank you for inviting us. It’s been lovely to see you.”

Judith pulled her into a hug. “I wish we saw you more.” After long moments, she released her and began piling the plates up. “Shame that man of yours is so dead set against marriage.”

“He’s not my man,” Lucy said and turned the tap on to rinse out the wineglasses.

“I’ve seen the way he looks at you. He’s yours, even if it’s just for now. Besides, you had no lipstick left when you came in from the garden.”

Without thinking, Lucy touched two fingertips to her lips, then dropped them when she saw Judith’s knowing smile. Lucy shut the tap off and leaned back on the bench to face her aunt. “It’s temporary. Even if he was interested in anything longer term, with the way people treat me, the expectations they have of me because of Daddy and Graham, the last thing I need is an older man who’s already well connected and wealthy. They’ll think I’ve taken the easy route again, found someone to look after me.”

“Maybe,” Judith said and scraped some scraps into the bin. “But I like him.”

“I like him, too.” Lucy bit down on her bottom lip. It was the first time she’d admitted to herself or anyone that she really did like Hayden. Maybe she was even coming to love him. But defining her feelings was a pointless exercise—no matter how she felt, their fling would end soon.

Judith smiled at her. “The one thing I’ve learned over the years about relationships is that liking each other enough is all that matters.” She tucked some of Lucy’s hair behind her ear then rubbed her arm. “It’s all that matters.”

Lucy smiled back, but didn't reply. From where Judith stood—thirty-two years into a happy marriage with her college sweetheart—things might seem that simple. But for the rest of the world, relationships were complicated, messy things that sometimes had luck on their side and sometimes didn't.

Maybe if she'd met Hayden in ten years' time, things would have worked out better for them—she'd have already established herself, would know who she was without being surrounded by strong men, and Hayden would have an eleven-year-old son and be more relaxed about having a woman in his life. Their age difference might not matter so much if they were thirty-two and forty-two instead of twenty-two and thirty-two. But things were what they were, and wishing for them to be different wasn't going to help her when it was time for Hayden and Josh to leave D.C.

Four days later, with one arm around Lucy's waist, Hayden shut off the faucet in her bathroom's oversize shower with an elbow and slumped against the wall, chest heaving. They'd made love in her bed, then he'd suggested a shower before they both went to work, but seeing Lucy's water-slicked body had made the end result of that idea inevitable. It was probably a good thing their time together was only a fling—if this arrangement was permanent, it just might kill him.

Lucy looked up at him with a satisfied gaze. "Your imagination is a beautiful thing, Hayden Black."

"I aim to please," he said, grinning, and summoned the energy to step out of the shower. He passed a fluffy blue towel to Lucy, but regretted it when she patted herself down and wrapped it under her arms, tucking a corner in to keep it in place. He let out a resigned sigh. Damn shame to cover up a body like that.

She glanced over at him, one eyebrow arched. "Are you going to towel off, or are you trying the drip-dry method?"

"Just admiring the view," he said, then ran the towel over himself till he was dry enough. "What have you got today?"

She walked through the connecting door to her bedroom and pulled pure-white underwear from a drawer. "More research into your background. Graham is going to run the exposé next week, whether I've got enough material or not."

She dropped the towel and stepped into the white panties. Hayden swallowed. "Good luck."

The idea of the exposé airing didn't thrill him, but in his line of work, it was a cost of doing business. He had no deep, dark secrets, no skeletons in his closet. And if they made up stories, he'd deal with that when it happened.

"Give me some hints." She'd put on the white lace bra and was sitting on a velvet-covered stool at her dressing table, brushing out her damp hair. "Did you cheat on a high-school history exam? Were you involved in a street brawl?"

"Okay." The mirror on her dressing table showed another perspective of her movements, giving double the impact and mesmerizing him. "This is the one and only lead I'll give you. I organized a boycott of the school cafeteria when I was a junior."

Her eyes brightened and met his in the mirror. "A radical political statement? Please tell me you burned a flag."

"Eight kids got food poisoning in the same week and no one would look into it. We boycotted until the school board sent someone in. They fired a couple of staff who weren't following safety procedures and tightened up the practices."

"Yeah, that's just the kind of story we need," she said, throwing him an ironic smile over her shoulder. "You'll come off looking like a hero. Fighting for truth and justice since you were a kid." Her words might have been flip, but her eyes shone with pride, and it made his chest swell a little.

He grinned. "Take it or leave it."

"I'll take it. Maybe I can find a different angle." She crossed to her closet, took out a pale green blouse and slipped it on. "What are you doing today?"

He pulled on his trousers, then socks and shoes, giving himself a moment to decide how much to tell her. Lucy had proved herself trustworthy in this investigation several times, but this information was a whole new level—today he was going to a judge to get permission to perform surveillance on Angelica Pierce. The slightest slip to someone Lucy trusted, like Graham, who leaked it to Angelica, would make the whole exercise pointless.

She stepped into soft cream trousers and secured the buttons before resting her hands on her hips. "Some super-secret mission?" she teased.

He rubbed a hand across his jaw. "It might be better if I don't tell you."

"You're joking, right?" she said, her voice incredulous. "I've done everything you've asked of me, even not telling Graham about Angelica being Madeline Burch. Why wouldn't you trust me now?"

She was right, but this was different. "You've been great on this investigation. The difference is you're helping out to try and clear Graham's name. If it comes down to it, you'll choose Graham over any other option."

"Of course I'll stand by Graham," she said, her voice

carefully controlled. "He's innocent. Are you telling me you've got evidence on him?"

He shook his head, conceding her point. "No, but I don't think it will be long. And if you had to choose between the truth and your stepfather, where would you stand, Lucy?"

Eyes blazing, she seemed to grow about two inches. "You're questioning my personal integrity now?"

The accusation hit him square in the chest, but he didn't waver. "Most people have a line in the sand somewhere. Many don't know where that line is until they reach it."

"And you, the famous investigator—who even as a child stood up for truth and justice—do you have a line?" She stared at him, waiting while he didn't answer. Then, suddenly, her eyes softened. "Josh," she said.

He nodded, every muscle in his body tight. He'd let Josh spend his first nine months being raised Brooke's way, against his better judgment. Nothing, *nothing* was more important than Josh. And there was nothing he would choose over Josh's best interests ever again. Not a woman. Not his career. Not his own life. Josh was his line in the sand.

Lucy's line was Graham. And Graham was tangled up with Angelica, he had no doubt.

"Tell me honestly," he said, sinking down onto the side of her bed and resting his hands between his knees. "Let's say Graham had done something illegal, not phone hacking, some other crime, just to take it out of this context. Hypothetically, if Graham had done something illegal that had hurt someone else, would you turn him in?"

She frowned. "That's an impossible question. No one could answer that without knowing what the crime was."

"That's an answer in itself." Hedging her answer just

showed that there were crimes she would cover up for Boyle.

She crossed her arms under her breasts and tapped a foot on the carpet. "Then you answer a question for me."

"Sure."

"Is whatever you're doing today legal?"

"Of course it is," he said, taken aback at the question.

She waved away his implication of being affronted without pausing. "Is it ethical?"

"To me, without question." Everyone had their own ethics and principles, but he was pretty certain his plan would be within Lucy's framework of ethics, as well.

She sat down on the edge of the bed beside him. "Then tell me what it is and I swear I'll help you."

Hayden looked at her, weighing the options, then made his decision. He could use her help, and if she'd given him her word, he could trust her. "I'm getting an order from a judge to put Angelica under surveillance."

"That's it?" she asked skeptically.

"If this leaks back to her, say, via Boyle, the surveillance will be pointless, so I have to be extremely careful. But understand, I have the evidence to get the judge's order for Angelica. If I had evidence on Boyle, I'd get an order for him today, too."

"Key word there is *if*. *If* you had the evidence on him." She arched an eyebrow. "You don't have it because it doesn't exist."

"The surveillance on Angelica will flush something out on Boyle." Though he knew nothing would convince her until he uncovered the evidence. "You still willing to help?"

"You betcha," she said without hesitation. "I want to be

there when Angelica incriminates herself and whoever's been helping her."

"You and me both."

Ten

"Hi, Roger," Lucy said to the ANS night guard as she walked Hayden past the security desk over to the elevators. It was just after midnight, so, aside from the studios where the anchors reported the late-night news broadcast, the place would be relatively deserted. It was the only time Hayden would be able to put the wiretap on Angelica's phone. As soon as he'd been granted the court order, Hayden had brought some tech guys from his company down to do some more elaborate work on Angelica's phone lines, but he wanted nothing left to chance with this case, so that meant also planting a good, old-fashioned tap on the phone, as well.

The elevator doors closed and they were alone, except for the cameras she'd told Hayden about during the briefing in his hotel suite. Josh was back there asleep and the nanny was staying the night in Josh's room. A rush of nerves filled her stomach. This had to work—the surveillance had to find who Angelica was working with and clear Graham's name. She sent up a little prayer that they'd thought of everything in their preparations and this would all go off without a glitch.

"The weather was lovely today," she said, making small talk. Silence would look suspicious for the elevator cameras. If they were caught, Lucy would tell Graham that she'd played double agent—luring Hayden to the office so she could show him some of the information she'd uncovered, ostensibly helping him, but really hoping to see if his reactions pointed her to further discoveries to help her exposé. Did that mean she was a triple agent now?

"Sunny and warm, which was nice for Josh," Hayden said, as if discussing the weather in the ANS elevator was the most natural thing in the world. The man must have nerves of steel. Though he didn't have as much to lose as she did. For him, this was a case—albeit one he felt strongly about. For Lucy, her whole family was at stake. Graham was all she had.

The elevator arrived on the eighth floor, which housed most of the journalists, but the skeleton staff on the night shift all worked on other floors. Angelica's office was down at the end, alongside the offices of the other senior reporters, and Lucy had a desk in the cubicles in the middle of the open-plan room.

"This way," she said, guiding him along a single-file corridor made by glass office walls on one side and waist-high partitions on the other. The moonlight through all the glass in the offices meant there was little need for lights, which was lucky, since turning on lights would only attract more attention.

"Which desk is yours?" His voice was low and it sent shivers down her spine. Even with all she had at stake, sneaking through a darkened room with Hayden at her back, asking where she worked in a deep voice, was enough to distract her from their mission. She shook her head at herself, but led him to her desk anyway, then held an arm out as if showing him a million-dollar view.

"It's neater than the others," he said, turning to survey the surrounding desks quickly.

She glanced over the surface—everything in its place, from the pens in the penholder to the little stationery box that held anything else she needed. "I like to be organized."

He arched an eyebrow. "I'm organized, but my desk is messier than this."

"Your desk is neat," she pointed out. And the room in his hotel suite he'd been working from had been so neat, so devoid of personal effects, that she'd had trouble getting a sense of him when she first met him.

"It's not a real desk—it's just for interviews on this case. My desk in New York has haphazard piles of documents and trays filled with papers. The way desks are meant to be," he said, the corner of his mouth twitching.

She thought back to the mountain of baby manuals she'd seen in Josh's room, and the way he'd spread papers over the coffee table when she'd been there at night helping him research. Organized chaos matched his personality more than the tidy desk she'd been judging him by. It was as if she'd seen a little further into the man inside, the one he didn't show everyone, and it made her heart warm.

"So where is Angelica's office from here?" Hayden asked.

"Just there," she said pointing to the darkened room across the narrow corridor. "With the way my desk faces, I get to see her smiling face all day." Of course, Angelica took every opportunity to scowl at her, or to say something cutting when she walked past.

The elevator pinged and they both stilled. As the doors whooshed open, Angelica's sharp voice filled the air. "No, that's not acceptable. If you want a credit on the story, you'll have the research on my desk by 8:00 a.m. End of discussion." Then a beat later, as if talking to herself, "Moron." There was silence except for Angelica's staccato heels clicking on the tiled floor, coming their way.

Lucy looked at Hayden, her pulse jumping. It was one thing to be found by a random ANS staffer, or to have their escapade get back to Graham, but Angelica was a different story altogether. If she saw them, there was a good chance she'd suspect what they were doing and be on her guard, ruining the plan.

Hayden grabbed Lucy's arm, pulling her down to the floor and quietly squeezing them both under her desk. To fit in the small space, she was tucked into Hayden's lap, her cheek resting against his chest, their legs intertwined. Her heart thumped hard and she could feel Hayden's matching beat under her ear, and knew it was only partly due to the chance of being caught. Their current position was 95-percent responsible.

Angelica's footsteps arrived at her office door, barely four feet from where they were hidden, with only a partition between them. She flicked the light switch and brightness streamed out, but it was still fairly dark under the desk. Hayden's fingers stroked along her arm, and even through the fabric the caress gave her goose bumps. She glanced up and found him looking languorously down at her, a devilish gleam in his eyes. She shivered.

"I want you," he silently mouthed.

"You're crazy," she mouthed back. His grin showed he was pleased with that pronouncement, and he undid her top button. She wasn't sure whether to laugh or melt. Then when his mouth covered hers, she didn't have to think at all. His hand inched inside her shirt just seconds before he froze, his mouth now a hairsbreadth from hers.

Another set of footsteps was coming down the corridor.

As they heard the footsteps turn in to Angelica's office, Hayden's hand moved away from Lucy's skin, and he redid her top button. "Later," he murmured in her ear.

She bit down on her lip. Later seemed an eternity away.

"Thank you for coming down," Angelica said. With the door open, the words were as clear as if Lucy and Hayden were standing right beside her. Hayden pulled his phone from his pocket and thumbed a button that she assumed started a recording program.

"What the hell couldn't wait for tomorrow morning?"

Lucy jerked as she recognized Graham's voice, but Hayden held her close against his chest, keeping her immobile. Meeting Angelica in the middle of the night didn't look good, but Graham worked crazy hours. There would be an innocent explanation.

"Something I've wanted to tell you for a long time," Angelica said, clearly relishing the words.

"Well, spit it out. I don't have all night." Lucy could imagine Graham checking his watch as he spoke.

"No?" Angelica asked, her voice silky smooth. "Not even for your daughter?"

"What the hell—" Silence filled the air as strongly as the voices had. "Are you telling me…?"

Hayden tipped Lucy's chin up, a question in his eyes, but she shrugged tight shoulders. She didn't know any more than he did, but whatever it was, she didn't like the sound of it.

"Mom always said I had your chin." Angelica's voice was casual, as if she was chatting in a café about the color of her nails. "Surely you've noticed that before?"

"Madeline?"

"Madeline," Angelica said, chuckling. "Now there's a blast from the past. I haven't used that name in a long time."

"Five years you've worked here. *Five years* without mentioning a thing. Why didn't you tell me it was you?" Graham demanded.

"And give you the chance to reject me a second time?"

"I did not reject you! I paid child support. I paid your tuition. I made sure you had everything you needed."

Nausea filled Lucy's stomach, threatening to rise. The only thing keeping her together was Hayden's soothing hand stroking her hair. Angelica was Graham's daughter? They were stepsisters? No wonder Angelica had always hated her—Lucy had Graham's love, affection and public acknowledgment.

"Oh, yes, I had everything," Angelica said. "Except for that small matter of a father. Seems you were saving up all that fatherly affection for your precious Lucy."

Hayden held her more firmly against him. A part of her felt sympathy for Angelica—assuming her story was true—but still, she desperately wanted to run into that office and save Graham from the poison inside his so-called daughter. No matter what he'd done, Graham was worth a hundred Angelicas.

"This has nothing to do with Lucy," Graham growled.

"You're right," Angelica said brightly. "It's all about you. In fact, you're the whole reason I'm here at ANS."

"What are you talking about? Of course you're here because of me—I headhunted you from NCN."

"I've heard you're having some trouble with the congressional hearings. You know, I don't think arresting Brandon Ames and Troy Hall is enough to appease them. They're after the mastermind."

There was a beat of silence, then Graham's voice was incredulous. "It was you."

Angelica chuckled again. "There's no evidence for that theory."

"You manipulated Ames and Hall. Brought out the worst in them."

"I think you have me confused with someone else. But whoever it was wouldn't have had any trouble bringing out the worst in those two sniveling hacks."

"And Marnie? You're the one who brought her in, as well."

"I wouldn't be surprised if she was involved," Angelica said, her tone clearly saying she knew Marnie was. "She's so desperate to make her mark. To shoot to the top."

"And you manipulated that to get her to bring the scheme to me for my approval."

"Not me. She must have done that all on her own."

Graham let out a sigh that sounded as if it came from the bottom of his soul. "Look, I don't want to talk about all that rubbish. Not when I've just found you again."

"And you were so obviously desperate to find me," Angelica said, her voice dripping with sarcasm.

"Maybe not at first. When your mother told me she was pregnant, it threw me. I wasn't expecting that."

"And then there were sixteen years of you still being *thrown?*"

"I'm sorry," he said gruffly. "But at least I'm not like our jerk of a president, who completely abandoned his baby, pretending she didn't exist. I paid child support. Paid for everything you needed."

"Paid?" Her voice turned malicious. "Oh, you're paying, all right. Good luck with that."

"Angelica—" Graham said, clearly confused, but he was cut off.

"Goodbye, Daddy dear." The staccato *tap-tap* of Angelica's heels sounded as she headed down the hallway.

Lucy flung herself from Hayden's arms, out from under the desk, around the partition and into Angelica's office, where Graham was standing as if struck by lightning. He looked up and his face drained of its last remnants of color. She stopped a few feet from him, not sure what to say now that she was here. They stood in silence, not even the sounds of other workers to disguise the emptiness that now stretched between them.

Finally Graham slumped back to sit on Angelica's desk. "So you heard."

"I heard," she said softly, everything inside her breaking apart.

"Lucy, I'm sorry. Of everyone who's been hurt or will be hurt through this mess, I'm most sorry about you." He looked down at his shoes. "I love you more than anyone on earth."

Part of her wanted to hug him and tell him it would be okay, but she'd be lying. And she couldn't make her feet take those last few steps to his side. "You knew," she said. "All this time I've been defending you, *believing* in you, and you've been authorizing Angelica's corrupt scheme."

He recoiled from the accusation, but didn't meet her eyes. "I don't know what to say."

"How about you start by saying you're sorry to Ariella Winthrop for letting her find out about her father's identity live on national television?"

He waved a wrist in the air. "That was an unfortunate side effect."

Her stomach dipped as she realized how little remorse he had. "Was it unfortunate that Ted Morrow had his name dragged through the mud, too?"

"No," he said, his jaw jutting.

She'd heard him rant about the president before, about everything from his policies, to his speeches, to how arrogant he'd been back when they went to school together, but she'd never paid much attention. This time she took him seriously, wanted to understand. "You hate him that much?"

"The truth of the matter is," he said, looking out the dark window, "I've been in love twice in my life. Once was your mother. The other was Darla Sanders, back in college. I thought she loved me, too, that we had a future, but one look from Ted Morrow and she left me without a backward glance. The bastard didn't even marry her."

She opened her mouth and closed it again, unable to believe what she'd heard. "All this has been over a thirty-year-old grudge?"

"Most of it was about good news broadcasting," he said, sounding more like his old self. "People have a right to know about the man who acts on their behalf as their president."

She planted her hands on her hips. "People also have a right to expect that their laws will be followed, no matter whose privacy is involved."

One side of his mouth hitched up. "You're your mother's daughter, Lucy. I'm proud of that."

The warm glow she would normally have felt at such a comment couldn't break through the tumult of other emotions filling her body to the bursting point. She rubbed her temples, trying to keep herself from falling into pieces on the floor of Angelica's office. There would be time enough for falling apart later, after she had some answers.

"And Angelica?" she asked. "Whose daughter is she?"

He heaved out a sigh. "She was raised by her mother, but it seems she's ended up with my ruthlessness anyway."

Hayden stepped into the room and all the breath left

Lucy's body. She'd forgotten he was outside the door, listening to everything she and Graham said. She ran the conversation back through her mind, praying she hadn't led Graham deeper into trouble.

"What the hell is he doing here?" Graham boomed.

Hayden drove his hands in his pockets, a picture of immovability. "I came with Lucy."

Graham turned to Lucy, his jaw slack. "You brought him here?"

She looked up at Hayden, unsure how much she was allowed to divulge. He gave her a resigned shrug, followed by a nod. She opened her mouth, but now that she had permission, she didn't know what to say. Couldn't think of how to explain. Hayden nodded again, encouraging her.

She turned back to her stepfather. "Hayden suspected you and Angelica were involved in the illegal hackings. I assured him you weren't and I was helping him so I could clear your name."

"By eavesdropping on me?" Graham asked, looking from one to the other, outraged.

Unused to being the target of her stepfather's displeasure, Lucy flinched. Then she collected herself. He might have dug his own grave—she had no illusions now about that—but this would still be hard on him. And it was only going to get worse. She could be tolerant of his emotional reactions under stress—he'd certainly cut her some slack during her attempts at rebellion as a teenager.

"Graham," she said gently, "we had no idea you'd be in Angelica's office."

Understanding dawned in his eyes. "You were after her."

Hayden nodded. "This time, yes."

"I guess you heard the conversation, too?" It was a

question, but Graham already seemed resigned to the inevitability of the answer.

"I did," Hayden said, his face neutral.

Graham narrowed his eyes. "Did you get enough on us?"

"On you, yes. Angelica didn't actually admit to anything." Hayden picked up a glass paperweight from Angelica's desk, looked it over and replaced it, timing the pause it created like the pro he was. "You know, it would help your case if you cooperated about her role in the hacking."

Graham groaned, then covered his eyes with a thick hand. "I can't do that. She was right—I've failed her in almost every way a father could." He dropped his hand and met Hayden's gaze steadily. "The only thing I can do for her now is protect her in this."

"It won't be enough to save her," Hayden warned.

"We'll see." Graham let out a slow lungful of air. "So what happens now?"

"You, Marnie and Angelica will be called to testify before the congressional committee. They'll have my notes, so they'll be able to ask the right questions."

"I'll make you a deal, Black," he said gruffly. "I'll confess to everything I've done if you'll keep Angelica's—and Madeline's—name out of it."

Hayden rocked back on his heels as he considered, then nodded and thrust his hands back into his pockets. "I don't have the authority to make that deal, but I'll take it to the people who do, and see what they say."

"I appreciate it." Graham scrubbed the pads of his fingers over his face and Lucy could almost see him growing smaller. "What's next after I testify?"

Hayden didn't blink. "There will likely be a jail term, and you'll have to sell ANS. The regulators won't allow you to keep ownership of a broadcast network once you plead guilty to the crimes you've committed."

"No," Lucy said, refusing to consider jail as an option.

"Lucy." Graham sounded heartbreakingly weary. "Sweetheart, it might be unavoidable once I testify."

"No," she said again and turned to Hayden. "If a deal can be made to protect Angelica, then a deal can be made to protect Graham."

"It's not the same thing," Hayden said. "There's nothing to bargain with for Graham's freedom. What would you have me do?"

"I don't know—as you've said several times, this is your area of specialty." She reached for Hayden's hands and interlaced their fingers, bringing them to rest over her heart. "You can save him. He's the only family I have. Please don't take him."

"Lucy, I'm sorry," he said, his voice strained. "There's nothing I can do."

Damn him, he even had the gall to look torn, despite this being the outcome he'd wanted from the beginning—he'd always wanted Graham's conviction more than any other. *Of course* he wouldn't help simply because the woman he'd been having a fling with asked him to.

She dropped his hands, straightened her spine and focused on the most important thing. "Can he at least go home?"

Hayden cleared his throat. "Yes, but he'll be called to appear before the congressional-committee hearing, probably in a couple of days." He turned to Graham, expression stern. "You won't leave town, will you?"

"Of course he won't," Lucy snapped, moving beside her stepfather as he sat on the desk, providing a united front. "Come on, Graham. I'm taking you home."

Graham's shoulders were rounded with defeat and when

he looked up at her, his eyes were as bleak as a winter's night. "Rosie's up in my office."

"Hayden, can I trust that you'll see yourself out of the building without stopping anywhere you shouldn't?" Her voice had an edge of contempt that she hadn't intended, but it was there anyway.

A confused line appeared on Hayden's forehead. "Sure."

"Then I'll say goodbye." She said the words quickly—like ripping a bandage off, it would surely hurt less if it happened fast. "We won't be running our exposé now, so you're in the clear. And you finally have the head you wanted on a platter. I guess we're finished with what we've been working on together."

He looked at her for a long moment. "I guess we are," he said and turned on his heel. She watched him walk to the elevator from Angelica's office door—he didn't glance backward once.

With every step he took, something deep inside her pulled, as if it were attached to him and was being stretched to breaking point. Their rules had made it clear that what they had would only last so long. Both of them had wanted it that way. Catching Graham meant their time was up. But when Hayden stepped inside the elevator, whatever had been inside her was now gone, leaving her empty. Hollow. Gouged out.

She closed her eyes against the emotion stinging them and turned back to Graham. She had a job to do—Graham needed her. She linked her elbow in his and pulled him to his feet. "Let's go get Rosebud and go home."

"Lucy," he said, letting her see emotion in his eyes without shying away from it for the first time since she'd known him. "I really am sorry."

"I know, Graham. It's okay." But her heart was dying inside. The only two people she loved in the world were going to leave her. One for—in all probability—jail, and the other for his life in New York.

She'd just lied to Graham, because nothing was okay. And she couldn't see things being okay again.

Eleven

Sitting on a kitchen stool in her pajamas as the sun peeked over the horizon, Lucy watched the early morning news, a steaming mug of coffee between her hands. It was blanket coverage of Graham's testimony yesterday at the congressional committee's hearing. She pointed the remote at the TV and flicked to NCN, where they were replaying yesterday's footage of Graham being taken into custody. He'd also been ordered by the Federal Communications Commission to sell ANS, or else the network would lose its license. What they didn't know yet was that Liam Crowe, a self-made media mogul, had already made an offer to buy ANS—that would be announced later today.

They were also reporting that Marnie Salloway would be testifying in a few hours, since Graham's testimony had been that she'd been the one who'd kept him in the loop about the hacking and brought new developments to him to get approval. She was expected to be charged by week's end. As Lucy had expected, Graham hadn't mentioned Angelica once, and hadn't been questioned about her. The prosecutors and congressional committee had taken the deal Graham had offered, including keeping his relationship with Angelica private, which meant the media hadn't picked up on the story…yet.

Lucy blinked away tears for Graham. She'd stayed with him the night she and Hayden had overheard his conversation with Angelica, the night her life had fallen apart. She'd taken him to his place and slept in a spare room. Or pretended to sleep—she'd barely had more than an hour's sleep at a time since then. He'd been taken into custody yesterday afternoon and she'd brought Rosie back here. She'd fallen asleep for just over an hour at about three in the morning, and now she was wide-awake again.

She couldn't stop thinking about Graham's miserable future, about his involvement in the illegal phone hacking, about him being Angelica's father. It was almost too much to comprehend, as if everything she'd ever believed was wrong.

And when she hadn't been thinking about Graham, her mind stubbornly turned to the one subject she'd been fighting to avoid.

Hayden.

Her eyes drifted closed and she saw his face, his smoldering coffee-brown eyes, his darkened jaw needing a shave at the end of the day. Her chest ripped open, painfully exposing her vulnerable heart. She had no idea how long she'd been denying it, but it was clear now—she loved him. And she'd never been more miserable in her life. Wasn't love supposed to be uplifting?

All her original reservations about getting involved with an older man and undoing her work to make something of her life were still there, but they'd been dwarfed by what had happened in the past week. The thing was, her love for Hayden was now tainted. It would always be smeared by Graham's arrest—she'd never be able to think about Hayden again without it being tangled up with the heartache of what had become of her stepfather.

What had he said to her that night in Montana?

"If we let it linger, it'll turn into something neither of us wanted. Something that might become bitter, and I don't want anything to tarnish the memories I'm taking of you."

It had happened anyway, even without them letting it linger. Now she was left without the sweet memories of her time with Hayden to keep her warm at night. They'd been ruined.

The best she could hope for was a little more time with him before he caught Angelica, finished the investigation…and left. He might not want to see her again after she'd been so rude the other night, and it wouldn't be the same now, but if wanting whatever she could have from him made her desperate, then she was willing to cop to the charge. She'd call him today. Maybe they could make some new rules. Or maybe she was deluding herself and everything was too tainted for even their fling to survive anymore.

Her cell rang, and she reached across the counter to retrieve it from where she'd thrown it last night. She wasn't in the mood to talk to most people, but she needed to keep an eye out for calls from Graham or the facility he'd been taken to.

When she picked it up, her heart stuttered. The number on the screen was Hayden's.

"Did I wake you?" The voice, so deep and familiar, made her ache.

"No," she said, her voice raspy. "I've been awake for a while."

"Can I talk to you?"

"You are talking to me."

"In person."

She squeezed her eyes shut. At this time of the morning, she didn't have her head together enough to face anyone, let alone Hayden Black, with all the conflicting emotions he stirred within her. She wanted to talk to him when she was ready, when her head was clear. Perhaps after another coffee—or three. "I can meet you in a couple of hours."

"I'm on the street in front of your place."

Her heart thudded against her ribs as she slipped off the stool and padded through to the front window. As she drew the drapes aside, she saw Hayden's rental car on the street. "So you are."

"Can I come in for a few minutes?"

"It's not a great time, Hayden." She needed a chance to talk to him about resurrecting their fling for as long as she could have him. And the time to convince him wasn't early in the morning while she was in her pajamas and had only consumed one cup of coffee.

"It has to be now," he said, and something in his voice reached out and pulled at her.

"Sure," she said on a sigh, knowing she'd probably regret it. It was hard to be seductive in striped pajamas after an hour's sleep. She disconnected and threw the cell on a side table. She didn't have time to change, but she ducked into her bedroom and grabbed her royal-blue satin dressing gown.

She swung the door open to find him standing there with a sleepy Josh in one arm. She stared at Hayden in his dark trousers, pale blue shirt and tie and dark suit jacket, her belly tightening. All she wanted to do was take those clothes off him.

"Sorry it's so early," he said, his thoughts clearly not on the same track as hers.

"Come on in." She leaned over to kiss Josh on the cheek, trying not to linger and sink into the scent of Hayden, then turned and walked down the hall to the kitchen. "Do you want a coffee?"

"No, thanks," he said, bending to scratch Rosie behind the ears, then depositing a rapidly waking Josh on the floor beside her. "I won't be here long."

She poured another coffee for herself anyway and took a sip. Any assistance to her mental alertness was welcome. "So this visit is both early and quick."

"I came to say goodbye," he said, his voice deep yet devoid of emotion.

Her stomach fell fast. She carefully placed the mug on the counter before she dropped it. He was leaving? It was too soon. Too soon. She held on to the edges of the counter for support.

"Hayden," she said, then swallowed. "I'm sorry about what I said the other night. I was upset."

His features seemed carefully schooled to give nothing away. "It wasn't anything you said, Lucy. I need to go."

"Before the investigation is finished?"

"It's for the best. I've become too involved. One of the top investigators in my company, John Harris, will be here by tonight. He'll be more impartial, which is what the investigation needs now." He frowned and looked down at Josh, who was petting Rosie. "What it always needed."

"And you're leaving D.C.?" She'd known this moment was coming, of course she had, but *please* not yet. She wasn't ready.

He nodded and a muscle jumped in his jaw. "The flight to New York is in a couple of hours. Our bags are packed."

She sucked in a breath and ignored the ache in her chest. There was no chance of a future for them—and if she'd had any doubts about that, he'd settled them at her aunt's lodge in Montana—so maybe he was right to leave now. Only ten minutes ago she'd been thinking that things between them were probably too tainted to survive even their fling with all its rules. Perhaps they'd even make things worse if they didn't make a clean break now. Wanting a little more time with him was simply the desperate need of a woman in love who was in denial about the future she couldn't have.

She lifted her chin and found a polite smile, determined to see him off with at least that civility. "Thank you for dropping by to say goodbye."

He speared his fingers through his hair and held them there, gripping tight for a long moment before dropping his hands to his sides. "Damn it, I hate this formality between us."

"We can't have it both ways, Hayden. This was only ever temporary." A blanket of calm descended to smother the tumultuous emotions that had been battering her. Acceptance. It wouldn't last long, she knew, but she was grateful for its appearance now. "Thanks for organizing Graham's deal to keep Angelica's name out of the hearings. I want to see justice catch up with her, but I know Graham would have hated himself if it had come via him."

Hayden nodded but seemed distracted. "It was a good deal for us—he gave a full and frank confession, and he named names like Marnie Salloway. We'll catch Angelica. The deal was only to keep her name out of Graham's interview. Now that that's over, all bets are off."

"But it won't be you who catches her," she said softly.

"No." He lifted his broad shoulders in a shrug. "John Harris will work the case. But I'll keep an eye on it from the New York office."

The casual way he was talking about leaving grated on her nerves. "So you're walking away."

"I'm taking my son home," he said pointedly. "It's the right thing to do."

"Is it so easy to leave me?" As soon as she said the words, she wanted to snatch them back. Pointlessly, she covered her mouth with two fingers, as if that could help. Where had that acceptance gone?

His eyes flashed fire. "Hell, this isn't even close to easy, Lucy. But yes, I'm leaving." He held one palm out, as if in surrender. "I can't give you what you need."

The words were like a match to tinder—all those turbulent emotions that had been roiling inside her finally had a reason to coalesce. "Who are you to tell me what I need?" she demanded.

"I'll tell you what I know," he said in measured tones. "I'm cynical and world-weary. A jaded widower. I know I'll never love with an open and unguarded heart, or with the intensity that I once did. My heart simply isn't capable of it—it's like an old, beaten-up, secondhand car. You deserve someone full of life. Optimism. Verve. Like you."

An ironic laugh bubbled up from deep down, but died before it reached her lips. He was telling her what she needed again. And he'd never been more wrong. Suddenly she saw everything clearly, maybe for the first time. Her love wasn't tainted—it just had some obstacles to overcome. But love took two. Unrequited love was a totally different ball game, and it seemed that was the only type he was offering.

"You're wrong," she said, staring him down. "But if

you're not even willing to stand by me and believe in what we could have, then maybe it is better that you go now."

He rubbed a hand over his eyes. "I've made a mess of this from the start."

"I fell in love with you, you know." She spoke the words lightly, more of an observation than recrimination. It was fair that he knew.

His face drained of color as if she'd slapped him. "God, I'm sorry, Lucy. So sorry."

Sorry? Her bottom lip trembled. If he said that word a third time she didn't know if she could bear it. "It's not your fault," she said more sharply than she intended. "It's mine."

His gaze stayed fixed on her face, obviously not fooled for a moment. "One more reason I need to leave. Once I'm gone I won't be able to hurt you anymore."

Inside her everything screamed, *just stay! Stay with me.* But she refused to beg. If there had been a moment for him to declare he wanted to be with her, it was when she'd told him she loved him. He'd simply apologized.

She wouldn't let the stinging at the back of her eyes turn into tears. All she had left was her dignity, and she was hanging on to that with everything inside her. She crossed to the sink and tipped the cold coffee out, then turned to face him, tranquil mask in place.

"So this is it," she said, crossing her arms under her breasts.

"Yes." He drummed the fingers of one hand on the side of his thigh. "I expect I'll be seeing you on the TV. Probably as a news anchor, but realistically, as anything you want. You have talent, Lucy."

After seeing what had become of Angelica, Marnie and Graham in the pursuit of ratings, the thought made her sick. "I don't think my future is in broadcast journalism. I'll be tendering my resignation to the new owner of ANS today."

His gaze sharpened. "What will you do instead?"

"I don't know. I think I'll take a couple of months off and find out what I'd like to do with my life." She was in no place right now to make life-changing decisions.

"Whatever you do, I know you'll make a success of it." The kind words, gently spoken, were almost harder to take than if he'd dismissed her plans. She pulled the sash of her robe tighter and held on to her composure by the most tenuous of threads.

"And you'll do a great job with Josh," she said truthfully. "He's a lucky boy to have you as a father." She was going to miss Josh like crazy. The little boy had wormed his way into her heart and even if she never saw him again, he'd always have a place there.

He nodded, then cleared his throat. "We need to go so we can make that flight."

He stepped toward her and she turned away, unable to stand seeing him that near and not have him. "Lucy," he whispered as he cupped the side of her face with his palm, then, without warning, he pulled her against him with his other hand and kissed her fiercely. The last shred of her control evaporated and she kissed him back just as hungrily. His fingers dug into her upper arms, and she welcomed the sensation, wanting to feel everything that was left for them. Lacing her fingers at the nape of his neck, she pulled down, never wanting to let him go, wishing the moment could last forever, holding him as tightly as she could. She felt her tears sliding down her cheeks and mingling with their kiss but was helpless to stop them. When his hand gripped her knee and urged it up, she wrapped a leg around his waist, desperate with the need to be closer.

Too soon, he wrenched his mouth away and rested his

forehead on hers, panting. Then, without a word, he placed a brief kiss on her forehead, picked up a smiling Josh and walked down the hall. Eyes squeezed shut, she listened to his footsteps fading as they got farther away, until her front door opened and closed. Only then did she slide down the cupboards to the floor and let the tears fall unrestrained.

Twelve

Holding the fracturing parts of herself together by sheer force of will a couple of hours later, Lucy walked through the heavy door a guard held open for her into a cold and drab pale green room. Graham was already waiting for her, seeming much smaller—shorter, even—with his shoulders hunched down, his lack of expansive movements. Unlike his usual warm greeting, his eyes were studiously locked on his hands, tightly clasped on the table.

Perhaps it was her own perceptions, as well. Graham had always been such a larger-than-life character to her—her stepfather since she was twelve, the owner of a national news network, a man confident of his place in the world. Now incarcerated while he awaited his court date to enter his guilty plea and receive his sentence, he was wearing an orange jumpsuit, stripped of all the trappings of his position and wealth. He hadn't even been granted the option of posting bail—with the seriousness of the charges against him, his private wealth and no real family to hold him, he'd been assessed a flight risk.

As she slid into the brown plastic chair, Graham looked up for the first time and the uncertainty there, the fear of rejection, made her heart weep. It hadn't occurred to her that he'd doubt her love and steadfastness.

"You're a sweet girl for coming," he said in a thick voice.

"Sweetness has nothing to do with it. You're my stepfather and I love you."

His jaw worked hard before he spoke. "Even after everything?"

"No matter what," she said quietly. "You've always been there for me and now I'm here for you."

He covered his face for long moments and when he dropped his hands, his eyes were misty. "I'm sorry, Lucy."

Seemed today was her day to receive apologies from the men in her life. "I can't say that I'm okay with what you've done at ANS," she said, "but that's only one part of who you are. You're also the man who took me into your heart when you married my mother, and kept me there even after she was gone. You're the man who wanted the best for me, gave me a job and kept me out of the dirty goings-on at ANS."

"That was always my stipulation—nothing was to touch you," he said fiercely. "Those involved were never to draw you into it."

That was Graham all over—he had honor, he just drew different lines about where it began and ended the than rest of the world. But she never doubted he'd prioritize her and protect her. Which would have gone down well with Angelica, she thought with a wry smile. It would have fed her hatred—not only was Graham like a father to Lucy, but he'd protected her while allowing Angelica to dive into illegal work.

"How's Rosebud?" he asked.

Rosie had whined overnight when she'd realized she wasn't going home to Graham, so Lucy had let her get under the covers with her. "Missing you, but I've been keeping her busy, so I think she's fairly happy."

"Thank you for taking her in."

"Having her has been good for me, too." A warm body to cuddle on the sofa this morning when the world looked dark had been priceless. She'd lost Hayden, the man she loved; Josh, the little boy she yearned for; and her stepfather, all in one fell swoop. Rosie had lost her human—her only family—so they'd been consoling each other.

"Lucy," Graham said carefully. "There's something between you and Black, isn't there?"

A denial was on the tip of her tongue, but why hide now? Hayden was gone, someone else from his company would be here soon to take over the rest of the investigation and the worst had already happened for Graham. There was no reason left to keep the secret.

She swallowed to get her voice to work. "There was for me, yes."

"Do you love him?" he asked sharply.

Suddenly there wasn't enough air in the little room. "It's not that simple. There are—"

"It *is* that simple," he said, cutting her off. "Do you love him?"

"Yes," she whispered.

"Let me tell you something. When I look back over my life, there are things I wish I had done differently. But my chief regret is about your mother."

She blinked. "I thought you loved her?"

"I did. A great deal. More than she knew. I should have

told her more. Cherished her more. She was the love of my life, but I spent my time building empires. I thought we had forever, but we only had seven years together. Too short. Much too short. She's gone, and ANS is gone now, too, so all that time I sacrificed from my marriage for ANS was for nothing."

"She knew you loved her," Lucy said truthfully. "She knew."

"Thanks." A small, nostalgic smile brushed over his mouth before he pinned her with his gaze. "Now it's your turn."

There seemed to be advice in his words, but it didn't make sense. "Don't you hate Hayden? He's the one who pursued you until you ended up here."

"If I never lay eyes on that man again it will be too soon," he said heatedly. "But much as I might hate him, I love you more. I'd give anything to make you happy, sweetheart."

"Thank you," she said past the tightness in her throat.

He looked directly into her eyes, not bothering to hide his emotions as he usually did. "If this is love, Lucy, grab it. Treasure it. Don't let anything stand in your way."

"What if he doesn't want to grab it back? If—" The pain of his apology in response to telling him she loved him took hold, until she was able to stuff it back down and take a breath. "If he's walked away?"

"Then he's an idiot, just as I suspected." He leaned forward in his chair. "But if you still love him, go get what you want. Life's too short, too unpredictable to waste a second of it."

Lucy looked hard at the man sitting across from her. This wasn't the same man she'd known—she'd always been a bit in awe of that man, who'd been a little distant, despite their closeness. He'd never talked to her about his relationship with her mother, never opened himself this way. Even though her world was crumbling around her, and she'd do almost anything to save Graham from being incarcerated, this—their first ever heart-to-heart—was like a small ray of sunshine shining through the parted clouds.

"He has a son," she found herself saying. "Hayden Black. He's a widower with a one-year-old son called Josh."

Graham's face folded up into a frown. "You're too young to become a mother."

Not long ago, she would have thought the same. Since becoming part of Josh's life, though, she saw motherhood and parenting differently, as something she'd relish if she had the opportunity. She'd been involved with babies through her charity for years, but getting to know Josh had been a new experience. And, no question, she'd fallen head over heels in love with the little boy.

"He's such a special boy. And he loves Rosie," she said, remembering how cute they were together. "The first time I met him, I had Rosie with me and he called out 'Goggie.' When I met him again the next day, he wanted to know where she was."

"You haven't asked me about Angelica," Graham said abruptly.

She hesitated, trying to catch the change of direction the conversation had suddenly taken. "That's your business. I won't pry."

"I never should have abandoned her as a baby." He clenched a fist on the table. "I thought I was doing enough by paying money to keep a roof over her head and food in her belly. Sending her to school. But it *wasn't* enough. I should have seen that at the time instead of being focused on my own distaste about being weighed down by a baby…or her annoying mother. If I'd raised Madeline, maybe things would have been different." His expression drooped, as if the weight of the world was on his shoulders. "Maybe she wouldn't have turned out so bitter."

She bit down on her bottom lip. Maybe Angelica would have been different had Graham raised her—he certainly should have tried. Though saying that wouldn't be helpful to a man already riddled with regrets, and in all honesty, was that the only problem Angelica had? She couldn't think of a single useful thing to say, so she went with the generic. "Babies are so precious."

"You obviously have feelings for Josh," Graham said, pointing a finger at her. "So you're poised to repeat both of my biggest mistakes in one giant blunder. Are you ready to walk away from the man you love, as well as a kid you want to be yours?"

She leaned back in her chair, folding her arms under her breasts as if she could pull herself away from the terrible picture he painted. "I don't know, but I promise I'll think about it."

He nodded, satisfied. "I know you'll do the right thing. You always do." He pushed his chair back and stood. "Now you go on and leave me here. You don't want to spend your days keeping an old man company."

"I'll be back to see you again before your court appearance," she said, keeping the tears that threatened in check. The last thing Graham needed was to think he'd made her cry. "Whatever happens with your sentencing, I'll be here for you."

By the time she made it to her car, she couldn't hold the tears back any longer. She rested her head on the steering wheel and let them come. Tears for Graham mingled with tears for herself as they slid down her cheeks.

If you still love him, go get what you want. Life's too short, too unpredictable to waste a second of it.

This time his words struck a chord deep inside her. Graham was right. She loved Hayden. It was as simple—and as gloriously complicated—as that.

She didn't care if Hayden had some ridiculous idea about their suitability or his heart's capabilities. She was going to fight for their love, fight for them. All the other reasons they'd thought they shouldn't be together, they were molehills, not mountains. Anything could be surmounted if they did it hand in hand. If she'd learned one thing from Graham's example, it was not to live with regrets. To make changes in her life while she could. Even if talking to Hayden again was destined to fail, she at least had to try.

She checked her watch—still early enough to catch a flight. She reached for her cell, dialed her travel agent and bought a round-trip ticket to New York. She'd just have enough time to get home, grab a couple of things and make the flight. She couldn't take Rosie, so she'd need to be back in D.C. tonight. If things worked out with Hayden, Rosie would be part of their permanent plans, but for today, she'd have to wait here. Excitement fluttered in her stomach. She knew what she wanted and she was going to grab it.

When a light turned red, she drummed her fingers on the steering wheel. First order of business—she needed to work out what to say when she saw Hayden again. He'd been adamant this morning, so she'd need the perfect way to explain that nothing mattered more than the two of them creating a new family with Josh and their future children. Words swirled around her head, forming into sentences to convince him, then fell apart as she discarded them. Maybe on the plane—she'd have a bit of time on the plane to get the words just perfect. She should be thinking about what to grab at her house so that went as quickly as possible. Missing this flight was not an option.

She pulled up in front of her place, grabbed her holdall bag and flung open the car door. As she stepped out onto the road, she hesitated. Someone was sitting on the concrete steps to her front door. Two someones. Her heart stilled. Two someones she loved. Hayden stood and picked up Josh, but he didn't make a move to come over to her.

Her knees wobbled and she leaned against the car for support. His gaze met hers but it gave nothing away. He'd come back—did he need something, maybe some more testimony? Had he left something in her house? Clothes? His phone?

The plan had been to tell him what she wanted for their future, but that was supposed to happen *after* she'd had time to get it straight in her head. Make the words perfect so she didn't ruin the chance. But he was here. Earlier than her plan. She was going to have to make the best of it.

She put her handbag up on her shoulder and set the keyless lock. Then she took a deep breath and pushed away from the car. One foot in front of the other. As she approached, Josh squealed and reached for her, but Hayden kept his hold on him.

"Hello," Hayden said, a slight frown line marring his brow.

She straightened her spine and found a welcoming smile. "Did you forget something?"

"Yes."

Her heart shattered and she only held herself upright through sheer force of will. He'd returned because he'd forgotten something. Though that didn't mean she couldn't convince him. "You'd better come in."

She moved around him and unlocked her front door. If she could get them inside, she'd have a better chance of having a fair hearing for what she needed to say. Maybe lock the door behind them. She pushed the door open with a trembling hand. Rosie rushed at them and greeted everyone with the enthusiasm of a dog who hadn't seen people for hours, standing on her hind legs and wagging her curly tail.

Forming her argument in her mind, Lucy walked into her living room. It was a safe place for Josh to crawl around on the floor so she could have all of Hayden's attention. Then she swiveled and planted her hands on her hips. "Before you get whatever it is you forgot, there's something I—"

"You," he said, voice deep and serious.

She stopped midsentence, mouth still open to form the next word. "Pardon?"

He put Josh on the sofa, where he was immediately joined by Rosie. Then Hayden looked back to Lucy, eyes intense. "I forgot *you.* As soon as the plane took off, I knew I'd made a stupid mistake. A colossal mistake. When we disembarked in New York, I found a flight straight back again."

She started to tremble. The hope was so strong, it was painful, but none of this made sense. "You want to continue our fling?" she asked.

"I want more than a damn fling. I want *everything,* Lucy." He took her hands and gripped them tightly. "I want to live my life with you."

The trembling inside grew stronger, until she could feel her lips quivering, and her fingers as Hayden's gripped them. All that she wanted seemed *so* close, but she wouldn't live with regrets. She wouldn't settle for anything less than the whole package.

"What about Josh?" she asked, looking down at the little boy who was rubbing Rosie's tummy. "I couldn't be with you and be excluded from your relationship with him. You said you'd never share him again."

"I was wrong." He dropped her hands and speared his fingers through his hair, looking nervous. "One of the things I thought about on that flight was that parenting a child with you would be a world apart from parenting with Brooke. It was fear talking—fear of being edged out of my son's life again. The best thing for Josh is to have two parents who love him. But I know it's asking a lot to take on me and Josh together. You should be—"

She placed a finger over his lips. "You're not about to tell me what I should be doing again, are you?"

His mouth curved under her fingers. "No, ma'am."

"Good," she said and grinned. "Because I love Josh. When you flew away, I was missing him almost as much as I was missing you. I want you both as a package deal."

His Adam's apple bobbed slowly, then he knelt down on her living room carpet and took her hands. "Lucy Royall, marry me. Marry me and Josh."

Joy bubbled through her body, filling every cell, every dark corner inside her until it was too big to be contained and seemed to flow out and fill even the air around her. But, aside from a smile, she managed to keep from reacting just yet.

"Before I answer that," she said sweetly, laying her Southern accent on thick, "I want to set some ground rules."

His mouth opened. Closed again. "Ground rules? You're killing me, Lucy."

She held up a finger. "First rule—no more thinking you know what's best for me."

"Agreed," he said, chuckling. "I failed pretty bad at that anyway."

"Also, I'll be flying back to D.C. at least once a week to

visit Graham no matter what happens with his sentencing, so I don't want to live too far away. Though I won't want to be far away after he gets out, either." She'd meant it when she'd told Graham earlier that she'd be there for him.

Not letting go of her hands, Hayden stood. "I expected you'd want to be nearby and I've had a suggestion. I'm open to setting up an office for my business in D.C. if you want to stay here. Or we could live in both cities—Josh has a few years before he starts school, so we don't have to be chained anywhere just yet. We'll work around Boyle's sentence."

After tracking Graham's crimes and being the one responsible for catching him, Hayden was still willing to work around the man's sentence, to change his business, if needed? For her. Because he knew it was important to her. In that moment, she knew he genuinely loved her. "You'd really be happy with that?"

"I learned a couple of things from my first marriage. This time I want a true partnership, where our lives reflect what we both want, what we both need. Graham is part of your life, so we'll include him. I'm sure I'll come to appreciate his virtues," he said wryly. "One thing I do like about him is he honestly cares for you. I can respect that."

Emotion clogging her throat, she wrapped her arms around his waist. "I didn't think I could love you more." It was almost too much, and tears of joy began to creep down her cheeks. "You know, he told me about an hour ago that I should come after you. I've booked a flight to New York. I was going to convince you to give us a chance."

He chuckled. "Who would have thought I had Boyle to thank for something good?" He tucked her head against his chest, smoothing her hair down. "Your house is too big for one person anyway—we may as well fill it up. Why do you have such a big place?"

"Build it and they will come," she quoted softly. Being an only child who'd lost both her parents, she hadn't been able to contemplate a condo or something small. "I think I've always been waiting for a family of my own."

"You have one now." His voice was as rough as gravel. "Josh, me and Rosebud."

Rosebud came trotting over at the sound of her name, panting with her curly tongue peeking out. Lucy looked from Rosie to Josh on the sofa to Hayden in her arms. And smiled. "The perfect family."

"So is that the end of your ground rules?" Hayden asked, leaning back enough so she could see his eyes.

"Yes." There was nothing more she could possibly want. She was ready to marry the man she loved. "I'll—"

"Well, I have a couple of my own before you answer my proposal." He pulled her down on the sofa so they were sitting with Josh—Lucy in Hayden's lap and Josh in Lucy's, with Hayden's arms around both.

She blinked. "You do?"

"First ground rule," he said, eyes narrowed, "no more secrecy. If I want to kiss you in the middle of a park, or on the steps of the Capitol, I will."

She bit down on the wide smile that threatened, needing to at least appear serious in the negotiations. "I think I can live with that rule."

Obviously bored with the lack of action, Josh crawled out of Lucy's lap and over to the other end of the sofa and began patting Rosie's nose, giggling when she licked his fingers on each pat.

"Second rule," Hayden said, bringing her attention back to him by maneuvering her to straddle his lap, then resting his hands on her hips. "There are no conditions on where we can make love anymore. Only being able to have you at your place was driving me insane."

She kissed a path across his jaw and was rewarded when he shuddered. “Another rule I can wholeheartedly approve,” she murmured in his ear.

“Then—” he cradled her face in his palms, bringing it back in front of his “—I think we might just have ourselves an agreement to get married.”

The intensity in his eyes, his love for her that was shining there unguarded, made everything inside her sing. Then he captured her mouth and kissed her, and she knew she’d never want more than this: being with the man she loved, who loved her, and the family of her heart.

* * * * *